COLONEL FITZWILLIAM'S CORRESPONDENCE

D. W. Wilkin

Regency Assembly Press
www.regencyassemblypress.com

REGENCY ASSEMBLY PRESS
LOS ANGELES, CA, USA

First Printing, July 2011
1 3 5 7 9 10 8 6 4 2

Printed in the United States of America

Table of Contents

ACKNOWLEDGMENTS

I have to thank my writing group for their encouragement in publishing and then refining this book. Deedira Bockhold, Elizabeth Durand, Anne Okamoto. My prepublication readers Deedira Bockhold again and Miriam Landres. My aunt Mimi (Miriam Landres) who did a tremendous job with the work, and has always had a good and often well deserved scold for my mother for as long as I can remember. The Regency and all its mores may not be so long forgotten as one would think of a time two hundred years ago.

THE WEDDING PARTY

As weddings go, Colonel Stephen Fitzwilliam thoroughly enjoyed the occasion. He stood up for his cousin, and was the representative of his father and brother. In fact with his young cousin Georgiana, they alone represented the family. His father, the Earl, was too ill to travel such a distance to Meryton at the time. His Aunt, Lady Catherine de Bourgh had made it known she was not about to condescend to recognize such an alliance, and was further put out that Stephen did.

Stephen had called for Georgiana at Pemberley and escorted her to London, where her brother Darcy was busy with his final plans and preparations for his nuptials. Darcy and Miss Elizabeth were bound for a wedding tour to Austria, as yet unconquered by the Tyrant. The Bingleys were to travel with them, the two friends inseparable, and during that time Stephen would act the responsible guardian of Georgiana, Darcy and his' ward. So Georgiana would live in London, and be close to his Regimental barracks, thus allowing the Colonel to be able to keep an eye upon her. He would have the aid of such fine a lady as Miss Caroline Bingley to help in this regard, and also the excellent Gardiners whose acquaintance he had made during Darcy's engagement the prior months to Miss Elizabeth Bennet.

The Colonel's circle was much larger, but he and Darcy had discussed thoroughly those whom Georgiana should meet and chaperone her, and these were the names they had settled on. Colonel Fitzwilliam could smile humorously as he looked to Miss Caroline Bingley in the third row of the church at Meryton, glaring, in her finest attire, for the wedding of her brother.

The Colonel knew that Caroline almost did not make it into the select circle of chaperones for Georgiana, but finally had because she was forever attached to Charles. Charles not only the best friend of Darcy, but also those two men's wives, sisters. Caroline would be a fixture in the circle for a long time. Though the Colonel felt sure that Elizabeth Darcy would be sending her many invitation to visit Pemberley in the years to come, for propriety's sake, Caroline would accept as few of them as possible.

The two women seemed to have the measure of each other. As Stephen had Miss Bingley's as well.

Caroline was near the end of her seasons and had not snapped up a man yet. The Colonel doubted that she would. Upon first being introduced to her, he quickly saw where her sails had been set. Now that port, Darcy, had closed to her, and Caroline deftly trimmed sheets and reset course towards himself. The Colonel was wise enough to see her intentions on her sleeve, though perhaps others could not. He extricated himself from her machinations.

Just days before, for the wedding at Meryton, the Darcy party and the Bingley party traveled together from Town. They were joined by the Gardiners who fortunately shared the Darcy coaches. It left no room for Caroline Bingley in them for she had thought to travel in the company of the Colonel. The distribution of nine people in Darcy's two conveyances, for the Gardiners numbered four children, allowed the Colonel to ride his horse, and that was a thing he proudly surpassed his cousin at. Darcy had many advantages, but Fitzwilliam was a better seat and his stables were better also, as the Colonel of a cavalry regiment should be.

At the first coaching stop, the eldest Gardiner boy, Jack, implored him for a ride and while the ladies refreshed themselves, the young lad showed himself fit in the saddle. The Colonel on the spot switched places with Jack for the next leg, but six miles, and the horse, Night, was tethered to the coach and four's team. The Colonel's man, Private Slade was atop the carriage with the coachmen and was instructed to pay close attention to the young Gardiner boy.

The gentlemen of the party thought the allowing of young Jack a ride grand largesse and the Colonel knew his cousin delighted in the favor shown to his future family. Mr. Hurst, Bingley's sister's husband, good-naturedly attempted a wager with Mr. Bingley over the lad's keeping his seat, but Charles would have none of it. Then instead Mr. Hurst offered the boy a half crown if he did keep his seat till the next coaching stop. Mr. Hurst was soundly berated by the Bingley ladies upon their return to the courtyard.

This however allowed Stephen to spend time with Mr. Gardiner and two of his smaller children in Darcy's barouche. He promised each child rides when they reached Meryton. He and Mr. Gardiner spent the time in animated discussion together where he found the conversation fascinating and his interest did not wander.

"Well sir, I do admit that the reel and the rod have held a fascination for me, though perhaps not such an attachment as you have attained. I have been more to hounds during my formative years, though these last few I have been to but three meets after the season," Stephen recounted to Mr. Gardiner who had just described the fine time he had at Pemberley enjoying Darcy's lake.

"Three meets a year with your other duties does seem..." The Colonel cut off Mr. Gardiner.

"I beg your pardon, you mistake me sir for I misspoke myself. I have been to all of three meets in the last three years after the season. Indeed I have spent more time at the streams of my Fathers', or at Pemberley and Rosings then I have to hounds. Though I have not done so there but little more than half of a dozen."

"Father would fish every day if he could..." the youngest Gardiner said.

And Colonel Fitzwilliam indulged the child, "We all would like to spend time at leisure should the chance permit, and your father has chosen a worthy study, for a fish is a tricksome thing."

The children giggled but continued to play with their toys, pretending not to notice the Colonel, though watching this new big person as time and opportunity permitted.

"Tricksome is a good description, though, I think if I had time for perpetual leisure I should not over indulge in any one thing."

"That is a very worthy sentiment," the Colonel responded, "I have often thought much the same. Moderation for all, excess for naught."

Gardiner reflected, "That is a concise summation, well put." Stephen nodded and happily the journey and conversation continued. By the time they reached the next coaching, Stephen had promised to tour the young Gardiners about the Regiment's Barracks. Upon returning to Town Stephen would also be extending invitations to the parents to dine with him and some select officers, for he enjoyed this new connection.

Should the Gardiners be forward and send him an invitation to dine, he would expect Caroline Bingley to remark upon it, or slander them. But, Stephen had the measure of the man, and from the polite behavior of the children could see that Mrs. Gardiner was quietly amongst the best of child rearers and thus understood propriety. Even with the marriage of their niece they were still not of the Ton. With their new connection, they still would not be in the right to send a first invitation to the Colonel, though should an entertainment be given for the Darcy's upon their arrival in Town, such would be acceptable, and even Caroline Bingley could receive such and take notice that it was artfully done.

No, a private affair without the attendance of the Darcys would have to initiate solely from Stephen as he sat higher than they. But he thought and felt that such a connection, though some of small mind would say was detrimental, as Mr. Gardiner was in trade, would be advantageous. The Colonel, amongst his acknowledged many faults, was even known to eat a midday meal with his sergeants and men to learn their thoughts and feelings. Further, he would make the Gardiners known to his quartermasters as the Regiment would benefit from doing business with this new connection as well. Mr. Gardiner's business would be able to outfit a part of the regimental needs, and that would be all to the good.

Stephen further reflected, though he knew that the Gardiners had dined once already at Darcy's town house in Berkeley Square, that expanding the Gardiners circle was something that Darcy would greatly appreciate. Stephen was determined to not only increase that circle to the Regiment, but he had certain friends that would deem meeting Mr. Gardiner a pleasure. The Colonel thought that Baron Moorden was an equally avowed angler, and would not think such a connection a slight. And though Stephen's father the Earl of M----K, would most likely not find the connection tolerable, for his father was at times much like Caroline Bingley in spirits, Stephen's brother the Viscount would humor him in this regard and also adopt the Gardiners. Already their circle had quadrupled amongst the Ton. The campaign was well commenced, Stephen reflected.

"Well young Jack, did you enjoy your ride?" The lad stared at his half crown from Mr. Hurst and realized that the Colonel spoke to him, but moments later, causing some good spirited chuckling amongst the men. Darcy clapped the Colonel upon the shoulder. In general his disposition was now become sunny and bright, as it seldom was before Miss Elizabeth Bennet and his engagement. Grander now, and it had been so for days.

"Yesss sssirrr. I mean thank you Colonel Fitzwilliam. I am mightily obliged," the boy said.

"No, not at all. You are under no obligation, and as I have promised the rest of you young men and ladies," he referred now to the three other children who stood brushing the horse down and holding Night's reins as it drank from the water trough. "When we get to Netherfield, and all are comfortable, you too shall have your rides."

Bingley, perhaps not caring that the ladies were just returning from the inn, or specifically that his sisters, Mrs. Hurst and Miss Bingley were close enough to hear, said. "That is very kind of you Colonel, and though when one compares your steed to the stables we have at Netherfield, one must state that yours is far superior. I feel sure we can mount all these young scamps at once, what say you young Gardiners to that?"

There was much huzzahing and jumping from the four children and Night was near to jumping himself if the Colonel had not quickly grabbed a rein from one side and laid a steadying hand upon him, whilst Darcy grabbed the horse's rein from the other. "And that my fine young fellows is one of your first lessons. Take care of your actions around these animals for though they are big and look solid, they take fright from such sudden movement as lads of three and six jumping near to their flanks."

The young children looked sheepish, "I am three feet nine inches..." Darcy and the Colonel heard that and found themselves laughing. During this Caroline drew her brother away and had a private word, Stephen observed.

Charles then said, "Indeed, I thank you sister for your remembrance. I am sorry children, I forgot that you shall stay amongst your family of Longbourn." The Colonel noted a smirk upon Caroline's face, further hardening him against such a countenance. A countenance that seeing it was being observed by the Colonel turned instantly into vapidness, as the lady transformed her features to look as pleasant as possible.

"Surely, though, Bingley, we can remedy that. I can take Night and such other horses as you make available and bring them to Longbourn so that the children may ride. But I expect that two gentlemen I know shall also make such a trip each day from Netherfield to Longbourn until the nuptials are conducted this Saturday. And they shall be making said trip upon the moment it is deemed the earliest appropriate time to call."

Some of the party of adults laughed. One of the Gardiner children ran to Mr. Bingley, who was then quickly surrounded by the others, to be implored to accept the Colonel's idea, while Mrs. Hurst and Caroline Bingley both tried to voice objections to such a plan.

"Earliest time indeed, Charles you have too much to do to prepare..."

"Please sir, the Colonel's idea is grand..."

"Darcy, that looks suspiciously like a smirk," the Colonel said sotto voce and the countenance of his cousin quickly changed.

Darcy responded, "Indeed Colonel, Miss Bingley must have the right of it. Charles and I would by no means call at the house of our intendeds any earlier than good sense and propriety demanded."

"Damned serious about it. I should wager with Mr. Hurst but I fear he would take me up on that, and I would render the disapproval of Georgiana. So I shall drop this line." Colonel Fitzwilliam raised his voice, "Now Children, you may count on it, at some time I shall arrive with the horses and possibly the bridegrooms. And you shall have your rides. Do any of you know how to jump? Indeed, no? It shall be a pleasure of mine to teach you, but do you know your soon to be cousin Darcy is quite good at jumping..." And the Colonel took the children to one side until all was ready to travel again.

Stephen saw Charles take Darcy aside and heard him enquire, "The Colonel seems to be carefree and easy of spirit. Is he always so?"

"Does he? I should think when he commands his Regiment he is entirely the opposite."

Charles paused and then said, "Yes I should imagine you have it aright there. But I was tempted to speculate that one reason we have become fast friends is that his manner and mine are similar. You have often remarked on the qualities I have just observed of the Colonel as being my failings yet we are the best of friends. I sense that you have found these challenges attractive for they reside in myself and the Colonel, and I recall once that Miss Elizabeth made the remark how she would like to see you adopt some of them. I shall hope that by the time we have seen the Alps in Austria you will learn to emulate me entirely." He smiled broadly and Darcy must have realized the extent of Charles' joke and gave him a grin to match. Perhaps the reason Charles had spoken so that he did hear such compliments.

Darcy replied, "Certainly, by the time we gaze on the Alps, I shall learn to make a joke. Indeed I shall endeavor to craft one between now and that august day. Is politics a safe subject for wit? Perhaps a societal satire?" Charles laughed back and soon all strode to their respective carriages as it was time for their departure.

During the last leg of the journey, the Colonel reflected that outings like these were not to be encountered often. He feared that the Continent would call soon, and he and his regiment would find themselves riding to the depths of horror. Reflecting on war generally seemed to make him melancholic, and for this he blamed his rank in the birth order. A junior son had little choice but to be employed in a service to King and Country. Certainly idling would not fit his character, but until he faced the hazards of battle he was not certain that he would be able to stand firm. He had little fear of blade work when controlled at his clubs. But the havoc of combat, with rules abated and the determination to destroy the enemy preeminent in the mind of all combatants, a fear formed in his depths. Until tested, he had no notion if he would pass or if he would fail. No notion if that possibility of failure would be irreversible. He had no notion if he would be able to conquer or at least constrain his fears.

Finally, Meryton, was reached and here a conundrum beset the party, for the Darcy carriages were set to go to Longbourn as the Gardiners would set down from there. But Caroline Bingley saw no need to, as she so forthrightly put it, "Intrude upon ones soon to be in-laws when they must be set upon with so many chores as would make one of the Colonel's quartermasters cringe."

Colonel Fitzwilliam had little choice but to nod at the recognition. The lady could attempt a passable smile, and the Colonel recognized it. He berated himself for not recognizing her many other dashing qualities. As a young lady of fortune and position she had several. But, with such intense scrutiny fixated upon his person, he was damned pressed to recognize them.

The conundrum raised affected Bingley the most, as Mr. and Mrs. Hurst voiced agreement that their carriage should proceed with out delay to Netherfield. Bingley did not feel the same. He wished to visit his future in-laws upon the moment, yet with no room in the carriage of Darcy, he ventured, "Well I shall be hanged if we go to Netherfield and I not pay my immediate respects upon the Bennets."

Darcy but cocked an eye at his friend, but the Colonel was swift, "Here Mr. Bingley, Charles, you shall have my horse and I shall venture to Netherfield in your place so as not to indispose the ladies. I beg that you do pay your respects for that is civil and as I have no connection at this point, tomorrow shall serve well enough for my first calling. Do not you think so, cousin?" Stephen had already begun to dismount.

"Why indeed that is a happy solution. Now Georgiana, how do you hold up, it has been a long journey." Darcy himself replied, while Charles, seeing an opportunity of others speaking to allow him to give his own sister the slip, was half out of his carriage.

"Why I thank you brother for your concern. Indeed I must say that any fatigue I have is banished at the thought that in minutes I shall be reunited with your fair Miss Elizabeth." Caroline Bingley surely had to think of the balance that the scales had thrown her way. Charles spending time with Jane, whom in three days he would be with for the rest of his life in any event, though Caroline would be able to limit her own exposure to the Bennets, yet she would have to develop a fondness for Jane, much as she adored her cat. Well, tolerated her cat. Stephen thought about the situation. He had seen Caroline Bingley with her cat once.

But on the other side of the scales, for the next few hours while the Darcys and Charles lingered at Longbourn, Caroline would have the Colonel to herself at Netherfield. Stephen had no doubts that her sister ensuring that they had privacy, would keep Mr. Hurst occupied with just the hint of a suggestion. With the hope of Darcy now past, the countenance of the Colonel, Stephen had already surmised, had risen as a monument in her sights.

"Very well, that is a capital, um you military men say, strategy?" Caroline said.

"Well I should not go so far as to say that." The Colonel helped Charles to attain his seat before a groomsman could attend them.

Under his voice so that the Colonel alone heard it, "My thanks on this." Stephen nodded to Charles in acknowledgement.

Stephen continued to Caroline Bingley, "But I will say it seems the happiest medium to please the greatest number of people. Now you young folk, I shall call tomorrow with the horses, so after your breakfast you do any chores that your parents have set aside for you, that we may have a good hour to ride, provided that is agreeable with you Mrs. Gardiner?"

"Yes Colonel, most agreeable," Mrs. Gardiner said, all smiles.

"I think cousin you shall not need my service for above a couple hours until Saturday, so I am at my leisure and should like to look about some of the countryside here as well," Stephen said to Darcy.

Darcy nodded and shortly the party split in two, the children waving to the Colonel until they twisted from sight. That action finally forced the Colonel to pay some attention to the two ladies in the carriage with him. Mr. Hurst seemed to doze in his seat, though the Colonel was sure that were the talk of a wager, the man would waken quickly enough.

"Now Colonel, you must tell us about your duties, for I am sure you must be very busy indeed with your regiment. Do you have many cannon in your regiment? How many men are there at your command," Caroline said.

Mrs. Hurst spoke at nearly the same instant as her sister, "When you march the men, do they always stay in straight lines. That must be tiresome indeed I should think." As questions continued, he nodded and smiled and looked beyond the ladies to glimpse what he could of the countryside. He had no need to answer for they asked another question before he would have to answer the prior one.

The journey to Netherfield Park took but a quarter of an hour more. He suspected that far more intelligent questions were at their command. Cannon indeed, for a cavalry regiment. He shivered inwardly.

But the air of vapidness that one cultivates has the potential of becoming the truth of ones personality, Stephen pondered. One must remember to use that intelligence that one has, else the world will label one a lackwit, and one's company will only be that of sycophants.

As Colonel, he regularly culled his junior officers over just such matters, forcing needed reflection and reform amongst them. Certainly having less nonsensical conversation in the Mess then most other of the horse regiments at His Majesty's command. Stephen shivered again thinking of the state of the officers when his Colonelcy was purchased.

"A very nice prospect indeed. I should consider this a good find, and Mrs. Bingley will be close to her parents and siblings. How advantageous," Stephen said.

"Yes, I should think that Jane will often have her family in to dine. Pity that I find so many social obligations in Town that I shall be unable to spend much time here." Caroline must have thought long and hard on how life was so shortly to change. Probably not for the better in her estimation.

"But certainly from what I have heard from Darcy, and even Miss Elizabeth who recounted much of her society when I met her at Rosings, there are very many felicitous people worthy of cultivating here, and I should believe that I would not want for lack of company, or divertimento if I were to do as Charles and take a home in such pleasant surroundings." The Colonel followed the ladies up the entry stairs to the grand hallway. Servants stood on either side, and the Colonel saw his batman had made it down and stood in line with the others.

The Colonel had sent Corporal Figgis ahead to take care of his arrangements and had Private Slade who would see to his horse. Slade was a deft hand as a groom, and though Bingley was sure to employ smart grooms himself, a cavalry horse would require that extra attention that the livery of Bingley may not have been aware of. So to be safe, his valet, one groom, and himself of course imposed upon the Bingley generosity as part of the wedding party.

Stephen's finances were such that a modest house, say of no more then four rooms, and some acreage, certainly less than twenty, could be had on the stipend allocated to him by his father. That he did much better in control of the finances of the Regiment, where he earned more then eight times as much as that stipend, meant that he could afford much better, but he was not one to spend it so grandiosely. He banked it, and even purchased shares in an East Indiaman. When he sold out, or was cashiered from the Regiment, then he would worry much more about his finances. In the meantime he endeavored to live on half his income from his various sources, such as his father, and the trusteeship of Georgiana, though in truth any monies from that were returned promptly as gifts to Georgiana.

That kindness, for his cousin Darcy knew of the financial straights of the Colonel, only further caused Darcy to look for ways in which to ensure his cousins' future was secure. Never spoken, but understood, the Colonel was the one amongst this generation of the family who was least able to afford the lifestyle they had been born to. Anne de Bourgh would have all her estates and trappings. Stephen's brother, the Viscount, would one day be Earl and share in that fortune. Georgiana was to have a dowry bestowed upon her when she married. Darcy of course had Pemberley and all the Darcy wealth.

The Colonel was apportioned 1200 year, a considerable sum to be sure, but not real wealth. What Stephen could make of fate, and should he sell his commission certainly another windfall would come of that, was all in his hands.

Whilst Colonel, the funds of the Regiment were his to manage and profit by. Stephen assured himself that his was amongst the three best cavalry regiments in England even as he did achieve some security from his control. It left him proud.

That nearly every other Colonel of his acquaintance showed a more lavish lifestyle then he did further left him self-satisfied. One thing that he and Darcy shared were a keen appreciation for the destructive force of money. Certainly their attendance upon their aunt de Bourgh had shown them that money was no clear indication of superiority despite protesting that it did raise one to the heights of society.

Upon entering Netherfield's hall, the Colonel did think it should indeed suit, and that the manor would be an addition to the family, for would not his cousin's sister be living here? Upon Saturday he would acquire Elizabeth as a cousin, and all her relations as his own, for he and Darcy were much more like brothers then cousins. Being but six months apart in age and having a shared view of the world, developed from long discussion whilst the Colonel was at Oriel and Darcy but close by at Trinity.

"Do you admire these surroundings, for I find that compared to our home in Town, they are less of a piece," Caroline was quick to say.

The Colonel had been a visitor twice at the Bingley home in London. "Well, when in the country I find that there is an openness of space that Town ill affords, of course. Now did you help your brother decorate here when first down last year, or are these trappings that of the prior owners?"

Previously, the Baron of Westock whose line had passed to the Marquis of Rhein, and thus the owner, did never venture to claim his holdings, had put Netherfield up for sale. "Sir, certainly you do not think that I have such taste?"

"No, of course if you say it is not so, but I find these paintings, these colors, even this choice of marble to be excellently done. Why I am sure my aunt Lady Catherine would agree herself, and should my mother visit, she too will provide her approbation. My mother's work at her house in Town also greatly influenced Darcy's home I believe you know. She helped Darcy's mother greatly with all manner of selection of art pieces." The Countess was recognized as a great influence on the arts during her day. That the colors blended together was a truth. That there was boldness next to subtlety was also true. It was not the Colonel's favorite color scheme however, and, certainly, in his home, he would not have it.

"Ah, I see," Caroline said. Clearly all she saw was that if she said white, he would say black, or if Caroline thought stop, he would respond with go. The Colonel had set himself up to be contrary to her. It was presumptuous of the Colonel to hope that is what she understood, but her demeanor turned as she gave her hat and gloves to a waiting servant. "Colonel, Fredericks will show you to your rooms. If you will forgive me, I am quite tired from our journey. I am sure Charles is not far behind us with the rest of the party, but I must retire to rest before dinner, and as the Hursts have already gone to their rooms you will make allowance if I do not escort you to yours."

"Not at all Miss Bingley. Go and repair your strength for you have suffered much from such a long journey. These marriages cause too much change upon our familiarity and all the world is new." He half smiled and bade her on her way.

Figgis was nearby as the butler Fredericks showed the Colonel to his room. Figgis commented that he was to be on one side of Georgiana, and Darcy had rooms on the other. The Hursts were also in this wing, but Caroline and Charles had rooms on the other side of the house. Darcy was in the very same room he had used on all his previous visits to Netherfield.

One objective that the Colonel was charged with was to solicit with Georgiana, as they would not need travel back to London for a few days following the wedding, to determine if other suitable homes were to be found in the area. Miss Elizabeth would no doubt wish to visit her parents on occasion, and Darcy had already looked to the future and saw in it trespassing upon the Bingleys, or worse, partaking of the generosity of Mrs. Bennet.

"That was ill done," the Colonel spoke softly to himself.

"Sir?" Figgis said from behind.

"Oh don't worry Figgis, just correcting myself again." The Colonel had become opaque in the matters of Miss Bingley and this was something he knew better than to be. He wanted to be translucent in his dealings with calculating women, just as Darcy was in his plans to find a house to take. Should one be found, Darcy had arranged it that none other suspect that he had employed artful means to discover one.

The Colonel had been too direct in his praise in maneuvering Miss Bingley off the scent. One thing he did not desire, with the Tyrant so close at hand, was to be making love to a woman. He feared that it was his lot to fall short of heroism and to give his all for his King and Countrymen. Nelson's line had not only been bandied about the fleet,, but the junior service now too had to live up to such a tradition. 'England expects that every man will do his duty...'

With such great expectations, Stephen knew that several of the sterner men of his rank felt that they would follow Nelson's example. The Colonel understood that the decorations; the foolish ones amongst those who had purchased commissions would never understand such cold calculation. He also knew that battle would favor each equally and as many of the men who just donned the uniform would return from war as did those of solid caliber he counted his peers. He was perplexed that no amount of training and readiness could give one surety of success against an errant cannon ball.

He certainly knew that his birth did not grant him such protections, nor did what little wealth he created or maintained. At times he wished for a better rapport with his men, but there was a gulf between them. Last he realized that his birth had placed him in such straits. Not for the junior sons to survive to lead great lives of idleness but to do the work of empire. To be the sacrifice that their elders who were born as heirs might live that fulfillment of ease.

Bingley had been blessed with no younger brothers as had Darcy. Sometimes they both lost sight of the condescension that came of that. Usually that reality did not bother the Colonel but on occasion, like greed, it reared its ugly head. The Colonel often thought that he had to turn this handicap into a blessing and by doing so, by establishing his own value in the world, then he would create for his own son a chance to succeed to a life of unearned leisure. A fine revenge indeed to he had against the foibles of birth.

That Stephen had treated Caroline poorly in his endeavor to be free of any entrapment with her was obvious and not subtle as had been his intent. Certainly at the first arrangement of the carriages he had succeeded admirably, for even without the device of the overcrowding of the vehicles, he was still a member of the Darcy set and would have ridden with his cousins.

That he could be perceived as snubbing her along the trip, well any set downs that he had delivered he told himself was in defense of the Bennets, though he had met but one. Certainly Darcy had reported no indication that the Bingley women were set against the Bennet girls, but every word of Mrs. Hurst or Miss Bingley certainly steered conversation towards the graces that the Bennet girls lacked by their accounts.

Stephen was glad he heard no remark of Captain and Mrs. Wickham. He had much to do when the ladies discussed the faults of the Bennet girls in front of Georgiana, for Darcy could not always bear the burden of their defense and Bingley seemed to deafen himself to those aspersions.

Georgiana heard them, however, and she did not need to become a part of the backbiting that the Bingley women indulged themselves with. Should they mention Mrs. Wickham then the young girl shivered and looked to her knights for protection. Her guardians were too quick to respond.

Darcy had not known how to ensure that Mrs. Bennet not mention the distasteful name whilst the wedding nuptials took place so Colonel Fitzwilliam volunteered his services,

Madam,

While I give you felicitations and congratulations on your youngest daughters attainment of marriage, I have a great boon to ask of you and your family. I will hope that what I am about to confide in you will not denigrate my reputation in your eyes, for I am hopeful that we shall form a great friendship through the marriage of your daughter to my cousin, and thus we are to be relations.

Some little time ago an affair of honor occurred between myself and another man whose name gives me pains to utter or hear, as even writing such a confidence to you does. I am all defenseless and in your hands as to the outcome of our future relationship. That this man was the son of my cousins steward and I have known him all our lives, that he purchased an ensign in the regiment of Colonel Foster which so briefly bivouacked at Meryton last year, that he has recently married and even with help provided by myself, secured an introduction to the very regiment he serves with now in the north, then to have an affair of honor stand between us is a hardship. I should ask that this indulgence of refraining from the mention of this persons name would do me a great service. That my distress is such, it is magnified in my young cousin, Georgiana, she being of a youthful nature and not knowing how much anguish lies between her beloved cousin and a man she has known since childhood, finds heartache at the impasse.

Mr. W... can no longer be a friend of mine, nor I of he. My cousin, he who is done such a great honor by your awarding him such a jewel as your second daughter, has condescended to my wishes to ensure that Mr. W... and I shall not meet, nor his name be spoken to me. That my cousin Georgiana has tender feelings on the subject also, it seems best to not mention the man to her either. I deem it a personal favor if that arrangement could be observed during the nuptials of my cousin...

Yours,

While there was no guarantee that even at that moment when Darcy and Bingley conveyed the Gardiners to Longbourn, it was thought that Mr. and Mrs. Gardiner also could hope to bring pressure with Elizabeth to keep Mrs. Bennet in check, especially around Georgiana. The Gardiners having learned all when their niece Lydia had been so indiscreet and willful.

The Colonel, who sat with his boots off resting in his well appointed rooms, wondered not how successful his letter was, but how all would conspire to steer the formidable Mrs. Bennet away from such distastefulness. Indeed that Mrs. Bennet was formidable was hearsay to him more from Charles Bingley whose admiration and respect, though not forced or unnatural was a little hollow in the Colonel's ears. He detected this hollowness in the choice of descriptions of praise which was heaped upon Charles' intended, or on Miss Elizabeth, whom the Colonel knew.

Darcy, upon reflection had let some of his torment seep through, "I once described the mother as not having discretion and to this failing, I plead error."

"I can not think of when you have ever mentioned Mrs. Bennet." That was truth in this context, but the Colonel had puzzled out his revelations of Darcy's character to Miss Elizabeth, and their withdrawal from Rosings so immediately thereafter. He knew that on one hand Darcy had saved Bingley from the family that he wished to condemn himself to also after time. It was true that he had never mentioned Mrs. Bennet by name in those regards but it was not hard to link all the circumstances together.

Then of course Mr. Hurst was much less discreet about it some months back, "Damn me, if Charles did not throw out the baby with the bath water. He passed up a damn fine woman just because the mother don't have no proprieties. Now don't let Louisa ever hear that I said this, you understand, but that girl would have been a credit to the family, done us all proud. Never a cross word, damned fine to look at. And the mother, well one need not take the mother with the daughter. 'Sides there are four other gels that she could live off of."

Well happy outcomes all around. Charles would have his Jane on Saturday as Darcy would have his Elizabeth. The Colonel would find a way to steer Caroline Bingley off of his scent, and spend his time chaperoning his ward Georgiana. She was near enough to the school room still that she had enough in common with the children of the Gardiners that she would help entertain them with him.

A sad fact of his society, that so many desired the children to remain in the school rooms except for a few brief hours of display when guests called. From what he had been told of the Gardiners, the children often shared meals with their parents, though that would not be the case at their stay at Longbourn. He had learned on his carriage trip with Mr. Gardiner that Mr. Bennet was very fond of his nieces and nephews and shared his library with them when they stayed at Longbourn, but he found the excitement caused by their dining at his table too much and so, except for the occasion of Christmas lunch, withheld the pleasure of dining with the children.

NEW FAMILY BINDINGS

A few hours later while relaxing in his room with a short volume of Livy, Stephen heard the arrival of the rest of the wedding party. In such a big house, sounds of people moving about were a constant deluge amidst the background of creaks and rustlings that came from all sides. Darcy knocked on his door once Georgiana was settled.

"Fitzwilliam?"

"A moment," The Colonel placed the book aside, carefully marking his place with the now tattered needlepoint his mother had given him at his seventh Christmas. "Please come in, the door is open."

The Colonel had time to put on his slippers before his cousin entered the room. Darcy said, "Ah, you are at your leisure. I do not mean to interrupt."

"Nonsense, I have no pressing business but to wait upon your needs this weekend," the Colonel smiled in reply.

"Thank you for your assistance. I but paused to further express my thanks for your kind treatment this day of the Gardiners," Darcy remarked.

The Colonel held up his hand. "No need to do it brown, I assure you. I believe these Gardiners to be the very best of people. I shall have them to my table and guests of the mess to boot." Darcy had been about to say something but his head jerked in startlement.

"On my account..."

The Colonel grinned, "I do much on your account, cousin, as do you on mine. But this shall be an enjoyment for its own self, as I am sure you agree. Your fair Miss Elizabeth, not withstanding, everything that had been related to me of the Gardiners has been amazingly proved true. Verified by my own ears, and eyes. They are the epitome of gentlefolk with circumstances yet to achieve their place in our society. Though I have no doubt should your alliance with Miss Elizabeth never have come about, we still would have seen the Gardiner children as leaders of the Ton before our time was done." Stephen reflected that he knew more about the confines of events then his cousin and knew that one could fall from the heights very swiftly should circumstances rear their heads.

Stephen had been in his early teens at school when it was brought home to him that his elder brother would want for nothing and have a life of leisure.

The Colonel continued, "Needs must be seen to and all that, I know whereof I speak. Mr. Gardiner may live in Cheapside now but will finish up in St. James's Square." Stephen did not want to be maudlin and dwell on his own need to have a career.

"Indeed, I find that we always have this subject at some point between us." Darcy kept his eyes downcast. The Colonel had tried to avoid the subject.

"We both know the way the world circles the sun..." Stephen said hoping to end the matter quickly.

"Then take your share of Georgiana's wardship. I do not begrudge you the fee," Darcy said.

The Colonel had a large grin, when he displayed it, much more often then his cousin, "I will take it soon as you do. Come! You know that is not who I am. I do well on my allowance and the management of the regimental accounts. My paymasters and quartermasters hate me for my scrupulousness, or rather making them account for the accounting. But I eke out enough that I shall not be destitute by any stretch. I may not be a first charger of the Ton such as you are, or Charles. I may not afford the letting of a house like Netherfield Park, but I shall endeavor to stand on my own."

Darcy shook his head a little. They had been over this rough ground before. "I shall remind myself to drop the subject."

The Colonel also shook his head, "And no doubt we will talk of it again. But let us move on. I agree."

"Indeed, I shall not convey Charles' thanks for your further adroitness this afternoon, for I am sure he shall convey his thanks directly. I should like to mention that Mrs. Bennet asked me about your letter in private once I arrived. I did point out to her how much this upset you, but the rift so much more upset Georgiana that she vowed to not speak the name of her beloved Mr. W., and she caught herself, and said no more on the subject. I am grateful for this as well, but I look to Eliza and Mrs. Gardiner to help rein her in," Darcy stated.

Stephen was pleased with himself. He said, "Yes. From what you have told me, I knew they would have to be enlisted in the campaign."

"I took the liberty of sharing your strategy with Eliza and she also confided in her aunt Gardiner. That lady also suggested that your confidence be presented to Mrs. Bennet's sister, Mrs. Phillips. That matter has been taken care of by my Elizabeth, but I think you shall find that it is an excellent precaution." Darcy nodded. Stephen knew that Darcy had enough of Wickham.

"I am, as I said, entirely at your liberty this weekend. Your marriage is the matter of the moment, all other concerns are seconded. That a frown on fair Georgiana's face would bring a cloud on the occasion I naturally will do all I can to keep the sun shining in all it's splendor," Stephen said referencing his classical education. The Colonel knew more than just the military.

"Now who does it too brown? Well, you have always barreled into the world at the charge, looking for glory." Darcy surely thought the 'charging' befitted the leader of a Cavalry regiment, but with a profession that had the goal of ending the enemy, it seemed a contradiction.

For a moment the Colonel was reluctant to explore a simile that related to his military occupation. He was silent. Darcy, perhaps infected with the too brief reuniting with his beloved, overlooked it.

Darcy said, "Indeed, well presently we shall dine and I must make ready." He paused, "About Miss Bingley..." Stephen contorted his face into his most pained before squaring it to his cousin. "Yes," Darcy continued, "I see you have formed some opinions."

The Colonel said, "Damned woman would be tolerable enough if she had not such a cutting tongue. And though Charles is your good friend, certainly you must see her faults."

"I am afraid that the family apportioned all it's good nature to Charles as you no doubt have ascertained and all of its..." Darcy searched for a polite word.

The Colonel cut to the chase, "Snobbery." Darcy gave him a

look. The two of them did not often hide behind the mores of polite society if truth was to be ignored. They had grown together and been such a part of each others lives that it was natural to be honest, sometimes completely so, with each other. But because each was a perfect example of the Ton, victims of their rearing, they often found themselves shocked and surprised that one would know the dark parts of the other's mind.

"Pride." Darcy finished.

Stephen noted, "And Mrs. Hurst has a large portion of the Bingley's humor and silliness, or perhaps the humor comes from long exposure to the eminently sensible Mr. Hurst." Pretending to sleep through much of the society of the Bingley women seemed a good honest defense.

"I do not know if I am able to hold a conversation with you," Darcy laughed out loud.

"Those were my exact words last Tuesday when I called upon you and we discussed your hare-brained wedding tour plans to Austria. But you are still not to be dissuaded there, I know." Now Darcy was forced to grin, for the Colonel had uttered the very same statement about conversations when trying to discourage his cousin from venturing onto the Continent at such a time.

"You are deflecting me," Darcy observed.

"Indeed not. Miss Bingley would be a good catch were she to but curb her words. She is pleasant to look upon. She has connections. And I am sure Charles will settle on her something grand to make it worth someone's while to take her on. I should imagine that were I in a marrying frame of mind, I could do far worse than Caroline Bingley. Easily would I continue the circle of all our friendships, though I expect as a bride she would be constrained to be polite to your bride, rather then warm and enveloping. After all, you shall always be the one that she originally desired or at least your fortune she originally desired," the Colonel grinned at that. They both knew, unfortunately that with Caroline Bingley, the latter was indeed the case. Darcy would always be one of her admirers that had slipped away.

"I am again chased from my thought. Pray allow me to finish this time." Darcy waited till Stephen gave him a silent nod. "I see that you have built some distance between yourself and the sister of our host. Indeed our hostess here. Charles, as you pointed out does indeed realize some... Very well don't look like that. He realizes all his sister's faults, just as you and I realize all of our faults and make allowances, so does he." Darcy held up a hand.

Darcy continued, "I do not know if he gives her set downs as we would want to do for inappropriate behavior, so do not ask. I should imagine that he does not. And though she may well be due for such a lecture, she acts in her ways. You have done an admirable job, as I said, placing distance between you. I know my duty and though I have concerns this week, I shall not abandon you to the lioness. Well not entirely." There was a grin then.

The Colonel sensed he was allowed to make a comment. "Indeed, have no fears on my account. I think perhaps I did it too strong upon our arrival, but I shall make amends at dinner. I can well take care of my own self amongst the marriage minded. She has passed her seasons and if she doesn't catch soon it shall be all for naught. I have seen these barracudas of the ballroom before, as have you, though I of course have had much more practice at deflecting them. Pity that you have never worn the Red, you would have looked damned dashing. Made all the schoolgirls swoon... I know, doing it too brown." And they both laughed.

"Now tell me all of your reception at Longbourn? Does the family warm to you?" Stephen asked.

* * *

The Colonel knew that arriving early in the sitting room before dinner would be the mark of a bad guest, as no one would be there to receive him or see to his ease. He was fairly sure that Bingley would have some spirits about, but he dreaded encountering the ladies of the manor. He did not relish allowing Georgiana to venture forth on her own, but found that she was taking care with her dressing and had spaced out her time to make her entrance but ten minutes shy of dinner. Darcy had chosen a similar strategy and the Colonel did wonder if Darcy had enlisted the aid of Georgiana's abigail in such endeavor to ensure that they would progress down to dinner together.

That Darcy had not included his cousin in this stratagem, left the Colonel to wander the corridors in search of a retreat where he would find safety from the Bingley ladies. A passing footman was kind enough, of course as a servant it was his place, to point the way to the snooker room. An open bottle and two glasses were sitting in regal state, with Mr. Hurst apparently already having paid his homage.

"Ah, Colonel. I expected some company before dinner, and this is as good a place as any to sequester ones self as any other. The library serves a purpose also, though I find either here or the card room refreshing and am little disturbed when I venture to either. Should you care to join me in a glass? It is enough to brace you for what we are to face..." Mr. Hurst was all good natured and friendly. More to the point he was animated and stood straight and true. When in the company of his wife or sister, the Colonel had not readily been aware that the man emerged to the foreground when so formidable a pair were also present. Here in the snooker room, Hurst emerged as his own self.

Nor did the amount of drink consumed, the perception being that two glasses had been drunk, seemed to effect him adversely. "Indeed, I believe the fortitude you provide is exactly what I should need. And if I may offer you one of these cigars? Yes, from the West Indies. I assure you. We have interests in several different plantations, though father has not taken outright ownership of nary a one."

"Quite right, wouldn't want to be accused of trade. Canny man your pater. Wish mine could say the same. He was in trade. Set me up right o'course. But still, you know, the stigma. Never can wash away the scent..." Hurst barked out a laugh. As much as he was upset by that, he still seemed to not take it as seriously as others would.

He was right. The Ton would cut him cruelly for his past, was true. Many would never look beyond the heritage to see the man. Certainly the Colonel knew that from practical experience. His parents could be, and certainly his Aunt were practitioners of that bigoted belief. He, having met too many idiot sons with perfect pedigree, and capable lads who couldn't find a trace of aristocratic blood in his service in the military, knew that one needed to see the man, not the lineage.

Breeding counted for something, Stephen would concede, but not nearly as much as was generally given credit. The Colonel knew that Hurst had more to him then he let the casual observer see. And possibly more than even his wife, who had been born to a family a few generations further from the hard scrabble of life than her husband would acknowledge. That Hurst presented one face to the Ton showed some shrewdness, for the Colonel indeed knew how vicious his society not only could be, but was more often than not. How often Stephen had been more ashamed of his friends and acquaintances, then proud. Oh yes, how great it was to be English.

"Well, to your health, Colonel, to your health." Hurst toasted after handing the officer his glass. For a moment Stephen thought his host would drink the entire amount in one swift toss, but he was mistaken. A good swallow was what passed the lips of the man. The Colonel did the same and was instantly warmed by the liquid, soon scorching into the back of his throat. Certainly one could taste the notes of iodine that permeated the strong stuff, but there were hints of lavender and cherries also, which the Colonel found astonishing.

"This is quite nice."

"Thank you, the Pater did do something right, we own the distillery and nearly the whole damnable town that goes with it. Well I shouldn't fault the Scottish for their ways, but the reason they are able to be so frugal is that they rob the landlords blind. I toured the distillery in my salad days, just after school, and all the maltmen must drink two bottles a day at least... And should you think this is smooth, and you don't have to be kind, I know that it is as liable to tear your throat out in one batch as be sweet as a lasses kiss in the next. The stuff those men drink at the distillery is the raw stuff, right out of the vats, not laid down or aged at all. Not that this here has been put aside for more than a few months itself, but I tell you the liquor they drink would make your hair all fall off, I swear it."

The Colonel smiled, he had heard somewhat the same from a few of the Scottish Officers he knew when they talked of the Whisky that was becoming more popular. That the Hursts owned a distillery was not surprising as there were hundreds of them. Every small family, village and town seeming to support the industry. "I hear rumblings that the government is thinking of giving the industry rules and regulations."

"Perhaps. Certainly should. But you know the government, in this lifetime, the next or that of our grandchildren. Taking the long view of things..." Hurst seemed to be optimistic as he smiled while elaborating.

"I take it you are a student of our Parliament and its glacial deliberations?" A hobby that many of the Ton pursued.

"I, no. Don't have the mind for it, I should think. Don't even have the mind for the Pater's trade. Do like the money though. Pater set me up to enjoy life, so I do. Can't see making my way at a thing, as don't know anything. Lucky to not be sent down when at school, only just, though. Could've gone the other way." Hurst took another swallow. Then looked about the room, cue stick in his hand, he moved it about in a small circle whilst one end stayed firmly planted near his right foot.

"Yes, I think you are, right. The ladies with their dressing most assuredly have given us ample time to play a game of snooker." The Colonel jumped ahead sensing the awkwardness of the moment for Hurst who faced an honest assessment of his life.

"What? That is... I was thinking... Yes you are quite right indeed. A game is just the thing. Say a shilling a point?" Always a gamesman, amongst gentlemen of their rank the stakes were quite acceptable and they laid into the competition. Hurst loosing the first round by three, and the second by two before an under-butler came to inform them that the ladies and Mr. Bingley were in the sitting room, and that the Darcy's were expected momentarily.

"Good game that," Hurst said as they entered the room where the others had all gathered prior to dinner. Two more rounds of the Whisky had been consumed but it was still not evident in their character for both men seemed to comport themselves with sober distinction.

"Yes," Bingley said, "You two had a game?"

"Indeed," the Colonel provided, "We were enjoying your fine snooker table. Mr. Hurst and I have had two wonderful rounds upon it, and I look forward to many more during our stay."

"Why that sounds grand. I should dearly love to join you for those rounds," Bingley said.

"Charles, certainly there are other duties for you to attend to prior to Saturday?" Caroline reminded him.

Charles paused for a second, "Yes, I had not forgotten. But there will be free time to spend with my guests. We do not dine at Longbourn but once prior to Saturday, and the Bennets also join us but once..."

"The Bennets join us?" Caroline asked.

Across the small table that separated them on a settee opposite, Georgiana cringed as did several others about the room.

Charles took another moment, "I beg your pardon, I must have forgotten in the rush of affairs since our return from Longbourn. I extended an invitation upon your behalf to have my in-laws and their family to dinner this Thursday and of course tomorrow we dine at Longbourn..." Charles had run out of words as he looked to see his sister's face.

"Charles... Charles.. Oh... How could you do so? I just don't know where to begin, why the house is not ready to receive guests... The servants have had no instructions... I shall have to meet with the cook first thing and see what we can do to accommodate so many people. Is there enough food here, or can we buy it in the village. Charles, you are a monster..."

Charles stood for a moment contemplating what to reply as the other members of the party looked about to other corners. Louisa Hurst looked at her hands not knowing which sibling to support, "Louisa, you tell him," Caroline instructed into the awkward moment.

"Indeed Charles you are very bad."

"Upon my word, I did not do this to distress you. It seemed to be the appropriate thing to do..."

Darcy had an interjection, "Come Caroline, if this is overwhelming for you with all that must be attended to for the nuptials, I am sure that we can have the Fox Tavern in Meryton accommodate us for an evening. Indeed, if this is dinner is too much for Netherfield to host on such short notice, I shall play host at the Fox." Darcy offered, but it was too much.

"No Darcy that is too kind..." Charles spoke immediately.

Caroline was not a moment behind. "You are too gracious Mr. Darcy. We shall do our best in the limited time Charles has allotted us. I am sure that it will turn out to be a memorable evening. And one that your in-laws will find quite grand in comparison to what else is available here." That line cut.

The Colonel added his own conjecture, "My mother, the Countess and I had a long talk but a month ago about Meryton and those surrounding it. Have you been to the Duke of Bedford's hunting lodge? It is Carton House and it is but twelve miles distant of Meryton. Certainly not part of Meryton society proper, but indeed a grand place. I was there once for a few days sport shortly after my years at school. It was a few months before I purchased the Colonelcy..." This segue led to a discussion of the grand houses of the surrounding neighborhood which showed up Caroline for thinking that Netherfield was the leading estate in the county. It was not, but it was certainly the nicest that was in the proximity of Meryton. That, however, did not connote to the idea that the inhabitants by birth or breeding were superior to their neighbors.

"So by my count, we have seven great estates all within a day's ride of the village. That is a goodly number, why from father's seat, there are but six within a day's ride, though there are many houses that I find more than comfortable in not only their appearance but also the camaraderie of their inhabitants whom I find refreshing, stimulating and the best of society. I should not be surprised if this little corner of the world has produced the same as the family estates, for have they not produced exquisite brides for both Charles and Darcy?" That the Colonel could step into the void and set down Caroline whilst praising the others was only furthering the problems of their relationship.

"That is a great many, there are but four near Pemberley at that distance, if I am right, Georgiana." Darcy did not want another to distract the conversation to the truth that the Colonel unveiled. Darcy knew that he was not being necessarily subtle.

"Oh, yes indeed. With Pemberley, there are only five houses that you would think of as great estates."

"Surely though none so great as Pemberley. Why I believe Hurst that is where you last saw Miss Elizabeth Bennet, not so?" Charles said. He too knew that there was enough diversion in the conversation that the pretense that Caroline had subscribed to was now moot. The conversation flowed from there and soon the group went in to dinner, the Colonel beginning a discussion of the great houses that he knew of from his fathers seat, to that of Rosings, and Pemberley, and the many others he had guested at.

When the last course had come, Charles looked to see that the nearly two hours of eating still was partnered by the discussion of the many estates that the small group knew of, "So Netherfield is a very good estate indeed, Bingley." The Colonel continued, "And considering what little I know of the grounds though you have related to me, I should think it quite a fine place indeed amongst those of my acquaintance. Set you up right proper as a country squire should you take to making improvements and letting go your house in Town."

"Why Colonel, we would never do that." Caroline said. That she existed as a complete dependent on the largess of her brother did not really allow her to assert herself this way.

Darcy, found a little to add, "No? There have been much times of late where I have thought whilst in Town how much I longed for Pemberley, that is home. I know that you could sense this differently, Miss Caroline, as you have lived your whole life entire in London, but do you not find there is a soothing calm to that which enwraps us here?"

Caroline could not but answer that, "Well Mr. Darcy, should I have Pemberley to lure me, I can concede your point. But here we must weigh the delights of Meryton with the, oh perhaps, grandeur that is London."

"There are parts of London and the society of Town, that I should argue are far from grand." The Colonel came back with. He looked behind the lady to the sideboard where sat the Port. Stephen made a bet with himself that within three minutes, the ladies would retire and the Port would begin to be passed.

"But how can one say that? Is it not the host to great Palaces, Nobility, Royalty, the center of the arts?" Mr. Hurst began to look openly towards the sideboard also, a turn that did not go unnoticed by his wife.

Stephen said, "I say that because while those avenues are open to us, a very few, London is inhabited by hundreds of thousands, no more than a million, who are separated from all that you call grandeur. Their lives are such that they can see our heights of glory and ever hope to succeed to it, but whilst trying to do so, they climb through a life that I can not begin to describe here in civilized society.

"This morning as we left Town, you could not but see the areas of the city where art, nobility, royalty is the furthest thing from the minds, and the ambitions of thousands who live there. We are privileged, and living in Town reinforces that at every turn. No. Here in the country, where one can actively work towards the betterment of ones tenants, I think is the best of places to be." The Colonel often contemplated how different his life would have paralleled with his ambitions should he have been the first born.

"Well said, Colonel." Charles thought to speak, and was echoed with a 'Here! here!' from Mr. Hurst.

Not that this was a set down to Caroline, though she immediately looked to take it as so. Charles, likely quick to know how his sister would react and ever striving to not ripple the waters, followed his first endorsement. "I have taken some interest lately in the tenants of Netherfield as the new owner, where on our first visit Caroline, you will remember, how we were uncertain should I" there was an emphasis to the pronoun, "like this half as much as Darcy often relates in his love of Pemberley. Of course with my beloved Jane, here the enchantment of the location has grown on me so that, I daresay, I am more fond of Meryton then Darcy could ever be."

Colonel Fitzwilliam thought that to be true. And noting the raised eyebrow of Darcy, he deemed that his cousin felt the same. But they both had witnessed Miss Caroline being curbed by her brother which was the correct manner of things. An opinion ill expressed that strove to belittle another's close held beliefs was often volleyed back in kind. Caroline had not been exposed to that, having ruled over her brother and the Hursts for far too long. And as reported to the Colonel not only by Darcy but also by Miss Elizabeth when at Rosings, he was sure that without some boundaries quickly enforced, Caroline would strive to do the same to Jane, once she became mistress of the manor.

Caroline took a moment to look about the table then said,

"Hmm, Louisa, Georgiana, it would seem that the men are ready to have some serious discussion about the tenants and the management of Netherfield. I fear that the conversation is more than we need participate in, shall we retire to let them enjoy their Port and discussion. Charles, we shall see you presently in the drawing room." With that she made to rise and the men all bounded to their feet. The Colonel it would be noted sinuously pushed his chair back and unfolded himself in a stance that was close to attention as if he was being inspected by the Prince of Wales, himself.

"Yes sister, we shall attend you presently."

The three ladies quickly departed, Georgiana looking to Darcy and the Colonel and both knowing that they would indeed have to attend the ladies after one brief round of Port. It would be better in the following two nights, as they would be in the company of many other ladies. But left by herself to defend against the onslaughts of the opinions of Caroline Bingley, for one did wonder if Louisa Hurst had any of her own, such a fate was not one a gentleman could allow to be endured.

"Just one glass I think. Pity I feel so fatigued for my normal want, Charles you know, is to have three or four whilst enjoying one of these cigars," Stephen said.

Mr. Hurst was right there with a response to that, "Capital plan that. I should be more than pleased to shadow you in such an endeavor." A smile beamed on his face. For certainly such a plan would take more than a good hour of discourse away from the parlor of the ladies.

"Fitzwilliam is quite right, if the fatigue of the road were not so prevalent, I too should think a few rounds before joining the ladies to be in order," Darcy said

"Hah," the Colonel projected, "And the next two nights we dine with the Bennets, I should doubt that any time shall be spent at table after the ladies depart either. I sense Hurst that then, when we are in no means fatigued, we shall find two grooms eager to be at the sides of their intendeds as soon as their father allows them to take leave."

Hurst laughed as the Port was passed to him, "I believe you are right, but as I have dined with Mr. Bennet, I should think that we might have a round or two when in his company. Having had so many dinners with naught but his clutch of womenfolk, I have found that he enjoys the company of men at table excessively. And now with two such fine sons to be to share those dinners I think this small pleasure shall be one he savors every part of enjoyment he can from it."

Darcy smiled as he poured but a small tipple into his glass and passed the bottle back to Charles. It now having made one trip around the table. "An excellent observation of our father. I believe that gives us a toast, Hurst. To Mr. Bennet soon to be made Happy with an increase of sons."

"Mr. Bennet." The others intoned and sipped from their Port. Darcy had taken so little that he had finished all of his.

There was an awkward moment of silence. The Colonel indulged himself in another swallow. Looked to Darcy who had put his glass aside and to Charles who toyed with his own. "Well Hurst it is you and I to either finish this very nice vintage, or to abandon it and join the ladies for Charles and Darcy are ready to join them, and today we do not even have the allurement of the Bennet brides..."

Hurst found that humorous enough to laugh at in a short quick explosion of breath. "If all the same to you, I should cast my vote for staying, though I fear I shall carry the lesser weight. And if I find myself standing alone on this motion, then perhaps I shall be able to spend time back in the billiards parlor for some span of time."

Charles knew his brothers inclinations well after these few years, "Indeed, you have full run of our house as you well know. I think that Louisa expects you to look to your pleasure for nigh on half an hour should you choose."

Stephen said, "There, then my observation is a right. These two grooms do hasten to rejoin the ladies in the hopes that the evening shall end quick and when day breaks be off for their intended's side again. Why to think that with a lifetime to be with the virtuous pair all but upon us this Saturday, that they wish to arrive at the moment as quick as can be, whilst not savoring every spare moment of freedom until the Reverend Dr. Thackston announces that they are married."

Darcy made to speak, but Hurst was the quicker, "You are correct in that observation. Why I have never known Charles to be so focused as he is now."

"You may joke about it, but I recollect how attentive you were to Louisa just prior to your wedding." Charles grinned but Hurst laughed again.

"Ah speaks youth, for though indeed I was attentive, I did still spend a great deal of time with my fellows before the blessed event." From what the Colonel could tell now, Hurst had relatively few friends outside of the circle that the Bingleys' provided.

"Well whatever the case, cousin, I expect that your observation is somewhat based on that which so often rears its head." Darcy said looking to the Colonel even as he pushed his seat away from the table.

The other men followed. Stephen said, "I am jealous for, and no slight to you Bingley, but I was captivated by Darcy's choice when at Rosings, also. But would I do it too brown to think that I would hanker to be attracted like a magnet to the side of my future wife. I think such a change in character would not be evident."

"Hence love slays all that has come before it," Darcy rejoined.

Charles nodded, "Indeed, and now let us join the ladies."

FIRST IMPRESSIONS

Leading a brace of horses and riding the elegant Night, Stephen set out for Longbourn. Night's sleek black coat shining, as the sun reflected from the mane, with well polished shoes and toes, Night knew that he was something to behold and proudly shook his head. The ride to Longbourn was pleasant.

Before this, though, Colonel Fitzwilliam had awakened at his customary time and found that Darcy had proceeded to enjoy his breakfast.

Georgiana and the Colonel thus were able to join Darcy as he finished reading the paper at table, a habit that Charles kindly indulged his guests for the same courtesy was allowed at Pemberley. Though, there, the paper was always a day late. Here at Netherfield, the proximity to Town allowed couriers to deliver *The Times* no later than nine of the clock each day. Many of the gentry around Meryton regularly received their news with anticipation.

"I say Colonel, much to do about the Tyrant," Charles began, as only he and Darcy were present in the breakfast room as yet.

Darcy caught his cousin's look of displeasure, "Certainly, the Tyrant is newsworthy and one believes the best way to deal with such a phenomena is to talk little about it."

"Ah, cousin, the ham is exceedingly good. I believe the cook uses a molasses base from the West Indies in her stock, and bastes the entire thing whilst it cooks," Darcy interjected before the talk led to the discussion of war.

"Good, I shall be a trencherman this morning, for I have quite an adventure planned with the Gardiner children." The conversation had been successfully steered away from the wars unpleasantness and Charles caught onto the byplay.

"Oh, yes, the children. I should think that the young miss Bennets might also enjoy a ride about the countryside too," Charles pointed out. He was keenly aware that his father to be did not have a stable of riding animals for pleasure.

Darcy folded his paper and placed it at the seat his cousin would take. Georgiana and the Colonel had gone to the side board to serve themselves of a vast selection of food. The Colonel did stack his plate, but no more then he would finish, though, it was quite a great deal. He wished he could store up the tastes and experiences of such a repast for the times ahead, when he would be campaigning and such largesse would be scarce indeed.

Georgiana had gone to her seat when he turned from the food, and he found a footman was sliding her chair in for her. "Do not all the Bennet ladies have much to do in preparation for the arrangements on Saturday?"

Georgiana added to this, "At first they were determined to make all the arrangements, but my brother is so good, he asked permission of Mr. Bennet to be of help in providing for the wedding feast."

"Georgiana, please." Darcy looked embarrassed but all at the table knew that was the extent of it. Darcy had hired persons in Meryton to provide all the food and prepare the assembly rooms for the nuptial feast.

Stephen said, "Oh I didn't imagine that the Bennet ladies would be cooking entirely for all of us, but I should expect that the brides and their sisters would have many tasks to do to prepare for such an event. Wedding clothes, helping pack for the wedding tour, all that sort of thing. If however, the ladies are able, I should be pleased to ride with them as well."

Charles looked at his guests, "Yes perhaps you are right, though I should think that my sisters would jump at a chance to ride your Night. So should I, come to speak of it."

"My dear Bingley, Night is at your disposal whenever you request him." Colonel Fitzwilliam thought ahead that soon enough Night should be in London while he went to the Continent with some lesser beast. Night was too pretty a mount to chance in combat.

"Very good of you."

Georgiana looked at her cousin with a small startlement. "Yes, you too Georgiana. Your seat is now quite capable of handling the brute." The Colonel acknowledged that the young miss had accomplished the ability to manage a difficult mount.

"Hmm," Darcy cleared his throat. "I wonder when we shall call for the carriage."

Georgiana looked up from her plate again, "Why brother don't concern yourself with the carriage on my account. I should prefer riding to Longbourn."

"Yes dear, I know that you would wish it, but I think that by the end of the day you might be fatigued and should wish to have the carriage available then." Darcy supplied. The Colonel ate and reflected that there must be some other motive, when a footman arrived with a note for Charles.

After quickly reading it, "It is from Caroline. She begs an indulgence that you amuse yourselves this morning and shall see us later after she has rested. She is tired from the journey of yesterday." The Colonel reflected that a letter from Mrs. Hurst should follow shortly also.

With the carriage at Longbourn, the chances of the Bingley sisters joining the wedding guests at the Bennet house diminished, Stephen thought. The Colonel nodded slightly to Darcy, who acknowledged the point.

It was then that Hurst arrived. "Oh jolly good, a full spread. Oh and Louisa is having a lie in. Not feeling at all well after the journey yesterday. Should be right as rain soon enough though. Hmm, I say a double rasher of bacon I think."

Approaching Longbourn, the Colonel could see the house. Not a grand manor as Netherfield was, but certainly functional enough. Perhaps four to six rooms. Very early Georgian. One small addition at some point. Otherwise a very good home for a county gentleman with no Town aspirations. He realized he would be happy with such a set-up but would like something a little larger. His father's estate had spoiled him as a youth and though not as grandiose as Pemberley or Rosings Park, the home of the Earl of M----K was much more functional than either of those. Certainly the art collection his mother had put together outranked that displayed in either of his relation's estates.

Here behind the carriage where Darcy and Georgiana sat, he enjoyed the prospect of the park of Longbourn. An entity with more than one secret location for quiet contemplation.

Charles rode his own horse just ahead. Hurst had decided to eat his breakfast and then spend the day at Netherfield wandering the grounds and looking to the shooting which he planned to indulge in once the marriage ceremony was wrapped up.

Just the four then ventured to pay a social call for a few hours upon the Bennets before returning to Netherfield and preparing for dinner. Since Dinner was to be at Longbourn, the Colonel believed that some suggestion later would be to send for their evening clothes, but he also feared that Mrs. Bennet would be ill prepared to extend that amenity to her sons and their family. The Colonel resolved to be surprised as the day unfolded.

As they neared the house, he saw the two youngest of the Gardiner children playing with an older girl. Coppery hair was tied with a loose ribbon. Her dress was not exceedingly old, but not in fashion. A shade of white and yellow muslin with a a red ribbon tied below her bosom that fit her figure with an emphasis in the right places. With the sun shining, Stephen got a very nice look at the form of her athletic legs and turned his head before Georgiana caught him gaping at them. The girl, or young woman, as he quickly interpreted, must be one of the other Bennet girls, for there was a resemblance to Miss Elizabeth.

A look towards Charles showed no exceptional joy on his face, so the girl was not the Bennet beauty, Jane. Though Stephen would be hard pressed not to say that she was anything other than a beauty herself.

Certainly her age was younger to Elizabeth in any case. Stephen thought that made her one of the younger sisters. Caroline had taken pains at one time to describe all the girls, and as was her way, did so in a deprecating manner. Not only did Night shake his majestic head, but so did the Colonel as he wondered yet again how one could be bred to a society of manners and be so indiscreet with them. That the Bingley girls were closer to their trade antecedents was evident in their manners and he wondered that if the affable Charles did not exist, how far in society they would get. Stephen's good manners, however, prevented him from investigating that vein with Darcy.

As the small party approached the playing children, they were noticed and all ran to the carriage to exchange hellos. While the Gardiner children were warm and friendly to Darcy, the young lady was much kindlier disposed to Georgiana. This was but a brief impression, for Bingley and he were upon them within moments. Here introductions were offered to the girl who was indeed a Bennet sister, Miss Catherine Bennet.

"Have you brought the horses for our ride Colonel?"

"Night is splendidly turned out today. May I ride first please?"

Georgiana smirked, because in their family she had been the young child always asking for such things from her older cousins and brother. And though each indulged her, it was by far the greatest ease to get the Colonel to bend to her wishes. Though for the main she seldom abused such.

"Indeed yes, we are here for a ride. Miss Catherine, it is a great pleasure. My cousins have informed me that you are a lively social partner, and a font for information of the neighborhood. I shall ask to enlist your aid in a mission most grave later, if I have your leave. But for the nonce these young ones must claim my previously promised attention."

She had perfect teeth he noticed when she smiled, and her cheeks dimpled more than Georgiana's making the tableau wholesome indeed. "Pray Colonel, with great anticipation my cousins have awaited your arrival here at Longbourn, for the entirety of their conversation has been of your promise to let them ride the greatest steed in all of England."

The Colonel had dismounted at this point and looked to the two youngsters, noting that the other two Gardiner children, with their older cousins and mother had emerged from the house to greet the arrivals.

"In all of England." He turned to lift the smallest into the saddle of his horse. "Nay, say in all Christendom, for does not your steed, young Geoffrey," he was fortunate to remember the names of all four children, "show you to your most magnificence. There, upon good Night, are you not fit to conquer worlds and slay the infidel?"

* * *

The other adults smiled and Kitty looked at the handsome officer before her. He was older then many of those of the militia that had been living in Meryton just the previous year. But he was also a Colonel. His family wealth could easily have purchased the office for him when he was young, though she had learned from Elizabeth that the Colonel had gone to university first, then waited for a few years before taking colors. He was thus somewhat seasoned, and this had all been a few years ago.

He was of an age with Mr. Darcy. Perhaps a year younger. The same height as his cousin and thus they were easily the two tallest men that Kitty had met. She, having reached the age of seventeen, felt sure she had stopped growing put perhaps there was an inch or two left within her. There was a soft brown sheen to his hair, so not as dark as his cousin. A great deal of hair that as he had doffed his hat blew about in the breeze. He had lines near his eyes, and she could see that they were formed from his smiling and laughter. She even heard such an example within a minute of their meeting for her cousin's the Gardiner's antics caused all to laugh and smile. Even Mr. Darcy grinned. The Colonel kept his face clean shaven and his sideburns were cut close, not the height of military fashion at all.

His eyes were blue, and very clear and light. Naturally he was fit as the youthful leader of a line regiment ought to be. That Kitty had seen very few line officers, for the Militia was anything but. She admitted that she found him impressive. He was in mufti, so she had to imagine what he would look like in his uniform but she had looked up in her father's library some plates of the Colonel's Regiment and recognized they were quite dashing. More so than the militia.

She had asked Lizzy if she had seen the Colonel in uniform and found he had promised to wear his regimentals to the wedding ceremony. Kitty could hardy wait. She would spend hours writing a letter to Lydia and make her angered that she had been unable to return from the north to attend the wedding. Kitty was not aware of the particulars that lay between Mr. Wickham and Mr. Darcy, but she recognized that if her older sisters chose Mr. Darcy over Mr. Wickham, then surely the odds favored Mr. Darcy being in the right. Consciously she knew that Lydia was too impulsive for not only Lydia's good, but that of the rest of her family.

Kitty recognized that Lydia had been very intemperate when she had run off with Wickham, but Kitty felt that she had been spared the ridicule of society, as her youth surely would shelter her from it. She quickly learned that youth was no armor against such scorn, and so had grown from the experience. Since the posting of the Banns about Darcy and Bingley and her two older sisters, Kitty and Mary had become slightly more desirable company for the unmarried men of the county, and, she was basking in the attention. Kitty knew she was considered more handsome then her bookish sister.

Her father, however, did not relish this new found attention, nor did her soon to be married sisters. Elizabeth was quite opinionated on the veracity and sagacity of her admirers. Kitty also had to admit that many were attracted now to her because her relations were to be amongst the first set of the Ton, and they quite wealthy too.

With the children gathering, it did not take long to organize a short ride for them, though the duration lengthened. Mrs. Bennet did not bestir herself from her sitting room to meet the new acquaintance of the Colonel, though Mr. Bennet was coerced by his brother Mr. Gardiner to venture forth from the sanctum of his library and was given to support the general opinion that the Colonel was a lively well mannered sort.

***

In Mr. Bennet's eye, the Colonel's chief accomplishment was that he not only kept the Gardiner children entertained and out of the way, but he seemed to also cozen his own children and the sounds of youth and gaiety distanced themselves from his house.

That he had children, Mr. Bennet did not regret. That they were all girls, he was not overly perturbed one way or another. That he had them trained to, on general principle, keep their outbursts to a nominal level was all that he had wished for, and found that he was only circumvented in this upon the great occasions when his wife went into an uproar over one trifle or another. That Lizzy and Jane did not follow his wife's foolish ways, and as he reflected that Mary would never be seen to emulate her either, it left but Catherine and Lydia to be the images of his wife.

Mr. Bennet had noted that with Lydia removed, Kitty had left off her childish ways and was much less troublesome. Kitty saw humor in simple things, and even showed great moments of kindness to all about her. Certainly a trait that she did not inherit from him, for Mr. Bennet thought of himself as somewhat acerbic. Mr Bennet recognized that he tended to look for such a touch when the fancy took him.

In all things, since the resolution of the conundrum of Lydia and Wickham had seasoned into the marriages of Jane and Elizabeth, Mr. Bennet reflected that life had turned for the better. Mary would stay and be a companion to her mother in her old age, for he did not think that she was destined for matrimony, though he could indeed be wrong, for but one year before he would have been hard pressed to believe any of his children would wed. Catherine, by inclination, it seemed, was on a course to marry someone quite like himself. A gentleman of little means and no ambition. And Mr. Bennet reflected that with certain compromises made, it could be a good relationship for all.

"Splendid fellow the Colonel," Mr. Bennet remarked as he returned to the library. He knew that his brother but waited to discuss the man and the impression he was making. Mr. Bennet further pondered, much as if his discourse was a game of chess, that by providing Mr. Gardiner with such a topic, they would easily converse and exchange ideas for more than a half hour and this he found would be quite satisfactory.

"Indeed I must agree," Mr. Gardiner said.

"He entertains the children with good grace and perspicacity." Mr. Bennet added. He was unsure whether he said it to be a conversation point, or if he truly believed it.

"He was very solicitous yesterday as we traveled. I also enjoyed some fine hours of conversation as we came up from Town," Mr. Gardiner responded.

"Indeed, he has a good turn of mind you say?" Mr. Bennet was ever in search of men that he could discourse with. He had found so few in his lifetime that any loneliness of spirit stemmed from that.

"I should expect that he is as well educated as Mr. Darcy and Mr. Bingley, and that I have found each to be bright, engaging gentleman able to hold an intelligent thought on a great many things." Gardiner elaborated. He hit the mark with his brother for Mr. Bennet had now completely reevaluated Darcy in light of the engagement between him and Lizzy. That Mr. Bennet had come to enjoy the times he spent with both of his future sons he found refreshing. In culmination, he had found two men who complimented his daughters greatly. One was all congeniality, perhaps the most memorable trait of Jane's thus emulated in Bingley who strove to ensure all were comfortable at all times. The other was reserved but quick of wit, and used a well founded education to advantage. Much the same as Elizabeth.

Mr. Bennet regretted that he had dismissed Darcy early on, and thus had lost months of good conversation. He made up for it now and looked to more opportunities to do so. With Stephen Fitzwilliam, Mr. Bennet surmised that he fell somewhere in between the always congenial Charles Bingley and the reserved and astute Fitzwilliam Darcy.

Mr. Bennet further reflected that their circles would commingle now, but that those times that they did would not be often. Certainly, not as often as Kitty would like. She had long passed the time of pining for the men of Colonel Forster's regiment, but now with another military man so close to hand, Mr. Bennet could see the signs he had witnessed last fall and winter. He certainly did not wish a repetition of those events and so would heartily wish Colonel Fitzwilliam on his way, when the wedding festivities were concluded.

* * *

The Gardiner children enjoyed their horseback rides tremendously and the Colonel had to sit with the littlest young boy, who was but five, in his lap for he was still too small to control such a big animal by himself. Soon enough though, it was clear that Night tired of the little jaunts with the children about Longbourn's park. "Now children, you have had a good deal of fun, but Night wishes his gallop also before we brush him down and then go to our nuncheon. Miss Kitty Bennet, should you like to do the honors?"

The Colonel was at that time mounted on his favorite and he looked down at the young lady. Darcy stood nearby and was engaged in conversation and holding the hand of Elizabeth as it rested upon his sleeve. Stephen saw his cousin turn hearing this and looked on the exchange.

Kitty said, "I thank you good Colonel. I should find the honor quite pleasurable indeed, but I am not dressed for riding, and your saddle is not equipped for me."

The Colonel recognized that he did not have a side saddle for ladies to ride, and seeing Mrs. Bennet's form looking to the park from an upper window of the house, had prompted him in this exchange. He received a nod from Mrs. Gardiner so slight that Jane, who stood next to her aunt, did not see it.

The Colonel thus reached out his hand, "My dear Miss Kitty, no need of a ladies saddle, nor of your being properly dressed for we do not go to ride with the Ton in Hyde Park and let others gaze upon us at the Serpentine. No, Night has never cottoned to that. Here, your hand and we shall swiftly away to give Night some exercise. The weight of both of us shall be the inducement my friend here needs to shake off the lethargy he has this day." That the Colonel's hand was there before her, it was but natural for her to take it and in a trice she was up and seated sideways on his lap in the saddle, much as her little cousin had been a moment before.

Charles thought it capital that the Colonel and Kitty were off at a trot towards the lane and exclaimed a burst of laughter that was clear. That the crease upon Darcy's brow was evident in contrast to the crinkles surrounding Georgiana's smile gave pause. The reactions from several about the park were in each of these modes. Either smiling at the humor of the two, or frowning at their impropriety. Stephen noted as they rode a circle about the grounds.

If the Colonel had been a cad, then further reflection from his friends and a scold would be called for. That he was a gentleman only slightly prepared the ground for a put down by Darcy when they returned to Netherfield. Further the wind would be taken from those sails as Darcy knew that the Colonel had no designs upon any young lady until the business on the Continent was to be completed.

"You are a devil, sir," Catherine said as the trot increased in pace.

"I, well perhaps Miss Kitty, perhaps. Shall we let Night have his head?"

"If it is safe," She said tightening her grip on the saddle horn and around the man's waist.

"Safe. Safe as houses I should think." Letting Night step faster.

The wind began to rush by and Kitty could feel the strong forearms of the Colonel also grip her sides as his arms reached around each side of her to guide the horse.

Kitty could sense that her perch was not as firm as when they but trotted, "Sir you mock me. This is dangerous."

"Miss Kitty, I am an officer of the crown. I swear to defend you from any dangers that we may encounter."

"I don't expect a French Regiment to pop up at Meryton Colonel, but there are spots along the lane that could stand some attention, and this is what I worry about." She shifted to replace her weight back on the lap of the Colonel.

He recognized that unless they achieved a much closer bond, the speeds which Night would prefer to charge about the countryside would be hazardous to attempt. And should he try to make Miss Kitty more comfortable and safe, he would have crossed the line of civility. He was not a rake. At least not as yet.

"Here boy, slow there, yes that's it. Very well Miss Bennet, we shall be more stately here for you are familiar with all these parts and I am a stranger." From what he could see though, he knew that Night was up to the conditions of the countryside. It was himself that was not. And as he thought it through, the only other lass he had ever allowed to ride with him in such a way was Georgiana. No other woman had ever excited and presented him the opportunity to treat this way at the same moment.

"You shiver, sir." And indeed he had. He had thought in counterpoint to his cousin Georgiana there was his cousin Anne who would never be allowed near Night. Let alone the chance to be carried upon the saddle in the same way in which he had Miss Kitty Bennet.

"Just a passing thought. Come, Night has had a good run to shake off the cobwebs for now. We must back to your home at the trot, then after nuncheon I shall ride this beast hard for his exercise."

Their return to the threshold of Longbourn was greeted with much cacophony as many had an opinion to offer. Stephen looked to Darcy and the stare he got only caused him to throw back his head and laugh with joyfulness. Such that some would also take up the glee, and others would be aghast at the explosion of sound.

When all was settled, the party did go to their nuncheon. The Colonel, a great favorite with the children, sat with Mrs. Gardiner, Mr. Bingley and Jane and the four adults entertained them throughout the lunch.

Mr. Bennet had been apprised of the inappropriate ride of the Colonel and his youngest unmarried daughter. His opinions of the Colonel, Stephen saw upon his face and they changed once again, now they returned to being favorable as Mr. Bennet saw his young nieces and nephews completely preoccupied with Stephen and Mr. Bennet's end of the table at peace with only adults.

The lunch also offered Colonel Stephen his first meeting with Mrs. Bennet. Here, he brushed aside all of Darcy's revelations of the woman and was completely at his ease with her. He considered her as silly as he considered his aunt de Bourgh. It was a different form of mind, but his mother had taught him the forbearance of dealing with frivolous women. The Countess had many in her social circle whom she had to acquaint herself with that were so.

The Countess had striven to ensure that her two sons could recognize the women who were not as strong minded as others. To embrace them, and to acknowledge that women would never have the same benefit of education that the Colonel and his brother had been afforded. Once that was taken into account, then the boys, now men, should be able to make decisions accordingly. His older brother had offered for a woman who was vain in her beauty, and in this regard the Colonel considered his sister to be that which his mother had sought to keep her sons well separated from. Colonel Stephen knew to relish these women, but to stay at arm's length from them, also.

Elizabeth and Mrs. Gardiner sat on either side of him and he was able to converse quite enjoyably with each. Mrs. Bennet had at first sought to pair the Colonel with Kitty, but Mr. Bennet seemed to quite easily rearrange the table. Mrs. Bennet thus found herself surrounded by her brother and Charles Bingley. It was Darcy who was ensconced between the young Catherine and his own sister Georgiana.

His young cousin was in quite good spirits, charming Mr. Bennet and also holding a conversation with Mary Bennet. The Colonel, long adroit at not only keeping a conversation going, but listening to the other conversations at table, found that despite her youth, Kitty was able to keep Darcy occupied enough that he did not retreat into quietude was amusing indeed.

Stephen said, "So Miss Eliza, this hare brained scheme of Austria surely must be all Darcy, for I have a dim memory that he has always wished to revisit the alps. We did both journey there some five years ago after our college days I recollect..."

"Why indeed he has informed me so..." She smiled sweetly at him.

"I detect by that statement he has informed you of far too much," He said, though he had a large smile as well.

"Oh I am not so sure of that Colonel. He did tell me that you developed a fondness for the biergartens," Elizabeth said.

'Is that how he put it? Indeed." He smiled at her. The Colonel had enjoyed his time at two biergartens. One had a very nice view of the Alps, another was next to a lake. They were not overly large, nor the very highest quality. They were comfortable, and Stephen had to convince his cousin to sit and have a drink with him there.

"Yes, Fitzwil... Mr. Darcy... Oh fie. That you are both Fitzwilliams does not make it easy." Elizabeth tried to look coquettish.

"No that visage does not become you." She laughed in answer to his own amused boom. "Why not call me cousin Fitz or cousin Colonel, or Stephen? In any event what else did Darcy lead you to believe about my fondness for Austria?"

"Oh, you know Mr. Darcy," She then betrayed a broad smile and then the laughter of the two at table carried, it was such that Mrs. Bennet became all inquisitive of the reasons for it.

"Nay ma'am, if you will beg my pardon, I should not be able to say exactly what the lovely bride imparted to me to set off such an explosion, though I fear that my manners must be quite lacking for such as our society. I should endeavor to curb these outbursts in future." The Colonel was quick to speak before Elizabeth gave all away.

"Mama, don't question the Colonel too closely, for some of what you hear may not be all together to your liking."

"Why I never, to be talked to by ones own daughter in such a manner. Mr. Bennet, I say Mr. Bennet..."

"Yes my dear?" He responded across the length of the elongated table.

Mrs. Bennet said, "I say that it is not too soon," the Colonel was finding it hard to maintain a straight face and this was noticed across the table by Charles who also had trouble maintaining his composure. "I say it is not too soon to be sending these daughters of yours to men who can tame them. I say. For all the years I have striven to raise them as is befitting. Daughters of gentlemen, indeed. Why I never! And that is all I have to say on the matter."

Mr. Bennet looked back to his wife. "Well yes my dear. Come Saturday we shall have the pleasure of that experience. Seeing our daughters tamed by these two wranglers here." He smiled and as always it was with benevolence.

Luncheon was followed by some quiet time in the sitting room, where conversation took place and a few hands of cards were played. The children, though, were quick to come, after some lessons in mathematics, for another turn on the mounts that the Colonel had brought. The young people, this time, all went forth to the park for a ride under the Colonel's guidance.

* * *

Elizabeth observed to her intended, "He is all at ease, just as Charles."

"Yes, Stephen has always had that way about him. You will have noticed the same at Rosings Park, I should not wonder." Darcy observed and thought back to the days when the Colonel had sung the praises of Lizzy as the only reason worth staying with their aunt earlier in the year.

"Yes I did, and I recall how contrasting your two manners were to me then, but now I see many more similarities." She smiled at him. He had no thought that she was being a tease, but that she truly did find more in their nature that was similar.

"You give me pause, for I see more of our differences," he told her.

"But then, Fitzwilliam, you are a man. Of course you see that. No doubt you think that you and the Colonel have different humors?"

"Yes. Of course we do," he said.

"No, that is not so, for each of you have both recited the same humorous story about a mare at Rosings Park and the Colonel's elder brother. Each of you, it is to be related, paused in the exact same places of the telling, waiting to deliver the climax and ensure your audience of their enjoyment," Elizabeth said.

Darcy paused and they watched the others at their leisure. He could not respond because Stephen was one of his closest confidants. This was based on much similarity of thought, though they did challenge one another.

"He pays attention to Catherine," Darcy said.

"Yes," Elizabeth agreed. This change of topic provided both of them an opportunity to reflect on what problems could arise from such attention. "She is somewhat changed from her earlier naivete." Elizabeth said with more conviction then perhaps was warranted.

"One but hopes that the Colonel also has grown in your estimation also." Darcy attempted wit, but the questioning glance from his fiancée left him to gather he had gone too far. "By that I mean to point out that Stephen, years before, did sow his oats..."

"And as his closest friend from that time, you did not? The Colonel did relate to me his remembrances of your trip abroad to Austria. It had a few differences to your rendition of that time..." Darcy tried to remember what he had told her.

He was again at a loss for words. Elizabeth smiled with a slight laugh, "Come now sir, you both were young and the Colonel was all proper in his account of your time on the Continent. I do believe that I have found you short, sir. There is a great deal to one's past, and there is a great deal that you will tell me, and a great deal you won't and I shall have no desire to know. We are to be one, and I take you entire."

"I am indeed the luckiest of men." Darcy kissed her hand.

"I shall never deny it." This brought them both laughter.

A SMALL GATHERING PRIOR TO THE CURTAIN

At first the Netherfield dinner was planned as a smallish affair. The Bennet family with the Gardiners and the Phillips, along with those guests staying at the great hall. And now that the families of Bingley and Bennet were to be united, the estate of Netherfield was referred to by those in the family as the great house, for Longbourn did not have quite the same history, nor the size. Five houses of Longbourn could easily sit within the demesne that was Netherfield.

To this, one could say that Pemberley was again some few times larger than Netherfield. The grounds were so, of a certainty. The house itself was but a little more than twice as large as that of Netherfield. That it was in Darbyshire was cause enough not to relate that estate to Longbourn. Pemberley was known in Darbyshire as the great house.

The Gardiner children were to stay at Longbourn for the dinner. Miss Bingley thus found the dinner arrangements manageable. Yet, it was soon made evident that Jane and Elizabeth's cousin, Mr. Collins with his wife, the daughter of Sir William Lucas, Charlotte, had arrived at Lucas Lodge. It took but a mere suggestion from Elizabeth to start Charles Bingley on the course of inviting the entire Lucas family to the festivities of the pre-nuptial dinner, which is what the Dining at Netherfield had now become.

Darcy had looked to his affianced with skepticism, for he knew that neither had much tolerance for the vicar in the family, though each did enjoy the company of the vicar's wife. Darcy realized that Lizzy was presenting a challenge to Caroline Bingley and further, it was proper etiquette to have those family members invited. Darcy had but a very few acquaintances invited to the following days festivities, Charles had many more, but by far the largest list had been comprised by Mrs. Bennet. Mr. Bennet related several times, "I had told Mrs. Bennet when sending letters to our friends advising them of this grand event on the morrow, that I should only really wish to acknowledge our happiness with a very few at most. I find her circle of whom we regard to be our friends, though, vastly larger than the one I acknowledge. In any event there were some letters I endeavored to ensure were delayed in transit."

Mrs. Bennet remarked back, "Oh Mr. Bennet you and your little jokes. That you would tease me about such a trifling, for Darcy and Bingley are entirely glad to show their abundance to so many of our circle. You fret my nerves sir with your teasing and to think we still have not heard whether the Untermans, Bakers, or Sherwoods are to attend tomorrow."

Mr. Bennet smiled, "Now dear, you shall indulge me that if they do not come to honor us, I shall not believe it to be a dishonor." He left her then. That this story was related a few times that night was such to provide warmth to the teller. This then left the small chapel to still be filled to an overflowing. Many were now the friends of Mrs. Bennet who had heard of the event and wished to partake of the bounty offered by the grooms.

That most would come from the near countryside to honor the wedding couples meant that they were in no way imposing upon any for a night's stay, in direct contrast to the Collins. But there were several families that were in the same circumstances as the Collins, staying in the neighborhood, and these learned there was to be a dinner at Netherfield.

Miss Bingley received polite inquiries, and callers all morning long. Proper manners begged that she invite several to the meal at Netherfield. Before one knew it, there were more than forty invited to the prenuptial meal. Little concern was shown by Charles, as he was busy with his own arrangements, and in entertaining various gentlemen who had arrived in Meryton to attend his nuptials.

Jane, who had many errands of her own to attend to, and little time to devote to any other duties, offered, as was her nature, to help Caroline in any small means that she could.

* * *

Caroline responded, "My dear sister, you are too kind, and pray do not take amiss that I call you sister today when tomorrow we shall be so. Yet you have so many obligations, and I trust that such a little dinner as we have tonight is well within my means to manage. 'Sides I have sister Louisa to rely on."

Jane said, "Yes, Louisa is a treasure. Oh, Colonel Fitzwilliam, you do not attend the men? I believe that Charles mentioned how he looked forward to seeking your advice on his new rifle." Jane had noticed that he had entered the room full of ladies and stood quite near them. Stephen did not think Jane realized that Caroline was finding another way to be uncivil.

"That is surprising, he only remarked upon this at breakfast," Caroline Bingley said.

"Ah yes," the Colonel smiled at the ladies. "But Miss Bingley, he made mention to us yesterday at luncheon what he repeated this morning at breakfast. And I have given my opinion of them. I do not believe you are acquainted with the man who gave this gift to Charles, Miss Bennet." Mr. Collins was also in attendance in the room and was the only other man amongst a group of ladies who had come to pay their social respects to the Bingleys, or who had come to solicit a dinner invitation, albeit by subterfuge, hidden behind the lace of societal mores.

Stephen was quite familiar with Mr. Collins as he guested often enough at Rosings Park to deal with the man and his much more charming wife.

Knowing that Miss Elizabeth had her opinions of her cousin Mr. Collins as well, and further planning to store the multitude of pontifications that Mr. Collins was sure to utter for later moments when his spirits needed lifting, the Colonel had left the safety and serenity of the other men, he went to rescue the women who were his friends from the torpor that Mr. Collins had the skill to induce.

"No Colonel, it was Sir Fairfax Chamberlain I believe who gave us those particular gifts," Jane said. "Two shooting rifles, inlaid with embellished silver etchings of pheasants in front of a ruined castle, on a darkly stained mahogany stock."

"Indeed, and such a good friend of Charles..." Caroline said.

The Colonel groaned, and then tried to cover his mouth for he remembered his promise to stop provoking Miss Bingley. "Sir, you have your own percipience."

"Yes, Miss Bingley, I am afraid that we are of two different minds. Have you met Sir Fax?" The Colonel knew that answer.

"Sir Fax?" Jane looked to the Colonel, and for this confrontation Elizabeth broke off from her imprisonment with Mr. Collins and came to this small skirmish.

"Yes. We used to call him Chamberlain of course, but he let us know many years ago that he would rather be called Fax. So we do. We are an overly indulgent lot," Stephen said.

"Of course," Caroline added, "Every time he visits the house in Town we only must call him Fax..." The Colonel looked astonished as he seemed to struggle with something to add.

Jane noted this and said, "Colonel the look upon your face, you seem taken..."

"Oh, yes, pray excuse me. It is just that..." he was still at a loss.

"Come Colonel, out with it, you certainly have not been shy previously, this week," Caroline baited, with some spite.

"Miss Bingley, I would well believe that you do also call him Fax, but I also know that he would go to great pains to ensure that he only visits Charles when he is certain that you are not to home. I do not mean to say he holds anything against you, personally, you understand. Sir Fax has been brought up to believe that women of our class have much to do in their lives, for his mother, Lady Chamberlain, was always sure to let everyone know just how totally busy she was at every turn. Thus I have been in the company of Sir Fax at the club when we are invited to dine at the home of one fellow or another. He ascertains first if, well I suppose one must put it, if it is safe to dine free of the fairer sex. That you have fooled him by your presence at table is what has shocked me so. I am all wonder at how he comported himself at dinner with women at the table. Or to say with eligible women at table. I have seen this once under the auspice of Lady Chamberlain and vowed to not repeat the experience." It was all true, though the telling made it seem fanciful.

Kitty had overhead this and tried to cover her laugh, which she did with some success. But Moira Lucas did not know the reason for her humor and quizzed her. The two talked discreetly behind their fans, so no other in the room could hear.

Elizabeth smirked to the Colonel, "Certainly sir you are not to reveal another scandal." Miss Elizabeth must have sensed that the Colonel did not want to attack Lady Caroline at the expense of Sir Fairfax, and had possibly embellished his telling in order to save face. He knew that Lizzy would be sure that Caroline had tried to embellish her own position in society.

The Colonel seized the opportunity. "Dear cousin, most certainly not. But one must know that Sir Fax knows very little about the ladies because of that. To my knowledge he has yet to dine in company of one, unless at his mother's house, and I assure you that very few ladies are invited to that house. I should imagine that his sending of the guns, and while excellent pieces to look at, they have many improvements needed to be good shooters, were his only gift but for a small book of poetry with gilt lettering on the cover and spine. I say this for he is at a loss to what to make a present of to a woman, and this has become his one trademark gift."

Jane gave a nod, "Yes that is so."

"And perhaps it was a book of the poetry of Marlowe? For this is what he not only sent the bride of my brother, but another the wife of Colonel Hanson, thus I have construed a pattern in my friend's character," Stephen said.

"It is so by Marlowe. I am astonished," Jane stated.

The Colonel turned his gaze to Elizabeth, "And knowing that your sister received the book of poetry of Marlowe, Miss Eliza, you perhaps kept concealed that you received the very same?"

Miss Elizabeth laughed with abandon, causing Caroline to turn her head away, and Jane to bring her fan to her face to cover her own amusement. "Why quite right indeed Colonel. Ladies we must be on our guard with the Colonel, he believes he can guess at all our secrets."

The Colonel inclined his head with his own smile fixed upon his vis.

"Now as to my friend, Sir Fax... I should not leave you with the impression that he would not be a good match, for the man has three rather nice houses, a modest income of more than two thousand a year, I should venture to guess, plus two barouches for Town. Once his mother takes to permanent retirement in one of the country homes, he should find his way clear to make some woman a damn decent spouse."

"You are very analytical in your description of the man. He is a friend is he not?" Miss Elizabeth reminded the Colonel.

"As to that, one has to decipher what one means by the word friend. I say Mr. Collins, I request your help in interpreting this conundrum. We discourse on the meaning of friendship." Stephen added the other man to the conversation.

* * *

Kitty and Moira Lucas had moved a little closer to the group to overhear the discussion. "He is a very forward gentleman, is he not?" Kitty said.

Moira noted, "Papa says he is talked about a great deal in the papers. His regiment is considered rather experimental."

"But how he talks about this other Gentleman, he was the same yesterday. He seems to acknowledge if a toad has warts, whilst his cousin Darcy would never avow such, but would keep quiet on the subject," Kitty said.

"Mr. Darcy is the very ideal of a gentleman."

"Certainly my sister thinks so," Kitty told her confidante.

"As does mine, and so should you, for he will be your brother before long."

Mr. Collins hurried to the little group as Caroline moved slightly away. A servant had approached to enquire on directions for that evening's dinner party and this served as a good excuse to leave the torment that the little group caused her.

Mr. Collins was as solicitous as ever. "By all means. By all means. Whatever I can do to be of service. Why Lady Catherine de Bourgh, your illustrious aunt, Colonel, remarked to Mrs. Collins just this past week before we made known our plans to venture to the nuptials, that I often can be found to be of help in deciphering just such predicaments."

Colonel Fitzwilliam said, "Yes I am sure my aunt did so, but I look to the training you partook of for the cloth. For the question I have is if I am indeed a friend to Sir Fairfax, or if my actions cast aspersions upon the gentleman."

"Why Colonel," Mr. Collins noted, "as the son of an Earl and Countess, and the nephew of Lady Catherine, I could never think that you would err by casting aspersions upon anyone."

Kitty noticed how the Colonel smiled before saying, "Indeed but I must say that my aunt's approbation has been earned when I traveled here to attend these nuptials myself. While thinking such an advantageous marriage for our good Jane is well and deserved, my friend Elizabeth here, whom I think of as the greatest addition to the family and bloodline in generations, though my mother of course does compare quite favorably, has not received the same opinion from my aunt."

The perplexed look on the face of Mr. Collins as he tried to say something caused Elizabeth to respond by placing her hand lightly on Mr. Collins arm and giving the Colonel a quizzing. He turned away and covered his mouth to hide his smirk. "Now Mr. Collins, you know I bear no anger within me for my new aunt, for she will be, come Saturday. I hope that in time she too will come to love me for my love of Darcy is such that, certainly, she must take joy of it."

Mr. Collins recovered, "Yes of course you are right, for there is no more accommodating or heartwarming creature than Lady Catherine, and though she might have a moment's pique at this arrangement, she will rally to the cause of your true love and embrace you as only she can so graciously do." From this statement it was decided that Mr. Collins had regained his abilities and sensibilities as far as he was able.

The Colonel having composed himself turned back to the group, "Now I believe we were discussing how much of a friend I am to Sir Fairfax for not only do I provide this fair assemblage with the façade of quirks he does present to society, yet I show also what has gone before, to the best of my understanding, to produce those quirks. Further I do highlight and solicit that patience shall persevere for the woman who truly would desire a match and that all in the end, Sir Fairfax, Fax, will be a dutiful, affable, presentable husband. A catch despite any quirks, and which of us men do not have quirks, eh Mr. Collins? Why I shall not reveal the grooms' trifling peculiarities as we are so close to their marriage, but I shall own to mine, and perhaps you might gift us with what you regard as your'n." Mr. Collins once again had that look of being flabbergasted.

"Indeed," Colonel Fitzwilliam continued once the moment's pause had let silence perch upon the edge of awkwardness. "That I do not indulge in great subterfuge, but just little ones, and am more direct than I think most men. I do not sleep late, but keep almost farmers' hours to the detriment of my parents who when I am, at home, are quite put out that the schedules of the servants must be rearranged to meet my needs. I am not overly bookish, though more learned then many another of my peers in service to His Majesty. I am rather proud of my seat, and believe to have one of the better ones of my set, but by no means the best and this prideful boast I believe is one more of my faults. I am not as handsome as my cousin it has been said, and I say, 'posh on that.' My dash makes up for the virtually imperceptible difference in our appearance," he smiled broadly.

As laughter abated, Elizabeth, who was soon to be wed to the more handsome cousin, came forth with a compliment to that, "Now Colonel, some in the most vain of circles might think that one's appearance is all that makes a man, and certainly my husband to be has much more than his looks to his good fortune. But it is so, his visage can be classically stated as more to be admired by the greater set of society, and your dash, as you put it, does more to carry your visage forward to match him." They apparently understood one another perfectly. Kitty thought the exchange of wit quite humorous.

Lady Caroline could not resist having thought of her own bon mot. "But Colonel, certainly, being raised at the County seat of the Earl of M----K furthers one's advantages of form, character, and breeding."

Colonel Fitzwilliam said, "Yes, and Darcy pulls my tail every chance he gets to remind me of the advantages I received being born to the aristocracy, and why he was one generation removed from such. For our grandfather, who knew us a little, devoted as much time to each of us before the title passed to my father. Grandfather was always fond of saying to Darcy what a handsome lad he was, and to me, 'There's my good stout soldier.' Even as a boy I was destined for service it would seem, and as a child carrying a couple extra stone." Now there was no evidence of any extra weight at all.

The ladies realized that they were being well entertained as they laughed again at the Colonel's stories. So much had they diverged from the discussion of Sir Fairfax and his guns that it was forgotten and no further discussion about Sir Fairfax came up.

This interlude with Mr. Collins and the Colonel in attendance upon the ladies passed well, and even Mrs. Bennet found time to enjoy a quiet moment with Louisa and Caroline while Kitty was near attending her mother. "I must thank the both of you upon my soul for such attentions that you have shown my dear, dear girls. Your graciousness touches mine and Mr. Bennet's hearts."

"Please Mrs. Bennet do not concern yourself so. We are glad of the chance to show our affection for dear Jane." Caroline said. Mrs. Bennet looked from her tea to Caroline, just as Louisa also spoke into the conversation.

"And of course Eliza, who we too look on as almost a sister to be since Charles and Darcy are much like brothers as can be. Why I own that my Hurst would be as close to Charles as Darcy is then we all should be happy."

Mrs. Bennet set her cup down in its saucer. "Yes, I should so like that for if you were to have the same warmth I find with my own relationship to my dear sister, Mrs. Gardiner, then you will be indeed happy." Mrs. Bennet looked across the room to where Mrs. Gardiner sat next to the Colonel in animated conversation, whilst a large group of young ladies stood nearby also contributing to their discussions.

As so many traipsed in throughout the day, the Bingleys were to forego serving any afternoon meal, and wanted to chivvy as best they could most of these callers away before tea so as to prepare for the dinner. Distances were such that all callers were no greater than thirty minutes by carriage from their homes and thus would have plenty of time to leave, refresh themselves and return if they had received the coveted invitation to dine that night.

Darcy and Bingley, along with several of their friends, though Darcy had but two aside from the Colonel in attendance, had come to pay their respects before their intendeds were to leave. Mr. Bennet said he had enjoyed a very agreeable morning in the company of the young men he was to take as sons.

"Ah Collins, I did not know you had come. Good to see you sirrah. And how fares your esteemed patroness?" Mr. Bennet fished for a good lengthy dissertation of obsequiousness. Kitty noted her father treated the man in the same vein as he did the

Colonel.

*　*　*

Eventually the Bennets bid their goodbyes as their visit had been more than two hours. At this time very few others who were not staying at Netherfield remained in Caroline's drawing room. This did necessitate that Caroline, supported by Mrs. Hurst remain as hostess to these guests, but allowed the men to show the Bennet party to their carriages. The young men escorted their affianced and future mother, whilst Mr. Bennet escorted his younger daughters joined by Georgiana and the Colonel. The Colonel paid some attention to Mary, whom he did not find as engaging as the three other sisters, but whom he had spent the least amount of time with. Thankfully the walk to the carriages was but a few short minutes.

"And so, you contend that the Roman classics have very little to instruct us whilst the more modern thinkers show great enlightenment," he summarized their conversation.

"Yes, that is so, while I find Reverend Godwin to be very profound about the nature of the four senses," Mary said.

"I would be remiss to not point out that I have only a fleeting acquaintance with the Reverend's work, but of the classics I am much more familiar." There was a teeter from behind him. He presumed it was Georgiana. Sensing a chance to divert from the path of the conversation he turned to include the two girls behind him.

"Cousin, you don't doubt my familiarity with the classics, do you?"

Georgiana smiled with a bit of mischief, "Not I, surely, for I have often listened to you quote the success of Caesar in his own words. Any military treatise you assuredly can recite."

Kitty sensed an opportunity to contribute, "Oh, I understand, the Colonel is a great one for the words of the heroes of the classical world, but what of the others, such as Cicero, the Gracchi... Those who used the power of language to incite men's spirits to great achievements."

Another titter of laughter came, this time from Mary, "I should like, sister, to hear you recite some elucidation from the Gracchi, or Cicero."

Mr. Bennet had been smiling at this all as they neared the door, to now find that he must speak, "Do not speak so yourself Mary, Catherine has made herself a guest in my library, on occasion, as you have so often yourself. I am sure that the Colonel nor Miss Darcy need to hear any rendition as to the shortcomings of either of your educations."

"Mr. Bennet, your daughter's education appears to exceed many of the young ladies of the Ton that I have met. I count myself fortunate indeed to receive instruction from Miss Mary Bennet and Miss Catherine Bennet," Stephen said.

Georgiana had been tutored to a degree that Mary would find a challenge to match, and of course Kitty could never hope to equal, but her spirit was such that she, too, begged Mr. Bennet to believe that she also felt the Bennet girls were very great scholars and how she knew that Elizabeth had great things to teach her. Georgiana said that she looked forward to future discussions on such matters.

This conversation took them to the carriages and their goodbyes were said all around. The Colonel later that day, before dining, caused a copy of Caesar to be sent to Miss Mary Bennet from his booksellers, and a copy of Cicero to be sent to Catherine. They would arrive but a few days after the nuptials, when the Colonel would have returned to Town.

COLDER CLIMES

That the prenuptial dinner party was a success was to be expected of course. Once again, there were those who had a good time, there were those who only noticed that they were together with those they loved, and there were those who felt the entire affair was so much bother that had to be endured for appearance was more important than enjoyment.

The following day was the wedding itself. All proceeded smoothly but for one instance. As the Colonel waited upon Darcy to dress for his marriage, the post arrived. Fredericks, the butler, passed the letters to be sent forth to the various inhabitants of Netherfield.

"Post, sor." Figgis said tracking his commander and employer down to Darcy's dressing room. The Colonel was immaculate in his best uniform. Figgis had cleaned and readied it the previous night, during the dinner party, and the final touches took but a moment in the morning. The Colonel looked perfection in the face within a hand of minutes, while Darcy had spent more than an hour on his dress and looked to spend near another before being ready to proceed.

As one of Darcy's men had come a moment before, the Colonel knew his would be following shortly. Two small missives and one letter were placed before him. He recognized the envelope and did his best to shuffle it beneath the other two. The smaller pieces proved to be one from Horse Guards and the other from his regimental adjutant. Both required his attention. The Colonel strove to deftly attend to them.

He failed.

"What's got you so fidgety. Surely you have not been mobilized?" Such news, though rumors began to fly about an adventure in Portugal, would assuredly be forewarned of in *The Times*.

"No, nothing of the sort." Stephen pretended to peruse the missive in his hand whilst covering the letter.

"You have a letter that you are trying to keep from my eyes, cousin. I can tell." Darcy now turned his gaze upon his cousin the Colonel, fully. Breeding, however, would not allow him to bait the man. Yet his eyes fell full on the envelope.

"Oh, I see..." Darcy's look turned as sour as Stephen's had become.

"Yes, our aunt has sent me a rebuke, I am sure." Now that he was discovered, the post from Lady Catherine de Bourgh came forward.

Darcy strove to shrug it off and returned to his dressing. "I am all anticipation, does our aunt take to scolding you now that she realizes her efforts fall deafly upon my ears?"

"You will forgive me if I put this off to later." The Colonel did not want to spoil the day.

Darcy however was of another mind, "Come it is best to confront our aunt and her perceptions of the state of things forthrightly, rather than thinking that best out of sight and out of mind." Darcy and his man were ready to begin work on his neck-cloth and the knot, the Fountainhead, was meant to be subtle and not take anything away from the wedding gown of Elizabeth.

"Darcy, you would not want to be put out by whatever I could impart from the letter, best to wait," Stephen suggested.

"And this is what you would advise your under officers should your opponents be pressing you?" Darcy riposted.

Stephen, in order to control his thoughts, stood and strode towards the window to look upon the park. "You are right, but the letter of course is addressed to myself, and should not be of any concern of yours."

Darcy waved off his man and paused to look at his cousin, "Shall we discuss how many times we have confided to each other the very contents of the missives of our aunt de Bourgh. Shall we recount how each of her summonses we cajole the company of one another..."

Stephen, well aware that Darcy wished him to jump to this bait, "Yes and not only do we take one another for protection from the severity of our beloved aunt, but also it would seem to smooth the waters so that we may pursue that which we hold dearest. Or, is Miss Eliza, and the wooing of her, something you felt up to the challenge by yourself last year at Rosings Park?"

Darcy knew himself caught short. "Yes, you are right. I felt my inadequacy to the challenge of Elizabeth who has an ease of friendship much as you possess whilst my nature is the opposite. I believed you to be my ambassador to friendship..."

Stephen turned back to his cousin with a smile on his face and motioned for Darcy's man to return to his work. "Wholly unneeded as you now well know. Your choice of wife compliments you entirely. That I could find such a woman... And of course the most important reason to venture together to Rosings, that we may keep you free, of Anne as your wife, something we are to ensure in the next few hours." That Darcy had thwarted the plans of his aunt and a plan his aunt purported to also be his mother's, to unite he and his cousin Anne, was an accomplishment well worth acknowledging. As indomitable a will as Lady Catherine de Bourgh possessed, that Darcy avoided a fate that he had never desired was indeed an achievement of note.

"I am not sure that cousin Anne will ever know happiness." Darcy pondered with his hands stretched out from his body allowing his man maximum access.

Stephen had opened the letter now and began to peruse the contents. "You generally see so much, though we have established you are a damnably bad judge of character. Anne is quite happy. If you mean that she shall not enjoy the happiness you are now to become part of in a marriage, that may be true, but our young cousin is not only content with her life, but enjoys it too," Stephen said.

Darcy turned to see his cousin reading the letter but chose to ignore it. "I fail to see that."

"Of course you fail to see it. You have always been too busy trying to avoid becoming thrown in her way, as Lady Catherine has tried to do. Anne is a great admirer of her estates at Rosings Park and takes enjoyment in things natural found upon it. Why I spent three frightful hours with her some visits ago, listening to her prattle about some moth or other that Rosings has and is found on no other grounds in the neighborhood."

To this Darcy nodded, for he too had heard mention of those moths more than once not only by Lady Catherine, in a disparaging remark, but also Stephen had remarked how he had been bored to insensibility by this lecture before. What the Colonel had not said was that Anne had spoken of the moth with a passion that bordered on affection.

The Colonel finished reading and folded the letter and placed it in his pocket. He hoped to betray no emotion on his face.

Darcy looked to his cousin. Stephen stared back and then sat back down in the chair he had first been ensconced in. He liked that chair as it clashed with the room, being in blues with gold stripes and a floral pattern running between the stripes. Not another piece in the room was such. Where in his rooms, everything was upholstered in three basic themes. Stephen was sure that the chair had been filched from another room to augment the matching set of chair and settee that were elsewhere in the dressing room. Dull shades of maroon with black borders he acknowledged in comparison to that upon which he sat.

"You know you will eventually tell me," Darcy said.

That summed it up very well. "Yes, I suppose I will. It is not as much of a slight upon you and Elizabeth as I expected. A slight of course, but Lady Catherine could truly have been mean spirited."

"One wonders if in childhood she was more like my mother or your father, and how she became so, so, so..." Darcy could not supply the right word.

"So bullheaded, opinionated, bigoted, and self centered? Father says she was like this in childhood. Less so, but still much more than he could stomach. It is only as an adult that he finds she is tolerable in small doses. Smaller than the doses we indulge in."

Darcy faced his cousin, the Fountainhead knot of his cravat displayed to perfection, as the valet and an assistant went ahead and helped the man into his waistcoat. Embroidered, with white thread and the merest hint of gold. The Darcy family crest and the Fitzwilliam, to a lesser extent, displayed throughout.

After another stare, Stephen sighed and began to summarize the letter, "She has decided to host a ball for Anne. She writes that my brother already has plans to be in attendance upon his wife's family, and thus this leaves me as the only man amongst her relatives that can be in attendance upon her. My parents will be at Rosings, for the ball shall take place at Rosings Park. As such I have been informed, rather than asked, to be Anne's escort to her ball. It is for Saturday next."

Both men knew that unless Horse Guards had other orders for him, which was unlikely, as a Colonel or any officer, could do very much what he pleased in regards to his mixing amongst society, then Stephen was bound to attend the ball. "Now you know all," Stephen concluded.

Darcy could not speak as he reasoned if Lady Catherine had decided this whim but six months previously, it would be he who would be cast in the role as escort to his cousin Anne.

"I shall have to send to Town for my dancing shoes and kit. As we had planned nothing of the sort here, mine are at quarters in the barracks." As the barracks was closer to Almacks than the small lodgings that the Colonel maintained in Town, when he attended Almacks to peruse the young ladies being run through their season, he stayed at the Barracks. He felt that the denial of luxuries on evenings such as that kept the perspective of auditing any future wife quite in its place.

Darcy's waistcoat hung brilliantly and the task of tugging the jacket into place began. Darcy's coat of superfine black wool was to do him credit as he stood in the church in Meryton. Bingley had commissioned his from the same tailor so the two grooms would look a pair.

"I apologize that you are placed in this predicament. My Lord Uncle, though, will not hold you to taking my 'place' and seeing Anne as your wife. He has allowed that he would never stand for an alliance between Anne and myself, privately, as much as his sister strove to see it happen," Darcy said.

"Yes, father has told me the same, though he also said to not pain our aunt, either. But I do not see any objection to Anne. If one must marry for money, as I should think I must if I would ever have any society to match you, say, or my father, then Anne is not without merits. Doubtless she would be up to the challenge of taming an old soldier such as me."

Darcy smiled, "You are nearly the youngest Colonel in the army lists. And you are some months younger than I. Old you are not." As Darcy had never considered Anne someone to make an alliance with, he had to be absolutely certain that Stephen felt the same. So the subject was dropped as Darcy finished his dressing.

The Colonel read the other two notes and found what he knew would be taking place. Soon Whitehall would be releasing rumors about the expedition to Portugal. The King's Own would be going. The highest ranked infantry regiment in the lists, counterbalanced with the likes of the Rifles and some Scottish regiments. It would be quite the collection of blackguards, brigands, and troops to make up an army.

That they found other topics to discourse on as they made their way to the drawing room where the other participants at Netherfield gathered was assured as Lady Catherine and her schemes, and the ever present weight of war were two topics best left alone. Georgiana could sense no strain by the time she arrived dressed in a grey and green ensemble that were meant to compliment Elizabeth's favorite outfit.

It occurred to the Colonel that when Darcy left for his honeymoon, he would also have to escort Georgiana to their aunt's, an oversight of Lady Catherine, for the vibrant Georgiana would readily eclipse the somber Anne.

As there was no help for it, he slowly smiled. He was also Georgiana's guardian and with Darcy away, her protector.

In the carriage to the chapel, Georgiana noted this, "You are thinking of something fondly, cousin?"

This sparked Darcy's curiosity also, for he knew of what weighty matters his cousin was faced.

Stephen said, "Indeed, I do. Your brother will indulge me, but whilst he is away enjoying the new found glories of wedded bliss, I believe that I must, yes that I certainly must, take you to the country instead of immediately back to Town. Yes that is it. We shall be off to the country..." Stephen looked to Darcy and raised his eyebrows, his cheeks high as his grin could not possibly become any wider. Darcy thought through what Stephen said, and then his chest heaved a few times as a light sigh emanated from him.

That sound grew as Darcy opened his mouth into what was a rarity from him, a chuckle. It was echoed by a deep bombastic burst from the Colonel. Georgiana knew she could put them to a scold, or join in. Darcy, who but a handful of times since their parents died, until he won Elizabeth, now engaged in a whole hearted laugh, and Georgiana chose to succumb and join the men. Soon the laughter carried, and in the Bingley carriage it was remarked on what good spirits the Darcy party enjoyed.

* * *

Four Days later Georgiana and the Colonel arrived at Rosings Park. They stopped briefly at the parsonage to allow the Collins a chance to disembark, for the Colonel had insisted that they use Darcy's carriage to transport the Collins' home. Darcy, having left his entire provenance to the direction of the Colonel would only suffer some indignation for the briefest moment that he had supplied largess to Mr. Collins when apprised of this. But then Darcy would remind himself that his sister found Mrs. Collins charming, as did his cousin, as did he. But, most importantly Charlotte Collins was the closest friend of his wife and naturally the use of his carriage as it was already destined to travel to Rosings Park was, of course, to be used also by the Collins.

Georgiana and the Colonel accepted an invitation to call back the following day, and society was established at the Park. The Colonel thought best to deal offensively rather than rely on any subterfuge, for once his aunt found Georgiana here at the Park, she would seethe and be vexatious. But to outward appearance, at least until the arrival of her brother, and the Colonel's father, the Earl of M----K, she would only be more ostentatious then usual. It would, of course, result in her trying to overwhelm the spirits of the Colonel to which she knew that success there would have to be tempered with her desire to see him as the husband of her precious jewel, Anne. So that left one to conquer whom she usually succeeded with, Georgiana. The Colonel's acceptance of a day at the Parsonage, which had Mrs. Collins thinking to invite them to dine, would further fret Lady Catherine and also keep Georgiana from their aunt and any overbearing pontifications which she might otherwise think to utter.

As the ball was but six days later, the Colonel now only had to find four more days to avoid any close acquaintance with his aunt or cousin Anne. He attacked the task with vigor.

On the day after he and Georgiana dined with the Collins, Mr. Collins agreed to accompany the Colonel on an inspection of the entirety of Rosing's Park, while Mrs. Collins helped Georgiana with alterations on the ball gown that had arrived from Town. That Rosings was large, was mentioned before, and certainly Lady Catherine would endeavor to describe, if not the largest estate in England, certainly it was nearly the largest in this and all of the surrounding counties, which in the main was accurate. It was the third largest in the county, and certainly could maintain that ranking of size in any of the surrounding locales. A good day could indeed be spent touring the grounds and seeing to the business at hand, but it would be with Mr. Collins in tow.

The Colonel was thus able to provide ample proof that the endeavor would take an additional day. It was all the talk when they returned to Rosings to dine with the Collins' and the Lucas' who had come to join their daughter as their youngest, Moria, who had formed a friendship with Anne de Bourgh, had found herself invited to the ball.

That lady Catherine was put out when that second day of inspection stretched to a third, she could only let her distemper remain under control as the Earl and Countess finally arrived. Having once before met the Parson, the Earl agreed how a third day would indeed be necessary to complete a proper inventory on all of Rosing's Park, as Mr. Collins would wax loquacious in his praise of the Park and the achievements of Lady Catherine to such an extent, that everything of course took three times longer. The Earl however did have private words later for his son.

"She only knows you from your visits. I know you well boy. I should not like my sister, even if she is a silly creature who married to a station which she has had to make grander all these years, to be any bit embarrassed. You befriend her sycophant, fair enough, the wife has charm and grace and makes up for him. But don't force a friendship to ruin a relation. Family is everything." Stephen did doubt that his father truly knew who he was become as a man grown, yet the Earl was keen on the game, so he must apologize.

"My word sir, I shall be a paragon henceforth," Stephen said.

"Good. Now another thing, Georgiana, surely Darcy did not cotton to this?" the Earl asked.

Stephen smiled, "Actually he did. Georgiana will not detract from Anne come tomorrow night. No more than usual. I am assured by mine aunt that Anne will have the most enticing gown that the coutures in London could produce."

"I shouldn't wonder if she looks like a pastry come tomorrow, but how will Georgiana not usurp Anne? There is no disguising vitality for morbidity," the Earl cut words to the bone in his anger.

That was a question that was unanswerable and Stephen had to let it pass. The silence led the Earl to his next line of enquiry, "How many months?"

A habit of the Earl was to not always provide those in conversation with him all the relevant pieces of the conversation.

"Sir?" The Earl also liked to have those junior to him acknowledging his station. The Colonel had noted that amongst those who outranked him, he did not employ the same tactic.

"Until you mobilize man. I have received half a dozen letters already about this Portuguese adventure. When your mother hears, she will be beside herself. Things have been mostly quiet except for the navy, and we didn't send you to sea, thank goodness."

Little England would never be able to stand up to the Tyrant alone. France and it's empire had caused so many men on the Continent to take up arms that the Colonel believed that their first battle should see them outnumbered by ten to one, for every peasant Frenchman had become a member of Le Grande Armée.

"I believe it will be less than three months, my lord."

"You are fully, what is it, staffed?"

Stephen translated, "Yes my lord, we are fully manned."

The father looked to his son, "You have all your provisions, no doubt, but I shouldn't think an extra three thousand to outfit your personal needs will go amiss. I will have my man send the funds to your bankers right away." A tremendous sum and equal to what the Earl gave his eldest son and heir, the Viscount each year. Not that the money would purchase invulnerability from the French Cannons. It would just assuage the guilt of having a second son that must face such danger.

The three thousand would purchase comforts for the Regimental mess and, as such, Stephen accepted it. He also knew that his frugality in regards to such largesse would leave a portion left over that he could use to secure more towards a future after his years in the Regiment. He would not think that he should face death and be defeated by it. He knew that in order to survive the upcoming war he would have to negotiate long and hard with the adversary, respectfully and forthrightly, else he would no doubt succumb. That fate was not one he intended, but to return was the only ambition he possessed.

"For your mother, keep yourself safe, it's all that I ask," the Earl allowed. Stephen knew that the Earl used references to the Countess to shield his own feelings.

"My Lord, it is my primary mission. I am assured that we will not attempt any rash acts of English Bravado, though I believe some of our general officers think this is still a game. That they have not learned from Churchill's example, last century, that warfare is for professionals is disappointing, but those officers who do not comprehend how serious war has become are those I shall avoid. I believe most of those will have relatively short careers when we face the Tyrant's army. It has proven to be the best army in all the world, certainly led by those who understand that this is not some sport."

The Earl waved his hand before he spoke. His father must have heard how his son tolerated no nonsense amongst his officers and how several had their commissions purchased so more sensible men could lead the Regiment. "Yes, well the Duke of Marlborough was exceptional. But this damn Corsican upstart has no breeding and I am sure that blood will tell in the end. I am gladdened that you are taking precautions though." The interview ended, the Colonel was thus free to enjoy himself.

His mother would be ensconced with Lady Catherine. Georgiana and Anne, who did get along with each other would be finding something to amuse them. His father would continue in the study to have a smoke and drink, so this left the Colonel at loose ends.

He chose correspondence, for he had little time to catch up on the frivolous letter writing that the Ton indulged in. When he had moments to write, it was orders back to his officers. Now he composed a long letter to Darcy, a longer one to Elizabeth, and two shorter ones to Charles Bingley and Jane Bingley. He thought after two hours had passed that a few last were needed and composed one very nicely for the Gardiners, one for the Bennets, and last for Caroline Bingley. A brief half page note to thank her for putting up with his gruff military manners during the recent festivities.

Due to the nature of pleasantries one engaged in these letters of no consequence, at least the Colonel saw them as such, he signed the letters, one way or another;

"with great expectations of seeing you shortly,"

or in the case of those he knew to be residing in Town;

"I look forward to the time when we may meet again when I am shortly next in Town."

That in some cases there was sincerity, for he did wish to meet the Gardiners, but less so the Bennets. And in other cases these lines were but normal form and not heartfelt at all.

Having finished those seven, he felt that he should show an exceptional friendship for Darcy's new cousins, and having developed a fondness for them, wrote to each of the Gardiner children. Once that road had beckoned, he sighed and composed letters to Mary Bennet, where he was hard pressed to think of a quotation from a modern philosopher and so settled for Livy. '

Truth is often eclipsed, but never extinguished.'

In the original latin as best as he could remember it. He was rather more full of joviality for the letter he wrote to Kitty Bennet after the somber one to Mary.

As it ran to three pages with recounting of his travel with the Collins, his time at Rosings Park ,and his impressions of all that had befallen him in the last fortnight, he wondered at his prattling on when Figgis came to help him dress for dinner.

"Sor, it be but an hour afore ye is to dine."

"So late already, why I just turned my hand to these after nuncheon." At least the Colonel knew it was directly after lunch and the interview with his father, sightly after two. And now, it was just past seven.

"E'en so, sor. I be thinking your mufti again 'night. The Countess be seeing enough of ye in uniform already," Figgis said.

"Yes you have the right of it. Here you lay it out and I'll bring this letter to a close," Stephen agreed.

He signed the letter hurriedly then, without much attention to what he had written, but knew that promising; "

> *I shall write again, when I return to Town, with all that happens at the ball,"*

may have been an act of ill thought.

For in all his correspondences that day, this was the only one he committed himself to another letter. Though it was expected he would write Darcy again, and perhaps some of the rest of that party on their grand marriage tour. He had not communicated more with any others, even upon the receipt of letters from them. He knew that the next few months he would be quite busy.

The Colonel would be much surprised if while preparing to march off to to war he would be able to break free of his duties, to dine more than twice each week at the club. Stephen certainly knew that once he returned to London, there would be no return to the country before he embarked for Portugal.

He looked forward to a couple of meals with Georgiana whilst engaged in readying the Regiment, and perhaps a few with the Gardiners, also. When he left for Portsmouth to embark, he would turn Georgiana's care over to his parents for the briefest of two weeks, before the Darcys returned, but this was to be expected. Georgiana did have the services of a governess and there was another who would stand as chaperone for her until her brother and new sister returned in addition to her Aunt and Uncle, the Colonel's parents.

That his mother the Countess was in attendance at Rosings Park had an effect on Lady Catherine that was singular and always worth noting in counterpoint to the times when she was not there. While Lady Catherine was still in the habit of providing her opinions on many subjects, the significance of another family member of rank was that Lady Catherine was no longer the greatest authority, or the preeminent figure of fashion. Or any of the other multitudes of situations where she had proven to be the leading light, by her own words.

One could note that at Rosings Park, the guest list was often varied, but very few men and women of rank actually did visit, nor was Lady Catherine often received in such homes since her husband died. That there was but one other estate in a twenty mile circumference from Rosings that had anyone who neared her exalted rank, or superseded it, and the Marquis of J---Y did not spend any great time at his estate allowed Lady Catherine to further live in a world she created with her preeminence. Those neighbors closer to the periphery of this circle were able to socialize with those who did outrank Lady Catherine or certainly had more Noblesse Oblige. Good manners prevented any from talking openly of her peculiarities, however.

The neighbors, both high and low, though none as high as the Earl of M----K or Lady Catherine, all accepted an invitation from Rosings Park for 'Such largesse, such a party,' Mr. Collins was all anticipation the next day in the drawing room of the parsonage as he entertained the Colonel, Georgiana, the Countess and the Lucas'.

"Why since I have been so fortunate as to be the Reverend here at Rosings Park, there has never been such generosity, even at Christmas when Lady Catherine takes every means she is able to ease the plight of the poor and opens the estate up to all of the village and her neighbors for a feast. Why that shall pale in comparison to this noble endeavor in what is surely, and my sister Moira and Cousin Georgiana, for now we are cousins, you will forgive me for saying, but what is surely the greatest honoring of any young lady, and by far the best match any young man could strive for." The Colonel shook his head a little, especially when his mother reached across to pat his hand. He was the only single man in the room.

"Indeed, our Anne," the Countess began and it looked like Mr. Collins was about to add more. He emitted a short squeak instead as Charlotte, his wife, stepped heavily on his insole and gave him a look that he seemed to recognize. The Countess was thus able to continue as if nothing had stopped her, though she did seem to fight a brief smile. "will no doubt carry off all the attention admirably. One thing that I always am able to say about Anne after we visit, or she comes to us, is that she has tremendous manners. She will thus be gracious tonight and I am led to believe that she is a very accomplished dancer. Certainly Stephen is quite good. I had a letter from Lady Jersey not very long ago telling me how, when he chose to attend Almacks, he was very much a credit to myself and that I should be proud of his abilities."

"Mater, I believe Lady Jersey was creating a fabrication," Stephen said.

Georgiana laughed, she had danced with the Colonel and knew him to be very good. Even better then Darcy when the Colonel gave into enjoying himself.

"Lady Jersey might be capable of such, but others have told me you are an accomplished dancer as well," the Countess said.

"I must elaborate for our friends the Lucas' and the Collins. What the Countess does not say is that Lady Jersey is convinced that I should be taken off the marriage market once and for all so that other eligible young bucks, preferably those with a title in their future, can make eyes at the young ladies. It would seem that when I attend Almacks, being without prospects and doomed to meet an early death in some heroic but foolish manner as we assault the little Tyrant and wrest the Continent back from him, the young ladies all would swoon and throw themselves at me, making any other suitors' chances damned small." The Colonel knew the game at Almacks. He did indeed go to see if any heiress was worth notice, who could excite his mind as well as his other senses. He found few that were allowed to respond, for though his connections were great, no mama wanted her dear daughter to be tied to a few hundred a year should the Colonel even be lucky to live through the coming unpleasantries.

"Stephen! That is quite enough," the Countess was angered.

Stephen's statement must have let the Countess realize the very real possibility that her son could be killed in the war. She did not ever accept his levity. Not comprehending that by making it light hearted, was the one way Stephen found the courage to lead his men forward to what certainly was going to be a very gruesome task.

"Oh your ladyship, we take no offense by the Colonel's remarks," Charlotte said into the taut exchange of looks between mother and son. "We have all become quite good friends with Colonel Fitzwilliam of late and know that some of what he speaks is close to the mark, and some is utterly exaggerated, but at the expense to get a chuckle or laugh that brings gladness to ones heart in a moment of strife. Lady Lucas and Father here, you will agree that the few times we went to Almacks, the marriage mart was in full swing and there was no match at all that I felt worthy of making, not until my good Collins came along." Charlotte had almost missed all her chances at a match, but the match with the Parson of Rosings Park not only ended up keeping her from spinsterhood, but brought so much more for the entire community. The former Charlotte Lucas brought kindness and sense to what was a community that was shaped to the whims of one without it. Slowly the entire area found their hearts lifted of what had been an unnoticed cloud and merriment once again shone throughout the county.

"Is she not the best wife one could ever wish for?" Mr. Collins said in a quiet voice to Colonel Fitzwilliam. It was quiet, but everyone in the entire room heard him. That the parson's eyes shone as he looked at his wife gave the Colonel pause.

"You are truly a fortunate fellow, Collins. To know such bliss. Fortunate indeed." He gave a clap to the reverend's shoulder and moved away. His thoughts turning to his profession as he looked out on the grounds.

"Georgiana, you have spent time this week with Anne. Is she all anticipation for tonight?" Moira asked. Though she had known Anne longer, since first visiting her sister after Charlotte's marriage, Moira found it easier to be a companion to Georgiana as they were very nearly the same age, but all of two months difference.

"From what I am able to tell, she is indeed looking forward to tonight."

"Certainly our aunt is," the Colonel added. That his mother then engaged him in a match of staring caused him to turn back to look at the gardens.

"Yes, Anne de Bourgh does look forward to hosting a splendid night for all. She remarked to us just a few days ago, is it not so Mrs. Collins, that she was anticipating your stay, Moira, and also yours Sir William and Lady Lucas. She fondly remembered your last time here Sir William. She found you very engaging in conversation," Mrs. Collins said.

Georgiana had not been present then, the Colonel and the Collins', of course, had been. What Stephen remembered was that though Sir William was a peer of age, she considered him common and did little to acknowledge his contributions to society. The others may not have remembered any condescension, but the Colonel recognized that Charlotte Lucas well knew his aunt.

"Why indeed Georgiana is right." He got the entire room's attention, "For my part, Sir William, I must say that there are few men of my acquaintance who fulfill the role of country gentleman so well. You are convivial, you are jovial, you are knowledgable, and all in all a splendid fellow. And I do not do it too brown. This last year I have met several of the connections of the new Longbourn members of our family and must say I find all charming and a real pleasure to have amongst my acquaintances. A few, such as yourself and Mr. Gardiner, I shall look forward to making great friendships with as we continue."

The Countess nodded. Stephen knew his mother wished her other son was as amiable with all of society as was he. She did not want him to be friendly with his foot soldiers, but that he had an ease with those of lessor fortune made her proud. She was reminded of her own brother, now dead, who also had an ease of manner with all men.

"Well, Mrs. Collins, we must thank you for your hospitality but the hour grows late if we are to return to Rosings Park and rest before the ball. Georgiana, it is time to say your goodbyes." It took but moments and the party from the great house was back in a carriage for the few minutes journey to the hall.

GIVE WEIGHT TO YOUR PARTNER

A ball can be a very tiring affair.

Physically, there will be a great deal of exertion.

Even if one never dances, there will be hours engaged in talking and spending eternities with one's neighbors and friends doing one's best to ensure that all those friends who expected to spend some amount of time with one exchanging pleasantries had those very same pleasantries exchanged. This of itself could exhaust one, as the wider one's circle of friends would lead to ever more people requiring, or demanding a moment's time until there were no moments left.

Stephen, fortunately, had very few acquaintances at Rosings Park beyond his family, and those friends from the Parsonage. Lady Catherine however was in her element as the doyenne of the county and here, hosting an event in honor of her daughter, she radiated pride as so many came to pay homage to Anne.

"My aunt takes pleasure in your triumph, dear cousin," Stephen said to Anne as he stood up with her a second time, half way through the night.

Anne was dressed in a shimmering blue gown, not cut low, for Lady Catherine would never countenance such a thing, but certainly it provided a fashionable representation of those young misses whom were of the first water. Young ladies whose beauty needed the artistry of the couture's of London to accentuate what little there was to work with.

Stephen was in his regimentals. There were a few others in uniform about the room. One retired general amongst them all. Stephen had even been asked, and then admonished, by Lady Catherine to do bring his officers to the ball, but Stephen deftly kept them from this fate.

"Mother enjoys the attention," Anne said and was quite correct. Lady Catherine always found those who paid her respect to be of the best that society had to offer.

"More than that, Anne. So much more than that." Stephen, of course, had been able to understand his aunt many years previously.

They exchanged places with another couple as the dance progressed. The Duke of Kent's Waltz was not some two hundred year old Renaissance number, but not even a decade old. As such, it was a great favorite of many. It gave ample time to converse with one's partner, and also some slight flirtation when crossing with a neighbor as the couples moved along the line.

The Colonel continued, "You have received a great deal of attention yourself this night." The house was crushed with many people, nearly to a fullness that it could not handle. That Pemberley or the Earl's main seat could handle more was without doubt, and that Stephen had been party to assemblies that had more at those locations was a fact. One not worth discussing in the hearing of Lady Catherine.

Anne laughed, "Fear Colonel. Surely you can sense it. The young men pay me attention not for any true regard, but because their own mothers have told them they must, or they shall be cut from the poor society we can afford them here at Rosings." There were many young men, nearly twenty by his count, that were of an eligible age and position to pay court to Anne.

"Anne, if you were to allow yourself such freedom to voice aloud more often these thoughts, the young men would pay attention more of their own volition," Stephen said. He was sure that Anne with some feistiness would become more alluring.

Anne said, "Surely cousin, you know your aunt? You do not expect she would tolerate that of me."

The Colonel chose carefully what to say, "Yes, you have led a life filled with as many dangers as I lead. Now I must contest that you label this society poor..."

She laughed, and he knew she laughed at him. "We may sit a good table, but the gentry have long since acknowledged that the reason to pay homage to mother is for her food and the depth of her cellars. My father did lay in a very good stock of wine, and that is one of mother's valid protestations. That we do indeed have one of the best collections of drink in the county."

Stephen could not argue that, even his father the Earl acknowledged the truth of it as well.

"Yes, but certainly these young men can see..." the Colonel dramatically looked about the room and he could not fail to notice that there were many young and lovely women in the hall also. The gowns they wore, in honesty were such that they offset the charms of their owners much better than Anne's. To spend such a fortune on a dress and to be eclipsed because of a want of beauty was a shame. The Colonel thought again that his society wasted their efforts. Anne's spirit deserved better than her upbringing at the hands of Lady Catherine.

"Colonel let us not mince words. Mother made her choices for me, and I always must do as she says. She has decided who amongst those here will be my suitor," Anne said.

The Colonel realized that he found this news to be a relief. "Pray tell, who is the lucky man I may call cousin," The dance, however, neared its end and some polite applause for the musicians left the men to escort their companions back to their seats.

"Why luck is a relative term. Especially here." Anne smiled and bordered on laughing as they neared her chosen seat. Stephen reflected that Anne did not often laugh at all. Anne was not seated near her mother, but her settee was within a line of sight so that they could be observed by Lady Catherine.

"I am summoned, it would seem." The two deciphered the look and use of fan to point out that Lady Catherine desired the Colonel to attend her. "Thus the intelligence of your paramour will have to wait."

"Do not fret so, cousin. All shall be made known to you shortly." Anne was not generally given to riddles, for though she was seldom an orator, except when it came to the rapturous regard she had for Rosings Park, this was very out of character. The Colonel looked back once to see that a new suitor paid court to Anne after he walked away. Most likely the man was her next partner.

"So what do you think of her now, eh? She holds up well amongst all these parvenus." Lady Catherine brushed her fan to encompass the entire length of the hall. Stephen knew his aunt spoke of Anne.

"Of course ma'am. Anne has always risen amongst society. It is but natural." A play on a theme he had been supplied by Lady Catherine many times.

This brought Lady Catherine's head around and she looked

deeply at him. "Darcy is..., Darcy would nev... Darcy, blast the man." Stephen stood attentively with a smallish smile upon his lips. She had not mentioned her other nephew once since he had arrived. Not to ask after his health, nor the details of the wedding.

She composed herself to begin again. "As you know, it was my fondest wish and that of my sister's to see Anne marry to Darcy. I make no pretensions but that match would have well suited this family and been a triumph."

The Colonel saw that it would have been a triumph for Anne, or rather for Lady Catherine. Stephen truly doubted how much Anne cared at all whom she married. "Yes ma'am I have been very cognizant of your desires about my two cousins these years."

"Be that as may be, now Anne is at liberty to form another alliance," Lady Catherine said.

"Certainly, hence this ball." Stephen swept his hand about the room. "Many eligible young men here who would do great honor to the family should Anne choose one."

Lady Catherine shook her head, "These puppies, why they have water in their veins. No, not like you or Darcy. You two have the Fitzwilliam blood and that tells, boy, as you know full well. We were with the Conqueror at Hastings, we were at Agincourt, Bosworth, Marston Moor and Edgehill. It is the blood. None of these boys should think of being an alliance for Anne."

Stephen was sure that they thought about it. Weighed the costs of being son to Lady Catherine and inheriting all that was Rosings Park. A new master could do tremendous things with the estate. It was large, it had a great income, many tenants, good prospects. There was just the pallor of staleness imbued throughout, that even this ball could not banish at present.

The Colonel did not remember his uncle the Baron all that well, but he remembered enough to recall how Rosings was more vibrant when he was alive. "So Stephen, what do you have to say?" Lady Catherine asked.

"Sorry aunt, woolgathering again."

"As if I shouldn't know the symptoms, as you seem to be lost somewhere on so many occasions. What do you have to say about our Anne?" Lady Catherine used her fan to point out the girl, now dancing again.

"She has done the family proud. A true Fitzwilliam credit indeed," he said.

"Of course she has. It is a shame Georgiana is not as mature as Anne, else she too would be a credit to the family." Stephen knew that Georgiana had more young men seeing to her needs, asking for her to step up with them. And scandalously flirting by asking for a third dance, which under severe instructions from the Countess and the Colonel she had been told to refuse.

Stephen was pleasant and said, "Indeed ma'am, but a few years and they shall be great rivals, though of course Anne will be wed before Darcy seriously entertains the notion of sending Georgiana forth to form an alliance."

"Damn to Darcy and his alliances. It is not his alliance that we talk about, but yours. Yours and Anne's," Lady Catherine said.

Stephen turned sharply from the dance and looked at his aunt. That he had definitely had heard. "Lady Catherine, I mistake your meaning."

"Come Stephen, you do not. You and Anne shall wed. I shall instruct your father that all shall be seen to this Christmas." Lady Catherine was known to smile, especially when she got her way. She was smiling then.

Stephen could see his parents further about the room. They were not close enough for him to beckon them over. "I am afraid aunt, that it can not be so. I am called to service to the King and Country. I shall leave from here to attend to my Regiments embarkation for the Continent. That alone precludes myself, or any other young officer, from marrying at this time." He knew that this protected him with an armor that Lady Catherine would not be able to pierce.

"Don't toy with me, Stephen. You are in need of an Heiress if you are to reach your full potential. Anne is Heir to Rosings Park. You shall marry Anne and come in to all this. Should have thought about this years ago. Darcy never needed an estate and so could act independent. You, however, are another matter." That she spoke truthfully about his prospects was forthright. The way she did so touched on his pride.

"If I were not bound for war, I should give this proposal of yours consideration, ma'am. But as I may leave my young cousin a widow before a six month is come and past, I find it advisable to stop any further discussion. Now if you will forgive me, I am promised for the next dance."

Stephen turned to take his leave, but even as he did so, Lady Catherine could be heard, "It will not be so easy as that."

Stephen went to partner a very pretty young daughter of a neighboring Baron. Her face was fresh, and hints of the color of roses glowed beneath hazel orbs. A gown of cream satin cut to reveal the hints of a firm womanly bosom.

Engaged in the dance, Stephen once again wondered at his aunt's machinations. Certainly Anne could never compete, handicapped as she was, by a mother who strove to outshine her daughter and all others around her. Anne could not succeed where her looks coupled with such a demeanor, made her seem more the relation of a mouse than of the highest in the land.

What fortune would be great enough bait to tempt any man worth the effort? Poor second sons in need of a fortune, tradesmen out to link with a title and the fortune and not particular about with whom they spent their remaining years. Anne had been destroyed, and what was left was something that was pitied even though not wanting it. All this too Stephen knew to be his aunt's grand design.

Stephen knew that any one to take Anne would be doing so not out of love. Any man who ventured forth would only do to Anne as Lady Catherine herself did. This ball highlighted that, for the men of the county were not worthy of Anne, if one used the same criteria that Lady Catherine used. And Stephen knew that Anne was such that she never could come out from the shadow of such a mother. Lady Catherine had seen to that.

If Anne was supposed to have a triumph this night, the presence of Georgiana would not have halted it. Anne could not outshine nine of every ten girls in the room. Lady Catherine no doubt hated every single one of them, even having already decided upon her daughter's fate. A fate Stephen would strive to avoid. Not that he expected to find love, nor a bride more handsomely dowered than Anne. However, he had planned in those times when he thought of it, to marry someone he could look at with fondness.

Another man of the exact same upbringing as he would no doubt jump at the offer. Stephen was beset by years of helping Darcy to avoid this fate, which thus transferred those same arguments and sentiments to himself. As the ball wore on, his thoughts were heavy.

* * *

Town provided release to the Colonel as he departed very early the following day. His parents would see to Georgiana's return to London, so he used as his excuse, the very real reason of needing to consult at Horse Guards immediately. That his arrival at the command center of the army was surprising to some of his superiors, for they did not expect him for a week, was quickly forgotten as readying an army for war was no easy task.

And one, certainly, which some very serious men did indeed diligently work at. Others who were supposed to apply such industry to the task, though, were quite frivolous members of the Ton. The astute officers, like Stephen, sidestepped these in order to actually get the job done.

Not always was there success, but for the most part there was. Stephen readied his cavalry regiment to as near muster strength as he could in the weeks that followed. Equipment was checked, repaired or replaced as needed. Ammunition was ordered in, and then ordered in again, as oftentimes the amount received was somewhat less than what was paid for, or as Stephen erred on the side of safety, what he expected the Regiment to consume in any active fighting.

It should not have, but it did take him by surprise to find in his first week several correspondences piling up that needed response. Not only from his cousin who was enjoying his marital tour, and lovely wife, but also Elizabeth's sisters as well as Caroline Bingley. Mr. Hurst too inviting him to dine with his wife and sister since Bingley was away.

Letters from Georgiana and his parents, the Gardiners and Mr. Bennet, which included an even longer reminisce from Mrs. Bennet. Mr. Bennet's begging his forgiveness for including that long length of gossip and prattle but, as his dear wife asked, he did so. He but asked that the Colonel peruse it in the kindly spirit it was meant. What gave the Colonel great pause, however were letters from Lady Catherine and from Anne.

"Figgis," he said to his dog-robber, "I have here a large pile of letters that I must attend to. I believe I have no pressing engagements and the duty officer should be able to see that we are relatively free this evening. Now I intend to plow through all this."

"Yes sor. Sorry sor, but are you sure that this is the wisest thing?" Figgis asked.

Figgis knew the extent of each letter, and he also knew that the Colonel was not a great correspondent. Stephen usually did save up things so that he could reply to everything at once. If only Stephen were wealthy enough to employ a secretary. Which of course he did as Colonel, but for some scrupulous reason, he only used the man for military matters and not personal ones.

"Yes, I am sure. Now as to my aunt, that charge must be halted at the source," Stephen said.

"If I may sor..."

"Yes?" That had caught Stephen's attention.

Figgis looked down and then back up, "A thing I noticed when we was at Rosing's this time." He paused for a bit and Fitzwilliam knew to hold back so the corporal would get moving. "Well, it was like this, the other servants, sor, they kind of knew Lady Catherine's plans afore ye. Kind of like, and I knew it would being upsetting to youse, so I did not say any thing. But I been a thinking and I talked to the head groomsman, Mr. Larsen. He and I get along pretty rightly and all. So I was talking to him about this here marriage ideer between youse and Miss Anne and all, and he thinks it would be no good either. That Miss Anne likes you and everything but that she likes Rosings so much that she would make no one really a good wife. And since Mr. Larsen knowing you as lad and all, he knows you need a flashy one, he said..." Figgis ground to halt.

Colonel Fitzwilliam thought about that and knew there was some grain of truth there, "And you agree, do you?"

Figgis looked back down at his shoes for a moment, "Aye, sor I think that the lads and all think that you deserve a high stepper. Er but as for Lady Catherine. We thought that she doesn't want to give anyone without some scratch, Rosing's, which is why she has settled on you. Not that you're being wealthy and all, since we as know that the Earl being only able to give you a pittance and all in his will, but that Lady Catherine would rather the pauper she knows and such.

"We sort of figured though that should another man of the First Water come out of the woodwork, well sor, we think that Lady Catherine might have second thoughts and all about you." Figgis finished.

The Colonel nodded thinking about that and felt that perhaps Figgis was right. If a man who had an estate and income to rival Rosing's Park offered for Anne, then Lady Catherine would forget all thoughts about Stephen. The trick was to find the man, make the introduction, and have the attachment form before Lady Catherine saw to the banns being posted between he and his cousin.

"I think, Corporal, you may indeed be on to something. Now the question is, 'who' would want to court Anne. Seriously court her. I couldn't go about asking my friends to do me the favor of shamming it just to keep me off the hook. Lady Catherine would smell that right quick. Not that she is as sharp as she thinks she is, but fabrications like that have a way of being found out," Stephen said.

"Aye sor, we thought so ourselves, me and Mr. Larsen. Now there was a man, before Mr. Collins took over as the Parson, Larsen was a saying. The old Pastor's son, but he'd have nothing to speak of, though he showed the same bent as Miss Anne and liked things sort of natural like. So p'rhaps a man from the Royal Society?" Figgis suggested.

The Colonel quickly began mentally going through his list of acquaintances who were also members of the Royal Society and could think of damned few who were worth their salt, or could even afford salt. "Very few unmarried men in the Royal Society are men of means, Figgis. Though I think you are on the right road. It bears thinking. But now to my letters."

The Colonel then began an industrious several hours of writing, leaving his fingers cramped and hand throbbing by the time he finished. His letter to Darcy was full of Lady Catherine's new campaign and of good Figgis' solution. The Colonel put Darcy to the task of unearthing a naturalist who would suit the bill also.

As he read the letter of Caroline Bingley he wondered just how he had ever endeavored to be tied to a dinner engagement, for Caroline reiterated Mr. Hursts' invitation to dine. She even implored him to coerce the inveterate Sir Fax to accompany him. This of course required that he write to Sir Fairfax and try to persuade him to attend the dinner, which actually would require a meeting first. The Colonel and Sir Fax would have to come together so he would be able to discuss, in glowing terms, the charms of Miss Caroline Bingley.

Good manners required he do his best, however it was presumptuous on the part of Miss Bingley to have asked that he do such. That he received her letter meant that he could do nothing but respond. That he received an invitation to a dinner from Mr. Hurst, an acquaintance whom he must acknowledge due to the connection from Darcy to Bingley, required that he do all that Caroline had asked of him. To use a sham excuse would be less than worthy. To not respond would be small.

Continuing with his correspondence, he found that he could respond to Lady Catherine with a brief thanks for his invitation to the ball, and then to his cousin Anne with a confidence.

"My dear cousin, you must understand that I did not retreat from you at the ball, but was fleeing in full rout. There is no doubt in my mind that our friendship has always been one not only based on our blood ties but also based on a realization that what we concede as common ground we find congenial. That we know the bounds of the ground and that we stay within its limits for those times when we have been together and are to be together, thus we are able to get along.

"Knowing this, I protest to my aunt that the very real possibility that I and the Tyrant may find our coming disagreement to result in my not being capable of returning to the land of my birth would cause an end to that friendship, and so any talk of anything further is something I shall not give heed to. My aunt's wishes in this instance are for naught, for I will not indulge her in a future that may be a fantasy.

"Know thus that in perseverance of our friendship, I remain..."

He signed it. He then turned to the next stack of correspondences. The Gardiners, both Mr. and Mrs. Gardiner had very nice and short thank yous for his own letters to them, and each of the children also. They even asked him to dine on any of three different dates. Here, he brought forth his calendar and wrote back that he would be glad to dine on one, and perhaps have them come to him on one of those where he would arrange for Georgiana to also be present, as well as a few other friends. Stephen would find that so much more pleasant than a dinner with Fax and Caroline Bingley.

He ensured that he sent a note to Georgiana about those plans. He knew she already looked forward to it, for they had discussed such plans while they were at Rosings Park. Each of them were surprised that they did long for the company of the Gardiners, for they both found them quite enjoyable.

Georgiana had already committed her brother and sister to inviting the entire Gardiner clan to come to Pemberley since their last visit to the area had been cut short by a few days. Georgiana had suggested to Elizabeth, who deferred to the younger girl, just which of the guest rooms and nursery rooms would be quite perfect for each. And the young Miss Darcy had thought of many plans and adventures for the children to have whilst at Pemberley.

That surprise would be sure to warm all the Gardiners once Darcy and his bride returned from Austria. Turning to his next letters, the Colonel found the Bennet girls had written. Mary quick to note that he had transposed two sets of letters in his latin quotations while Catherine's letter was of a different nature entirely. Written on plain stationery as all the Bennets of Longbourn had, no hint of scent about it. A contrast to that of Caroline Bingley's which was an elegant eggshell piece that was full of her perfume.

"It was with happiness that I unfolded your letter and spent many languorous hours sitting in the shade of the tree in front of Longbourn reading it with great pleasure. Your many characterizations of our cousins who traveled with you and of your aunt and cousin at Rosings leads me to have many moments of merriment..."

More followed in a similar vein until the Colonel realized he had spent a half hour reading her four pages through three times.

Shaking his head, he bent to respond. Another hour later he realized the clock approached five and he had four pages of his own on his observations of the ball and other events of the last few days spent in Town.

"It was with the greatest pleasure that I devoured your letter. I look forward to the gastronomic delight of your next course. Yours..."

and with a great flourish he signed the letter with all his rank and right honourables that he could muster.

The next two days he spent engaged in duties but on the third he took himself to his club before dinner with the Gardiners. As he entered he asked of the liveried doorman, "Hendricks, is Sir Chamberlain amongst the members in, at present?"

"Why, yes sir. He arrived perhaps an hour ago. He is in the senior member's lounge." That there were two lounges, one for members who were admitted under their own aegis labelled senior, and a junior lounge for those members who were legacies was a novelty, here, as to their naming. Though these lounges only took on meaning in the event that a new member was brought to the club for his first gathering to meet the members in the lounge to which he most assuredly belonged.

"Reading his papers, no doubt."

"Yes sir, he is well through his stack."

Sir Fairfax was quite at his ease with his papers, and his drink. When he finished one paper, he would read another, sometimes four or five a day, and felt he was very well informed. Few, though, engaged him in conversation regarding current events so this acquired knowledge was very much kept to himself.

Both Fax and the Colonel were legacies at this club. Fax actually did not belong to any other, whilst Stephen belonged to three. "Thank you Hendricks. I shall take a drink there then."

"A seat for dinner, then?"

"No, dining with friends. Just stopped for a drink." The Colonel paused, "and it happens that we have a new trooper these last weeks who is doing quite well." Hendrick's nephew had joined the regiment. If the Colonel had not brought up the mention of the lad, Hendricks never would have.

"Very good sir, I shall have your drink fetched presently." Hendricks had already passed the Colonel's coat, gloves, hat and cane to two other under doormen. Now he motioned to an under butler and relayed instructions as the Colonel advanced up the stairs to the senior lounge.

Fax sat reading his paper, a drink, most likely, the second, sat at his side, half finished. He looked relaxed. Sir Fairfax Chamberlain was a man of routines. He rose at half past eleven each day. After attending to his bath, he breakfasted at one, which was followed by either a ride or promenade in the park. From there he would walk the High Street, or any other street of merchants, in sequence, Oxford, Bond, browsing. Settling into a chair, it did not matter which one, he invariably popped his head into either of the lounges and then the library, bar, or reading room, and chose to sit in the room that he first came upon that was quiet. If he had no pressing evening engagement, he would stay ensconced in the club, dining at ten, and returning to his home at one.

The only days where this varied was the Sabbath, where he attended services, instead of a trip about Hyde Park, and of course he could not frequent the shops. He took Sunday dinner with his mother. Or on those evenings where his mother had him to her home for a meal where he would be put on display for some young miss or another. Sir Fairfax Chamberlain was not motivated to attend the theater, nor the opera, nor an art exhibition, nor sporting match, nor a hunt, nor play billiards, or cards, or attend a lecture, or go to a salon.

"I say Fax, how the devil are you," the Colonel said when he espied his former classmate. "Haven't seen you since I went down to Darcy's wedding. Great fun that." In order to engage Fax in conversation one must just say his name to get his attention. Then he would be the most jovial of fellows.

"Why indeed Fitzwilliam, it has been quite an age. Now how was that august occasion? I am afraid I was all tied up in a bother here with my affairs, you know."

Stephen smiled and sat in a chair he had pulled over to be close to Fax. "Indeed, well I shall report that you missed a splendid occasion, for there was great camaraderie and fellowship. You have met Darcy's good friend Bingley I am led to know?" At the nod of agreement, "Yes, well, Bingley was up to the stuff as host opening up Netherfield to us all. I shall tell you and his little sister, Miss Caroline Bingley, was our hostess, her allure is quite captivating, and she did the Bingley's proud indeed."

Stephen paused. As he knew would happen, there was no hint of care, recognition, or any other facial expression in indication that Caroline Bingley held meaning to Sir Fax.

"Yes, well the grooms, they stood up to the mark you say," Fax said into the awkward silence.

"Indeed they did. I say, have you met Bingleys' brother Hurst. A gamesman I find and a kindred spirit for you, I believe. I spent many hours conversing pleasantly with him. Indeed I am certain the two of you should get along famously. He is much like the old rogue of ours from university Roger... Roger..."

"Roger McMaster! Why I haven't seen that old son since he was sent down," Fax smiled. McMaster and memories of the man was sure to do that.

That was a certainty. McMaster had ended up going overseas with a position in the East India Company, and had not been heard from since. McMaster still owed the Colonel about 100 pounds from bets and loans that he needed to make good on. As McMaster and Fax were inseparable for weeks at a time, the Colonel would be willing to wager that he was in to Fax for a great deal more. Fax however smiled at the remembrance of his old friend and Stephen knew that whatever he was owed, was but a trifle compared to what was owed Fax and others.

"Hurst seems to be somewhat more stable, and I should think that it behooves me to arrange an introduction," Stephen said.

"Indeed, you say he is Bingley's brother. Why I wonder I have yet to meet him. Bingley is the nicest of fellows. I sometimes wonder how such a stalwart gentleman has been able to put up with your cousin's cold waves, though I allow he seldom sends those of us who are intimate with him those glacial glazes. Ha-Ha." Fax most likely found little bon mots at Stephen's expense which he shared with Darcy.

"Indeed, that is in my estimation, the best of things about Bingley. That he remains friends with such as Darcy, and ourselves." Stephen added. Fax looked about not sure when a comment, such as that, was directed his way if it was a compliment or not.

"Now the Bingleys. Well you know Charles has two sisters and the one married to Hurst, quite a pleasant and agreeable person. Never a word contrary unless it is directed at Hurst, of course, in some teasing fashion. Oh, I don't mean to bore you with these tales of domestic bliss, but I thought you would find it nice to know about such of our friends where there is a good match. We shall observe both Bingley and Darcy when they return from their marriage tours and I hope shall have just as pleasant things to say."

Fax nodded, "Indeed I am always hoping that our friends match up well. You know, I shan't be a bachelor for ever."

"Indeed, I had heard that your mama takes this well in hand. Planned better then any campaign I go on that is thought up by Horse Guards," Stephen said. His line was baited. Now just needed to cast and hook the fish.

"Ha-Ha, but no my mama does not take such an interest..." Fax tried to deflect attention from his mother.

"Oh, I beg pardon, for I had not heard anything but how she played a tune and you my old friend, were often found dancing to it. Why I said just the other day to Rodgers, you remember Rodgers, well never mind, I said to Rodgers, that this can not be. Fax is of strong character. He would not let his mama point him like a hunter after a fox."

Fax studied his drink, "Yes quite good of you to say so. Fox indeed..."

"That's a hunter, and do you know, talking of hunters, but Hurst has just brought a pair. Finest bitches I've seen in a long time. We should go round some day and have a gander at them, I'm thinking."

"Sounds smashing. You know how I like a good pair of hounds. Why remember that time at Wayford Hall. Why we had a damned good time then, I do say. I do say." Stephen had secured some interest with Fax, now he was to see if it would take hold.

Another half hour of light discourse with Sir Fax and he excused himself and went to Cheapside in search of the Gardiners.

He did notice the circumstances in which the Gardiners lived, for he was born to notice such things. He knew that his father would never venture to this part of town. He also knew that Darcy had spent some hours in this home already. That not only had he endorsed the residence as quite comfortable and not at all pretentious, should circumstances allow, Mrs. Gardiner would have a quite fashionable home.

Stephen was thus already prejudiced to think much the same. What he found quite surprised him. The home had a modern wall papering and oil paintings covered these walls. A tastefully done portrait of the houses' mistress adorned the main and only drawing room, to which he was shown, but opposite was a painting to which he was familiar. "A Grenville, I believe?"

Mrs. Gardiner looked down at her lap, "Yes but only a poor copy. I had the chance to see the original as a girl at an exhibition, and remarked my admiration to Mr. Gardiner shortly after our marriage. He most worthily gifted me this piece upon our first anniversary."

"Mr. Gardiner you are a romantic also, I surmise."

"Oh no, do not credit me there. I just do what I can to make Mrs. Gardiner happy." Stephen smiled. The young boys sat with stiff backs, and the young girls tried to look ladyish before being sent to bed. "Now boys, on Saturday after next you are to come to my regimental headquarters, for we shall have a treat. I desire that you attend me at nine, and though this is early, we shall have you looking your best for there shall be such a to-do, and I think you shall find it quite fascinating."

The Crown Prince was to attend and inspect his troops in a full muster. His Highness would not arrive till after one, but Stephen felt the boys would find entertaining the soldiers preparations. "And Mrs. Gardiner I should invite you and the girls also to attend Georgiana that morning after eleven, and then my carriage shall escort you all to join us. Now you must save your appetites this day for you are to have tea with someone quite special and I shall be introducing as friends for the briefest moment to someone whose acquaintance I think shall be rather unique."

He saw Mr. Gardiner raise his head, for that gentleman had cottoned to what the Colonel proposed. "Oh, Colonel Fitzwilliam, I do not know if this is at all appropriate..."

"Nonsense there shall be a large pavilion for tea and not only Georgiana and some few others who are known to you, I believe the Hursts, though not Miss Caroline Bingley shall be amongst our guests for tea, but the families of all my officers, for they are not all bachelors. There are even several young gentleman in these families who are the same age as our two little lads. And some young misses too... Why I do believe..." The Colonel reached into an inside pocket, "Yes here they are, a letter for each of you. These two are from the children of Major Sendler, this from Captain Fortescue's daughter Miss Megan, and here from Sergeant Bell's young lad who is off to attend Ipswich School next year. Mrs. Bell will be seeing to the tea and I have been quite proud of all of Bell's little ones." The Colonel was paying the fees to send the boy away to school as he had proved himself quite good at the parish school near the barracks. The Reverend Mr. Dems had come to plead the boys case. With a patron, the boy could make something of himself, and so the Colonel took that charge.

The children retired shortly thereafter eagerly looking forward to the upcoming special day. They had badgered the Colonel for many minutes but he would not add one word to his surprise. His steadfastness had them all laughing as Mrs. Gardiner finally brought the visit to a close and sent the children to their beds. This left the adults a few minutes before they were to dine, and the Colonel thanked his hosts for such a wonderment as a evening spent alone with their family.

"Colonel, pray do not give us too great a praise for we do realize that, for a bachelor, children can be much of a trial."

"Mrs. Gardiner, I can not fault that statement, except in one instance in my experience. That instance is here with your family. Now that Georgiana is grown, and she having always been a single child amongst us older cousins," he didn't remark upon his cousin Anne, "your children are the exception to that utterance. Not only well behaved..."

The parents quivered, for they were to believe perforce that the Colonel ignored the faults of their children, "But also an absolute joy to be around. I shall endeavor should I be blessed, to have my wife and I emulate your own efforts in the raising of such pleas-ant, nay such a happy, family."

He smiled and one could see that it rose to his eyes. Mr. Gardiner came to him, "Thank you sir," and extended his hand which the Colonel took and firmly shook.

"It is I who thank you. I also give you thanks for honoring me with this dinner. I have looked forward to it since we spoke of it at Netherfield. I shall tell you what else I look forward to, having you reciprocate the honors and join Georgiana and I for dinner at my quarters upcoming..." The butler entered then to take them to dinner and the Colonel and Mrs. Gardiner made plans for such a little visit later in the month.

CANNONS ROAR

"In the midst of our trials and tribulations here, it was a refresh-ment to receive your letters. I had to stop at the fifth, and thus have three more to go, because I desired to pen you a response, for you have given me so many precious tales, that I fear should I not pen the first letter back now, I shall lose myself completely in all your anecdotes of those who are known to both of us."

* * *

Kitty had written him several letters which had arrived after the victories at Roliça and Vimiero. Battles won under the command of Sir Arthur Wellesley. Then command changed to Sir John Moore.

Stephen found quite a pleasure to break the monotony of nothing happening as Christmas came. The Army had advanced into Spain by this point, and rumors that Napoleon himself was in Spain had begun to circulate. Sir John, certainly, had not said any of that when Stephen attended staff meetings.

"I am pleased that your sisters' return from their marriage tour allowed you a brief fortnight in Town. I had a separate letter, and only one to the many I have received from you, from Georgiana, to tell me how much she enjoyed both Mary and your company in attending, three drawing rooms and how envious she was that you were able to attend two balls in Town. We shall all have to console her that next year, when she comes out, she shall find even greater pleasure. That she has only emerged to dance at family balls, such as the one in honor of our cousin Anne which I wrote you before embarking here, I am cer-tain that she will be quite taken, as you were yourself, by some of the social negotiations that occur at balls in Town."

One of Kitty's letters had observed that at the ball of Baroness Freedham, the young people clustered in three corners of a trian-gle. Along one length of the triangle was the orchestra, nine pieces. Along the other two were settees filled with matrons who glanced from one couple to another and then would be seen to talk long and hard of the prospects of the couples as unattached people stood up with one another.

Between these lounges of matrons, small clusters of the fathers stood and talked about politics or the war in which he was involved. The inquiry over the three generals and the Convention of Cintra was some of the most talked of news. Kitty imparted this second hand for she had to quiz Mary who, as often as not, wasn't dancing unless Mr. Bingley or Darcy offered to stand up with her. Though, Kitty related, some few others did so at each of the two balls.

"I am delighted that you met Sir Chamberlain Fairfax. Inspecting with Mr. Hurst his hunters, as you wrote. Sir Fax does need to be more in society and I think that the small time you spent with him, you and the other ladies in your party, surely will improve his society. I have received a letter from Miss Caroline Bingley that also told me of your quarter of an hour meeting. I should not wonder if overtime Sir Fax does not meet you and your friends when you are once again in Town."

The letter from Miss Bingley was actually presented in quite a different tone altogether, for it mentioned at the third page;

"and Sir Fax paid us the greatest compliment just this last Saturday,"

the letter postmarked but two weeks after Stephen arrived in Portugal, shortly before the first clash at Roliça.

"That the hunters of our brother Hurst did indeed attract him to our kennel, but it was our allure that kept him captivated."

Those remarks had stirred a memory in him, for the words sounded more poetic then Stephen had heard Miss Bingley ever utter to this point. That Fax had spent some few minutes, for he was sure it was less than the quarter of an hour described by Miss Bingley, and that his inclusion of that detail would exact the truth of the matter from Kitty when she wrote back.

"I cannot fathom what has Darcy out of sorts when you talk of news of our little outing here on the Peninsula. I received but two letters from him. One postmarked prior to his return to town, so yours on his demeanor are much more informative. That he should take a scold to you for enquiring what the men at the clubs are discussing would be by his nature and to be expected, despite his love for you and Mary.

And surely allowing her to be the vanguard of your campaign for information is the strategy a great general would fashion. But learn some history from me, and that you will grow to adapt to, is that the nature of Darcy's scolds are more directed at himself, for he would not be ever so ill-mannered to direct a scold at a person he knows. I believe one could make reference to some whom he has every right to give the cut direct to, and we can say that presented with such an opportunity, Darcy still would elevate himself above such an action and be seen more pure because of it."

That he spent time defending an action of Darcy in his own letter gave the Colonel pause. He would rather not be using his time to do such, and so turned back to discuss other matters which Catherine, Kitty brought forward.

"You say Mrs. Darcy, our Lizzy, has been given the choice of a dog as a present, and she looked quite astonished at the gifting. Then without a by your leave, in typical Lizzy fashion, asked for a Mastiff. I should have liked to see my cousins phiz then. It must have been quite astonishing. I am certain he expected Lizzy to be contrary to choosing a small dog, but not one so large."

He had used his information gleaned from Elizabeth's letter to him and Kitty's to admonish Darcy for his indulgences to his new wife. To Darcy he wrote:

"I should not offer Lizzy a choice of horse, sirrah, as your next gift of largesse. Certainly she has pin money that she may purchase any suitable mount and is a good judge of horseflesh that her choices can be made without your guidance. But should you do so, I should expect

long letters informing me of your being the proud owner of a Destrier able to storm into battle carrying the hardiest knight in armor, even if only meant to carry your Lizzy."

When he returned to his letter to Kitty, it was more along the lines of how pleasant it was to receive these letters in the field.

"We left Salamanca earlier this week and I fear shall continue in our pursuit of the little corporal. It became certain this week that he is in the field against us here in Spain. We have definite news now that Madrid has fallen to him and that our allies, are defeated.

"In any event, I must relate to you how your letters cheer up this old soldier and give me something to look forward to at the end of a long day of campaigning. With but a few days till Christmas, I shall endeavor to celebrate with your letters and the fond memories of all my other friends from my time in Meryton."

Such was not to be the case for as the next few days proceeded, the army faired worse. The morning of Christmas Eve brought news that decided General Moore to change his advance to a retreat towards the coast. The rearguard fighting winning actions but, still a retreat nevertheless.

Finally Corunna was in sight and the army encamped waiting to be relieved by ships and transported to safety. However, before that event could take place, a battle ensued.

* * *

The battle of June 16th was much talked of in such locales as Longbourn and Netherfield where the Bingleys were wintering near their family, the Bennets.

"Charles,"

"Yes Father," he replied to Mr. Bennet after the two sat down in his study at Netherfield whilst all the ladies gathered in the long hall.

"Any word from Spain? Last we heard the army was at Salamanca. The girls are worried," Mr. Bennet said.

"No, I have heard nothing. The Hursts join us tomorrow and perhaps they will have word. There has been nothing in *The Times* recently," Charles said.

"Damned business, this. Darcy has had no news either. I have had word from the Gardiners also, and they too hunger for news. Well no news is no news. Now I must warn you, Mrs. Bennet still is not in the mood to forgive you for not being with us this Christmas. She will recount how Darcy and Lizzy made much of their time and came here on their way to Pemberley which added days to their travel of course. I shall not scold you, for I believe your choices were very diplomatic in regards to your sisters. But as you know, Mrs. Bennet sometimes speaks before she thinks of all that should be thought of."

Charles smiled, Jane had shared three letters admonishing them for spending Christmas in Town. "I believe Jane and I have plans to put this issue to rest. If you will indulge me, I expect that as you enjoy your sherry, in but a few moments we will be interrupted. Even though my room is as much my sanctuary as your study is yours, I should think that the ladies shall not respect its sanctity today." Charles hinted, but was not about to spoil the surprise.

Mr. Bennet nodded and sipped from his glass when a very few minutes later he heard the siren call. "Mr. Bennet! Mr. Bennet! Oh such news. Such news. Mr. Bennet!" Mrs. Bennet could be heard distinctly.

The door opened so quick that it all but caromed into the shelf of books next to it. Mrs. Bennet had clearly been rushing, three daughters behind, though they seemed to have proceeded somewhat less hastily. "Oh such news, such news. You will never guess Mr. Bennet. No you will never guess, but such news, I do not think I should be capable of being happier. Oh, Mr. Bennet!"

Mr. Bennet looked from his wife to his new son, and then to his three daughters as they came upon the room. "Yes Mrs. Bennet, I should be delighted to try and guess should you allow me."

"No upon my soul but how could you, for you are a man and know little of these things so of course you cannot guess. Upon my word, I am out of breath and must sit down." Which she did. Jane had looked to her husband who shook his head as if to say you do not need any permission, and then she followed her mother into the room.

"Here my dear, give me your hand. Oh so precious a daughter

we have raised Mr. Bennet. So precious. And you dear Charles, what a husband! Oh yes indeed. What a husband. Such news. And won't Lady Lucas be all in a gather when she finds out, and her Charlotte more than a year married and still waiting." Mrs. Bennet spoke so quickly she did not seem to pause to breath.

Mr. Bennet cleared his throat, "Now my wife, you have some trifling bit to impart to me. Pray is it about the war? For, Charles and I were discussing it."

Mrs. Bennet gave her husband a look that was what one expected from drinking sour milk, "The war! Pray what do I care about the war. Our Wickham is nowhere near that whole business."

"Mama!" Mary exclaimed.

"Oh Mary, and you too Kitty, don't take on so. I know there are those whom you are fond of in Portugal," Mrs. Bennet said.

"They have invaded into Spain, Mama. They have faced Napoleon himself." Kitty spoke up. But then Jane looked to her younger sister and then tilted her head to the men. Charles reflected it was enough to remind all that once Mrs. Bennet found a topic, it could become a focus for an entire night.

"Mrs. Bennet?" Mr. Bennet enquired.

"Oh very well, but do not think Mrs. Bingley I did not see you give a scold to your sisters, despite your expecting. I have been giving them scolds much longer than you have. Now Mr. Bennet, you shall never guess..."

Mary was the first to speak, though Kitty clearly giggled and Charles had a small smile he tried to hide, "But Mama, you just told Papa."

Mrs. Bennet said, "Told your father, why I did no such thing. Now Mr. Bennet, you shall never guess what our glorious Mrs. Bingley has told me."

Charles could see Mr. Bennet smile as he said, "Why Mrs. Bennet, I am all ears, for you are right I shall never guess it, though I should hazard that were I a better listener, our middle girl may have the right of it."

Mrs. Bennet looked puzzled, and then rebounded, "Our middle girl is Mary and you do spend too much times engrossed in books so perhaps you do know many answers, but not to this, eh,

Mrs. Bingley. Well Mr. Bennet, seeing as you can never guess, I shall tell you. You are going to be a grandpapa. Such news, we must celebrate." Mrs. Bennet beamed happiness. Charles and Jane had discussed at length that they thought she would be happy.

"Indeed." Mr. Bennet, who had been standing since the ladies had barged into the room, walked to his daughter Jane and kissed her upon the cheek. Then strode to Charles and shook his hand whilst grasping Charles' shoulder. "Well done, well done, indeed!"

This turned the talk for the rest of the evening to domestic matters and all discussion of news of the war was curtailed. Mrs. Bennet had much to say to her married daughter as well as the two who were unwed. She asked six times if Jane had written to tell her other two sisters, and had been answered six times that Jane had not. Jane and he knew to inform Mrs. Bennet first to give her joy in the telling. Mrs. Bennet had volunteered to write those letters and upon returning to the drawing room after dining, while the men drank one glass of port, she composed her letters out-loud to her daughters Lydia and Elizabeth.

Going back and forth between the two letters, this process continued long after the men joined them and the letters were finished just short of the parties' need for retirement. The Bingleys had asked that the Bennets stay with them the night. Thus the evening was fully consumed at Netherfield by the blessed news. The next day the letters left early taken by servant to Meryton so they could be carried by post messenger. The household stirred and gathered to share the breaking of their fast.

It was while dining that a letter arrived. "From Darcy. He, Lizzy and Georgiana shall be joining us, also, today. He writes there is news from Spain. They stop one night on their way to Town and asks if we could host them and inform you, Mr. and Mrs. Bennet, that they stop with us and ask if they may have us all together at once. He says that he and Elizabeth can not afford a longer visit then the one night."

Charles knew that Mrs. Bennet had resigned herself to knowing that Darcy was much more comfortable with the accommodations of Netherfield then that of Longbourn should the Bingleys be in residence, and had all but stopped mentioning how this did slightly perturb her, "Well it does seem fitting, since you dear Jane do have so many servants, that if the Darcys are to descend on Meryton and put us all to an uproar for the one night, that Netherfield host them. Why I shouldn't wonder if Darcy does not travel with four liveried men for his carriage, his valet, groom, and Elizabeth with her two maids and abigail. I should not wonder where we would put them all." One would have to relate that during Christmas when the Darcy's did sojourn at Longbourn, Darcy had his servants stay at the Fox Tavern in Meryton so as not to be an imposition on the household.

Mr. Bennet, remarked that from his studies of his son Darcy, he believed that the letter informing them of the imminent arrival left somewhat more to be said. As Charles continued to read from it, he also began to believe that was the case. Mr. Bennet just nodded.

"They shall soon arrive and shall tell us all, won't they Charles," Mr. Bennet said.

Charles nodded then. "Yes, you are correct. Darcy and Lizzy will have more to relate when they have come."

Mr. Bennet inclined his head to his married daughter, "I am afraid, Jane, we will be your guests then again for dinner tonight. But we must still remove back to Longbourn so that there are rooms for Lizzy and Fitzwilliam, as well as the Hursts as was planned."

Jane quickly did some math, "Why no Papa, you shall stay another night, so as we all can have as much time with Lizzy as able, we have rooms a plenty, and Mr. Darcy's favorite room is at hand for him and Lizzy. Charles? Yes, you see, it is all arranged." Mr. Bennet had seen the nod that Charles gave to his wife, full of happiness.

* * *

"Brother," Kitty addressed Charles, "Mr. Darcy mentions war news?"

"Indeed, though *The Times* last night had scarce anything. The army retreated and some small victories had been attained, though nothing much greater as you will recall. Sir John Moore leads them back to Corunna where he hopes to make good his departure from Spain, I shouldn't wonder," Charles told her.

They had all discussed this before as it had been the news for days. Sir John knew that a fleet of English ships awaited him in Corunna and so strove to make it there. All knew of the one letter Kitty had received from Colonel Fitzwilliam postmarked before Christmas, though she but read excerpts from it.

Her mother would ask that she do so nearly each day and then would spend some time admonishing the Colonel for not having writ all of them, as he had done so in the past. Mr. Bennet would then remind his wife that from the news they had heard, it was not only quite an achievement for any in their family to have received one letter from the Colonel's hand when the campaign was in disarray, but that they had it on good authority from Darcy, that the Colonel had not even written his own mother since the early days of November. And that no letter had arrived for the Countess since then and so they must consider Kitty of being recognized of a single honor.

Each time this was stated, her mother would then go on to praise the Colonel for his sensibility in the friendship he displayed to Kitty. She would also reprimand Colonel Fitzwilliam for being so injurious of a mothers feelings that he had neglected his own mama. Kitty would just smile knowing that much more than half of the Colonel's letter she would never be able to share with her mama, nor any sister, save perhaps Lizzy, for it was so scandalous. The Colonel's wit shown through near every line, and this would be ill thought of if repeated. But in the quiet of the night, she would reread parts that were memorized, and do her best to hold her laughter quiet.

"That Sir John is much admired, it is true. But we do dither here, and we dither there, and we dither everywhere. We waited in Salamanca for weeks indecisively. We made a hash of our march through much of this countryside. And our allies... Do you remember when we were in the drawing room at Netherfield, and it was so quiet you could drop a pin and hear it? The only sound was Hurst as he snored. Everyone afraid to speak until Lizzy turned to your father and asked if Darcy's largesse for after the wedding ceremony was all taken care of? That is our allies. No one wants to speak, or act first. That the little corporal could come into Spain so easily is obvious..."

Charles spoke his thoughts as the table was cleared of their dishes, "I should imagine that *The Times* will have more to relate. I shouldn't wonder that Mr. Hurst shall be able to bring us the paper, otherwise we shall have the news tomorrow morning when the paper arrives from Town."

"Perhaps mama, I can go visit mine aunt in Meryton to see if there is any news in the village?" Kitty looked to Mrs. Bennet for permission to visit Mrs. Phillips.

Before Mrs. Bennet could speak, however, her father did, "Now dear, I do not think that is needful. Certainly Mr. Darcy has written that he has news. We are to receive the paper soon enough, especially should Mr. Hurst bring it. And I should desire it if you are to hand when your sister arrives, since Charles and Jane have so kindly asked that we stay. I am sure Jane, you could use a hand in making your preparations for your guests." Jane looked to her father and nodded. Kitty knew that but an hour's preparation with the servants would take care of such. She could not decipher his meaning and it did not seem that Jane could either. Jane was well enough adept that she need not speak against him, though.

"Yes, Kitty, I should appreciate your help and Mary's too. There is much to be done. Do you not think that both Lizzy and Mrs. Hurst should like an arrangement of fresh flowers for their rooms?" Jane said. Mr. Bennet's smile led one to believe he had achieved greatness.

The family spent the day around Netherfield in various pursuits. The ladies looked at fashion plates and commented on how various garments would be for Jane's lying in period. The men walked about the house and grounds, not straying too far. Charles had not expected his sister until the middle of the afternoon, but it was not easy to predict when the Darcys would arrive.

It was the Darcys who arrived first. Only one carriage, the coachman and with Darcy's valet sitting atop the coach. Darcy, Lizzy, Georgiana and her governess were the only occupants. Lizzy it was later related, having told her husband that in the interests of speed, they could make do with out the trappings of their position in society. As Darcy handed Lizzy and the other ladies down from the carriage, the rest of the family gathered and greeted them. Hugs, hearty handshakes and chaste warm kisses from one to another depending on who acknowledged whom.

Even as this occurred three more carriages came up the lane. The Hursts and several personal servants had arrived. In addition, Caroline Bingley followed her sister Louisa stepping down from the carriage.

Less hugs and chaste kisses were exchanged and the handshakes were perhaps not as hearty. With Caroline's arrival, Jane instructed servants to prepare a room, which truth be told, she had anticipated and previously had made ready. Despite Caroline's prior protestations that she could not tear herself away from Town, Jane expected that left alone she would, of course, travel to be with all her family. Jane thus had ensured that a room, a very nice room, was reserved for Caroline. Jane did not say anything about the matter, except as Kitty helped her earlier, Jane said a good hostess should be prepared.

Lizzy was apprised of the momentous news that the Bingleys had to share, by their mother who went on in such a voice that soon all had been made known to the assemblage before even entering the hall. Mr. Hurst had brought the previous evening's paper, but that had arrived that morning. He had nothing more to add, just rumors. The gentlemen then retired to Mr. Bingley's library.

* * *

"This is old news," Darcy said as they entered the library. The account of the battle of Corunna was writ large and held much of the paper.

Hurst said, "Yes, Charles mentioned your letter saying that you had news of the war and were to Town."

"My Cousin, Stephen, the Colonel. He was shot at Corunna," Darcy replied.

"My God man," Hurst exclaimed. "The casualty lists are in the paper but I paid them little mind. Is he mentioned there?" Hurst had given the paper to Mr. Bennet who was looking at it. He shook his head, no.

Bingley had more presence, "How is the Colonel, he survived surely."

"Yes, I understand he is wounded in the shoulder. We travel to see to his recovery. My uncle would have him to home, but the brief note I received, dictated by Stephen, suggests that he shall be obstinate. Father, may Georgiana and her governess stay with you for a few days as Lizzy and I see to my cousin. I shall then venture to fetch her when we are sure of his arrangements."

Mr. Bennet knew of the closeness between the two men. Lizzy's father seemed to weigh his great distress as Mr. Bennet was surely aware that this would subject his beloved sister Georgiana to the direction of Mrs. Bennet. "Do not fret so, Fitzwilliam. When you are ready, write and I shall escort her to Town myself."

"Or, I will accompany her and father, too," Charles added.

"Thank you father, Charles. That relieves me of a worry. I know how much Georgiana gets along with your daughters, sir, and this is an aid. I shall be much more able to focus on my cousin's needs, as shall Lizzy."

"I find it damned peculiar," said Mr. Hurst. "There is no mention of Colonel Fitzwilliam in the casualty list at all. I had just penned him a letter last Tuesday, though I doubt that he got it with all this rot going on. I wrote to inform him of a new hunting rifle from Couches I got recently. I believe I told you about it, Charles..." Mr. Hurst stopped when he looked up from the paper to see the other gentlemen looking at him. "Right, sorry that."

"You say he was shot..." Charles began, "And I caution you, the ladies will want details, unless Lizzy is telling them now of all you know."

Darcy paused, and then nodded, "She most likely is. I know Mary and Kitty will both be concerned, and either Lizzy or Georgiana shall sketch for them the particulars of the situation. I received two letters. One written on the morning of the battle, just as I had received from Stephen's hand before Vimiero. He detailed out certain instructions in a few brief paragraphs, and a synopsis of the battle he was set to face. He did this, too, discussing in two lines a hellish retreat across northern Spain, some thirty of his men dead or incapacitated, and the loss of one officer. For all that he wrote, he was still healthy then.

"That I received a second letter, also, which let me believe he had come through unscathed for it was apparent in the first letter that they were to face a battle, outnumbered by the French and in poor position with their backs to the sea. As I say, a second letter in his hand surely meant that he had lived. Yet this second letter was not in his hand, I discovered when I opened it. And neither was it in his clerk's.

"It started thus;

'I live. I am holed in my right shoulder. I write as we cross to Plymouth. Come to Town, I do not want the Countess to make a fuss. We won, but near a hundred of mine perished. A damn wretched business.'

And that is all. Lizzy has the letter, for she knows that Georgiana would cajole it from me."

Darcy paused, and to this Mr. Bennet, who had sat quietly during the retelling now said, "Amazing. He deserves my admiration. Indeed. I am at a loss…" And Mr. Bennet could say no more. Darcy knew Mr. Bennet had lived so amongst his books and the small world of Meryton, that these events were writ larger than he.

Darcy saw that Charles could see the path that his thoughts had taken him. Charles said, "You go to install him in your town house for his convalescence. I should think he will put up some fuss at being moved from his lodgings, but it is clear that his rooms are not adequate to the care your home in Town can provide. I should think also another solution would be to use Heather Court, if he could convince his parents to allow him."

Darcy briefly smiled, "This is a side you do not know of my cousin, though knowing me, you should expect he shares a similar notion. We do not like to be fussed and bothered over much when ill. He caught a fever a few years ago whilst at the Earl's seat and the Countess was such an attentive nursemaid that he snuck down on the third night to the local Inn to recuperate for the rest of the duration. If he were to remove to Heather Court, he would be ill pressed to keep his mama at bay."

"Well this I can say, you are both too proud over such matters, and I believe you Fitzwilliam, have come to know it this last year," Mr. Bennet said over the foolishness that he was hearing.

"Indeed sir, your daughter said much the same to me on our carriage ride here. She too takes your line, and I can see how she has the correctness of it, yet Stephen is still Stephen and doubtless could further elucidate why he wishes to heal without the attention of mine aunt."

Darcy was not even sure, since the Colonel's name had not been reported in *The Times*, if the Earl and Countess knew of their younger son's injury.

If Stephen had not informed them, then Darcy would be doing that the instant he had met with his wounded cousin. An ill thought crossed his mind which he could not conceal as it played upon his face. "That looks like someone swallowed some three day old fish, if ever I saw." Mr. Hurst had noted Darcy's visage as well.

"There is something else?" Mr. Bennet asked.

Darcy looked at the three men, and knew they were, even Hurst, to be trusted with some of his confidences. "I do not worry upon mine aunt, the Countess, and her reaction that such news will portend. I have a concern with regard to mine other aunt, Lady Catherine de Bourgh and how she will respond to such news. I fear that the Colonel will have even less regard for her temperament and ministrations then he would for the Countess'."

"Yes, Charles, and of course, you Hurst will not have heard," Mr. Bennet said, "but my indiscreet daughters..."

Charles raised his hand, "Actually father we have both heard my younger sister has apprised us for not only did Mary and Kitty receive letters from the Colonel about his sojourn at the Ball, So too did Caroline, and of course Georgiana was there. When all four were in London recently upon Darcy and my return from our wedding tour, we received various reports from your married daughters of the attachment that Lady Catherine has decided for the Colonel. And of course how the Colonel has decided to perceive this attachment."

Mr. Bennet said, "Perhaps you know more of this then I. I know my youngest but one to be less than completely discreet, and was surprised when Mary had something to add. Naturally, well perhaps not naturally, but I did not let them indulge in their discussions in front of me, and I did instruct Mrs. Bennet in this instance that no further discussion was to take place under my roof."

Darcy smiled, then said, "Yes sir, and I do believe that the girls and Mama did follow that, for they complained bitterly how strict you had become. But this did not stop the little vixens to discuss some of this as they paid social calls about the neighborhood. Or when in Town to stay with Lizzy and I."

Mr. Hurst was nodding. When Mr. Bennet looked to him the man said, "Your daughters had come with Miss Darcy and Mrs. Darcy to pay a call upon Jane and whilst I sat with my paper, they could talk of little else, asking both Georgiana and Mrs. Darcy to opinion upon Lady Catherine and Miss Anne De Bourgh. Mrs. Darcy did then at one point exclaim, 'enough.' She stated then, that they not only were all relating parts from their correspondence with the Colonel, but they assuredly had no meat in their recitals. Not one of the chits who compared letters were able to produce any hint that Lady Catherine was seeking a specific match for Miss Anne, nor was that match the Colonel."

Darcy said "Yet I fear that this must be the case."

'Mine aunt, Lady Catherine has the notion that now that you have flown the coop, the only man of quality available to her for Anne, is I.'

Darcy quoted. He explained that those words had arrived in Vienna from the Colonel in one letter to Darcy.

Mr. Bennet said, "How so Darcy? I believe the girls have related to me that they pieced together that Anne was in need of a husband, that the Colonel observed that the local gentry to Rosings Park were in fear of Lady Catherine and so maintained a distance, and, that they expect that the Colonel's agency must be to facilitate a match from the most eligible of Town." Mr. Bennet believed he had understood the position quite well that the young ladies had come to. "It is having seen Lady Catherine's treatment of Lizzy before your engagement that gives me pause for the Colonel's privacy. Though it is apparent that I must further instruct the Bennet ladies in what I consider appropriate for discussion." That all three men nodded must have given Mr. Bennet the feeling that he had let his duties lapse. He shook his head as he often did when contemplating a scold for his daughters.

Darcy then said, "One must also think, father, of mine cousin and his letters. Certainly they provided us all with a view of Anne's ball for we have compared some of his letters. Indeed did we both not find that the passage he wrote to me, and to you and Mrs. Bennet were the same right down to the punctuation!" This provoked a laugh.

Mr. Darcy knew that the Colonel's correspondence to all had included some showing of the truth, but that only the letter to him had stated exactly what the precise circumstances were. Darcy had pierced this together and found that Georgiana also had become convinced that Lady Catherine also wished a match between the Colonel and her cousin Anne. Mr. Darcy was most firm in instructing his sister to talk of that to no one and he was certain she had not confided those suspicions to any soul, even though some discussion amongst the ladies led towards those conclusions.

"Quite a problem indeed, no matter what one thinks for the Colonel, I should say. Perhaps one can take solace in that Lady Catherine does not have a residence in Town," Mr. Bennet remembered this.

"She does not, but she does believe that my uncle the Earl, shall set aside room for mine aunt if she ever does need them. Not these last five years has she, but the rooms I believe remain as her right, to her mind." Darcy did not mention that this understanding had been his burden, but upon the announcement of his engagement to Lizzy, Lady Catherine said he should put his mind to rest that she would never darken his door. Elizabeth had learned of the suite that Lady Catherine previously used at the Darcy townhouse and insured, it, too, remained ready for Lady Catherine. Should word ever reach her ladyship that the suite was used by another, that would surely destroy any rapprochement.

"In any event, whether the Colonel shall allow the ministrations of his mother, which he seems disinclined to, or any other lady, it does seem somewhat strict to close one self off to such attention." Bingley uttered and when the other men looked to him, they realized he had not grasped what they had.

Darcy chose to mention it with grace, "Yes Charles, perhaps the wound is worse then Stephen has allowed. It is possible and I beg you to not mention these fears to any of the ladies. I expect Lizzy worries what conclusions my mind has jumped to as we left Pemberley with all dispatch. But she has kept my attention from this and deftly ensured that Georgiana does not stray down these dark paths."

Charles nodded sagely and then poured a round of sherry for all. Then recalling the women, the men sought their company explaining that they had determined a course of action. Georgiana staying with the Bennets and the society of the Bingleys and Hursts being much welcomed at that moment in the country. Darcy observed that Jane clutched Caroline's hand and ensured she did not speak against the men's plans, and Mr. Bennet was quick to interject and stop Mrs. Bennet the minute she cleared her throat, "Now my dear, certainly you can see that Georgiana will be a godsend to us in our nearly empty house, I believe it is three daughters I have lost in so short a time but it is hard for me to keep track, there used to be so many underfoot."

"Underfoot indeed, why Mr. Bennet, how many times have you mentioned to me how you find the quiet refreshing now that there has been such a leave taking from under Longbourn's roof. But I still..."

"Yes Mrs. Bennet I may have said that, but you know that is in jest." The look upon Mr. Bennets face was hard to read, "And to think our Jane is soon to be blessed with a child herself. Is that not wondrous, I am still all amazed at what changes shall take over all our lives. Why Mrs. Bennet should not you and the ladies plan a visit to Lady Lucas with such news. I do believe she shall be happy to receive it, and Georgiana can renew her acquaintance with Moira Lucas..."

Mrs. Bennet's eyes took on a sparkle as she planned, "Why yes indeed. Lady Lucas does not know your splendid news, dear Jane. Lizzy I do not suppose you and Darcy may have anything to add? I am sure that the waters of the Balkans..."

Lizzy spoke, "Alps mama, we were in the Alps, and Darcy and

I hope to give you the same glorious news that Jane has in time mama...

THE STRONG MEN ARE ALWAYS THE WEAKEST

"I do not need that foul smelling concoction. Please, Lizzy, it is bad enough that I shall be on display for the rest of the day, but to drink that..." the Colonel struggled with what he could say in polite society. He lost, for the only words that came to his mind were ones that one could not say.

"You shall drink this Colonel, or I shall tell your doctor." That threat was one that the Colonel honored. It was several degrees worse than the first threat, having Georgiana include such news in letters to Lady Catherine. The second degree was letting the Countess be informed that the Colonel refused his medicine. The third degree was letting the ladies who lived in Berkeley Square know of the Colonel's refusal to drink the healing liquid. And the last was letting the physician know, for the doctor could, and would, keep him on medical leave, away from his Regiment.

"Very well, but I shall have to list you on the Regiment's books as the sternest sergeant we have." He made a face as he choked down a little more than half of the foul liquid. Then he reached for a very large glass of sherry to cut the taste. Resolved, he drank the rest.

Whilst Darcy told him he had been fearing that Stephen had a debilitating injury, the reality was not nearly so bad. Towards the end of the battle a ball had lodged in the meat of the Colonel's right shoulder. The surgeon had tried to attend to it immediately, but the Colonel had waved him off having the doctor see to the men first. Hours later, the Colonel was made unconscious so the surgeon could extract the ball and bits of debris from his clothing that had lodged in the wound. In all, a successful operation, and the stitching to close the wound was in a nearly straight line.

Stephen suffered from a slight fever and blood loss, and the muscles around the arm were slightly atrophied and needed to be retrained. All this added together, caused the Colonel to need to convalesce. A fact recognized by his family and friends if not by, himself.

The Colonel shivered on the settee where he spent the early part of his days. This piece of furniture had been purchased by

Mr. Darcy's mother and was grey moiré with red half inch stripes that had a slight tendency towards pink. With the Colonel ensconced upon it, covered with a large dark green blanket, it was hard to see the patterns. It was repeated in two adjoining chairs across a small table that barely could fit a tray with three cups and a teapot upon it. Behind the settee, another set of four chairs faced one another, and then a small bench lay athwart one of the two great floor to ceiling windows that faced the west side of the house. The fire was well stoked each day so that before he entered the room the temperature was warm but not sweltering.

The Colonel would later in the early hours of the afternoon, go to the nursery, which since Georgiana had her own adult rooms, was now vacant. It had been turned into a recovery studio and here the Colonel would work his pained shoulder in a variety of exercises to increase its strength. He could now handle his sword but had no real control. The same with a quill. He was fortunate to be able to use a pistol, however, to the same skill he had before. He still was a very good shot.

The week in which he had been recovering at Darcy's Berkeley Square house had shown marked improvements. After the third day, Darcy had allowed the Bennets to descend upon them. The Countess had seen her son for a brief half hour interview, satisfied herself that Lizzy and the professionals were giving the man the dispassionate care he desired, then retreated to her own town home. The Earl had made one appearance. The Countess came each day, spent from half of an hour to not more than two hours with her son, and then departed. She allowed as how her visits and correspondence kept Lady Catherine at Rosings Park. But she feared that upon hearing that the Bennets stayed at the hospital here at Berkeley Square, Lady Catherine might be soon to come to Town.

"If it is true, that mine aunt, Lady Catherine, should come to Town, I do not think to see her come to pay a social call upon you, Mrs. Darcy," the Colonel said. A letter from Horse Guards lay upon his lap, somewhat ignored.

"I believe you have the right of it. Now pray attend, the doctor has proscribed that you take a drive in the Park this afternoon for he wishes you to have fresh air. The Countess will call for you and the young ladies, she informs me, to escort all of you to the Park. This shall be quite an entertainment for Mary and Kitty as they have not been to the Park but once before with Darcy and myself when we brought them up after our travels."

The Colonel nodded. Lizzy said, "Pray attend, do not move your head as if you listen when you think upon all else."

This got the Colonel to listen more closely. He said, "Yes, the ladies and I shall be ensconced in Mama's carriage. Is that it. I, to be displayed like a museum piece so the world knows I live. I am sure the Ton discusses my recuperation as much as it does some of the other senior officers."

He stopped short on brooding on those men who had been lost from society. It was a subject he and Darcy had talked of once, but had never raised to the ladies. Stephen though had been informed that the Ton did speak about such matters in many another drawing room.

"Yes, you shall be as a museum piece, and further, if you are a good museum piece taking your air, and continuing to improve, the Doctor has left the determination up to me if on one of these days we shall have the carriage take you to your bivouac. Perhaps even today.

"There you may be allowed, should I desire, to engage in possibly an hour's discussion with your subordinates. Or not, should you remain petulant and continue to sulk as you have. Mary had a decided opinion on your actions of yesterday. My sisters are all here only at your request, and I do believe it was such as to ensure that the house would be full of my relations so that no other could encamp here, but you must learn not to be short with them sir, for their feelings are easy to wound."

The Colonel realized that after dinner, one in which a light repast was served each night in order to facilitate his recovery, and in which the entire family complimented him by also consuming the same, he had been decidedly short of temper the previous night. He had brooded on the pace of his recovery for he had hoped to be further along. The light repast also did not improve his thoughts, for Lizzy had control of the menu each day and refused to alter it to his whims. All three men had been losing weight, but he had an ally in slowing this reduction. Kitty not only scavenged in the kitchen for herself and Georgiana, but also was able to sneak a sweet each day to the recuperating Colonel. Darcy and Mr. Bennet did not think to supplement their diminished meals and had lost nearly twice as much weight as Colonel Fitzwilliam.

With his temper short, then Kitty had remarked that Town in the Winter in no way compared to the Country, the Colonel had been dismissive of this. His mind was on returning to the barracks and seeing to his Regiment. He had elaborated his cutting remark in the drawing room with a second, in poor taste, regarding that there was no comparison to Town, else why would so many of the country rush madly towards its light. Speaking a certainty allowed for no differing opinion and this was his crime. Gentlemen always allowed each to their own opinion, and graciously insured that no one's opinion would be invalidated.

"I had addressed my remarks to Kitty, and late last night penned a note, though its legibility may be such that a translator from the Foreign Office may have to be called into read it, asking for her forgiveness."

"My manners are that of a cur, my words are that of a beast, I beg the greatest bit of mine honor to apologize."

Stephen had employed the use of the under-butler last night to deliver the small note. An hour later a reply arrived.

"In forgiveness I shall pat you upon your head next I see you, or shall I scratch you behind the ears?"

Kitty had used her abigail, something new while ensconced at the Darcy's town home to bring her reply. While Stephen did not expect the below stairs to be discreet, and was assured that Kitty would not think that servants are apt to gossip, he bid the maid to attend and paid for her discretion and the return of a missive to her mistress.

"I am afraid that a good scratch would be too risqué now or ever, and a pat on the head is no fit acknowledgement for a hunter. Perhaps

for a ladies terrier, but not for a foxhound."

The abigail returned with another missive, much after all were further abed, and he dismissed her with another two guineas. He found though this missive needed an answer and so had to summon and bribe the under-butler also, this was becoming much more expensive then the penny post. Kitty had admonished:

> *"Sir, I believe having been wronged, it is I who shall determine what breed of canine one currently resembles. Have no fear, I can recognize the difference in your very bark, since we have seen no bite. As for a hunter, I should think one would remember remarking that it has been sometime since one was last the hunter, as you have regaled before. That but three times these five years, or perhaps my memory is fading? I should not make a remark upon that if I were to stay in one's good graces."*

He dozed between these notes, for one could not call them letters. Prior, their letters had run to pages. But his rest, which he needed to heal was sorely interrupted this night. That the writing made him work his injured shoulder was most likely a good thing, yet he did not use it arduously in the composition of these short notes. He found the payment of such funds to keep the servants free from starting tales much more painful. His last to her, with a final note to curtail until the morning was penned, with an intentional last word.

> *"Indeed I submit to be any manner of dog for which you name my breed. The punishment that shall be inflicted from your kind and delicate hand shall be taken with grace, yet as member of the four legged species I claim one attribute as the evening now passes and the second hour of the day has been greeted. I claim the attribute of being dog tired and must curtail all until anon, for fatigue has claimed any sense of play that yet remains. I am your obedient puppy..."*

His conversation with Lizzy filled him in on what happened when he had left the previous night and gone to write the first of the letters that were exchanged. "Kitty was kind enough, after

Darcy chased you to bed, to forgive you. Mary however was in a fit and my mother did not do much to discourage her of those feelings."

The Colonel realized that he could say little to that. He knew that asking Mrs. Bennet to Town, which was an imposition on Darcy already, was his responsibility. He had met her and had understood all of Darcy's objections that had been made known to him, and those he had deciphered from long acquaintance with his cousin. In spite of that, he found a certain charm in her predictability of the society in which he lived.

"I shall endeavor to apologize to Mary with your mother present, and I am sure that each shall appreciate that effort. I believe Kitty prefers the correspondence, a reverse of both their natures." And in this understanding it was possible that the Colonel was correct for Lizzy nodded.

"Now that you are settled, and have had your medicine, your cousin begs me to remind you that we attend the Bingleys this evening and shall be leaving you to your own devices. My father spoke to staying here to keep company with you, but Fitzwilliam reminded him of how much pleasure Charles derives in his company."

"Yes I shall miss that. Your aunt and uncle Gardiner are also to attend I believe..."

Lizzy handed him his stack of that day's correspondence, and he shuffled through it till he came upon several envelopes in a pale green color, all of the same size. Lizzy recognized them as from her cousins and their parents. "That the children write you each day I believe shows their regard for you, though they shall be at home with their governess this evening."

"Yes, young Jack has written as to the unfairness of it all..." Stephen smiled.

Lizzy returned the smile and said, "And I believe he must also write a line or two of you relenting in your orders and allowing them to visit."

The Colonel thought for a moment, "I should imagine that if the doctor prescribes that I am well enough for the Park, then I should be able to relent in my proscription and the children may come visit. We may then present Jack with the bullet that was taken from my shoulder." He had requested to see it more than ten times.

"That shall please them and it does show that you are healing." Lizzy went to the rope pull to summon a butler.

"The girls will be up in a moment or so. You are ready?" Lizzy asked each day. He was appreciative of her taking him in hand, and also steering his mother to her own house. He had heard that Mrs. Bennet even pointed out that Lizzy was an excellent nursemaid for this task, to the Countess, for she was able to tend the Colonel with some dispassion. A case in point being that the Countess would have allowed her son to forego his horrific medicines. This might then have prolonged his recuperation.

His nod allowed Lizzy to take her customary seat at her desk and begin some correspondence of her own. The Colonel reread the note from Horse Guards. The Regiment's status for the return to Portugal was questioned. They wanted to begin to reinforce the small amount of troops left there in April. Sir Arthur Wellesley, having been exonerated of the Convention of Cintra, was to command.

His shoulder was pained, though, he knew physically, he was able to walk, stand, exert himself each day. His control of a Saber however might not have returned by the time the army returned to the Continent. Further the recruitment efforts to bring his unit up to strength went poorly. The retreat from Portugal and losses on the battlefield made it difficult to find men willing to hazard such an adventure. Though the Regiment had fared somewhat better then many another.

"Well, look at him today, the picture of health." Mrs. Bennet said upon entering the room, followed by her daughters and Georgiana. The three young ladies carried vases of fresh cut flowers; lilacs, lavenders, daisies and roses, that they had been arranging in the first floor foyer. Each day they did this before entering the day room.

They each curtsied and the Colonel nodded in acknowledgement. He was well enough to get up, but having been arranged so carefully by Lizzy each day, he did not. Stephen resolved on the morrow to not allow her to fuss him into the settee, but, for him to sit in a chair like any other healthy man. He then would rise in greeting the girls and further distance himself from the sick room.

"Thank you Mrs. Bennet, and how are you this day?"

"I am well sir, though I must say I long for the country and Meryton. Once you are recovered we shall away to there. Mr. Bennet has never much liked Town and though I was a great favorite here in my youth, I must say that as a soon to be grandmother with those days so long past, Town holds little allure for me now." That Mrs. Bennet should say such elicited a look from Lizzy.

She continued "I see you there Mrs. Darcy. And should you wonder at such remarks. I have heard that you should wish to be in Pemberley more than you should wish to be in London."

Lizzy shook her head a little, and the Colonel smiled. "Now Mama, that is in context. While the Colonel needs our support there is no place I would rather bide then here."

Stephen stepped into the developing battle, "Why indeed Mrs. Bennet, Mrs. Darcy, I should thank you each again for giving up such great comforts and serenity as your country seats offer to attend to my small needs. Your great kindness and sacrifices to me are such that I can never repay, and you young ladies, to give up your comforts when the season is just beginning to stretch its legs, and my recuperation chains you to this house, I applaud and salute you each. I also beg your forgiveness for any boorish activities on my part that I uttered last night."

Mary looked about and believed she could contribute, "Why it is we who must thank you Colonel, and of course dear Lizzy for hosting us. The splendour of London is so enormous that I feel consumed just being here. Why not two days ago I was at the British Museum's department of Printed Books with Papa and there were thousands upon thousands of them. Why I believe even Papa had his breath taken away.

"And the architectural achievements of Mr. Wren and Mr. Jones..." Mary found that her audience had wandered. The Colonel had surreptitiously glanced to the letter in his lap. Georgiana and Kitty had picked up a series of fashion plates and Lizzy looked to her correspondence. It was Mrs. Bennet who added the next bit, a matter of habit.

"Yes, dear that is all well and good and I am sure we will wish to hear more later." A few words that the Colonel could recall having heard more than once when Mary spoke.

Kitty gave him a moue. "Sister, the Colonel does tease a little, I think. He is just like a spaniel I think. He knows we have been able to go to four salons, already, and though we have turned down two balls, he knows that we shall yet avail ourselves of at least that many before we return to Longbourn. Why just last night he instructed us to take advantage of the tickets his mother, the Countess, obtained for us to Almacks, even if he was unable to escort us, and Mr. Darcy graciously said without hesitation that he would do us proud and chaperone us to the assemblage."

Lizzy put her pen down, "Oh my dear, I love that man to distraction, as you have remarked, but I do think there was some hesitation upon my dear Darcy's part." She realized that if she did not make the remark, the Colonel was sure to find something humorous to interject and that could start Mrs. Bennet once again.

Georgiana had also gotten used to the game, "It must be how Lizzy says, surely you remember. My brother is so good natured that he will take us to Almacks, for he has promised that this is to be my season too, but he has always been reluctant to attend that establishment." The Colonel's grin was something that Georgiana wanted to cut short as well.

Mrs. Bennet said, "What are you all on about. We are to go to Almacks this Thursday, and I do not know why you carry on so. We have all your fittings tomorrow after breakfast with the dressmaker and I should say you must thank your cousin again, for he and Darcy and Charles have all seen to ensuring that you three young ladies shall look your best. Colonel you are far too indulgent of these three girls, why to outfox my sons and make them also buy dresses for the girls alongside your generous offer. I shall never forget the look on either of their faces."

Mrs. Bennet had only thought that the Colonel had caught the two well heeled men off guard, but he knew the cost of a dress to each young lady was but a pittance to some of what he had gathered in Spain. Following a retreating army before retreating himself, he and his officers had found a few thousand guineas worth of spoils. He was easily able to spend five hundred on the young ladies and his cousin and Mr. Bingley felt compelled to match it. Especially since Charles had brought the subject up, 'I shan't want to hear Caroline say one word about Kitty or Mary's dress...' Stephen had responded, 'Easily solved, for I came into a little money before being shot. I shall buy them each a gown to wear about, and Georgiana too, as she is my ward.' Then it was 'Nonsense we can't let you do that, Lizzy and Jane would give us a scold...'

Soon settled that the three men would commission a dress for each. Stephen stole a march on the other two men by announcing his gift before they had the chance to do so, as he saw the three ladies first in the drawing room before all the other family could assemble together. Not that he generally intended to upstage Darcy, for the times when he was able to do so were few and far between since embarking on their adult paths, but that these occasions did arrive was a source of some pleasure to the Colonel.

The season was ever a topic of conversation amongst society and yet this room held little of that discussion which Stephen had found refreshing. He had lived in London each season all his life. Except when at university, Darcy, had lived but half the seasons whilst he grew to adulthood and was home from school, and then less then half as an adult preferring the solitude of Pemberley.

Mrs. Bennet talked incessantly when the subject came upon them of her part of a season whilst younger. Lizzy had once remarked to Stephen that this influenced Kitty, but had no meaning to Mary who was much concerned with the joys of the physical London and not a care for the society of London.

Lizzy had a brief glimpse of the end of the Season upon her return from her wedding tour the previous year and aside from desiring to meet that part of society that Darcy did approve of, she had little desire to go to the theater or opera nightly. A rout or ball, if an intimate gathering of Darcy's friends, or a small dance that he delighted in was enough for her, she had told Stephen.

Darcy then for his part had told him that he found this aspect of his wife, who he deemed much more social then he, a pleasure, for it did not force him to a new height of society. The

Bingleys though were vastly different as they did enjoy the social whirl, but Charles felt the longing for Netherfield more so and had made plans with his wife's consent to dissect the season into small bites with long interludes at his new estate.

Darcy did note a concern in regards to Georgiana as this was her first season, and he was amused that he should think of it as his wife's first real season also. He knew that he would have to present her correctly to society and that this was an area where his wife would be treading on new ground. Darcy told Stephen that his mother, the Countess, was readily able to provide suggestions and since the death of his and Georgiana's mother had taken on certain aspects of the confidence of a mother to Georgiana. Her guidance provided some key help in this aspect.

With Georgiana's season planned, with much briefer interludes at Pemberley than the Bingleys would partake of at Netherfield, it seemed only natural that Darcy do his best by his two new unmarried sisters and see if they could be launched as well. Darcy told Stephen he had formed this opinion and had expressed some little remark to his wife. The wounding of his cousin had seen all plans put in abeyance and the care of the Colonel being seen to now as the preeminent concern.

It happened that once the Colonel had asked for the Bennets to companion Mrs. Darcy and see to the lightening of the monotony of his recovery, that Stephen should then propose the obvious. He suggested that Darcy launch all the girls into the season, expanding upon the little efforts that the Bingleys took at the end of the last season.

"Tonight a nice quiet dinner after our ride in Hyde Park." The Colonel went over the itinerary. "Tomorrow, what is planned. Was there not an outing again to the Museum, then the day after Mrs. Bingley's drawing room followed by the theatre?"

Kitty muffled a giggle.

"Why indeed Colonel, you are very well informed as to the girls plans." Mrs. Bennet looked to the man. Stephen believed she was comparing him to her three new sons and dressed him up and down. But a look crossed her face and perhaps Mrs. Bennet had heard about and Anne de Bourgh and Lady Catherine's desires.

"Oh Mama, look to Kitty for betraying all plans," Lizzy said. "You must see that the two of them are peas in a pod with their heads together making all sorts of plans to keep Darcy on his toes."

The man himself walked in at that moment. "I should think that I am often upon my toes when standing or walking." A small humor for Darcy, but it brought a grin to the faces of his intimates and was lost upon the others.

"Good morrow Mrs. Bennet, my dear. Ladies, Cousin. I have just left father ensconced in the library where he believes he has found three tomes that you may wish to peruse, Mary, at your leisure..." Darcy could no more finish that sentence, then Mary had stood and begged everyone's forgiveness but desired to attend her father at once in the library.

Darcy and the others were used to such abrupt comings and goings with the girls for if the morning was to be social, Mary had little desire to be in the room, and if the morning were to be musical, then Kitty would ask to take her leave. If the ladies felt that attention was needed to their needle skills, then Lizzy all but gave permission to Georgiana to find another task for she was sorely lacking in those skills. Her governess' had felt that an heiress of her stature need not bother with the accomplishment of such a mundane task.

"Well cousin," Stephen said, "I should think that your good wife and her very accomplished family have seen expeditiously to my recovery, why, not an hour ago, the discussion was how quickly I would be attending to my regimental duties and be out from under your ardent care."

Lizzy looked sharply as Darcy said, "Indeed, cousin, for your primary care giver and I had some similar discussion this morning and I was informed by this gracious lady." Darcy bent to kiss his wife's hand. "That all felt that perhaps by weeks end, you might sit with your officers for a half hour at most."

Stephen said, "To cast no conceit to all my healers, but surely as I am able to sit with the family all day, I should be able to spare more time with mine officers?"

Darcy knew who ruled here, "Indeed one would think it, but surely you must admit to knowing men, as we have discussed many times these last weeks, who proclaimed that they had fully recovered, returned to duty, and were dead the next day. I should sorely not like to see that happen to you."

Stephen nodded, "'Sides," Darcy continued, "I shall not believe the surgeon shall allow your return to duty until he and I both are convinced that you may defend yourself capably with sword and pistol, sit a horse and perhaps get in and out of your uniform coat." That task too was still difficult to manage as the pain flared when the shoulder was flexed as one put on the tight fitting garments of the uniform.

"I am overcome with your arguments. I shall retreat here to my settee for the rest of my days."

"Well perhaps for a few more weeks, Colonel." Lizzy added. He knew she wished that he was able to heal as fast as he hoped, and that the process would take longer than the war was surely to do. Lizzy had not said it, but she had talked around the subject that if he were to die, Darcy would be ill effected as if he were to lose a brother.

"Lizzy, could not the Colonel accompany us to the theatre? He is the only one who knows the play well and he would be such a great guide for all of us." Kitty tried to entreat her sister. All realized that the desires of the Colonel were seconded to the orders of Elizabeth.

"I should think that the Colonel still suffers from exhaustion easily. A full night might be somewhat much."

The Colonel advanced into this sally, "You are to use Mother's box, is that not so?" When Mrs. Darcy nodded. "I should imagine I would be able to attend, and if sitting in the back, I could take my ease without much notice."

Kitty laughed and Mrs. Bennet was quick to add, "You and Mr. Bennet both." All understood this to mean that if the need was upon them, they would find an opportune to time to nap during one of the acts.

"And was it not you raving about this particular play? Why may I quote, 'The language is sublime,'" Darcy continued, grinning, a sight that warmed all, "yes sublime was the word you used. Then you stated that having seen it twice already, by this particular production company, though Ms. Sallis has replaced Mrs. Trent amongst the cast, you would gladly see it a third and fourth time."

This brought more mirth, "Mr. Darcy, I should think the Colonel's praise is what set us on our adventure to this production." Mrs. Bennet was enjoying this too, for it had been several years since she had seen a play in Town, and to sit in the Earl's box, that was something she was going to be able to tell all in Meryton about for many months to come.

"You are all quite right. Why should my keeper here let me join you, I shall be your most stalwart guide through the intricacies of the plot. Though, being but human, I believe we have an adequate contingency plan should the too frail flesh fail."

Elizabeth stepped in before her sister could say anything more, as it did appear she had some bon mot to add, "Now we have had enough of all this discussion. First we shall take today's ride in the Park as a preliminary to any other strenuous outing. The Colonel already looks forward to a possible stop at the Regimental offices and should that occur, we may find our patient wearied so much that any outing up for discussion as far off as the day following tomorrow may not have left enough recuperation time at all."

Lizzy was not used to stopping her friends, her family, in so decided a fashion, but all discussion ceased leaving a space composed only of silence.

It took some moment for the Colonel to think of something as he shuffled the letter upon his lap, "Oh I say, Cousin..." And with that the room returned to discourse again. Mrs. Bennet asking to see what Kitty had in her lap, being correspondence from some of the young ladies she was meeting on her sojourn this last week in London. Darcy took a seat next to his wife. Georgiana then sat down to the pianoforte to play a light air.

DUTY CALLS

"Thank you, Sir Arthur, I shall call upon you tomorrow." The Colonel shook hands with the commander of the expedition back to Portugal as the intermission neared its end. Already ushers were gently reminding the patrons to take their seats for the last act of the play.

Arthur Wellesley gave Stephen a nod to accompany the firm handshake and with another to Sir Fairfax Chamberlain, he was off back to his own box. Fax had also shown up at the first intermission, holding back for the ladies to clear out of the box and see to the refreshments that they, with Mr. Darcy and Mr. Bennet, went in search of.

Mrs. Bennet might have stayed to meet such a social paragon as General Wellesley but she had caught and understood the look from the Colonel, as well as the gentle guiding hand of Mr. Darcy that led her and Lizzy from the box. The ladies all curtsied and quickly walked away with the other men folk allowing Sir Fax to overcome his awkwardness and speak at length to Stephen.

"Mother had me come tonight and what a fortune to find you here. I have called some at Berkeley Square but you were not receiving yet." Stephen recalled one card and had sent a brief thanks to Sir Fax for having stopped at the house.

"Yes, I am thankful for your care and concern, Fax. It has been a hellish time as you may guess, but you must know that the young ladies have made the pain of recuperation bearable. Whilst I defy anyone, even you, to argue otherwise. My coz's young relations have provided the most agreeable diversions to the boredom of the sickroom."

"Hmm, yes I am sure..." Sir Fax, Stephen knew, had no basis for an opinion and so found it hard to contribute to the topic.

"Now I must tell you, I believe you have met the young lady too, since I left for the Continent, for I was informed by Hurst that you have, Ms. Caroline Bingley. What an incomparable woman, don't you agree? She is handsome of features and of nature, and has contributed to my recovery even more than these good girls of mine..." Stephen waved towards where the ladies stood talking across the corridor.

"Ms. Bingley, why yes I do recall meeting her once when looking to those bitches of Hurst's. Fine animals, indeed. Why, I offered for one on the spot and Hurst turned me down. But he did promise me one from the next litter. At an exorbitant sum, though. I shouldn't wonder if he were to make a living on his charges..." Stephen nodded heavily and knew that Fax was steering away from talk of the ladies.

"You are quite right, Hurst does seem to find some means of a living from his breeding, though of course I expect his marriage settlement played well with his purse. I should think his sister Ms. Bingley should be dowered as well as his wife, don't you?" Stephen was not smiling and seemed all serious but his eye was caught by first Kitty, and then Lizzy before he had sense to look upon his companion.

"Father once advised me in a similar vein. Handsome women with fortunes are priceless rubies, I believe he said," Fax shook his head as he said it.

"Very admirable, saying that." Stephen smiled. His own father the Earl would never think to say such. Of course the reality was that the Colonel would be fortunate to find such a wife, and Sir Fax was not in need of such a lady. Fax was already enjoying his wealth, which was fairly comfortable.

"I have seen this Ms. Bennet before I think. Yes the tall one there next to Darcy. I recall her. She is somewhat handsome." Stephen saw that it was Kitty he mentioned.

"Indeed, she does show well, though, young, I should think she may form an alliance in the next few seasons," Stephen said. He realized he was being protective of Kitty.

Fax laughed, "You amaze me, have you not noticed that our young ladies are forming attachments much more quickly. Why I should think Ms. Darcy shall be snatched up before you blink twice." Fax smiled at himself reaching for his handkerchief so he could polish his quizzing glass.

"I don't think I take your meaning Fairfax," Stephen was a guardian of Georgiana Darcy.

Sir Fax made a half step backwards. "I am sorry old man, I have got your hackles up, I see. Oh, yes, of course. You were away most of the year. And you are in uniform. Tell me, are your younger and junior officers forming engagements? Does it seem that there are a few more than perhaps there were two, three years ago?"

When Stephen nodded, Fax continued. "You see, you men in uniform are forcing a rush to marriage. And the young gels I think are all agog over you Soldiers and Sailors. Why the fashion set have a hard time getting a gel's attention once she has been escorted about by an officer."

Stephen looked across to the three young ladies with Lizzy and Mrs. Bennet. There was a small cluster of other men about them. A few talked to Darcy and Mr. Bennet, but most sought the attention of the ladies. Those closest to the girls were predominantly in uniform, two were subalterns of his own regiment, that he had performed the introductions on, at the earlier intermission.

It left much to ponder as the ushers moved all into their seats and the curtain rose on the last act of the play. Stephen found himself looking to Kitty and Georgiana and then over the railing into the main hall. He counted the sets of staring eyes of the young men clearly locked onto his box and at the ladies he accompanied, rather than the play on the stage.

The next morning the Colonel rose early, much earlier than other members of the household. Henry, the under-butler who was first awake to attend to his duties and relieve the night man, heard sounds emanating from the nursery and found the Colonel hard at his exercises. The Colonel reassured the servant all was well.

Two hours later as the maids began to gently glide through the halls to awaken their assigned ladies, they found the Colonel striding the main hall with a purpose. He was fully dressed in his regimentals, his horse already having been summoned. Within minutes of this he was off about his business.

* * *

When Mrs. Darcy walked into breakfast to find her husband in one of his quieter moods, she knew to pause and make him cheerful before carrying on with any other task. She had encountered his black moods often enough whilst they courted, at least, in hind sight, one would call their tumultuous past a courtship. Elizabeth knew that lightening his spirits would do much for the enjoyment of Mr. Darcy, and all that he knew and encountered that day.

"Well Darcy, should I be as Lydia and ask you if you like my new frock. Only seven and six while I am sure Lady Haronbent had one of a similar cut for all of fifty guineas." She was not frugal, but she would not spend her husband's money without some use of sense.

He laughed. She said, "Well not quite the warmth to which I had hoped, but I perceive that you find some mirth in my triumph." He laughed again.

"No my dear, but I appreciate your objective. Yet I fear once you are made aware of my information, you too might countenance a frown." He waited for her to be seated and served her coffee before he regaled her of the whereabouts of her charge.

"That Stephen has recovered to a certain degree, it is true, and certainly being waited upon by so many women has not hurried him along a course of expeditious recovery. But I am greatly put out that he should take matters into his own hands when he is under my charge," Lizzy said.

Darcy smiled, "Ah, so you, too, have a darkening mood when thinking on my cousin."

"Was I not given the responsibility of his recovery?" she asked.

"Indeed my dear, and I believe the Colonel is of the opinion that you have succeeded. His doctor may not agree with the patient's diagnosis, but that is as may be. Stephen has gone off to his regiment to hurry things along, as he puts it."

Elizabeth looked to the side for a moment, "I blame Sir Arthur..." Darcy nodded as the door opened and Kitty entered the dining room.

"You blame Sir Arthur Wellesley, whom we met last night?" She seemed quick on the uptake that morning.

This remark gave the Darcys pause for with out context it did seem a very forward statement to utter.

"Yes, apparently the Colonel has been spurred by his interview last night to rush back to duty. I expect I shall have to fetch him when I finish my breakfast, for he is bound to have tired himself."

Kitty sat, she too was in a new frock. Her's of cream yellow, a red ribbon around her waist and small dots throughout her bodice. This dress had been made from the remains of Georgiana's and Mary's ball gowns. Kitty and Lizzy both thought the material too fine to go to waste, and the dress maker obliged readily enough for a nominal sum. That Kitty's day dress would never be seen whence the other's Ball gowns were displayed made the piece presentable.

Kitty said, "Well, that is quite disagreeable, and the Colonel praised Sir Arthur so much. Yet I am convinced that you too little credit the Colonel and his health at present. I think he has shown much in the way of improvement and believe his strength is able to bear the weight of a full day. Why he did not fall to slumber at the performance last night at all, yet just last week, we had such a hard time keeping him awake whilst we played charades."

Darcy smiled. Lizzy knew he too had nearly fallen asleep during Charades. Darcy then allowed that his cousin displayed much less fatigue this week over last. "My cousin has been known in the past to put up a good front as it were."

Kitty smiled, "I should think Mr. Darcy that the trait runs in the family." Lizzy covered her mouth and Darcy smiled back at his wife and sister.

"I believe you may have the right of it Kitty. You have caught me out entirely."

Lizzy now gave voice to her laughter. "Kitty you do show some perception of late. I can not imagine what has brought forth such a change." Kitty looked to her plate. "But as may be, I do concur that the Colonel should be fetched. Perhaps a note following breakfast asking whence we may collect him for a ride in the Park?"

Kitty clapped her hands, "Indeed that would do well to kidnap him back home and certainly be a salve for his pride. Oh, I beg your pardon."

Darcy's face did not display any look of vexation however. "Quite right, Kitty, quite right. You address the problem square on. My cousin, and you would acknowledge all of our clan have an excess of pride. If we are filled with sin, that is the one we lay claim to, my dear?" Darcy tilted his head to accompany such a question.

Lizzy had covered her mouth again, but uncovered a smile that was luminescent. "Oh, I believe that some members of the clan have found their way to expelling that sin." Georgiana entered then and Lizzy continued, "And of course some have never had that character trait at all. Good morning my dear, did you sleep well?"

Pleasantries with Georgiana and then the others who arrived to break their fast diverted the conversation from the industrious and missing recuperative. Though at some point the empty space at the table was noted by Mrs. Bennet. A few, or nearly twenty, "Well I never" and "What can he be thinkings" and Mr. Darcy was able to excuse himself and compose the letter to the Colonel, suggesting that the carriage fetch him with the ladies, so that they should have their ride in the Hyde Park.

* * *

The Colonel was very fatigued whilst he reclined in his seat. Elizabeth sat at his side, while Mrs. Bennet was able to sit on the far side of the row, facing forward. Opposite sat Kitty, Mary and Georgiana. The Colonel recalled that their carriage had stopped next to one occupied by Mrs. Bingley, Ms. Caroline and Mrs. Hurst once, and some pleasantries had been exchanged, yet he found difficulty with his eyes at that moment. His eyelids were weighted with his fatigue, and he was sure his utterances were less than coherent.

He did recall that questions directed to him seemed to have been answered for him, either by Mrs. Darcy or Kitty. For this some gratitude was mumbled. Soon, once the Bingley carriage had passed on, the Colonel felt a sharp pain, radiating from his ankle. A certain sign that the Ms. Bennet across from him had used the point of her toe. The Colonel shook his head a little to clear the cobwebs, and he felt a good bit of pressure on his instep. Another sign of his attention being sought by the young lady. He then noted that his left bicep also was being gripped rather firmly, though certainly not causing near as much pain as that from his foot.

He looked forward and saw not a hundred feet distant Sir Arthur Wellesley upon a horse with an aide at his side. They were in the midst of a conversation with Sir Fairfax Chamberlain and there seemed to be no hope for it but that the Darcy carriage was to bear down upon them.

The Colonel closed his eyes tight once more, "Yes, Kitty, Mrs. Darcy, I thank you. I am quite recovered."

Mrs. Bennet, "I should hope so, why your General is but there and you were insensible with Mrs. Bingley and her companions." Stephen believed that was probably the most perceptive thing he had known her to say.

"I pray you will forgive me. I expect that the air shall help to brace me up," and he leaned outwards of the conveyance and took several deep breaths as they came close to his friend and to his commander.

"I pray Sir Arthur, I give you good day."

"Why Fitzwilliam, I did not expect to see you or Chamberlain so soon after last night. Though it is good that I have found you. Save me a posting, I should think, though have to follow this up with something official at any roads." Wellesley paused and this allowed some of the social courtesies to then take place.

The aide clearly searched for a piece of paper from a small lather satchel he had. "Ladies," the general said to the group after having acknowledged each, "I must send my compliments to Mr. Darcy for allowing such an assemblage of beauty to grace the Park this day." Sir Arthur wasn't a poet and did not pretend to that line. He believed himself to have said all that was needful.

"Now Fitzwilliam, here it is, your sailing date. You will be in the third convoy over, and that should give you some extra days to prepare. I received your readiness report this morning. Quite punctual, your ensign was. Had to make him wait while I finished my eggs. You are still seven officers short and some ninety men. But all your equipment is purchased and in stores, so that is a good show. You are not the worst of my regiments, but give me men Fitzwilliam, men. There's the thing." He stopped and looked pensive.

"I can do that sir, but it won't be the same this time." Sir Arthur knew instantly to what he referred.

"Yes, I know." Sir Arthur nodded twice. "Well it is our lot.

Now, there is Harrington. I must away. Ladies my compliments."
The general nodded again to them as a group and cantered forward.

When the general was out of hearing, Sir Fairfax had pleasantries to exchange. He was courteous to all the ladies and acknowledged Kitty last. This was a slight grain against decorum as
Georgiana was youngest amongst those in the carriage.

"I say, but Sir Arthur is very much concerned with your recovery, he all but badgered me as to your health. Was very put off
that I had no better of it than he did from our meeting of last
night." Fax finally imparted when he had a chance to direct this
intelligence to the Colonel.

Fax did not wait for a reply though, "So ladies though we do
not have much sun at the moment, do you not find today's
weather bracing." The mud was not too thick from the mornings'
rain, but there were indeed suggestions that wet weather would
be revisiting before nightfall.

The ladies briefly murmured some replies, but then Fax added
to his insights, "And you young ladies, how do you find this season? I do believe Miss Georgiana, Miss Catherine, mother shall
have sent invitations to you each for a small party she has endeavored to have at Fair Winds House this next Tuesday. I told
her of our meeting of last night, and she was quite insistent on
asking you to attend. I do hope you will not disappoint.

"Mrs. Bennet, shall these fair ladies have your blessing and
your escort to my mama's? I know you shall find the invitation
awaiting you, but I would be honored to carry your acceptance to
my mother." Fax was all attentive. Stephen now was quite awake
and looking hard upon his friend.

"Why Fax, this is quite the road for you. I have not seen such a
side before. Is everything well at home?" That Fax was so out of
character, put Stephen's guard up.

Sir Fairfax looked annoyed, "Indeed Fitzwilliam. Well enough.
Perhaps we may talk more later at the club." Which said, meant
that Fax had his guard up as well.

Elizabeth, after shifting quickly in her seat away from the
Colonel, and then looking at him with her own expression of annoyance, added to this conversation. "I do not believe any of our

party has had the pleasure of your mother's acquaintance as yet, Sir Fairfax. Though mother, Jane was saying, that is Mrs. Bingley, was saying that she did have this pleasure not too long ago, prior to the Christmas festivities. Have you met Mrs. Bingley, Sir Fairfax?"

"Why I must beg your pardon, for if I have, I am such a poor study that I have entirely forgotten the honor, though memory does stretch that I believe I have met Charles' wife, indeed. It is so. How could I forget such when she is one amongst so many lovely ladies that do you worlds of credit Mrs. Bennet. Why I believe that Mother intends to invite Mrs. Bingley, also, to her little soiree." Stephen knew Fax long enough to know that Lady Chamberlain hadn't. Though now she would of course.

Stephen saw opportunity, "Why then, Mrs. Bingley must attend, for her mother and sisters shall be there. Should not, also, those other ladies attached to Mrs. Bingley also grace this wondrous party? For, indeed, I know Miss Caroline Bingley has such warm admiration for your mother. While just last week I had a letter during my convalesce from Miss Caroline that discussed how she had encountered your mother at Gainsborough's gallery and they had a great talk, indeed." Stephen looked to his cousin's wife as he finished. He hoped Lizzy would catch on.

She nodded, "Yes I remember some passages being shared from that letter, though I shall have you know that, contrary to what one may think from acquaintance with the Colonel, he does have discretion. Yet I digress, It does appear, though, that Miss Bingley is a very great admirer of Lady Chamberlain, and I am sure that once we all have the pleasure of her acquaintance, we Bennet clanswomen shall be so, also." Lizzy did understand.

"Good to hear, very good to hear. Then I can proceed to my mama and tell her that the party shall be a success for the very best of this year's society, whom I have met, shall attend."

Fax was stepping back to make his goodbyes, when Stephen added, "I shall see you later at the club, I am sure Fax, but you must not rush to fast too include my charming cousins and caregivers to your mother's party. You must grant them time to peruse their calendars before they write an acceptance to your mother. Daresay should I come upon you one day in the Park and ask you to some party or another, you, too, would beg leave to consult your calendar. Fact, I can recall just such an instance not so long ago..." Sir Fairfax nodded, remembering, but he rallied, smiled brightly at the ladies and said his farewells.

* * *

Darcy entered from his dressing room in his lounging robe, over his bed clothes, coming to his wife's bedside for the night. "Dinner at the club did not tire our soldier too much I gather, though you returned somewhat earlier than I expected." His wife reached into his robe and placed her hand around till it gripped her husband's back.

"Mmm, yes we did leave somewhat early. Wagers began to be placed on certain aspects of the war abroad, and our erstwhile allies, and Stephen did not wish to stay. Nor, for that matter, did I."

"Understandable, he has been very serious since first away to the Continent, and moreso now that he has suffered his wounds," Lizzy noted.

Her husband lifted a lock of hair from her forehead. "You comprehend him well."

She nodded to his smile. "Was Sir Fairfax Chamberlain at the club tonight?"

Darcy was caught by surprise, though he pondered often how observant his wife truly was. "Indeed, he was. How did you know?"

Elizabeth told Darcy of all that had taken place in the Park, "And though I believe it does signify that Sir Fax made invitations to all of our party, the Colonel was somewhat intransigent regarding it."

"There were more words this night on the subject, and after them, neither of the two men had much in the way of discourse with one another," Darcy replied.

Elizabeth waited for more. Darcy realized that his wife wished it and withheld until he was poked quite hard and recanted his silence. "Yes, I shall tell, though no more probing with the finger of displeasure."

"Said finger shall probe anon if no elaboration comes forthwith," Lizzy told him.

He smiled and had a smile in return, "Sir Fax approached us early and began to question the Colonel in detail as to the plans of our household in regards to the social calendar, even to the exclusion of converse with myself."

"Yes. One should not ask the head of this house what is to take place, for he seems to never know." Both knew that he and Mr. Bennet were keenly cognizant of every movement in their households, and chose to allow such with as little interruption to their own schedules as was possible.

"In any event, Stephen was fairly certain that the ladies of our household and of your sister's might indeed be well engaged until next Christmas. He would have it, though one finds Miss Caroline Bingley with a great deal of time for some social events, according to my cousin, though that he has intimate knowledge of Charles sister's society, I find difficult to fathom."

She looked to her husband and reminded him, "They do correspond, you know." Elizabeth believed that Darcy did not know.

"He writes her? I find that hard to believe."

"And yet it is so, for a man who is quite busy with the affairs of his regiment, and his convalescence, he does have a great deal of time for letter writing. He writes mine aunts, and all my Gardiner cousins, as well as my uncle. He writes to many another including your Aunt de Bourgh and your cousin Anne, as well as the Collin's which I should not tell my mama, if I were you, for she would be put out. I believe he writes all at the Bingley household, though not daily, as he does with some such as my Uncle Gardiner, and should we not be here in the house with him, I believe the Colonel would be a great correspondent with us. Why even so, he has written letters this last week twice each to Georgiana, Mary, Kitty and Mama."

Darcy took all this in, "And yourself?"

"He does not write me, for he says he tells me all, anyway, so why place it on paper," she said.

"Indeed, I am no longer amazed that he should be a party to the societal schedule of this household through the winter holidays," Darcy said.

"Come sir, that is an exaggeration, though I expect that he should wish to keep some young females free of Sir Fax's society."

"What do you mean?" Now Darcy looked surprised.

"You know full well. Sir Fax must marry, it was said, even before our wedding. And it would seem, recently, he has lost his shyness about women, and is inclined to explore where the company of women will lead him," Lizzy said.

"Do you mean Georgiana?" Darcy did not looked pleased.

"It is possible, though I expect it is Catherine that has tempted him."

Darcy pulled away, "Kitty and Sir Fax?"

"Don't shake your head. Kitty has new influences Mr. Darcy." Darcy thought for a moment and realized that the girl, once led about by her younger sister Lydia, was now less likely to be found in foolishness with Elizabeth, Jane and now Georgiana as her companions.

"Yes I see that, but is she fond of Fax? Why I can't see that, or Georgiana for that matter." Darcy was shaking his head.

Elizabeth's small smile told him much, "I expect neither are fond of your school friend in that manner, though I believe your cousin to have some great fear of it. He does seem to direct Sir Fairfax to be attentive to Caroline Bingley often."

Darcy shook his head, "Sometimes my cousin forces too far. I should not wish that on Caroline, who, despite all, is the sister of Charles."

Elizabeth's nose wrinkled. "I should believe that it would be a good match for Caroline, and that the Bingley's would see it as such."

"Oh yes, yes. Fairfax is heir to a decent fortune, as nice as Charles, himself, I should allow. And that would put Caroline Bingley to the place in society that she wishes to occupy. But it would not suffice for Kitty. Fairfax will not be constant to any woman. Not that he would be found in the petticoat line, but that he would do his duty for an heir and then find some other interest that would make family life far from satisfying."

"I believe you, the Colonel and I have all found this same quality. Perhaps, even Caroline Bingley has, too. Perhaps, she sees this as the life she would choose. But I expect you are correct about Kitty, though, perhaps, not about why Stephen wishes to intercede between Kitty and Sir Fairfax," Lizzy said.

Darcy stood to pace, after a three lengths of the room, "Do you believe he is forming a tender for your sister?"

She smiled. She let him continue. "You do believe it. Would this be awkward, we may need to discourage this."

She held up her hand, "Stephen grows strong and will return with the army to Portugal and Spain soon enough. I fear for him, but believe that this shall displace any affection between the Colonel and Kitty. Of this, distance and time will cause any affection to fade. Sir Fax though may be a tenacious suitor. He has not shown interest in any woman before you have told me and may not understand how to conduct oneself should he encounter no interest being returned," Lizzy said.

"Hah, you equate my friend to your cousin Mr. Collins, as memory serves. Fortunately, he was made aware that your resolve was intransigent, though I expect your sister to not share such fortitude. And, certainly, I have witnessed Kitty to have some lesser affinity for sense than you possess. This pursuit by Fax will bear watching." Darcy thought it amusing.

"Yes, Sir Fairfax to be retained as a friend, and to be matched with a suitable mate as well as our girls finding suitable partners."

Darcy shook his head as he reached for his wife. "You, my dear, are very much accomplished at this," he said.

"Are you surprised, I have had much study at this. Pray sir, you laugh. You full well know that the machinations of my mother was the best education one could possibly hope for."

Darcy's guffaws stopped short, "That is one battle I would not want to fight. Should your mother find a baronet with an interest in her daughter, I should expect she would wish to pursue such a match, despite the objections of all others."

Elizabeth paused, "I had thought of that. I believe you do not count upon the strength of my father enough. He may have failed in one matter, but he persevered in many of his other campaigns."

Darcy had grown to not show a look of distaste whenever the subject of Wickham came up. He had resolved to be forgiving in the matter, though he should never meet the man again. Yet he knew that with so many Bennet connections, the subject of Lydia would arise upon occasion. Though Mrs. Bennet had become good about not speaking of the man in front of Georgiana.

"Besides, should you and Charles show mother a united front on any subject, she readily takes your side, or have you not noticed. She even reveres your two thoughts and opinions over that of my father. What is that black look for?"

"I do not recall ever opining differently than your father. And now you laugh?" He pulled slightly away from her.

"You and Charles have not, but, let me observe that, I have had a lifetime to know of my father's thoughts and you have had but a year. There have been some things you have propounded upon that my father has not held the same view. Mother has come to support those same."

Darcy nodded, "Ahh, I see. I had no intention..."

"Father knows that. He would never say a thing. But, I believe you take my point. Should mother wish to have Kitty, or Mary set her cap at someone who may not prove entirely worthy, she can be dissuaded. I should not expect you or Charles to use this power of yours for any nefarious means, howsoever," Lizzy said.

He was holding her again. "I should hope never to do so."

"Good, 'sides, I should expect mother to not take kindly to Lady Chamberlain if what has been related to me is at all accurate. You know Mother does not take well to those who greatly condescend to her."

"Ha, ha... Indeed I do. Indeed I do."

THE FRONT

"The General was kind in his words, gentlemen." Colonel Stephen Fitzwilliam spoke to the assembled officers of the regiment. He had written a letter, the previous evening, to the wife of Captain Carter who had died in the battle. Missing, also were two leftenants who had sustained wounds which precluded their attendance at this meeting he had called in his tent. Talavera's costs were hurtful.

"Three battles of importance in the last three months. We showed off well though the entire army paid a great cost yesterday. More than one in four killed or wounded. Our losses considerably less. Gentleman, I shudder to think what our 'allies,' do." As he paused there was a brief, gruff laugh from most of the assembled officers. "Yes, allies, will do to provide for our men, as they have provided rations so well for us." Promises of aid had come to naught.

"Therefore, I want to ensure that we take every man with us, and be damned what the general staff should think. We do not have much in the way of horse transport. We must repair that, and Leftenants Smyth and Jeffers, that is your job. Take the animals from the Spaniards if needs must. I have talked to the surgeon. Mr. Harvey believes that we can get near everyone of the men safe away should we have two days to make our preparations. I believe we won't have that, though. Marshall Soult is fast approaching. I should believe we are to march for Portugal at first light."

His men stood in complete silence. He asked of them an impossibility. If the surgeons proclaimed some men needed more time to mend than they had, surely that was the case. Stephen had never been like this before. "I surely would not give these orders did I not think it necessary. Further, I have been brevetted to Brigadier and the seventeenth and nineteenth will now fall under our purview. Major Carstairs, you will see to the seconding of two gentlemen to serve as aides for myself from our regiment. Lieutenant Colonel Parker shall see his duties increased as I coordinate the three battalions on the march."

The meeting continued much the same. What was readily apparent was the need to get their unit cohesively together and begin preparations for a march coming straight after their hard fought victory. When the Light Brigade had arrived that morning, with trumpets and fifes playing, having marched more than forty miles in one day only to miss the battle, they did not realize how lucky they had been, despite their aching feet.

Stephen had seen the cost of the battle, and knew were there many more such victories against the French, that there would not be much of an English army left to fight. Wellesley had kept such thoughts to himself. Yet the more intelligent amongst the senior officers all thought the same.

In the following days, the precautions taken by General Fitzwilliam proved valid. The Spanish allies abandoned the wounded left in their care to be captured by the French. Mr. Harvey and the other medical staff had not been pleased with Stephen's orders, but when news of how the other woundeds' fate turned out, they then kept their opinions to themselves. Their charges suffered, but miraculously, only two additionally succumbed. Losses from Talavera were less than twenty men, all told.

"This retreat, for we can not characterize it as anything but, has been wearying on the spirits of the men. We have marched long and hard, fought well against adversity. Seen our erstwhile allies prove as close to false as one could expect without betraying us, and, yet, the men still find time for some levity. I encourage my officers to follow that lead, and now with two more battalions under my command, new officers I must challenge to look to what little good we can make of it. The losses in the two regiments I have had added were much greater than in our own. Hence the amalgamation of the units under my command. It is a great honor. I believe I am up to the task. We consistently are placed in the van of the army, or but one remove from it, hence Sir Arthur trusts us to do our duty.

"I shan't trouble you with much of the details of life amongst us at the moment. It has been better, and never worse, I fear. As such fine ladies should not hear of it, and your previous missive asking for every detail must be rendered obscured by the reality of that which we face. I know you sit there and if Mrs. Darcy is in the room you will drop the

letter into your lap at this juncture and look to your sister, with an 'I never!' but you must trust me on this. Some of what an army faces is not fit to be described, for it is unsettling. Further, as you argue with Mrs. Darcy, 'But there are women amongst the army, some of them quite well born.' I can see and hear your sister in her wisdom remarking, 'Yes, but they most likely will balance their choices of being amongst the fine young gentlemen with the horrible realities of battle, and on some days regret their choices deeply.'

"This is how I must leave it with you, for Kitty, some of what I have seen and what I have done to other men is such that I am shamed of doing, and haunted by what my eyes have beheld. I should not wish this on my friends, nor those who are not my friends. That I have taken the life of those whom are mine enemies shall never be right, despite being a necessity, and now as I reflect that you raise your head once more from reading the letter and pass this to your sister to read, I must attend to my other duties. As I expect that you shall share this with the rest of your family, please tell them that I an unable to include any other letter, or any more length than this for a retreat does not afford one a great deal of leisure for correspondence.

"He remains your affectionate champion, this time it would seem," Elizabeth remarked to Kitty who held a handkerchief to her moist eyes. They were alone as Kitty had sought her elder sister out, solely. Kitty had adjusted to the splendors of Pemberley for the Darcys had the entire family for a fortnight.

He, Mr. Bennet, Charles Bingley, Mr. Hurst and Mr. Gardiner were fishing with the younger Gardiner boys. No one but Elizabeth and Kitty knew that a letter had arrived from the General.

Kitty said, "I suppose we will have to get used to calling him General Fitzwilliam."

"Dry your eyes, and use your kerchief. Mama shall discover us soon. You are correct, though, it is a singular honor and reflects well on him. Despite his distressing news, we shall celebrate his success."

After blowing her nose twice to clear it, "You are right we should celebrate. And anything we write to him must be full of cheerful news. He has too much of the bad to dwell upon," Kitty said.

Elizabeth nodded, "That is quite observant, Catherine. I am proud of you, indeed. As I see by your smile that you rally. We have met some officers now, and you will remember the militia and even brother Wickham. Do you not think that amidst this adversity, of the men we know, Colonel, or General Fitzwilliam shall be the best of men to see it through?"

"I can think of no other," Kitty said.

Lizzy agreed, "And neither can I. Which I say not to allay your fears, but because it is truth." There was one thing that Kitty held back from Elizabeth. The General had included a small hair comb, tortoise shell with fine ornamentation and a few small jewels of pearls and garnets, with the letter as a gift. He said he acquired it during the normal course of war. Kitty kept it hidden.

It did not go unnoticed later that day as the family gathered that something had occurred, and soon Kitty, following Elizabeth's lead, shared much of the contents of her letter.

"Why I must say that he shows a great regard for his trials..." Mary said. But any further comment was lost whilst others took the floor. The men had read much of the retreat to Portugal in the papers, and knew of the many losses suffered at Talavera, despite it's being a great victory.

The ladies knew of these also, despite the men trying to keep such from them. Mrs. Bennet had the right of it when she exclaimed to one and all and especially Mrs. Gardiner who sat with her on a settee, "Why we need not worry so, for there is little that we can do for him, and the General now is certainly amongst the very best of men whom we know."

Darcy noted that his cousin requested that he send letters to his family in regards to the matter, and Elizabeth took it upon herself to send letters to the Colonel's friends with whom she had become acquainted. This included Sir Fax, and saving Charles the need, a letter to Caroline Bingley, who had not come to the fortnight at Pemberley, though she had been asked.

Kitty wrote this to the General when she replied to his letter;

"Doubtless your correspondents will inundate you with many letters in the days to come with scolds for not taking the time but to send us one missive whilst you found yourself harried to Spain, much as at

last Christmastime.

"Elizabeth informs me that she expects a letter, herself, from Lady Catherine de Bourgh at any moment scolding us for receiving news from you when as your letter to me said, Anne writes you, diligently, each week. I have yet to meet your cousin, but Georgiana and Elizabeth tell me much of her plight and I know that, when able to make your aunt happy, you shall set your cousin free from the shackles she endures...

"There, I now see you with a look of horror on your face as you so well related my expressions when last you wrote. It is sometimes said that opposites attract and do well together, though I think you and your cousin Anne shall do no such thing.

"I have put you to the blush I am sure, and now you laugh for you see the humor in my teasing, though I am shamed that it is at the expense of your cousin and scold myself for such poor manners. Well, you know me, I don't scold myself too heavily for I have gleaned from those of your'n here and your letters that neither you nor she desire a marriage to happen. I expect that if Anne were able to ever attend her cousin Darcy, and by happy circumstance I should meet her, we should get on as friends. I have found what great delight, as you relate, she takes in Rosings Park. To me, Pemberley is also a wondrous spot. I have spent some hours in company of the keeper of the grounds and with my brother Darcy in learning the history of the estate.

"Elizabeth, abetted by Father, say I have never shown such interest in Longbourn, and they are correct. It is something I intend to amend once I return home, though Elizabeth has asked that I remain as companion to her and Georgiana for most of the summer. Mary is to go with the Bingley's to Town. Mother is very pleased, in her way, for she desires my brothers to put us in the way of a good marriage. Darcy allows as how it is possible that such will be achieved, and that in the following season, when Georgiana is to be presented at court, I too may have a moment to shine."

Now that his brigade had encamped and a regular mail had arrived, he reread the letter that was dated following his last sole missive to Kitty. There were near thirty other letters all told from his correspondents, and three from Kitty, two latter than this one he had read four times now. Countless maneuvering had seen to the safety of the army and the fall and winter looked to be hard with inactivity and boredom.

Some of his contemporaries had already made arrangements to return to England, for the nonce, turning over the commands to those more able to stand the monotony of leading while in bivouac. They would ensure their return before the campaign season began again. Unless dire emergency called him away, the General was determined to stay the course.

"General, sir?"

His batman had laid out his best uniform, for he and some other senior staff were to dine with the Earl that evening and some of their noble Spanish and Portuguese allies. Sir Arthur had been granted that most prestigious title for the victory of Talavera. "Yes Figgis?"

"Sir was thinking like..." Figgis was now a sergeant but no braver when discussing sensitive issues. "Well its like this, with them other officers and such going back to London, p'rhaps we might be thinking that is a grand idear also."

"I do not really think that is so wise, for the men aren't able to take leave in England," Stephen said.

"Ah but sir, they knows how it is..." Figgis looked at his feet.

"But, what we know is that if we and our officers are to lead, sharing their same hardships will make it easier when we must lead them into the worst of the battle," Stephen knew that for a certainty.

"Yes sor, I mean, no, sor. Ye see sor, it's like this. The lads and all have heard sumwat of yer troubles wit the ladies an all. They be wishing to see you tie the knot with a high stepper an such."

"Figgis, I should think that you know my circle of acquaintances does not now include many high steppers," General Fitzwilliam had to think hard about the last time he had the chance to make love to such a woman.

"No sor, I mean to say it does, sor. Why that Miss Caroline she being one, and o'course there is Miss Catherine, and then if youse was to marry a cousin, there is Miss Georgiana, though I think you'd be not thinking of her as she and you being more like brother and sister in yours affections, an such," Figgis rambled on.

Stephen, again, was struck by how much time, Figgis, and by extension, the rest of his command had time to speculate on his interaction with the fairer sex. "Figgis it does not seem appropriate that I receive so much advice..." Stephen began but had no chance to finish.

"Oh I know it sor, but ye see it is the men sor. Why some of the other Regiments, they have officers wives to make things more genteel and all. And now youse a general and all, and Colonel Bently of the nineteenth and Mrs. Colonel Bently being sometimes gracious to them other officers, but not treating the lads and all very nice, why the Mrs. Major Dalmer of our regiment feels right out of place, she does, now she being outranked, an all."

Stephen could see that the matter had some seriousness to it. "I could not ask the married officers, or men to send their womenfolk back to England." He wanted to, but it would go against the grain, and it would not be an order easily followed.

"Indeed no sor. But a good lady for youse would set the example, and Mrs. Colonel Bently would be falling in line and all."

Stephen had personally seen the wife of his subordinate make somewhat of an off colour scene in noticing the men and their coarser ways. "So, you, the men, that is, have selected for me some candidates to choose from."

"Well yes sor, the men were particularly pleased when the ladies came to a visit last April when we still in London. The men still talk about it. They be often talking about the day you took Miss Kitty for a ride afore the wedding of Mr. Darcy and all."

Stephen smiled, "And, this they learned, how?"

"Why your favorites sir, the Gardiner children be relating the story many a time when they be a visiting. They also be great favorites of the men an all," Figgis said. A big smile on his face.

Stephen had to nod over that. The two boys once invited to attend the Regiment, and certainly when meeting the Crown Prince, were considered very great favorites of the Regiment since. And they certainly had related the story of Stephen galloping off with Kitty so long ago.

He looked at the letter in his hand, the men also were no doubt aware of whom he had sent private correspondence to, as it would not be possible to keep such a secret. He was definitely doomed.

"So the men have a new cause, to see me wed. That a lady can be installed in our hierarchy to save them from one who does not appreciate that their common life needs some indulgence from us. But more so that we have a light to bring culture to our little circle here in Portugal.

That is what they say, yet I tend to think that is to humor themselves. You have had exposure to our men on their best behavior, when under discipline. I however must allow them moments, more so than polite society might expect, where they can loose themselves from those restrictions so that they may find ways to forget that we are in the midst of a war, that they have seen horrors and that the next battle may be their end.

Perhaps, that is the true difference between the men and we officers, that we may not show those feelings as readily, or must conduct ourselves in a more discreet way when we choose to find some solace away from the tragedy of a war. In any event, a woman of quality, here to share our burden, is now the true mission. As with mine aunt, Lady Catherine, I am able to resist their campaign.

I sense your little smile as you think I turn my reflections to something that I have avoided. Yet I must report that a letter has arrived amongst all the others that reached me, from my parents. They, of course, admonished me for sending all my previous news just through you, and though they allow that you, and your sisters, seem to be women of great sense, they were not completely pleased that I should send news to one source. Yet that is not the main of their letter. Mother allows how an alliance with such a near cousin as Anne should not be a consideration, for she recognized that as she termed, 'necessities' for a marriage were not between us. The Earl, however, had an entirely different view of the matter.

He allows as his sister has made such a determined argument for the merit of the marriage, and that my hopes for a provided for life based on my achievements might not bear fruit, that the consideration of her proposal should be considered with seriousness. I sense a weakening in his resolve that I should not marry his niece. I see you realize that I fit all of these thoughts on one page so that you may keep it to yourself and now I see you nod your head, then shake it as if I should not *have to write this for you do understand."*

"You hold something back," Mary noticed.

"Yes. Not everything that the General has written, I am meant to share." Kitty said.

Elizabeth looked to her sisters even as Mary turned to her mother, "Mama, do you not think that is impertinent? That the General should write to Kitty with private thoughts."

"Mary, you have your own letter from the General, and I expect that there is a possibility that what the General writes might be of a comment upon one of our family that Kitty knows would be ill to share. Certainly he has written Mr. Darcy and myself with items that I can not share with you either," Lizzy said.

"It's always like that. You and Jane have always had secrets..." Mary stammered out.

"That is unfair Mary." Mrs. Bennet was want to say.

"No mama, Mary is correct, but I think Mary if you examine yourself, you may see that you too have some secrets?" Elizabeth's smile allowed Kitty to read more of her letter in quiet. After, she allowed the others to share some of the General's letter and they shared their letters with her, they were able to hold a discussion regarding the letters overall.

"He is in good health, and better humor then when he wrote after the battle," Kitty thought to comment.

"Indeed, I did not know he could be so low afore. Certainly when he recovered from his wound he was not in such spirits." Mrs. Bennet added.

Later, the men, for the Darcys had come to Longbourn for a short visit, and the Bingleys of Netherfield were also in attendance, had some more insights into the particulars. "That my cousin has seen his share now of battles is undeniable, and certainly some men are able to stand such. But there are some instances where I can only sense that it is overwhelming," Mr. Darcy said.

Their father, Mr. Bennet who had begun to enjoy his role as paterfamilias, now that he had sons to support him in conversation, had his own thoughts. "I believe Fitzwilliam you have the right of it. I know that I could never stomach what our General now must endure. You know me for a man who likes his library and his quiet, though heaven knows I have had little of the latter these many years. Should I have been thrust into the situation where I would have to stand amidst the volley fire of cannon and musket, stand steadfast in the face of an the enemies' cavalry charge, I should be found wanting."

"Indeed father, and you would not be alone, for I too would be feeling the same," Charles added to the conversation. Such conversation now passed with much admiration of the General and his efforts on behalf of the nation.

"Here is something of passing fancy, Caroline, you might appreciate it," Charles added later when they had retired after dining, to the drawing room. "I have had a letter from Sir Fairfax Chamberlain, who has requested a fortnight with us. It seems that London had become a dead bore and knowing that we have our entire party here, who he now deems as his closest friends, he wonders should he be too forward if he could impose on our company for some time, p'rhaps a fortnight."

Elizabeth's eyes flashed to her husband, Darcy saw. "Why Charles, he invites himself to stay at Netherfield?" Darcy clarified.

"Indeed, he posts down tomorrow."

"Why, we are but three days more here Mama. Then we shall be on our way." Elizabeth had originally thought to leave Kitty back at Longbourn at this time. "Though I am wondering, Georgiana and Kitty, you have both gotten on so well at Pemberley. Should not we maintain our arrangements and, Kitty, you return with us to Pemberley?"

Mrs. Bennet was aware of the great condescension of this gesture, "That is a grand idea."

"I am afraid then, Jane, that we are leaving you with but half of our society to entertain Sir Fax." Elizabeth stole a look at Caroline Bingley who was smiling, something that she had little done of late. "But with Mary, Mrs. Hurst and Miss Caroline you shall have ladies surrounding you to ensure that Sir Fax is nobly entertained."

"And thus Georgiana and I were spirited away shortly into his

visit. Sir Fax partnered me for three dances while Mary played on our last night which we supped at Netherfield. But then Miss Caroline did monopolize him. Georgiana and I spent the evening looking over the caricatures in the folios.

Sir Fax did not seem to understand that we were to travel to Pemberley and seemed much disappointed by our departure the following day. Why, he rode to catch the carriage and Mr. Darcy had to have Hemmings stop us entire. It was such a scene, and Lizzy must stop and scold me for remarking on it, Sir Fax all disheveled and Mr. Darcy out of sorts, for this, certainly was not the thing, just to ride hard to catch us, to say his goodbyes.

Why I am sure that we had said our goodbyes the night before. I, of course, had returned with my parents to Longbourn. But I believe that in departing from Netherfield, it was made clear to Sir Fax that I was to join the Darcy party to travel and stay at Pemberley.

I do like Pemberley. Mr. Darcy and Lizzy have given me a room all my own next to Georgiana. Lizzy says that if I take any frights whilst living in it, it is because it had been previously given to Lady Catherine's use.

'Stuff and nonsense,' I hear you say and I echo your thoughts. The room is wondrous and has a very fine aspect. Georgiana says that her own is not as nice, though of course you and I both know it is better. But my view at Pemberley is such that Longbourn pales entire. I could stay here forever, but we are promised to London, the month after next, for the start of Georgiana's season.

She says she has little intention of enjoying it, and certainly as a companion this is quite different than ever Lydia, that is Mrs. Wickham, and I ever considered prior. We always would beg Father to allow us to stay with aunt Gardiner, but I had done so, but twice, and only whilst still in the nursery. Here, now, I have been to London twice, since the wedding and shall go a third time. It is grand.

That you shall not be with us shall make it somewhat dull. That you so easily were able to get a chuckle, or raised eyebrow from Lizzy and Mr. Darcy. Even get Father to laugh, though he would deny it, through your convalescence. I still shudder to think of the pain you must have had in your shoulder and here allowed all these women to descend upon you. Your mother was so gracious, I still know not why you would not allow her to care for you. I think, sir, that deserves pun-

ishment, and I struggle to find a sentence that is suitable to such a crime. Were I a magistrate, such as your father, I should come to one more easily.

"Well, that tears it," Viscount Wellington said. The Spanish had suffered a great defeat at Ocana. Several senior officers were gathered with the supreme commander before dining that night. Amongst them General Fitzwilliam stood with thoughts far away.

There were many murmurs about just deserts, bad lot, and other dismissive comments on the Spanish. It brought Stephen from his reverie. "I beg your pardon, sir, but that puts a great burden on us. That our erstwhile allies should be destroyed is no cause to be flippant. Many men who fought for the freedom of their country are now dead, let us give them some respect, poorly led or not."

Wellington looked to the man he relied on to keep the center of his line steadfast. A trait that paralleled his voice here. "I should say that General Fitzwilliam is right. They may have caused us distress after Talavera, but it will go worse for us now without the aid of men and munitions that we should have expected with their support." This put an end to the discussions along those lines.

There was a brief pall of reservedness over the proceedings for a few minutes but then General Picton began on a story about a trooper in the Life Guards who felt that he could spend a day riding everywhere backwards. That, of itself, caused the pre dinner gathering to lose its tenseness and gave the officers a chance to relax. Viscount Wellington had noted before that with such gatherings, his senior men were able to distance themselves from the distasteful job that they were required to do. Sending men, who were under one's command, to death was not the most calming of tasks.

During their dining, shop was not discussed as they had ample opportunity to discuss their profession throughout their long barracking. "Gentleman," the Viscount got their attention after the loyalty toast to His Majesty, "I should think that we are seeing the wearying of all of the troops, officers and men, alike, due to this inactive winter of ours."

Nods met his assertion. "Though we can not rotate the men back to England for recuperation, unless we were to pay off an entire regiment, and I feel I shall be needful of them all come the spring, perhaps certain select officers may rotate back..." that Wellington, as he now was being called, indicated that there were some officers whom he desired to remain in England, rather than be with an army was clear. It would be a way to get those who were better as parade officers, than fighting officers back to London where they could preen and strut.

That got a very well received approval. The Viscount had his plans made. He included in those plans travel, by a select group of seniors, as a reward, for them to travel between the winter camps and London carrying dispatches whilst there was no campaigning.

"Though, I doubt that Viscount Wellington will include me on the list of officers taking his private correspondence to Horse Guards, for, though I believe I am well regarded, I am not a true favorite. I do not have private meals with the General as some do, nor do I have many private interviews. If we meet once a fortnight, I consider it normal. Though I have been told by fellow officers that he often has words of carefully selected criticism, I have yet to hear it.

My men, I believe, are no worse at finding trouble than many another brigade. I do my best to keep them occupied with activity. We have built much better quarters than our tentage allows and have contributed greatly to a project of Wellington's. It is fortune that allows us to be camped north of Lisbon. I fear that the men, if given more leniency then we already allow them, would disgrace us.

I can not claim that my boys are wells behaved, but I feel that they show well against some of the other lads here in the field. In this last month since our Christmas revelries, I have had only eleven men entire, in the three regiments, brought up on charges. I am told that this is the least amongst all the serving units. My own regiment had but two men on charges.

Yet they all do feel the need for action. Our edge grows dull as we wait for the campaigning to start again. From your last letter I gather that your season is progressing well. Two dances, three recitals, and the next one, with your sister, Mary, as the main performer. That is a great honor indeed. And from your comments, you expect it to be well attended. That it precedes a recital to be held with Georgiana later in the season is a careful bid to strategy, so that two girls now thrown so close together may not detract from each other. I applaud Mrs. Bingley and Mrs. Darcy in their management of the details, as you have related them.

That you felt that perhaps something might go amiss, is now for me to give you a punishment, should I be in London. I expect both ladies will give very great creditable performances, and that my acquaintances will relate of them with favor. A London concertina by a respectable young lady in a fine home is nothing to take lightly and many of society will find that it is an honor to attend. You must do all you can to make the two ladies feel as if they are the most important on that special day of theirs. I have already written to my man of business that great heaps of flowers are to be purchased and are set to arrive to honor the ladies, each. Now what great cultural showcase has been decided for you?"

Lizzy said, "I do believe, sister, that soon these letters from the General will become of a private nature and you shall have to withhold all from me and the rest of the family."

"You tease me," Kitty said.

"And should I not? Some of this tone seems to me that General Fitzwilliam has a tender for you. Certainly his letters to myself, Darcy, even Mama do not take on so, as she related last from Longbourn."

Kitty giggled. Lizzy continued, "I would not think this so amusing, were I you. I might be inclined to confine you to the house here for a fortnight should I deem your respectability to be put to the question with an officer with such an acknowledged past as our friend the General."

"Tosh, you do it to brown, Lizzy. We have heard all of the General's past and there is little that is truly of a scandalous nature, though perhaps there was a little that came close. Certainly nothing like Mr. Wick..." Kitty stopped and looked to ensure no servants were in the room.

"Yes our brother Captain Wickham. It is just us. Lydia and her husband are in the north. You have the right of it. Captain Wickham has a much more notorious past then the good General. Do you see that in this last round of letters he makes no mention of his part in the recent dispatches we have from *The Times*. I shall send him a scold for that, for Darcy shall make light of it."

"They are barely out of their winter encampment and begin once again their assault on Spain and the French. I do not see how we should bring this up, for did we not desire to talk about anything but his military preoccupations." Kitty reminded Lizzy of her own rule. "Ah, I have caught my sister at a loss for words."

Lizzy recovered then, "Don't smirk. It is not becoming. And yes you have the best of me. I was it, who set the rule that we should only provide good cheer in our letters to the General."

Georgiana and Darcy entered then. "Good cheer, what, are you still dissecting Stephen's latest, it has been two days." Darcy knew better, for he had seen the phenomenon of his cousin's correspondence consume the household for up to an entire week. It also spurred letters to the various others connected to the General until by the time those were responded to and a second answer received, new letters arrived from Portugal, starting it all over again.

"General Fitzwilliam is ever a pleasant topic with us," Kitty said.

"Well here is something of news..." Darcy began.

"Fitzwilliam, you said I may tell." Georgiana interrupted her brother.

He paused and bowed, "Yes I did, pray proceed."

"Oh it is so fun. My cousin Anne is to come stay with us so that we may show her some entertainment here in London." Georgiana seemed please.

Kitty looked at her sister and saw that emotion played across her face, as did Mr. Darcy who was opposite. "That does sound grand indeed Georgiana," Kitty said. "When does she come?"

"She is due here week after next." And the two young ladies went to discuss the itinerary of Anne de Bourgh.

When they left, the married Darcys were alone, "And this is strange news indeed."

"Yes, Elizabeth, you will forgive me but Lady Catherine has been ill disposed enough to invite my cousin upon us."

"That I took for granted, but the question remains, why?" Lizzy asked.

Darcy lifted his head, "Ah, for that I have an answer. Mine other aunt has written how we are the veritable center of all things concerning her younger son. How our household seems to know all about Stephen, and apparently Stephen has written but thrice to Anne since our wedding. It would seem that Stephen's favoring us with the majority of his affection has left mine aunt to believe that she should send Anne here that she may be a part of that affection."

"Well, despite the suddenness of the endeavor, I should think a sojourn here amongst us shall due Anne quite good," Lizzy said. Elizabeth seldom used a fan, but at this point she did have one to hand and had taken it out to wave with some vigor.

"Do not fret yourself. I should imagine we can not expect a long stay. Mine aunt will not venture to your house, at present, and the separation from her daughter, I do fear, can not stand a lengthy time," Darcy said.

Lizzy smiled, "In this, I expect you are right. Lady Catherine does need someone whom she may instruct. I fear that we should invite the Collin's to visit also. Perhaps they may chaperone Anne to us."

Darcy broke into a fulsome laugh, "You are quite the creature which is why I cherish you. But let me ask this, do you feel saving your friend Mrs. Collins from Lady Catherine is a fair exchange for having me host Mr. Collins?"

Elizabeth looked to her husband. "Yes, for the short time that you will bear this burden, it is an imperative and I think we need hear little more on the subject."

"Very well. I shall be the grand host indeed, but I fear we should limit our social activities at this time to more family and home events, don't you agree?"

Elizabeth's laughter, "Oh most assuredly, most assuredly, indeed," which put an end to the episode.

"As you can only imagine my surprise at such a gift. I now believe it is because Anne de Bourgh had such an excellent mount, though she rode in the Park but once. My mare is all of eleven hands and she is

quite spirited. She is a compliment to Georgiana's and I initially thought Mary would be so very jealous when she heard of the gift of Mr and Mrs. Darcy, but the Bingley's had given her a new present, a flute. For as they put it, she aspires so to music and poetry and fine writing. They even have provided her with a tutor.

A flute of course in no way compares to a horse, I should say, though Mary has taken no notice, for she does not like to ride at all. Mr. Darcy, however, says my seat shows a good foundation and that I may improve it greatly. He feels that I may even rival the very best in the family, of which I believe him to mean you, General.

In any event Anne's stay was not as long as had been proposed barely a week longer than the Collins were with us. Mr and Mrs. Collins returned to Rosings Park by way of a fortnight at Meryton, so I believe Anne was at home with her mother more speedily, and the tales we have of Lady Catherine being overcome with the vapors, was a short lived episode of but three days.

Now, you have been jollied by my letter, I have no doubt, but I will take umbrage at your last letter in which you chastised me for my cultural pursuit of small stage theatricals. The gentlemen here, including your close friend Sir Fairfax Chamberlain, have all proclaimed that I have a presence and quality.

Perhaps you decided to reprimand me as something that you thought was not becoming a lady of quality, but I assure you this is quite the thing in our circle and it does seem to be one area where I show better then my sisters, Georgiana or Anne."

* * *

Stephen reviewed the letters from Kitty as his only solace during the last days of summer. He knew that the eve of battle was upon him and his men once again. And despair was his constant companion at the moment. Vastly outnumbered by the French and their greatest generals, his hopes were that some miracle would ensure the British could remain sustainable. General Craufurd had survived against the best of Napoleon's Marshalls, Ney, at the bridge of Coa in late July.

Tomorrow at Buçaco loomed another battle. These gambles, though, could not last forever. At sometime fighting a numerically superior force that had been under arms for more than fifteen years, was going to tell. The British were bolstered by their Portuguese allies. Were it not for those, the odds for the following day would be a disaster. The only advantage he hoped for was that they could keep the high ground. His orders placed his brigade in and around Soula and here he would wait to take the advance of the enemy.

Stephen held that packet of letters, a goodly sized bundle, and wryly considered that he did not use it to be a correspondent of note. Now more than a year's effort, showed that he was a regular at it. The men no longer wagered on his courtship to find a lady, but he had taken the mess in hand and ensured that the wives of the various Colonels attached to his division, for he had become a Major-General, did in no way try to rule the roost.

Several of the other Generals were busy with their staffs and various commanders ensuring that all was in readiness for the following day. Stephen had walked around his command for an hour prior, ensuring that hot meals were being served. He and his commanders had gone over the details and made preparations for the battle, in such detail, that there was nothing left to be seen to. It was possible that in two of his regiments, the Colonel and their staffs were a bit more active, for some felt the need to over-manage the details, but as general he would not interfere. He certainly did not like it if he was brooked with when he acted as Colonel, and knew that now, he could only provide so much in the ways of orders and guidance.

In any event, his thoughts had turned to England, and those whom he loved. He had made it part of his talk with the soldiers that he had spoken with, as they ate their evening meal. That the battle tomorrow was all part of keeping the tyrant from the shores of their beloved country and the terror that would be unleashed upon their loved ones should Bonaparte ever reach England.

Better a war fought on foreign soil than their own. And, in this, the army had been fortunate. Tomorrow, they, too, would be fortunate, and their efforts would be noticed not only in London, but in Paris. One day Bonaparte would grow weary of the English and their tenacity, and this is the motto he left his men with, 'tenacious like a bulldog with a bone.' That is how the Grande

Armée would see them tomorrow. That the troops of his division would get their teeth into the enemy and not let go until victory was declared.

THE TON

The comfort of Pemberley embraced the Darcy family. Fitz-william Darcy finished recapping for his wife, sister and Kitty, the news from the letter he had received. "He of course signed it, and I am to understand one also was sent to the Earl."

"But he writes that it is not a terrible wound?" Georgiana was very inquisitive.

"Yes, a graze is how he puts it," Darcy said and did not look very concerned.

Elizabeth stood up and went to pull on the bell rope. She thought some refreshment might be of use. "I shouldn't worry, we would have heard much more if the injury was serious enough that he needs convalesce in England again. Now we must consider our holiday plans, for they are nearly upon us."

It was some few weeks 'til the holidays, but the family was deciding whether to travel to Netherfield. The Bingleys wrote that they would be suited to hosting the entire family. Kitty, however, was decidedly looking vexed.

"Jane has written that, should Netherfield host, not only the family shall attend but some certain others she has thought to invite," Kitty mentioned.

Lizzy said to fully inform Darcy, "It is so. Would you like that we make a change of plans and have everyone here? I should confess my love, that I would not be perturbed by such a thought. Jane did miss being with all last year as they stayed in Town, again. Thus, I believe she wishes to have everyone to Netherfield. But we have not had a chance to bring in the Yule here at Pemberley either since our wedding. I should like to be hostess to all for such a celebration at some time."

"We did venture to Longbourn for the celebrations last year too, and that is twice now since you have become mistress of this house. But should you have such celebrations here my dear, you will be asked to invite your own list of our nearest and dearest to celebrate the yule." Darcy had a look that spoke to his thinking of many thoughts, several that he held back from expressing.

"Oh that is so droll," Georgiana began, to her brother's dismay.

He did not like that she had developed some backbone since she had come out in society. "We shall have to send for my aunt Catherine, and I rather think she will attend, since Anne had such a time with us in London. It is past time that Lady Catherine make amends with Mrs. Darcy and I shall write her at once. It is more than two years now. My aunt, the Countess, I shall encourage to, also, take Lady Catherine to task and in no time we may be one happy family again. This has gone on long enough, I shall but mention that I heard one word about this strife amongst us in London during last season, and soon the entire Ton will know that the de Bourgh's guest at Pemberley for Christmas. Lady Catherine is loath to be made an ondit, I assure you."

Kitty chuckled, and the rest followed suit. Darcy nodding to Georgiana's excellent plan. "That seems agreeable, but I should believe that Jane is the eldest daughter, and, perhaps, her household should be the host first?" Darcy made mention.

Georgiana had grasped Kitty's hand, "Brother, Mr. Bingley wrote of a particular attachment recently, once we left Town, to Sir Fairfax Chamberlain. Should he be invited to Netherfield, it could be an awkwardness."

"Pray excuse me," Kitty stood and hurriedly left the room.

"There, you've done it again." Georgiana said, and then rose and went after her companion.

Darcy looked to his wife, "I have done what?"

Elizabeth smiled indulgently, "Kitty does not wish to meet Sir Fairfax. He has been looking for an opportunity to speak to Kitty, alone. Georgiana has been my aide in ensuring that this does not happen. Kitty does not know how to refuse him, for Mama has made it seem like a great match. Jane knows little of this, as Kitty had only sensed the problem a month or so ago." Elizabeth however had sensed the problem earlier, and had gone to lengths to lessen the presence of Sir Fairfax in their London circle for much longer than that. Kitty, however, was sure, in her heart, that she did not long to spend her life with Sir Fairfax Chamberlain and had told Lizzy so when she saw how Sir Fairfax had set his course.

"Now that is a fine development. I must say that thwarting your mother is not something that many Bennet girls seem to have embraced. Why there must be one amongst you who has been a thoroughly rotten example..."

"Mr. Darcy, you do it rather brown, do you not think, and at your poor wife's expense," Lizzy thought her husband deserved a set down.

Darcy crossed to take her hand and kiss it, "Ma'am, I wrong you with my tease. I stand reprimanded."

"Indeed sir, now we must solve this problem," Lizzy said. She smiled, forgiving his transgression instantly.

"I fear that, this year, Sir Fairfax has become much more our friend, then in previous years. Now I can attribute the reason," Darcy said.

"Posh and twaddle, sir, I informed you of his tender many months ago." He stepped back from his wife hurriedly. She was not angered at Darcy. Just befuddled how he and all men could be so obtuse.

"This does bother you. I shall endeavor to treat it more seriously. I did, indeed, put some distance between my activities and Sir Fairfax', but I am afraid the suspicion that the Bingley's would have him to guest for the holidays is most likely accurate. Charles and Mr. Hurst both have found common grounds of discussion with the man. Hurst is flattered by the attention he receives and Charles by their lively discussions of current events. Though, I also expect, that both he and sister Jane believe that Sir Fairfax might find a suit towards Caroline Bingley an answer to their hope that Caroline make a match." That would be a happy event. Except that the man was besotted with Kitty.

"Now, with little Charles, the Bingleys wish to see their home life more theirs alone. Do not worry so, dear heart, when our new arrival comes this spring, I shall not endeavor to have Georgiana marry any earlier then she feels she must, and leave us," Lizzy said.

"Thank you my dear, I did not expect you would. Nor should I ask that we send Kitty away as one of our companions, though should Mary be burdensome to Charles and Jane, perhaps we should ask to guest her with us more permanently," Darcy did not seem overly joyed at the last.

"Indeed, one day we may wish to do that. But for now, I believe Jane sees Mary as a help mate, especially when Louisa and Caroline are not motivated to lend a hand." Lizzy knew that was truth. She did believe one day Caroline would not be so bitter, but Jane's goodness easily overcame any want of character in Caroline.

"Harumph," Darcy cleared his throat, "My dear, did you not once mention to me that there was a certain stratagem, since I lend this inception to the General, that Sir Fairfax was also being directed towards Caroline Bingley? And further, Caroline herself would like to do something with such."

A light laugh emanated from Lizzy, "We gossip like two old fishwives, Mr. Darcy." He nodded to this. "But yes, you are correct, I believe that the General thought to create an alliance there from an early moment. Certainly Caroline acted as if upset with the General from his actions at our wedding. And, was no warmer, in Town. While every opportunity to meet Sir Fairfax in the early days of our acquaintance, did seem to have Caroline about."

"I had noticed the same. If but this Christmas we were able to have the Bingleys entertain Sir Fairfax, whilst we had the remainder of the family here." Lizzy looked askance at her husband, and he knew that she preferred to be with her family entire. Having risen to the ranks of the first circle of society, she did not abandon her family that remained behind.

Letters left later that day for various parts of the country informing select connections of the plans for a Christmas at Pemberley, and soon responses came pouring in. Yule at Pemberley was to be a success. Not one person refused, and Lady Catherine in a terse acceptance, said she was very much intending to see how Mrs. Darcy managed the legacy of her sister.

The first days of December saw the family readying for an influx of relatives and friends. Mr. Darcy came to his wife one morning shortly after the post arrived, even as she asked her sisters in the sitting room, Georgiana and Kitty, to leave her for a moment as she seemed unsettled by a letter she read.

"Ah, I've found you," Darcy said.

"Indeed sir." Darcy stopped and saw the paper in her hand.

"From your sister Jane? I have one from Charles," he said.

"Yes, our great schemes were for naught. We shall have the Bingleys with us, a mixed blessing it seems." Darcy had not expected that from Lizzy.

He said, "Yes m'dear. It seems that we are ever dancing around the social mores of our family and our society. Why I am tempted for you to invite the Collins and the Lucas's we should even have a few rooms remaining to accommodate the spare stranger that descends upon us."

"Well as we need have rooms made up for Sir Fairfax Chamberlain, in addition to the usual Bingley retinue, I should greatly enjoy the comfort of Charlotte Collins, and she has yet to be invited here."

Darcy knew they avoided that main point, "I have had several hints in correspondence from mine Aunt de Bourgh that she would welcome such traveling companions."

"I had composed the letters yesterday and thought to ask you this morning if we should send them." Elizabeth smiled and he nodded in good humour.

"I believe that Mr. Collins being here, if we must have Sir Fairfax, and you must own that aside from his tendre for Kitty, he is a good fellow to have in a parlor, once he has read his papers. In any event with Mr. Collins here, an example might be provided in the event that Kitty and Sir Fairfax cross paths," Darcy said.

"Ha, ha. You believe that Kitty should follow my technique at refusal should that become necessary," Lizzy said.

"Perhaps. But a few words to Sir Fairfax might send him off the scent. If needs, I shall be blunt with him," Darcy volunteered.

"You make me laugh again," Elizabeth said as she composed herself once she was done with her fit. "Trying to look the stern demeanor when we talk about Sir Fairfax does seem like a contradiction."

Darcy replied, "Yes. But he is a friend, or at least one in our set that I tolerate for his insightful thoughts on the current events."

"Oh, I admit that he has something to recommend him, and certainly if Kitty leaned towards a person who cared about current events, then a match between the two is something I also would encourage. Oh do not look at me as if you think I am my mother," Lizzy said.

"I am sorry, but my looks seem to incite you to heights of hilarity or the depths of self reflection," Darcy stated back.

"Oh I see your smile, and your apology is not accepted. As for your looks, they incite me to many different depths indeed."

"Now you have made me laugh," Darcy said when he too had regained his composure. "As for a match, I agree that Kitty and Sir Fairfax Chamberlain does not seem a good set."

"Yes, you and I are good. For despite what many people think, we like people, and thus have much to discuss as we interact with our society. You may have some study of current events, though not to the extent of Sir Fairfax, and I might have some inclination to other talents that you do not possess, but nothing that is so clearly defining as Sir Fairfax and his love of the news."

Darcy responded next, "Then what do we see as Kitty's raison d'être?"

Darcy did not think his wife would pause so long, "Well of course she has taken to theatricals, but you will remember two years ago, she was very like Lydia, enamored of men in uniform."

Darcy said, "Yes, I can recall your mother relating how prior to the marriage to your father, also, had that same attraction. But I have noticed this last year, that there were no gentleman callers for Kitty who were in uniform, though Georgiana did have two."

"Captain Walters, and Lieutenant Smith, the Honorable Lieutenant Smith." They both smirked at the young man's self importance. "Georgiana, I believe, does think favorably of the Captain, and he does have some successful campaigning to recommend him."

"Yes, I have written to his Colonel, but I've told you that before. Did I mention the response I received? No, well the young man does have his head on his shoulders, though I shouldn't call him too young, as he is but four years my junior. His father is in trade of course, but respectable, owns some clothing manufactories and a few ships, I understand. Third son and all that, so was not destined for the business, though his Colonel writes that the lad does have a head for what's what. Not full of nonsense like some we know in our set," Darcy said.

"You are letting your snobbery run away with you. You have had him and the Honorable Lieutenant, each, twice to dinner, you must certainly have your own thoughts?" She asked

"Well yes, I should like to keep the Honourable Lieutenant well away from our sisters whilst I have no objection to the Captain. Though my reservations would be that I already worry overmuch about the General each time we read of a battle, so if we were not to have another member of the family in uniform, that would be fine with me as well," Darcy said.

"Indeed we all have taken the same partiality about the General. Mama has even taken to asking about him so many times upon any given day that we wonder for her memory, for this is the first sign we have that she is so distracted that she forgets of what we have informed her," Lizzy said.

"Yes, well now I think we had best break the news to Kitty. Better for her to be prepared for this."

Darcy had stood again and paced in short steps.

"You had best let me do that dear. She is my sister and I think I shall know how to best handle it," Lizzy said.

Darcy paused in his pacing and sat down. "Thank you m'dear. I am quite sure you shall be better at it than I. Well now that is taken care of I shall go have a word with Jones, the gamekeeper. It is rather cold for fishing just yet in the lake, but I think we can arrange some entertainments for the guests." Elizabeth knew that this meant the male guests. All entertainments of both sexes together were placed in her hands.

* * *

Georgiana had been with Kitty the entire day and after they had left Elizabeth the second time that day, she knew her close friend was in quite a state. "Mr. Darcy all but promised that Sir Fairfax would not be a guest with us this season."

Georgiana couldn't refute that. "He did explain the circumstances."

"The circumstances do little to make things right," Kitty said.

"Often that is the case. I believe the older we are becoming, the less we always find the world to our particular liking," Georgiana said.

"Please don't give me a scold just now, Georgiana, I shall be better later, but just now my emotions speak first."

Georgiana reached for Kitty's hand, "And I think should your sister Elizabeth hear a statement like that, she would be proud. Indeed I know that this is a blow. But it is a big house, and will be filled with many people. Sir Fairfax will not make such a goose of himself, that he would do anything beneath society's notice, so all shall be well." Kitty hoped Georgiana was right.

"That is what your brother said." Kitty sat and turned her head away.

"And Elizabeth added to it with her story of Mr. Collins, how if Sir Fairfax does bring up any subject that is unpleasant to your ears, you but best be firm and let him know that such a conversation should not be discussed and you will not hear of it. Elizabeth also said she would consult Mrs. Bennet on the matter and ensure that your mother be apprised that Sir Fairfax has ambitions and qualities that are not near to the greatest of your suitors."

"That ploy would cool mother's ardor, that is so," Kitty smiled at the thought.

Kitty looked towards Georgiana, who after looking at her hands raised her head back up, "Well at least for a half hour, surely." That brought forth a laugh from both, and Kitty realized that her distress would have to be borne.

I had been looking forward to this Christmas, but now it is with trepidation. I should wonder how I will survive for I have done nothing I can think to show any special favoritism to the gentleman. At this point, I am beside myself on what advice and from whom I should seek it. Lizzy has often sat beside me to give me some guidance, but it is hard for me to listen, for I feel that she is somewhat culpable as is your cousin, Mr. Darcy in forcing another meeting with the man.

They have both confessed to me that should I not wish to be allied, as they put it, with the illustrious lordling, and I know he is a societal leader in your set, then they shall back me. When I have gone to approach Father about it, and he looks at me and says 'what do I know of the peerage. Best write to your friend the General, seeing as I waste so much paper in that line already. I would begrudge you that' he carries on 'if I were not keen to hear of his exploits and health,' and always then Father goes quiet, and hands me thruppence to go to the stationer and purchase more paper. Even while we are at Pemberley where Mr. Darcy has insured that I have a very adequate supply of paper with my own engraved initials now upon them. And, sir, I am surprised that you did not remark about this the last time I received a letter from you, how my stationery has certainly taken on a new character. I fear your mind drifts in its attentions to me.

But enough of my tease, I fear that you shall receive this letter in too short a time for a reply of guidance before Sir Fairfax descends upon Pemberley. Thus I sit here thinking what a letter from you would say. "Do not be obtuse when dealing with Sir Fax, for he needs to be brought right to the point. He tends to wander in his mind, if left to his own devices and spends so much time reading the news, that he has some trouble keeping the appropriate day in perspective."

The house was by no means full of all its intended guests when Sir Fairfax Chamberlain arrived at Pemberley. There were quite enough people gathered, though, that Kitty had been able to be about other areas removed from Sir Fairfax's meanderings on the day of his arrival. They then did not meet till dinner, where Kitty arrived almost upon its announcement. As Lady Catherine and the Countess of M----K had yet to arrive, Darcy had the leisure to say, "Mama, if you will excuse me tonight, I believe it is my turn to escort Kitty into dine, as I have received instruction from Mrs. Darcy in this matter, saying I show too much favoritism upon some of our other members, and have quite forgot Kitty and Georgiana."

Kitty had been in the drawing room all of half a minute and Sir Fax had but bowed a greeting to her. "Well of course Mr. Darcy," Mrs. Bennet began, and realized that she had sat at his side twice in the three nights that she had been at Pemberley so far. "It is only fair that you honor all of us ladies, equally, in turn."

"Then my dear Mrs. Darcy, will you arrange us all?" he said to his wife.

"Yes, of course. Sir Fairfax, as our newest arrival, will you accompany me. Very good. Now Papa, I think Georgiana tonight, and Mama, Uncle Gardiner..." with not much effort, Elizabeth soon had the entire party sorted out. Kitty found herself spared by being seven persons removed from Sir Fairfax and on the same side of the table. The Darcys handled the matter quite adroitly.

When Elizabeth signaled for the ladies to retire, and Darcy kept the men for half an hour at their port. Elizabeth and Mrs. Gardiner controlled the conversation in the drawing room while they awaited the men. It was but five minutes before Mrs. Bennet made an effort to mention Sir Fairfax, "I must have entirely forgotten that charming Sir Fairfax Chamberlain was to be a member of the house this week."

Elizabeth and Darcy had withheld that information, so her forgetfulness may have relied more on her never having been informed. "Yes Mama, I am sure I wrote you an exhaustive list of all of our attendees? Well it must have gone astray then, did not you get the copy aunt?" And Mrs. Gardiner was able to reply that she had, though Mrs. Phillips, Elizabeth's other aunt found she too was in such a state of ignorance.

Lizzy said, "You do know then that tomorrow we should be joined by the Earl and Countess, the Viscount and his wife, and Lady Catherine and her entire party which shall consists of the Collins?"

"Yes, I am. Why sister and I have talked at length about this invitation to Mr. Collins," Mrs. Bennet replied.

Lizzy said, "Now Mama, you must remember that despite the entailment of Longbourn to Mr. Collins, ever before we were acquainted with him, we have spent the holidays with Charlotte, who was Charlotte Lucas before. Why I confess that even these last months I am growing fonder of Mr. Collins."

Mrs. Bennet gasped and looked to her daughter with eyes grown big. In that awkward moment Kitty chose to cough. Jane quickly spoke into the silence, "Are you feeling quite well, Kitty?"

"Yes, Jane..." she responded. This was lost as Georgiana spoke a little louder than her normal want, "It does seem that you are a little pale, dear."

Elizabeth nodded as she now spoke, even before Mrs. Bennet had yet to utter a response to the remarks about the Collins, "Why I do perceive that Georgiana is right, you do look a little white. Now we can not have you coming down with a cold. We have seen what colds do at house parties, is that not right Mrs.

Bingley. Come, now, off to bed with you Kitty. We shall make your apologies to the men when they come in from their port and cigars. And Mary, you will be extra quiet when you go up, of course you will. Come I shall take you up and Mama, would you summon a footman to send some hot plasters up to Kitty and Mary's room? Thank you..."

Elizabeth had Kitty out of the drawing room so quickly, that others could not remark upon it. Kitty and Mary were to share a room, as were several others for the house was full, even for a house as large as Pemberley, which boasted many guest rooms. Georgiana was to share with Anne de Bourgh, upon her arrival, and the single men were also doubled up. Mr. Darcy had suggested this arrangement to ensure that nothing untoward would occur to anyone's mind. Knowing Sir Fairfax, Darcy said he doubted that thoughts of carnal pleasure had yet to be noticed by the man. Pursuit of marriage had only emerged for the baronet due to the pressure from Chamberlain's own mother, and the co-incidence of his acquaintance with Kitty.

"Thank you, I really do not feel my very best..." Kitty began as they walked up the stairs.

"Posh and bother, Kitty, I know you are perfectly well. Now we'll put you to bed, and you can have some quiet time alone before Mary comes up. Perhaps two hours. I shan't be able to keep you entirely free of Sir Fairfax, but Darcy intends to have a word with him."

Elizabeth provided a light grip as she guided her sister forward. "Oh I just don't know what I shall do," Kitty said.

"You must be strong. And you must plan for what you will say if Sir Fairfax solicits a private conversation," Elizabeth told her.

"No, Lizzy..."

Elizabeth stopped, even as they approached her room. "I am sorry my dear, but take my example, there are some men who will make an offer and should you choose not to accept, you must be firm. Our father is not such a man as can readily discourage suitors. Certainly our mama encourages certain suitors, nay any suitor for her daughters. Despite you having three married sisters, she shall never stop her quest to see all of us wed."

Kitty opened her door, "I know you to be right, though I am

distraught over it." Lizzy could see that Kitty looked like she could become ill because of her current emotions.

"Yes I know. When we lived at Longbourn, I had never thought that we should be thrust into such a situation, yet you remember how it was with Mr. Collins and myself. Now that Town plays such a part of our lives, we can not return to our obscurity. I fear that it shall be harder for you and Mary then it was for Jane, Lydia and I. Not only shall you have offers because of who you are, but because of who your relations are. Your new brothers are men of stature, and they shall provide you with callers whose sincerity is questionable."

"Those are not the only type of suitors that shall be steered my way," Kitty said.

Elizabeth realized her sister already understood what she spoke of. "Indeed. Know this then, you are in a position now, that you may choose your future. Though, whatever man anyone of your relations feels may best be your match, you have my support in choosing your own. One might even say that despite Mama's best plans for all of us, we each have chosen our own husbands, Lydia, Jane and I."

Kitty smiled, "Yes, the Bennets lie between those who expect an arranged marriage to preserve ones bloodlines and those where providence forces an arrangement to keep poverty at bay. Sometimes one actually can not tell which part of society one is from. We all knew that Mama was set to barter you to our cousin Mr. Collins to ensure our futures even though she expected Mr. Bingley to make Jane happy."

"Perhaps," Lizzy noted that some insight had come to Catherine. "Yet we seem to have all done surprisingly well. Now should you and Mary choose men that shall ensure your happiness, then all shall have turned out splendidly."

Before speaking in response, Kitty paused, then sitting upon the bed she said, "I understand. But, I now have to think of something to say to Sir Fairfax." Elizabeth left her sister to her thoughts. Returning to the drawing room, she found the men had yet to join the ladies and when they did finally arrive, Mrs. Bennet related how Kitty had retired for the night. Two ladies provided entertainment upon the piano forte and there were three ballads presented as the group socialized. With the arrival of the last of the invited guests set for the following day, even more evening entertainment would be arranged, but, soon enough, the residents and guests of Pemberley retired to their rooms.

Lizzy stayed long at breakfast the next day for Kitty took refuge in the schedule that women in a country house maintained. She and Mary took their time with their toilette and came to break their fast long after the men had done so. Kitty this had the assurance of yet more hours free from a confrontation with Sir Fairfax. To be sure, Kitty seemed to hope that such an encounter would not occur, but the likelihood of a private meeting greatly outweighed her escaping one as Sir Fairfax had gone to such lengths to ensure himself of an invitation to the seasonal gathering. Lizzy did not think her sister could escape such through the whole of the celebrations at Pemberley.

* * *

Darcy took it upon himself, as the men rode out to enjoy the estate grounds, to guide Sir Fairfax off to view a particular area of the grounds. He was able to broach the subject that he and Lizzy had discussed. "I say Fax, I have a rather delicate matter to bring to your attention."

The two had stopped their horses and looked back towards Pemberley. It was grander then Sir Fairfax's ancestral home. "Well, Darcy, pray speak, I shall give your problem my full consideration."

Darcy patted his horse's neck, "No, let me not mislead you that what we discuss is as world defining as Nelson's victory at Trafalgar? But I believe that you personally must be made aware of something that has become very obvious to myself and Elizabeth these last months."

"Pray, continue." Sir Fax stood tall in his stirrups to stretch.

"It is this. You must know that we have taken Kitty to our breasts to not only companion Georgiana, but also to expose her to society. You have met her parents, and whilst I esteem them greatly, Mr. Bennet will be the first to admit that London and the Ton make him feel like a flower uprooted from the soil."

Sir Fairfax smiled. Fax had clearly noted this. Though the men rarely indulged in what the Ton offered, all could recognize that

Mr. Bennet was comfortable here in the country, in an uncrowded world. "Yes of course, but surely you do not scorn your relations."

"Indeed I do not, for I spent many hours battling with demons raised by what the connection would entail. I had the advantage that some may not, that my relations are slightly more distant than many of our contemporaries, such as yourself, for my parents have left Georgiana and I orphans," Darcy said.

Fairfax nodded. "I believe I see your point. Yet, surely, your example and Bingleys are such that the height of the Ton can take those of lesser society and raise them up."

Darcy shook his head, "Is that the case or do those who proclaim me friend talk about my new relations in parlors when we are not there? You probably would not know since you seldom go about the circle of such society, but think to comments you may have heard from those in your mother's clutch of friends." Fairfax shook his head, for any slurs on the Bennets were comments he had ignored at the time.

"Well, personal observation would show that while Elizabeth and I receive many invitations to events, when my in-laws arrive in Town to spend time with us, we receive almost none," Darcy pointed out.

"Come now, Darcy, you make our set seem to be rather shallow," Fax observed.

"I know that you seldom go to those events that you are invited to, but surely you have heard at the club who attends what," Darcy knew the man was not entirely unaware of what took place amongst the Ton.

Fairfax shook his head again, "It is not meaningful. We have such great events shaping the world that these little parlor games are small. And surely you have said that Elizabeth and you are accepted readily into society. Why, your wife is amongst the finest ladies of my acquaintance."

"I thank you for that, but I ask you to pause and consider your purposes and what consequences they may bring." Darcy caused Fairfax to stay, for he seemed anxious to resume his ride.

"Of course, of course. I have been thinking much lately of items more personal than the doings of our great empire. I shall add your reflections to my thoughts." The topic apparently exhausted, the men resumed their ride.

* * *

Later that day, Kitty did exchange greetings with Sir Fax for a space of time, as once again all gathered to meet for dinner. Kitty found fortune that he did not ask for a private audience and seemed a little preoccupied.

Elizabeth had arranged once again to separate Kitty from the nearness of Sir Fax at dinner and so while the Earl of M----K escorted her into dinner, Kitty was escorted by his son the Viscount. Darcy had, on his arm, the Countess this first night of their attendance, and behind him was Sir Fax with Lady Catherine. Lady Catherine and Elizabeth had exchanged their own brief sentences, on the surface all pleasant but one could still see some tension between the two.

The third day of his visit to Pemberley Sir Fairfax achieved what he had come for.

"Ah Miss Kitty, I have been searching you out." He had found her in the music salon where Georgiana and Anne de Bourgh were to join her. "I have spent the morning in quest of your whereabouts and a chance encounter with Miss de Bourgh and Miss Darcy have led me to you." The two ladies had followed him to the room but ten paces behind and when he entered and quickly shut the door, they were loath to enter.

"Sir, I do wait upon the ladies for we are to practice some pieces for tonights' entertainments."

"Yes I had gathered so. But pray a mere moment's indulgence." He stopped her and motioned for her to return to her seat. She had risen when he entered and was looking to find some ease whilst they were alone.

"I have spoken with Darcy and he has allowed that I should examine my feelings close in my great regard for you. I have done so and have concluded that you shall be the best of companions that I mayst find in this life." He turned slightly from her so that she could not see the fullness of his face. He clutched at his handkerchief and she could see that it had lost all of its pressed and starched form.

Sir Fax continued, "At first I can only say that your bright countenance awoke me from the stupor that I found myself in, when in the presence of your sex. Later this attraction deepened from that of the vain reflections to the compatibility I see as I engaged you in conversation of the affairs of the world. I make no secret that this is the dearest thing to my mind and heart, at least until I entertained you residing there. That you were able to credibly discuss the world's weighty burdens intelligibly and passionately, as I do, brought you ever closer to my tender affections." Kitty clutched her hands one to the other as she composed herself to remain free of any sign upon her face. She was sure she had never spoken with him at length about world events. He mostly spoke while she politely listened.

"That this warmth has grown within to a fire and now consumes me, though I know that sounds like the trite words of a youthful lover, it is nevertheless how my feelings have evolved. I ask that you give me leave to announce that you have made me the happiest of men. I pray you take my hand and allow me to regard you as my dearest."

She rose from her seat and turned from him. Sir Fax said, "Pray, what's amiss, I know you have some regard for me." He had not advanced far into the room and was some several feet distant from her. The bulk of the pianoforte was between them.

When Kitty turned to face him, she had composed an answer, "Sir, you do me too much honor, for I am but the daughter of a country squire. I have not aspired to the heights of society to which you are enjoined and so your solicitation gives me pause to consider what affections we do have for one another..."

"There, we are to be happy," Interrupting her, Sir Fairfax beamed.

"Hold, sir, I pray. Do not let my words cause you to run victorious, nor flee. You have been a friend these many months and you share with me the world of affairs that few other suitors or men who have shown interest, have been able to enlighten me. For this you have a tie to my affections." She held up her hand for he had started towards her. "Yet this affection has not blossomed into one which I can allow that it shall give you joy. Sorry, I am, that the affection I hold has grown little since our first meeting."

Unsteady on his feet, Sir Fairfax swayed a little, "Pray sir, I beg you sit. I do not mean to discomfort you, yet I wish you to know the feelings you proclaim are not returned. I do not say that there are no feelings, and since I am but new to the society of Town perhaps I do not know what feelings of rapture are, but my feelings for you are the same as those I have for Mr. Darcy or Mr. Bingley. Certainly should I give you joy, these should be more, just more than that." Kitty was certain about that knowledge. She understood a little about love.

He composed himself, then said, "Perhaps you are right. Perhaps in time feelings will grow between us."

"Sir Fairfax, certainly we are friends, enough, that you would not expect me to ask you to hold your affections when the world awaits either of us. Should another come between us who may make you happy, this would only bring me joy, knowing my good friend had found such. I should ask that my friend would think the same for me if such was to be."

He could hardly protest such, "Yes of course I would wish it."

Kitty said, "Then there it all is, for I pray you to understand that unlike my sister Lydia, whom you have not met, I know I have not found that love of any man that I should have were I to wish joy. This may be because of my life till recently in Meryton, for you know Jane and Elizabeth were much older than I when they met their husbands and found themselves passionately in love. Perhaps it is for the best that we have met while I am yet unsure of my feelings regarding love and desire in the companion of my heart, for when I recognize these emotions your friendship shall be as a guide."

She realized that she was leaning towards giving too much away and had to compose herself to stop. If she didn't take care with her words she might say something that could lead to too much hope for Sir Fax.

"Well... Well... I ah see... Yes that is I see your point. If you will excuse me, I have some correspondence to attend to..."

"Yes of course, please be free," she gestured and he left with abrupt, jerked movements.

* * *

"Elizabeth, I just had a long talk with ..." Darcy walked into his wife's dressing room and motioned for the abigail to leave, which she did hurriedly.

"Sir Fax? Yes I am sure you did. Was it as productive as yesterday, when you told him not to pursue Kitty?" She was cross.

Darcy stopped. "Yesterday did not go as well as my expectations. I seem to have lacked clarity."

A long look greeted him. "Sir, that is understated."

After a deep breath, Darcy said, "What do we do now?"

"Pray, what has your last encounter with Sir Fairfax revealed? And before you relate a long tale, I have also spoken to someone and know all about his offer and the refusal that it was met with."

"You have spoken to your sister?" He looked at her, with some wonderment upon his features. He had previously shown how his own approach to the matters of love were fraught with difficulties. That he was now happily married proved that his own love was able to overcome the obstacles that he had placed in his own path towards the joy he now owned. But as an agent of Cupid, or one to see to the success of his family's and friend's rapture, her husband was still inept.

"Yes, Kitty came to me hours ago and told me everything so that I was able to find my Mama and ensure that she did not speak as she is normally want. I should not have her giving rise to food for Caroline Bingley, or your Aunt." Where as Mrs. Bennet recognized that her daughter Mary was want to discourse at length on subjects that few wish to engage her in, the mother of so many girls still did not realize that not all thoughts one had, needed to be uttered in polite society. Some were definitely best left unspoken.

Darcy said, "Oh I had not even thought of that. In any event Sir Fax is removing to the Inn and will be posting up to Town in the morning."

"Nonsense. You must go and fetch him back this instance. We are all friends and now, but few know of his offer. If he leaves and returns to Town, all the Ton will be gossiping about it for weeks. Kitty has not told your sister, though Georgiana and Mary suspect. By the end of this yule gathering I shall ensure that no tale creeps back to Town. It shall be our little secret and all reputations shall be intact."

"I am not sure that Sir Fax will see it that way," Darcy said.

"Darcy, you must convince Sir Fairfax, and you must be direct. If he returns to Town his mother will find out and he shall be berated by the old harridan, there I have said it, she is much more formidable than even Lady Catherine. Sir Fairfax is too gentle a soul, a lost soul in his world events, but a gentle one to continue to be castigated by such a woman. If only the man took an interest in such as Caroline Bingley. Why she dotes on the title and connections he brings. And if anything that is what she is most fond of in a man," She said. It was a true estimate of the woman. A harsh one, but valid.

Darcy looked about to see if the abigail had truly withdrawn. He relaxed his tense and stiff shoulders when he saw they were completely alone. Both had talked of Caroline this way before, but they had not matched Caroline to Sir Fairfax. "I do not think Sir Fax has ever considered anyone but Kitty as a partner..."

Lizzy said, "You know that to be true. But even in one of the General's letters Stephen made mention of this months ago. Sir Fax needs a woman to provide him heirs and allow him to read his papers all day long. Kitty would be at the end of her wits should she be that companion, for she needs to have someone to do things with. Being a child of five she never was much alone. While Caroline Bingley sees herself as a doyenne of the Salon and wants but a husband to set her up in society as such. How did the General put it;

"If Fax and Miss Caroline were wed, two friends would end their days realizing that they had provided each the ultimate happiness, yet all of us would be made happy immediately from such an event."

And then he admonished us not to share that with Charles and Jane."

Darcy took a deep breath, "I have not either, though my letter back to Stephen scolded him most grievously for putting those thoughts on paper." Elizabeth smiled, she had read Darcy's stern lines and had not told him that the letter that followed from the General that had been addressed to her contained a critical analysis of her husband's ability to put a scold onto paper.

"Darcy must do better when he wishes me to act propitious. 'As to the matter of your thoughts on Miss C. Bingley and Fax, why Heavens man you can't be writing that, one simply doesn't,' Now Lizzy you had promised me that by the end of your first year of marriage you would be taking the stiffness out of my cousin, but here we have evidence that he is backsliding something terribly."

"Why Darcy are we talking of Caroline Bingley? You came here to discuss Kitty and Sir Fax, and Kitty is definitely closer to my heart. To be sure, ensuring that Caroline weds will make life an ease for Jane, but that is not our present concern."

Darcy shook his head, "Yes, Kitty. She refused Fax, as we knew she would, but he seems to think that Kitty is currently incapable of love."

"Yes, she told him so. She is young and is certain she has not been overcome by this illness that certainly possesses us. Now hurry to the Inn and fetch the man back. Dinner is just over an hour and you shall have enough time to make it. Later you and I shall interview Sir Fax and set him to rights. He is a lost soul but it seems he has become our lost soul." Elizabeth dismissed her husband who nodded and turned to leave. She called to his back, "And send Millie back to work on my hair," Lizzy referred to her abigail.

Darcy left understanding that her directions were logical and well thought out. Their marriage had begun to divide up tasks and duties, and those considering the emotional lives of those they touched was directed by Elizabeth for she had a much firmer grasp on them. He had talents that were utilized elsewhere.

FAR FROM FRIENDS

Being at war in the year of 1811 was telling for Stephen. The monotony of the previous year for him, when so much had occurred in Town for his family and friends, was something he had begun to dwell on. His position as General was such, that unless action was upon them, he had much free time to brood.

His latest letters were fairly current and he had all the news of the winter at Pemberley that the entirety of his correspondents had partaken of. That coincidence, that everyone he wrote to were all in one place together made him realize that his world was not with his men, but with those at home in England. His father's last letter showed flagging support for a war that continued on and left his son in danger. That Stephen's brother the Viscount had developed a cough since winter that had not gone away, seemed to be cause for concern, and some days he could not leave the house. But his father's last letter was such to put the General to greater thought.

That duty is expected of us all, it is important, and that those sons who shall not inherit, we look to raise the flag of empire in any forms, from warrior, sailor, rector or peacemaker. Even as a servant of the government, heaven forbid. Your uncle, my brother, had also done duty in India for King and Country, and I have fond memories of our times together when we were lads. I never saw him again after he left, dying in Calcutta, as you know. I do not write you thus to distress you, but to enjoin you to not leave my last memory of you be from April two years ago. I desire that you return, hale and hearty from your service.

I have made arrangements with your brother and we have found land and a house for you when you do so. I have cut back my spending and your brother's these last two years that we should acquire the place and have done so in your name. So the manor of Combe Laud is yours, seventeen miles south of Town, and just off the road to the locality where the Bingleys and Bennets live. Indeed Mrs. Bennet was she who first touched on the grand manor and once I saw it, I knew it would be perfect for a county seat for you. Now be brave, be safe, and come home to take it over.

The General had been touched at his father's bequest. When he had left the family to take up a career in the service, he had little hopes of a sizable income, and thought if he were to receive five hundred a year, he would be lucky. After his years on the Peninsula, he had amassed some fortune, and he knew that he would be able to afford his own manor should he live until the peace. Now that he did not have to purchase one, his money could go farther. He would have to find out more details of Combe Laud for he hoped that his father's choice would be something to his liking. Certainly his father's ceremonial home was quaint, but not at all close to the glories of Pemberley or Rosings Park. Neither of which he had become wealthy enough, in his campaigning to afford.

General Fitzwilliam was also concerned about his brother's health. For the Viscountess had mentioned it, which was to be expected, but so too had the Viscount. And though the brothers were distant by some years, they did not discourse on such items unless they were of a serious nature. Illness was an item not discussed by men unless very serious.

As a General he now found that more time was spent behind his desk than in front of his troops, a bad habit. But, in order to maintain the army in the field, or in garrison ready for a battle here on foreign soil, someone had to authorize and make decisions, and Lord Wellington used his officers in just such a way. Stephen glanced out the open window of his office and saw the last effects of winter being shaken off. Soon they would be on the move again and he was determined that this year should be the last they were away. He fervently hoped that Wellington thought the same and that this year the French obliged. Turning to his duty, he did his best to put thoughts of Town aside.

* * *

"It is strange," Mrs. Bennet remarked to her second daughter. "Your father and I have not had any correspondence from the Colonel, the General for ages. Why we received one just after Twelfth Night, and none since." That it was May pointed to the length of time since that missive.

"I should not consider it strange, *The Times* tells of news of the campaign mother. The General has left his winter camp and marches on the French. I am sure he is quite preoccupied."

Mrs. Bennet looked to her daughter, "Your father lets me believe you to be the smartest of my children, and I am quite sure he is correct, Lizzy. But don't think that I am always bereft of my senses and do not know all that occurs around me. Something has happened to the General, or to his spirit. I am sure that your sister no longer receives letters from him, and I do wonder if she does write them. Viscount Parkes does now take up so much of her time. But tell me, when was the last you or Mr. Darcy received a letter from the General."

That Mrs. Bennet showed sense and caring in her question caused Elizabeth to think before remarking something to put her mother off. "You are right, he has been very quiet since the holidays. We had a half page, after, wishing us a blessed new year and since then I have sent three letters that have gone unanswered. Kitty had received a letter once after my last, but she expressed to me that it contained little of substance."

"There, I knew I was right. His spirit is low and must be raised. I know, we shall send a gift package. Where are the girls? Out riding in the Park, I shouldn't wonder. Darcy has spoiled them with these animals he has given them, though fine specimens, and better than your father could ever afford. But Mary has a poor seat. And Kitty, well I fear this new set you let her carry on with. I looked to you and Darcy to keep her in check. I am certain that I shall have to take her back to Longbourn."

Elizabeth thought she would like little better just then as well. Viscount Parkes was the son and heir of the Marquis of Sloane. Handsome, rich, well dressed, and in pursuit of her sister. What surprised Elizabeth was that Mrs. Bennet was not encouraging the match. "Mama, I distinctly recall writing to you about Viscount Parkes..."

"Yes you did, but you made no mention of his past. Why the one thing I can say about all my sons is that they are men, indeed. Why not a one has caused me any bother." Mrs. Bennet conveniently forgot much of what had gone on during the courtship of all her married daughters when, at various times, each of the men's wooing had given her the vapours.

"Mama, Viscount Parkes' past is not often spoken of. Mr. Darcy says he has reformed himself," Elizabeth said. She was not sure she believed it to be true.

"Yet, I find that he is all for show. He certainly looks better than Captain Wickham, but underneath that pretty exterior, he is not a much of a much, I tell you. And, I am surprised, Lizzy, that you can't see that. Why it was your aunt Gardiner who sent me a letter, after I had so many from you calling the match fortuitous. Why? After that horrid affair at Pemberley." Mrs. Bennet referred to Sir Fairfax Chamberlain's offer for Kitty.

"Mama!" Lizzy was glad she and her mother were alone. Her parents had arrived the day before, and Lizzy had no inclination why they had come to Town. Now it was all too clear. Lizzy had written her mother the instant to let her know that a rather well connected man had shown an interest in her youngest unmarried sister. At first this prospect seemed rather a happy circumstance. On greater acquaintance with the Viscount Lizzy was not so sure.

Not much had been said about the Ton in their ondits regarding Kitty and Sir Fairfax. Though it was certainly noted that Sir Fax was not seen at all amidst the Darcy's set as he had previously been wont to do.

After a short retreat to his club and the comfort of his favorite chair surrounded by his papers, it was noted that Sir Fax had become a frequent guest of the Hurst's and to a lesser extent, the Bingley's, though only on nights when Jane Bingley's sisters were not in evidence. Though always about on these occasions was Miss Caroline Bingley. That, too, was noted in the Ton's ondits.

"When I related the name to your aunt Phillips, she had all the horrid history of Viscount Parkes. Why such a bounder has shown interest in our dearest girl, I cannot fathom." Lizzy remembered how when all their fortunes were once hinged on Jane's successful match, Jane had been the dearest girl. Then when Lydia was first to wed, she had been the first amongst the sisters in her mother's words.

"Mama, please don't get the wrong idea. Lord Parkes indeed has a reputation, and past, but Fitzwilliam has made inquiries also. Whilst I have other reservations about the appropriateness of such a match, it is clear that his lordship is now above re-proach. The worst report that we seem to have is, that he was younger. His lordship had been sent down from Oxford. Though no great recommendation of his scholarly abilities, many in his social set could claim a similar educational experience. His parents also are leaders amongst their social set and great friends of the Royals. He has been left to his own devices with ready money."

Mrs. Bennet shook her head and took up her hat which was next to her on the settee. She was adding ribbon to the piece. "Your aunt Phillips has it that his lordship was seen with, and ca-vorted amongst, the theater girls of Drury Lane." That disaster, if true, was akin to accusing the man of utilizing the services of women of ill repute, for many of the actresses supplanted their meager incomes from the stage with private performances in their boudoirs.

"And to that extent," Lizzy nodded, "That is what Fitzwilliam has uncovered. But, Mama, many men in that social circle have spent their time in the arms of the ladies who strut upon the stage. It is no shame to their character, and many, I have learned, consider that a furtherance on their education. Darcy has assured me of some men in our own social circle, also, though few, have been known to have been taught some lessons at the playhouses."

Mrs. Bennet shook her head, "Don't be wise with me. I should never expect it of the men we know." Lizzy had to think how she loved her mother's naiveté.

Lizzy shook her head. She knew of several of the men in the families around Longbourn, whom Mrs. Bennet counted as friends, had previously led lives that would have taken them to the same circles to which her mother damned Viscount Parkes. A man Mrs. Bennet, had yet to meet.

At this juncture their husbands joined them and the discussion was left for talk of the men venturing to one of Darcy's clubs that day. The ladies were planning to amuse themselves with so-cial calls before all gathered to go to the theater that night.

"Mr. Darcy, I should ask a question of you, that I have asked of Lizzy, though have gotten little in the way of an answer. It has been on my mind this little while and I do worry about so much, that I fear you can put it to rest."

"Mama, I should think that it best left unsaid," Lizzy said.

"Unsaid, why ever for? Certainly Mr. Darcy will elucidate me?" Mrs. Bennet said.

Darcy looked between his wife and mother. Catching the expression upon Lizzy's face, "I should think that if we have a delicate matter before us, perhaps Elizabeth is right. I must profess some squeamishness to discuss womanly things." Mr. Bennet raised his eyebrows and as was his practice, turned his mind to other matters.

"Oh Mr. Darcy it is nothing of the sort. I merely want to enquire about a particular friend of yours," Mrs. Bennet stated.

"Mama, I did not say that the Viscount was a particular friend of Mr. Darcy's," Lizzy said.

"Viscount Parkes, what has Viscount Parkes to do with the price of figs? I am not talking of the Viscount. Though I have some questions and opinions on that subject and I shall be plain, indeed, upon it. That to lead our daughters, your sisters down such a path is a dangerous game. A dangerous game indeed. Should such a rapscallion pay court under my house, I know that Mr. Bennet would have words, is that not right my dear."

Mr. Bennet shook his head and rumbled deep in his chest, clearing some congestion there, "Yes, of course my dear. No more rapscallions for the girls. Married enough of them off to those types already, of course not to say you are a rapscallion, Darcy. Least ways Lizzy has assured me that you are not, and that excellent grandson of mine proves that there is some mettle about you, my lad. But, is that right my dear?"

"Oh Mr. Bennet, you know my meaning. We came up to Town to see the babies, and to stop this nonsense of Kitty and that rake..." Mrs. Bennet began.

"Mama, I have been telling you that Viscount Parkes is not a rake. He is a very proper gentleman," Lizzy wanted to believe that.

"With a past as degenerate as his, how proper can he be? But never mind him. I shall take a firm hand with Kitty and we shall soon have that mess sorted out. Your cousin, the General, sir. That is whom I desire news of. Why, just before we came to

Town, my sister, your aunt Phillips dear, and I were rereading the last letter we had from the General and I then remarked that it did seem a bit dated. Why even Mr. Bennet has shared some news or other about the war and some battle that the General had been involved in. And yet he had not written to your father and I to share his recollections of it. And every other battle or event of import since he left after his injury, now these two years, he has shared with us."

Darcy had turned his attention from her mother. He surely had to regard himself fortunate that she shared more matters of the mind with her father than with her mother. "Yes ma'am, I understand you to be concerned about the lack of correspondence that General Fitzwilliam has sent your way, and certainly unanswered also are letters that Lizzy and I have sent, also, to my cousin. His greatest correspondent has always been Kitty, and in this regard also I believe her letters have dwindled..."

Lizzy had something to add to that. "No, they have stopped altogether. She too has noted that, but the last we talked of it was some weeks ago. She told me then that she had written three letters over the course of several weeks and they had been unanswered. I do not know if she has written much these last months..."

"Because she is cavorting under your very noses with that rake, Viscount Parkes." Mrs. Bennet was angered. It was quite noticeable, as she directed a look straight at her daughter.

"Mrs. Bennet, I ask you to ease your mind about Viscount Parkes. A past he has, but in compliment to your daughter, I have taken precautions that he can not circumvent. You also know that Georgiana is being courted by a handful of men? I have winnowed out the fortune seekers and have left three men of good standing, character, and mind. These all have been taken into mine, and Charles Bingley's confidence to ensure that they also regulate our Lord Parkes and guarantee nothing untoward occurs when Kitty is not under our personal purview," Darcy said.

Mr. Bennet looked up. Here father said, "Charles understands the seriousness?"

"I have made him fully aware of it, and he it was who found means to enlist the suitors of my sister into our confidence. Kitty is protected by respectable chaperones at all times, as are Mary and Georgiana. Have no worries there," Darcy said. Lizzy was assured he was correct else she would never have countenanced their going out into society. It was so different than that of Meryton that she would have worried otherwise.

"Yes," Mrs. Bennet said, "But the General. How does he fare?"

"Certainly, mother, there has been no mention of him as a casualty in the lists in *The Times*. For that, we can be thankful." Mr. Darcy paused for a moment. "When his letters dropped off, I found that I had no other correspondent within the army and struggled with how best to communicate to my cousin. Certainly your observations have proved correct, no one really has had word from him these three months or more." Lizzy knew Darcy was worried as well.

Mr. Bennet shifted, "But you were just telling me about..."

Mrs. Bennet saw that, and Lizzy too knew of what Mr. Bennet spoke, yet it was very recent. "Sorry father, I did not explain to you how I came upon the information." Darcy said for all of hem, "Just this Tuesday I received a letter from a new correspondent. Mr. Hurst has a friend, General Allen, whom he wrote to on my behalf, though I delicately guided his hand in the writing of the letter. And the Brigadier was kind enough to pay a social call upon my cousin and, as he put it, 'gave him a swift kick in the...'" Darcy smiled as he began the last, then she saw her mother's face.

Mrs. Bennet looked to Lizzy as Darcy abruptly stopped. "Fundament mother. Darcy showed me the letter. I believe Brigadier Allen pointed out how the Earl of M----K had the wherewithal to put a bee in the bonnet of the Viscount of Wellington that none of the family had heard from the General, and that could lead to censure from his peers, though I believe not many of Wellesley's commanders believe writing news to us here in Town to be of tremendous import, they do perform it as a duty," Lizzy elaborated and Darcy was able to resume the narrative.

"Where we stand now, is that mine Uncle and Aunt received a short letter yesterday. As Brigadier Allen said that they and we should. So I expect all of us to have a letter, perhaps not verbose, but some statement of his health these next few weeks," Darcy summarized the matter.

"But why has he stopped writing for so long?"

"My dear," Mr. Bennet responded to his wife, "I have tried to help you understand that a battle, and the General has seen a few now, leaves a man's soul pained. Death stalks violently upon those fields and for want of an inch and a miracle, each participant, the General included, faces that he too could become but a memory in such an instance." Darcy nodded. Mr. Bennet had explained this to him before and though previously he had thought little of the romance of battle, in terms, such as this, it was stripped of all its flowery prose.

"Oh, do not be such a high and mighty. Your father has been getting this way more and more now that Longbourn is so quiet. I am sure that all our cheerful letters have quite taken General Fitzwilliam out of himself and given him pleasure in knowing how we get on without him," Mrs. Bennet said.

Darcy cleared his throat, but Lizzy replied before he could speak, "Actually Mama, that seems to be the heart of the problem. What we have from Brigadier Allen, at least what he was candid enough to share, is that several of the officers, and now we must number our good cousin amongst them, have become heartsick for two fold reasons. One that as dear papa states, war is barbaric and has all the horrors that are beyond my imaginings. And the second, that we remind our loved ones with our silly writings just how much they miss by not being here amongst us.

"Not just the silly daily goings on," Lizzy continued, "But also all manner of simple joys such as walking the dog without fear that one shall be shot at, or that someone you are responsible for is not sleeping with a moth eaten blanket to cover himself and hasn't eaten a decent meal in a fortnight. That one can spend languorous hours over ones toilette after sleeping till two, as several of the dandies set do, is much missed in the bare fields of Spain and a military camp."

Darcy muttered and one could barely hear 'like Viscount Parkes.'

"I fathom that you believe that our letters make the man desolate, not joyous?" Mrs. Bennet said, with a shrewd insight.

The three others were astounded, "Oh don't be such puppies.

Why with your big eyes. Your aunt Gardiner told me that she thought this was the case, that the General had become desolate at the society he is no longer a part of, countered with the tragedy Mr. Bennet remind me of when I should bring the subject up. She advised me that I should not allow you to get me in a bind or else I should cry and had me confront the notion many weeks ago. Your aunt, I fear, is one of the few I trust to tell me just what Mr. Bennet means when he instructs me." Lizzy had not thought her mother paid much attention to Mrs. Gardiner these many years.

"It is so, and that guidance of our good sister makes her ever more endearing. I should shudder to think where my mind would have wondered these many years, without someone whom we have both been able to seek counsel with," Mr. Bennet said.

"You do go on Mr. Bennet. Now that you see that your aunt knows the right of it, what ever shall we do? Mr. Darcy, Lizzy. Surely the General is in need of some cheer?"

"Oh Mama," Lizzy looked away. Despite her aunt's edifications, Mrs. Bennet still was obtuse.

"I do not think there is much in our power to do, Mrs. Bennet," Darcy spoke into the silence. "My cousin showed that ever present family pride as he withheld his letters to us so that he would not be forced to dwell on the source of his discouragement. It is unknown whether he has read any of the letters we have sent him since he fell silent. Though we wish it otherwise, there is no way to coerce him to correspond. Even the tactic we have employed with General Allen is no guarantee beyond the letter the Earl received."

"Well that is a fine way to look at things indeed. I must say that you all have left us with little in our basket. Why I am sure that his letters to Kitty were what kept her occupied and free of the advances of such a fast man," Mrs. Bennet said.

Elizabeth looked back to her mother, "Mother, Viscount Parkes is not a fast man."

"Certainly not, who ever said, but I am certain that he is, what do you people say, 'a dead bore.'" Mr. Bennet looked at his wife and realized that she had repeated something he had heard as they sat in the coach traveling to Town.

"Lizzy, I believe your mama is foxing you something dreadful," her father said with a smile.

"La sirrah, why ever would I fox my own daughter." Mrs. Bennet had a small smile upon her lips.

"My dear, with such five vexatious children as you have reared, and now the grandmother of two and a third on the way, as Jane and Charles have announced, I can only admire you as you get some of your own back. Your mama is funning," Mr. Bennet said, very certain of himself.

Mrs. Bennet looked at her husband, a pose she often gave him, "And now you've gone and spoilt it."

The couple held their respective faces in place for some seconds before they broke the stern visage with laughter that Darcy joined in, followed last by his wife. "One of the best things for us old married parents has been getting you young misses married off. Then pawning the last two upon you, giving us a home to ourselves. It has been so long, why, I think we had quite forgotten what it is was like before we had you children," Mr. Bennet said, and smiled at his bride.

The Darcy's had no time alone to themselves for they had been escorted on their wedding tour by the Bingleys. They then returned to the guardianship of Georgiana, and the sponsorship of both Kitty and Mary as such occasion demanded. The arrival of little Fitzwilliam ensured that they would be surrounded by family for the rest of their lives together.

"I should think that these last two that you have desired married, shall be upon us soon. When they ride in the Park, they return near this hour," Darcy remarked.

"Very good then. I shall desire some time with my daughter to give her a proper scold." Mrs. Bennet said, and now Elizabeth struggled to decipher if her mother was at all seriousness.

Mrs. Bennet did get her wish later that day after the party had dressed for the theater. That conversation certainly did seem to affect Kitty and other members of the party were able to note it. "Kitty you are too quiet. Why look at the finery of Lady Melrose. Is not that taffeta a little ragged there at her left sleeve? Why, it will be all over Town tomorrow." Georgiana tried to get her companion to speak in a sentence instead of the monosyllables

Kitty had uttered since leaving her audience with her mama.

"Yes," Kitty said in acknowledgement of the frayed sleeve, and that was all. Mrs. Bennet, if one observed her visage, would be said to have a smug look about her, and Mr. Bennet scowled behind his wife while trying to concentrate on something his son in law was saying. Elisabeth had her own arm firmly wrapped about her next younger sister's, refraining Mary from walking next to Kitty and having any of her own conversation with the Bennet's fourth daughter. Long acquaintance with the two sisters about her, gave Elizabeth the knowledge that keeping Mary in a position where she could not make a commentary on her family, would be a blessing.

So Georgiana was left to accompany Kitty, closely, as they entered their box at the theater. Georgiana knew something troubled her friend, but was also wise to know not to confront her on it.

It was the second, the last intermission of the evening when Viscount Parkes accompanied by a few friends came forward to be presented to the senior Bennets and renew his familiarity with the others of the party. Mr. Darcy was all proper as he introduced all to each other.

Mrs. Bennet was surprising herself, "Yes Viscount, one has heard many things about you, but most how you have taken a shine to our precious jewels."

His smile was bigger than any other man Lizzy had ever seen sport, "Your precious jewel outshone any I had seen in the shops at Oxford Street, Mrs. Bennet, when she first came to my attention. So striking, I completely stopped what I was doing, though luckily my horse knew what it was about as I saw this lovely complement to your artistry as a parent, in the Park. I endeavored to meet her and have also come to know her sisters. That such gems were mined under your gentle hands, attests that I now have met the finest of all England's, um, miners…"

Some laugher, though that seemed forced, came on top of these words. Viscount Parkes clearly looked to Kitty, while she looked away. "What say, Mr. Darcy. A man who flatters me. And also pays particular attention to one of my daughters. Should I not find joy?" Mrs. Bennet said.

Mr. Darcy was shaking his head as Mr. Bennet turned his back and held his hand to his face, before turning back. Kitty still looked away.

"Well Parkes, I think that Mrs. Bennet is on to you. As you know she has become wise with three daughters happily married, is that not correct Mama?" Darcy saw her nod with a thin smile and so felt confident to continue at her game, "Now she puts you to the test. You are to be audited and watched in certain ambitions that you seem to have formed lately without having said anything along those lines. But you know this is what every good Mama would do. Kitty surely knows this as she has seen a full season. Though I think this war has played some havoc with the normal course of a young lady's season." Lizzy wondered if her husband was correct. If their friends who wore uniforms for England were in Town, instead of away, would things be different.

"Indeed it has," Mrs Bennet added. "Why I have one son who is a member of the military and Darcy's cousin, who is close to us, is serving under Wellington now."

"Yes, General Fitzwilliam. Kitty has mentioned him and his particular kindnesses," the Viscount said.

"We are all very fond and concerned about our General. He has done much fighting and been wounded countless times. It is quite alarming." Mrs. Bennet looked ill. Kitty still had not turned back to the conversation. Her hands tightly clutched her program and fan.

The conversation had gone from the Viscount's admiration for Kitty to a discussion of another man. An incomparable other man, as he was off in the Peninsula putting his life in danger. Knowing that this was a time to stop, since regaining the conversation back to himself was unlikely, the Viscount withdrew.

"My word Darcy, is that the best of society these days? Why you showed twice as much confidence as that one." Mrs. Bennet said as she leaned to her son-in-law.

Darcy smiled graciously "Indeed mum, I perceived instantly that the prize was so great, only the grandest amount of showmanship would have you gift Eliza to me."

Mrs. Bennet looked down her nose at him as she paused, "Yes

you are quite right, only the most deserving and diligent of suitors stood a chance. Why I can not think why our cousin Mr. Collins should think I ever encouraged him in his advances. Tsk, in any event, the best man won the prize for I can't think of Lizzy ever being happier. Now can we see that young man making Kitty the same?"

Darcy nodded sagely and caught his wife's eye. "Early innings mum, early innings yet. Perhaps the Viscount will grow more enticing with time."

"Not should he have twice as much as you Darcy. Not twice as much. Young so and so is very full...Oh Kitty, we just were discussing that this production is not half as good as what we saw that night when the Colonel took us to the Opera? Do you remember. How happy those times were. Why he was so gracious to have us up to the house whilst he recovered from his wounds back, what, now two years ago. Why so much has happened. Jane with two children now, Lizzy and Lydia each with one. The time does pass quickly, is that not right Mr. Bennet?" Her mother took liberties in counting for Jane's second baby was a few months away.

"Indeed Mrs. Bennet. Indeed. Why it seems but an instant since I was courting you..."

"Oh Mr. Bennet, you make me blush. Such a thing to say to a woman who is a grandmother now four times. An instant indeed," Mrs. Bennet said.

Lizzy saw the little smile Mr. Bennet allowed himself at bringing such pleasure to his wife.

"Dear General, it has been such an age since you have written. And I find it has been far too long since I have written also. So much has happened these last months, I just don't know where to begin. I know that everyone we know has sent letters to ensure that you know how you are missed in our society.

There are so many fine men I have met in uniform that I do wonder why your General Wellesley will not let you return to us for even the smallest bit of time. I believe though that soon we shall see you. Our new friend, Viscount Parkes says that it will be so. He and several of his friends have spent much time with us these last months and even today we spent a wonderful day on an excursion to Somerset House. Viscount Parkes and his friends do so much in entertaining Mary, Georgiana and I, it is quite wonderful. Why, we see them nearly every other day. Sometimes we see the Viscount and his gentlemen friends twice in one day. Such was the case just yesterday.

I am sure that my mother related her excursion here to Town in her last letter to you, for she had told me she would. For near a month it was good to have my parents here with us. I even believe your cousin Mr. Darcy has come to appreciate at least one side of my mother. They did seem to spend much time together and I believe spent even more time with little William. He is a darling boy and has taken to saying such cute things. My mother even spent time teaching him your name. I hope I have not spoiled a surprise, so please act accordingly should the occasion arise. Mama however spent time holding a plate of an officer and had William say your name, 'General Fitzwilliam.' Though we have not discussed it, I begged Darcy to allow me to peruse your family tree. I wanted to ensure that none of your illustrious for- bearers had named a son William. Though I found to my chagrin that as recently as your father's grandpapa was so named. I pray that you set in stone that your children and theirs, through eternity shall not be labeled with such. I shudder to think that should my father have been blessed with a son, as you know my mother's dearest wish, that such a to do would have been if a Bennet would be saddled with Benjamin and thus Ben Bennet could have haunted the corridors of Rugby or Cambridge.

Mary remarked that she thought it strange how Mama did not teach William to say her uncle Wickham's name, but I feel Mama was being quite pragmatic. It is much more likely the lad will meet you, and not his uncle, I should think. None of us have seen Captain Wickham since his wedding though, we did see Lydia early in the sea- son. She came to Town for a fortnight to shop, but left her little baby, George, at home with the Captain. I should want to teach little Will, to say Georgie Porgie, but I am sure that all would give me a scold. Well perhaps not you or Mr. Darcy, but Lizzy would say I was un- kind, and Lydia would have her revenge by teaching the little one, who by account of Lydia's maid is quite a round butterball, to utter Silly Willie, or some such and the two cousins would take an instant dislike to the other. I should think, though, that no matter what I am to do as an auntie, the outcome would be the same... Our William will grow to have the best of both his parents, and little George will be hard pressed to overcome what his parents have blessed him with. (On pain of a severe set down, you are sworn to secrecy on these thoughts of mine.)

I find this letter to be such a length it is as if you sat beside me and I told you of all my little gossips and conceits. Stray thoughts and deep concerns. Lizzy said I must write you and write you and write you. Oh, so many times, and I hope I have done it justice. I, and we all do miss you. Why without you Bingley and Darcy and even Mr. Hurst offer little for us young girls to laugh and be gay with. Viscount Parkes and his set do make us laugh. Mr. Darcy and the other men of our family do not get on all that well and so I know if you were here in Town with us now, all would be happy. I wish you well and safe and long for your return to all our company."

A MAN OF GOOD BREEDING?

"By your leave," the Viscount bowed and retreated from the study.

Mr. Bennet sat back and shook his head. He sat this way for surely what must have been a quarter of an hour. As the clock in the hall sounded the hour, he stirred. Roused from his pondering, he penned two notes and called for Mrs. Hall. She would have the boy to run them to catch the evening post, another would take a letter to his son Bingley's house.

"Mr. Bennet, oh Mr. Bennet, you fill me with such pleasure," Mrs. Bennet said.

"Indeed, Mrs. Bennet, and how is that?" he asked his wife.

"To dine at Netherfield, why Jane just had us to dine the night before last," she said.

"But, Mrs. Bennet, we dine with the Bingleys twice a week I am sure." He nodded sagely. Charles had responded instantly to his letter that day.

"But we always dine on Sunday and Thursday. I can not think of the last time Jane had us dine on a Tuesday," his wife said.

Mr. Bennet paused as he straightened the shirt collar before he placed his cravat around his neck. Not as fancy as the younger generation would do, but a serviceable piece of linen. "Why surely we dined on a Tuesday but three weeks ago, if not a month. Was not Mr. Bingley and Mr. Hurst entertaining a friend from Town that weekend? A Sir Foretly?"

"Yes, Sir Gerald Foretly and his wife. Particular friends from the club of the Hurst's I believe." As Mrs. Bennet had not been invited to Netherfield to meet these Foretly's, and had used the pretext of visiting her grandchildren so that she could meet Lady Foretly in Jane's dayroom on that day, she did have a little to add.

"Yes that is the last Tuesday we dine with them, though why Jane should open her house to such a disagreeable woman and monstrous children, I shall never know." She continued, "But Mr. Bennet, this sudden desire to dine at Netherfield, how splendid you are."

"I have another surprise for you my dear."

"Yes Mr. Bennet. Why, you are quite the generous one, with all these surprises," she said. He knew that she was aware Viscount Parkes had called upon him earlier.

He smiled, as was his way, "Don't be to hasty m'dear until you know what I have in store. I have asked the Darcys to come to us here, and I have asked the Gardiners also to come down to Longbourn. I should think that the Darcys will be gladly welcomed to Longbourn, but I needs must consult with Fitzwilliam, your brother and Charles all together about an important matter and 'twere best done quickly."

Mrs. Bennet showed all happiness at the idea of all coming to Meryton, "All the family here, it shall be very nice. Why Mr. Bennet I can not fathom what has come over you. Surprises and gathering the family all together. Why you are a changed man," she said. He was sure she was jumping to conclusions.

Mr. Bennet nodded and finished with his cravat. But when his wife turned away to have Mrs. Hall help her with her hair, he found himself shaking his head, troubled by the day's earlier development. The Bingleys proved that night to be very cordial and Charles was quite agreeable to helping his wife's father with the difficulty that lay before him.

"Dear General, I understand how desperate the New Year has been for you, while it has been so long now since we last saw you. Your last letter was so brief I was convinced that you were writing, once again, upon the eve of a battle. I saw your mother, the Countess, later that week and she compared her letter from you with mine and we realized you had writ near enough the same to each of us.

I know that I have become a very poor correspondent of late, but I am sure you can guess why. I wrote somewhat of it in my last letter. How Viscount Parkes was so attentive to my sister, Georgiana and I that we were having a very great season indeed. It was a surprise that when we returned to Pemberley after the season ended, who should visit for a long weekend, but the Viscount.

Oh Mr. Darcy was not at all happy at that, and neither was Lizzy. I should think that if the acquaintance had been smaller between the Viscount and our household, he would have been asked to stay in Lambton. But it was so fun and gay while he was here, at least until the last day of his stay that long weekend. Then there became a tenseness between he and Mr. Darcy, that was even more prevalent then it had been before.

As you will remember, a previous occasion at Pemberley Sir Fairfax did me an honor which I could not, in good conscience, grant him joy. Now that he has offered for Caroline Bingley, though all has ended happily there. Now on this day at Pemberley, dear Henry offered for me, and I did accept him, though my sister was quick to point out that my father's blessing was a requisite.

Henry was quick to be off to Longbourn to seek my Father's approval and Mr. Darcy bundled us all up with intemperate speed to also follow to Longbourn. I was torn between waiting for my heart's desire to return to me, and for my Father's decision. I did not know whether we would pass my Viscount in his haste to return to me. Lizzy, however, was quite perturbed with all this and set me down for a scold.

For the first time, ever, she gave me a scold. Well, she has given me scolds, before, but this time it was quite severe. Mary, of course, echoed her, but so did Georgiana, which was quite unexpected. How they all believed that the Viscount was quite an unsuitable match. I knew that Mama would be happy at the notion, I marrying a peer. So our journey to Longbourn, though fraught with coldness, I knew, would be redeemed by my Mama's happiness.

We arrived to find, though, that Papa had not given an answer but wanted time to consider whether to acquiesce to the proposal. Without his blessing, I could not run away to Gretna Green, nor do I think that Henry would carry me off. For, at times, he is consumed by propriety. As things stand presently, Father took counsel with my brothers, and decided that he would consider the proposal one year hence.

I can not believe that Father, of anyone, would give heed to the dreadful rumors that are spread about Henry, but he said that a year with nary one ill word raised against Henry's character and he would be a fit husband. I spent three days arguing with Father, but all, even Mama, were arrayed against me. Aunt Gardiner, who was staying at Longbourn summed matters up, 'A man may reform from Rake to Respected, but jumping willy-nilly to his side is ill advised, and you my dear have all these who love you to ensure the advice you receive is wise. If it were another Rake, such as our good friend the General (here she

*referred to you sir,) we would have nothing but joy for we know un-
derneath his rakish behavior, a solid man is formed.*

*'Of your Viscount, he has a reputation that is blackened, and we
all watch to see that he has redeemed himself through his own actions,
rather than the act of marrying a woman of good repute to do so.'
Finding I could not argue, any more, nor cry myself silly, for I have
given that up, I was forced to acquiesce. Now though I may meet the
Viscount when supervised by Lizzy, Jane or Aunt Gardiner. Georgiana and Mary are not considered of enough gravitas to be my duenna.
If ever there were another maid in all of England so beset upon as I,
I do not know who it could be."*

The General took out the letter again and read it. He had read
it up to three times each day these last two months since it had
arrived. He had also began corresponding again to all his loved
ones back in London. All, but Catherine Bennet. That had not
gone unnoticed. He had received a second letter a month prior
scolding him for writing everyone but she. Then, another that
implored him to write for his letters to his kith and kin had held
little back.

A most recent one to Lizzy had related the lack of good hy-
giene after so long at war which led to his fears not only for the
men contracting disease, but of he also. The letter rambled on
about not only his fears about the enemy running him through in
the next encounter, but just war itself being an enemy which
could defeat him, in detail.

Kitty's letter, as many another, led him to believe that Lizzy
had shared many passages with all his friends. He also was led to
believe that his own observations regarding the future betrothal
of Kitty had not been shared with any but Darcy. The General,
however, should not have been in any state of mind to brood
upon the young lady.

He had no claim to her, and she had very little to recommend
her to him. They had spent a brief time together in Meryton, and
then again in London while he recuperated. He had no ties to her
and, she, none to him. That her future marriage would be a vexation to his loved cousin Darcy was one that would do the man
good. He had too easy a life and having turmoil caused by his

relations was good for his soul.

"Damn, but, Darcy has done well," he said aloud, though none would hear him in his tent. He glanced through the opening and saw the siegeworks of Badajoz. Soon enough, perhaps even the following day, they would assault the city. Wellington had said as much. General Fitzwilliam's division had been making preparations these last two days and the men grew anxious with worry. Soon enough the dance with death would be upon them. The General bent to write another letter.

This time, he would write to Kitty. He would tell her some things her young ears had not heard and should if she were to be now treated as an adult. He had written more than six times since her letter of engagement to each of her family or their friends. Now he took his quill and gave her his mind.

> *"I come now to a passage that I see you crushing and tossing away, for the truths I have told you of myself I will expand with the truths I know of your paramour and his set. In my society, there were both men of good will and temper, such as your brother Darcy and Bingley. They will tell you well of me. But you know that is not all of who I am, as I have related. I am the second son of an Earl. I have had mistresses. I have named them to you in the earlier passages, and I have little regrets in my time with these women.*
>
> *There are other societies to which I became a member, and to which I thank the lord I am no longer a part of. That I had the sense to decide that they were too fast, even for myself. I came into contact with your Viscount in just such a set. He is my junior by more than five years, though his cousin, Baron DeWitt is of an age, and is a friend. The Baron is the son of your Viscount's Mother's brother. He came into his title when we left school, and despite that, DeWitt went on to university. Parkes was sent down on his third day. Something that he is rather proud of. That he caused the disgrace of a Don's wife is not common knowledge. I believe he spreads it about that he lost a bet and was seen without clothes on in the commons. That too is true.*
>
> *I tell you this as but first, that you should know fully what I know, what others think they know, and wish to save you from embarrassment. Should you hold your lover to such a high standard you should ensure that he answer to all his faults. Mine are the three mistresses,*

the one night of gambling that cost me six hundred pounds, and thus never repeated beyond a five pound stake, and being caught drunk before I took the colours, nine times. Since then, I never have more than a half bottle of wine, three drinks, or any thing that will cause me to loose my faculties.

That cannot be said of Parkes. Even here, as I sit at Badajoz, I hear tales of him. He has another cousin, Major Parkes, for they share the same grandfather, and it being made known that his cousin was to marry my cousins' sister, he has presumed on the alliance to make himself known to me. He is in the Guards of course, and he shows that it is a good fit. He was with your fiancée-to-be but a month before he came to us, here. This but five months ago. He says he has met you. After a night at the Opera where your mama was with you, the gentleman went to their club and the seven of them drank, if I have it correct, five cases of wine and champagne, nine bottles of scotch, and each a half a dozen yards of ale. The Major assures me he was quite sick the next day, as was the Viscount. Toasts to you and your Mama and the other ladies of our acquaintance were numerous. I had to remind the Major that should he ever have the audacity to do the same in my presence I should be sending my seconds to ask for the time and weapons as I would be calling him out. One does not do this.

You are a woman, and I am not one to scold you for having a heart that has made a choice. I should be the last to do such as my heart has been locked away by the Ocean as I spend my days here with the sounds of guns, and the smells of death. I give you what little advice, or knowledge that I can. Your family, some of whom we know to be wiser than either of us, have your happiness to heart, and, they, you should give some weight to. I have more I could write about the Viscount and his set, for twice I found myself with them. From all accounts of my friends, those events were tame. I ask for you to be sure in not only your heart, but in your mind that the course you desire, that you are counseled by nearly all against, is the correct course. Use the time, the remaining months to think with your head, and not be led by your heart, for this is the wisest and most important decision you may make."

"What an infuriating man," Kitty remarked to Georgiana.

"I would say that you have finally come to your senses, dearest friend, and speak of your intended fiancée. But I am sure that you refer to my cousin the General, as you read his letter once more."

Kitty smiled at her closest companion, "And that I have said the same a dozen times this last fortnight."

"That you should know his character traits so well, on such little acquaintance, I should wonder at. How strong is your affection for my cousin, the General?" Georgiana asked.

Kitty looked at Georgiana and there was no smile, "Do not jest. Henry would be little amused by such." Kitty referred to Viscount Parkes.

Georgiana smiled now, "And good for that! Your Henry is too much the peer and too little the man, in my opinion, and I will say it again despite what pains it causes. The General, though not so his elder brother, is quite the reverse as well you know." Georgiana having lost her temper, quickly turned from her friend, then turned back after she was composed. "Forgive me, dear heart, for losing my temper. I worry for you so, and I worry about this alliance of yours."

Kitty bit back her words, and then after a pause of some time staring towards Georgiana, nodded. "Yes I know you worry, but do not fret, my heart tells me all is right with my Henry."

Georgiana shook her head and there was another silence that stretched beyond brief, "Come, we must choose another subject else we shall be at odds again. I remind myself I have promised amongst all our family to not distress you."

Kitty mouthed thanks but there was only silence as Georgiana stood up, "Oh, what for another subject? Perhaps we should go to the library and choose a book, Shakespeare's sonnets, or some such, that we may divert ourselves," Kitty said to make conversation.

"We cannot. The post came but a quarter hour ago and Mr. Darcy has locked himself therein."

Georgiana paced and then walked towards the window to look out upon the square. Kitty found herself unfolding the letter from the General once again, and started to read it once more. "Oh, when will Lizzy and Mary return. Such a dreary day. And, nothing on our social calendar. We should pay a call on someone. Perhaps Caroline Bingley. We can listen to her regale us about her latest plan for married life," Georgiana said.

Kitty looked up. She said, "Sir Fairfax will marry her." Kitty's expression was wasted on the back of Georgina.

"Yes, but when. One delay I can fathom, readily, for being called to the country the week before the nuptials is plausible enough. But, a second delay, because he had broken out in spots and could not leave the sickroom. And no date to reschedule, though Caroline has all sorts of new plans for her house and the redecorating goes on apace. It is such a wonder," Georgiana said. She now sounded like a Bennet sister, Kitty reflected.

Georgiana turned into the room and witnessed her brother in the doorway. "You two young ladies, at one time, had more civil things to occupy your conversation with, I am sure." Mr. Darcy paused. *The Times* was rolled up and clutched in his hands together. His coat sat high on his right shoulder, not snugged down to his frame.

He continued, before Georgiana could beg forgiveness, "Your sisters, they are out? I have news and best you hear it now, for soon all our society will know it." He looked down at his feet and realized that he choked the paper. "It is Stephen, General Fitzwilliam. He has been wounded at the taking of Badajoz. Apparently, their were many casualties in the assault. This was followed by rioting after our troops had captured the castle.

"It is in the paper, that is all I know. I must ride to Horse Guards Parade and enquire if more is known. Stephen is listed as severely wounded, which I fear is better then saying he is dead, but it gives little hope." Kitty observed that Mr. Darcy wrung the paper again.

"That is all?" Georgiana asked. Kitty could hear how worried she was.

Kitty knew she herself could not speak. Kitty was sure she was even more nervous than Georgiana.

"I leave at once and shall endeavor to find all that is known." Mr. Darcy turned and before either of the girls could say a word, he left.

Georgiana sat down hurriedly. She turned to look at Kitty, her lip quivering and tears laying rivulets upon her cheek. Kitty however stared at her own hands. So tightly were they clasped together that the letter from the General was crumpled, and it took her a month of moments to notice and relax her grip upon it. She deliberately pulled the letter into some semblance of form and carefully used her hand to iron it flat. Then began reading it again, very slowly and with dedication, "...Infuriating man. Infuriating man!"

'Lizzy says that a man with a limp shows a certain longevity of will, for all elders walk with the use of a cane, and that you should not be ashamed by it. As your friend I write this to you so that you will be ready for the society of your loved ones when you return to us. Mr. Darcy writes us that your humor has a dark side to it, but, as you have recuperated in the week he has been with you he informs us, it has turned somewhat warmer.

I am unsure if you have shown him your heart, or, if you are putting up a good front. That he has gone to fetch you, you must allow is a sign that he cares, and that Mr. Hurst, Mr. Hurst of all men, accompanied him to help with the arrangements speaks well of Mr. Hurst. But, I think he, also, fled his sister Caroline whose impending marriage raises its head once more. Or, not, as Sir Fairfax, one hears, also volunteered to accompany the gentlemen to help with the arrangements to bring you home. As you see, Sir Fax is not with you. The minute Mr. Hurst returns to Town, which, of course, shall be when you do, we shall finally see Ms. Caroline wed, or, not, should Sir Fax find means of avoiding the altar once more.

One does wonder if I had accepted his offer, though we both know that was never to happen, if he would have been as irresolute? Here in Town, that is not our only story to relate. I must allow how spending time with Caroline is more of a trial than usual at this juncture. Many mornings, Jane arrives with the children and spends a good deal of the day with us. You can speculate all you wish if this means she is avoiding calling. You, I am sure, have already guessed what I believe.

After the news of your injuries arrived, and Mr. Darcy left for the Continent, our society took on further additions. Your aunt, Lady Catherine, and cousin Anne have come to Town. They are staying at your parent's townhome. We see her quite often, as your mother has invited us at least twice a week and sometimes three times each week, for different reasons. Just last night we were there for dinner and the Gardiners had been invited by your Father, also. I believe that it is your Father who desires that the dinner table be kept full and lively. Anne confided in me that, should there be no social calls for dinner, the Earl will dine at his club. She said the Countess seems less than civil to your Father after such.

Anne was confined to her room for a week, once they arrived here in Town, and Dr. Jaspar attends her each day, even now that she is well enough to go out. She does not go to the Park for riding, or in a carriage. Your aunt ensures that when in society, it is approved drawing rooms such as ours here, or the Bingleys, both of which I regard as surprising, for I remember her irritation the night she came to Longbourn before Lizzy and Darcy's marriage. Now, that day seems so long ago. It was but a few days later that Lizzy told us of her love for Mr. Darcy, and then you arrived for the wedding. Oh, what happy days they were. Why, my cousins, the Gardiner children, were speaking about it and your horse, Night, just last week. There has been no news of your most loved horse, and they ask as to its health also.

My parents have written that they intend to come to town when a date has been ascertained for your return. Mother has become a great correspondent of late, for I receive a letter once a week from her. Father writes, every third day, with some instruction. I am ever doing errands for him and his library. I am frustrated that he does not ask for Mary's help or Lizzy's as they have a more natural bent for this task. But, I am ever at the booksellers' stores and stalls, looking to add to his collection."

* * *

"I see that Kitty realizes that the Bennets have her well in hand. I am surprised that she does not write me again of Parkes, for her previous letters have praised him tremendously," Stephen said.

Hurst choked, Darcy looking at him sharp, "Yes, I should expect my sister to sing his praises to you, once more, after you related certain traits of character and some of his less salubrious past actions. I believe some of the passages from your letter were related to me, more than once an evening, upon occasion..."

"Posh, you know the young miss would ramble on and on about that damned letter. Why, she in her way, was just as annoying as Caroline has become over this marriage to Fax... Ha! You smiled Fitzwilliam. I saw it. You must be coming round, I dare say," Hurst laughed. Much pleased with himself, Stephen was sure.

Stephen let the smile slip, and took another step. The pain of which ensured a grimace, instead of any thought of pleasure. The cane took a great deal of his weight. He took another step, a third, and finally reached the chair. Gripping the side and then, an arm, he eased himself into it and beckoned the serving maid to deliver his ale.

"So, Kitty related my last letter to our set?" His teeth clenched, he talked through them, giving rise to a hissing sound.

Darcy replied, "Yes, though, some, she kept private. Many of the letters she has received from you she has shared some, or all, and some none at all. Is this not what you intended?" Darcy gave him time to relax from his pain.

The General said, "Indeed, though my last letter had some of Parkes' history that, perhaps, others should not have heard."

Hurst brought over another ale to replace the one that the General had drained. "Many of us had tales or anecdotes about the Viscount, though yours had the validity of something other than being second hand..."

Darcy sat across from the General, "I believe Parkes had found some way of dismissing previous stories, that were related to Kitty, as of little consequence, having reformed his character. Or, that the tale had grown since the occurrence and, due to envy, his detractors had made it seem quite worse than it had been in actuality. With what you wrote, he could scarcely deny it."

When the General had sat his glass down, Darcy nodded, once more, and waited. The General struggled to his feet with an audible grunt. He then began his slow walk to the writing desk and back. "You understand that I could do this without you both watching me," Stephen said.

Darcy's head jerked back, "Yes, we realize that, but I am sure that Hurst will agree, we have little better to do then spend our day with you."

Hurst had buried himself in his glass of ale.

"Ensuring that I exercise," Stephen said.

"Yes well," Darcy made a small comment.

Hurst now looked at Darcy, "What your cousin does not want to admit is that, before we left Town, he was instructed to see to your recovery. Even my wife spoke to it, your ward, her friends, Mrs. Darcy, sister Bingley, of course your mother..."

"Hurst could recite every woman of our acquaintance, but this would bore you. The ladies, who worry for you, task us to return you hale and hearty to their care," his cousin said.

The General had reached his seat once more, and settled into it with satisfaction. "Well, certainly, I am better. Soon we can embark upon our journey home," though Stephen was unsure if he wished to return to England.

Hurst nodded and tapped the left pocket of his waistcoat with his right hand. "I go to negotiate with a Captain Samuels tomorrow. We should sail, before a fortnight is past, when Captain Samuels next returns."

"Dearest wife, we are due now to take ship, in three days, for home. This letter shall be aboard the last ship before ours is made ready, so, after this letter, we shall be the next to return from Iberia. Hurst has been a good companion for myself and Stephen. His humor and ease helps Stephen to smile. It masks many moments of pain that Stephen carries.

This is something that all should prepare themselves for. Stephen still is unable to sleep peacefully the whole night through and takes laudanum to ease the pain. He has lessened his need for it, but still uses it each night. His doctor says that, with time, and this could be many more months, Stephen will see his need diminish.

I am encouraged in his recovery so far. His right leg, saved from amputation and of some use, though he shall always walk with his cane, and his left leg shall always bear the signs of his wounding. I have witnessed the changing of his bandages, now finished, and must relate that it is an unpleasant sight. Better, though, to have him alive, with such wounds.

His gait troubles him still, and he is rather embarrassed by it. I believe, no, I know and shall not coddle the truth between us. Stephen will not be venturing into society, nor wishing for society to come to him because of it. He wishes to remain in seclusion until his gait is near enough normal to be of no concern. Hurst and I have tried to talk against this view, but we have failed. We shall return to England and take Stephen to his new county home that the Earl purchased for him. There he will recover further without visitors but for family. He has made us aware that he considers me family, but would be uncomfortable if you, or the boys, were to accompany me to Silverponds as he has named what was Combe Laud.

Stephen spent some time explaining himself on this, and assured me it was not a slight to you. He fully intends to exclude himself from Aunt Catherine de Bourgh for some while, and would do the same from his mother, but knows he can not deny her visitation. He believes a note to his brother will forestall the Viscountess from visiting, and thus aside from mine aunt, the Countess, no woman shall be seen at Silverponds. He is that particular at the present. I believe this shall pass.

Your last letter had little of news of the boys in it, and I scold you for it, for aside from the anguish of separation from you, our sons are missed most. I shall do my best to stop briefly in London, though I fear we shall but pass through quickly and your next letter to me will best be addressed to Silverponds."

"The General does not want the presence of ladies! How dare he? Why I have been inquired of by everyone in society about the General's health and recovery and to be remembered to him these last three months as if I were some special friend." Kitty was all excitement and paced back and forth. Reading Lizzy's letter had worked her into a state. "Even Henry has cried enough, for he is somewhat jealous, I believe, with some satisfaction."

"He has indeed?" Lizzy reached for her letter and folded it neatly. "Whyever should Viscount Parkes be affronted at your care and consideration for such a friend, and sorely wounded friend as, the General?" Lizzy knew that the Viscount was due to pay a social call later that day. She did not look forward to the event. "Never mind that. When Viscount Parkes attends later to-day I am sure we shall hear his opinions on the matter."

"You wrong him Lizzy..." Kitty started.

Mary made a sound, "Oh Kitty how can you say that. The Viscount lets his opinions be known on every subject that is discussed." Lizzy was always taken by surprise when Mary's common sense was rendered at the perfect instance.

Kitty looked down, then back to her sisters. "It does not signify." She paused, for the briefest of times, while shaking her head. "In any event we can not tolerate this attitude of shame from the General. There is no help for it, we shall journey to Silverponds and rally him out of it."

"Kitty!" Georgiana sounded mortified.

Mary covered her mouth.

Lizzy noted when all three of the younger ladies turned to her, that they once again expected her to solve their problems. "We shall not. Why, I can concede your thought as valued, for the General should not let this feeling that a disfiguring wound is a humiliation. My Fitzwilliam would have let me know if such a course is one which he would have me pursue, or allow you to."

Kitty looked to her sister, "I understood that from your husband's letter also. However, I am going to ignore it and journey to Silverponds. Once there, I shall set up the house for General Stephen's return. When he arrives I shall berate him to accept that there is nothing less about him because he has received this wound. I shall not leave until he believes it and acts as our friend of old." The look on Kitty's face was not that of a child in any particular. She was a mature woman now.

"And how shall you do that?" Lizzy said. "I wonder how you shall journey to Silverponds, for it is easily more than forty miles from London."

"Ah, I understand that I shall not have leave to ask for the carriage." Kitty smiled broadly, "But, you must realize that since you, Lydia and Jane were married, Father has given Mary and I an allowance that I have been able to save, for you are kind enough to pay for most of my expenses. I have nearly thirty pounds accumulated and can use that to pay for my journey, in comfort, I am sure."

Lizzy nodded, "If I should forbid you to go?"

Mary had put her hand over her face. Kitty was undeterred, and, shaking her head, "I shall defy you. And further, if you were to write Father to also deny me, I should disobey him. Perhaps this is unlike the families' opinions about Viscount Parkes. Your opposition, there, I have submitted to. Here, however, I am sure you believe me to be right. We know of other officers and men who have returned wounded, many of them have a hard time returning to society. But, all good society has accepted their situations."

"Not all," Georgiana said. Lizzy could agree their were a few people they knew who were of such small mind.

This caused Kitty to say, "Yes, there are some whose wounds cause some accustoming to. The General may have such and we must go and assure him of our affection and that we will think of him as the same man we have always thought him. That amongst our society, he is not only a hero, but an integral part of it."

"Very well, go and pack. Mary, Georgiana do you wish to accompany Kitty?"

Their answers left Georgiana packing to go to Silverponds, and Mary readying for a stay at Netherfield where she would join the Bingleys who had retreated there until the week of Caroline's wedding. Lizzy, too, packed for she would continue to chaperone the girls who were in her charge. Her one significant pleasure of that day was the note she left for Viscount Parkes, turning him away from the house that was now become empty to him. It took less than two hours to arrange for the ladies to start their way on the road to Silverponds.

SILVERPONDS

"It is a nice prospect, and not overly large, as has been said. Manageable I am sure," Stephen said.

"Yes, house staff of nine, I believe, with seven serviceable rooms at a stretch. Library is intimate and should provide comfort and solace, though I believe you will need a fire there throughout winter," Darcy said. Hurst had left them in London but promised to visit after the wedding of Caroline had finally been concluded, now, planned for a fortnight hence, but one could not be sure that Sir Fairfax would keep to that schedule.

It was some four hundred yards of park from the lane to the manor. Built, originally, at the end of the reign of Charles II. An addition was added behind the right side during the first George, and then a later addition returning back so the house was shaped in a giant U, around a courtyard. The courtyard was over twenty yards itself on one side, and nearly thirty on the length of the main house.

"It is a quarter of the size of Pemberley, perhaps smaller," Stephen said as he took in the entirety of his new home.

"It is just such a property as I would hope to acquire should I have had to find a home for myself. There is a river beyond the stables there, and fifteen or twenty tenant cottages on the property. This, and nine or ten other landholdings, along with the holdings of Sargrave just down the road, make up the seat of Borethampton. The member is in his fifties and perhaps you could stand for his seat one day," Darcy said.

"Darcy, a life of politics? I should never. Besides I shall not be venturing into public for quite some time." Stephen rubbed his right leg. As long as there was no sudden jostling, there was not much pain.

The carriage neared the entry stairs of the hall, and Darcy could see the servants lining up to greet the new master. Then he saw something else and turned his head.

"Nice proportion of servants. Did you arrange this, or was my father responsible?" Stephen said.

"Sorry, what do you mean?" Darcy asked. He was bothered by

something.

The General waved towards the maids and cooks lined up. "One matronly cook, I see, but her assistant and the maids all look young and quite lovely. This has my father's touch all about it."

"Yes I am sure that he must have had something to say about it. I believe the servants all came from your parent's estate. You have a stables here that is quite large. One of the previous owners was a member of the hunt set. Quite a fiend about it all, I believe, and so were you to take to your riding again, you should be right at home. I believe that much more than my mother in law's recommendation sold the Earl on this place. That, and how, with little effort, this home can be reached on the Earl's way to Town and back. He remarked to me how he had been passing the house for the better part of his life and had no expectation as to how charming it was," Darcy said, then looked back to the road.

"Ah here we are," The carriage stopped. "Darcy? Wait, no... That's Kitty. And Georgiana... Who else is here!" Stephen was overcome. The pain in his legs forgotten for a moment.

Darcy turned back from looking out the window towards the lane. "I assure you I wrote Lizzy and told her that no one was to meet us. That your recuperation was to be conducted in solitude. Only your closest family to visit and, only, at your invitation."

Arranging himself deeper in his seat, the General's voice was a hissed whisper, "I think I should take that girl over me knee and give her a good thrashing with the back of a hair brush. Don't laugh, isn't that how one punishes willful girls?" The General's right hand was held out straight and he waved it sharply at Mr. Darcy twice.

Darcy stopped laughing and whispered, himself, "Yes, when they're five. I shall get out and send them off to the Inn. Then escort them back to Town after we have you settled..."

There was a knocking at the carriage door, "Are you going to come out, or shall we come in and fetch you out?" Kitty's voice came through. From his position in the carriage, General Fitzwilliam could see the top of her head. "I think I should also mention we can hear a bit of what you are arguing on about, and, Mrs. Norwood wants to get back to your kitchen. She is right in the middle of preparing luncheon."

Having faced the French cannons for four years, being wounded three times, and seen violent death innumerably, facing Kitty was not nearly as horrifying. He used his left hand on the door latch and took hold of his cane. Leveraging himself, with a grunt, he slowly maneuvered himself out and down. A technique he had neither perfected, nor mastered, yet, but he was able to proceed through it without falling and ending up on his face.

He turned to the young ladies first; Kitty and Georgiana. He noticed that Lizzy stood at the top of the stairs. After acknowledging the ladies, Kitty took charge and introduced him to the servants. He then proceeded up the stairs, Mr. Darcy and the two young ladies following. Straight into the drawing room. A tour of the house would be conducted in stages later.

"I do not even know how to begin..." the General, of course, started thus.

Kitty held up her hand, "Best that you don't, then. Let me assure you that we are all here because of my determination that we come to you."

Mr. Darcy looked to his wife. She remained quiet.

"My wishes were..." the General started, once more.

"Your wishes are of little concern for you made them known without clear reflection." Kitty was firm. "We know many men who have become disfigured by this war. We welcome them in society. But you are alive. I am so thankful that you lived. Your company is something I value and will not have you stay shut in your room denying me of it. I told Lizzy that there was nothing she could do to stop me from coming here to convince you of it."

Stephen slowly shook his head, now ignoring all the others but Kitty, "It is not for you to say..."

Kitty interjected, again, "Your thinking is muddled, General. I am not being some willful miss, either. You are hurt in body and in your mind. Both injuries may be with you for all your days. But the world still has much joy in it, and you can take part of it. I am here to remind you of that." Kitty had gotten up and now she approached him and gave him a modest kiss on the cheek. "Come Georgiana, greet your cousin too and remind him he is living." With this, as encouragement, and he completely speechless, she, then Lizzy, last, all gave him sisterly busses on the cheek.

"I am quite overcome with your arguments, Miss Bennet." The General fell back to polite society's catch phrase. Then he showed his old self, "But you ladies have paid great honor to my left cheek and my right feels all quite alone by this show of welcome." Kitty laughed and clapped her hands, and then bent and gave the forlorn right cheek a kiss also.

"Stephen!" Mr. Darcy said.

This was followed by "Kitty!" from Lizzy.

It caused the General and Kitty to both laugh and Georgiana to giggle.

"Don't scold, Darcy. It seems I have returned home." The General said. As he shifted his weight, the pain of his injuries were plain upon his face. Kitty and Georgiana quickly positioned an ottoman for him to rest his leg upon, under Darcy's instructions.

"Mind girls, ladies" he corrected at the cool looks he received, "I am much less than I was when last wounded, and in your sister's care."

Lizzy looked him over, "I fear that your recuperation shall be longer this time, cousin."

Darcy had some to add, "I have arranged for a London specialist to come twice each month to supervise, and shall make an appointment with the local doctor presently."

"Already taken care of, Mr. Darcy," Kitty said, "I have everything in hand, and this time, instead of Lizzy, I shall oversee the General's recovery."

As Mr. Darcy looked to his wife, who shrugged her shoulders in resignation, the General had his opinions to express, "Miss Bennet that is too much graciousness for one such as I..."

Georgiana giggled again, "Kitty said you would say something like that. I have lost a ha'penny."

That caused more mirth. "I am so predictable, then?" Stephen asked.

Kitty was all smiles, "Not just you, but all the men of your family. I won a half crown from Lizzy as to the composition of the servants that your father chose, too." Once more, laughter engulfed the room.

* * *

By the end of the first week, Stephen knew all the names of the servants, had established the routine of the house by setting meal times, and which rooms he preferred to use. The General had explored the house and could find his way about fairly easily. His routine limited his movement up and down stairs to but two trips a day, for climbing stairs was still the most painful part of his convalescence.

He had now been more than a fortnight at Silverponds. This day found him walking with Kitty and Georgiana to the stables, his first trip that far, and the first time he had walked so great a distance in one session without stopping.

"Well I think we should have you sitting a horse today, too, you have done so well." Kitty was again complementing him on his achievements. She had a much different manner of encouraging him to recuperate than Darcy had, in Portugal.

"We have yet to reach our goal," he said. His struggles for breath clear.

Georgiana remarked, "But we have certainly gone more than half way, why I can see the horses in their stalls through the door now." That view was clear to all three. An under-butler and gardener were close to hand in case the General encountered difficulties.

"See them. Smell them, more like! I don't think one stable hand is enough, General, you should see about a second as soon as you are able." Kitty had the audacity to point out.

Stephen paused for a moment, but then started again. "You are doing quite well. It is a long walk, but almost there. And it is the last part of the house you have yet to see. Then we can start on a tour of the grounds."

He gave a wry laugh, "I think that I shall spend time in my courtyard garden and take a tour of every flower, bush and rock..."

Kitty said with a cross look, "Yes, a distance that can be crossed in a few paces. We shall never have you striding down Pall Mall, if that is your desire. No, tomorrow we shall walk from the main house to the lane. By next week we shall be paying a call on

the vicar, who has asked that you review his notes on the ser-
mon..."

"Let us not take this lord of the manor role too far," he said.

The girls had been talking of little else for three days since the
Countess and Earl had arrived to see their son. The Darcy's
stayed another day and then had departed to join their own sons
at Netherfield, but planned to return soon. The Earl had brought
news that the Prince Regent had acknowledged General Fitzwilliam's role and sacrifices in the war, with the title of Baron. A
ceremony of his elevation to the peerage would take place within
the year.

Kitty talked on, "And why not? The only other titled land-
holder nearby is Lord Morton who spends nearly all his life in
Town, or at his two other country homes. Everyone has remarked
on it. You will be the biggest thing in the parish and, deservedly,
so. Lord Morton thinks himself a dandy though Brummell would
never espouse it. And the man had no thought of service, but
idles his time and money on frivolity." The last week had seen
visits by all the neighbors of affluence in the parish to become
acquainted with the General, and Kitty had taken matters in the
drawing room well in hand there also. The Countess of M----K
even relied upon her to pour tea and serve the General's guests,
as he and the Earl watched, with amusement. The Earl had
leaned over to his younger son and quietly reminded him, "Your
mother does not let the Viscountess pour, even in your elder
brother's own home. This is a fine situation, indeed!"

They had reached the door to the stables and could see several
stalls full of horses, and many empty stalls also. There were
horses from both the Earl's carriages that were now at the hall,
and for a small runabout that had been purchased for the General. Georgiana and Kitty each had their horses stabled here, as,
too, were a couple of the horses that a manor house needed in
order to be run properly.

"Here, is that Night? How the devil did he get here? And, he is
well?" The General had not seen his horse since falling at the
siege of Badajoz. He forgot his pains, though his grunts as he
hurriedly hobbled to his charger, reminded the ladies that he had
them. As he closed on the animal, "Here, boy, why look at you,

still magnificent..."

"It was Mr. Hurst. He says that when they first found you at the surgery, your aide pointed out your personal articles and Night. Mr. Darcy did not know how they could look after you and the horse and your other belongings, but the next day all was attended to." Georgiana had the information, "Mr. Hurst had seen to all the details. There is a scarring on his right haunch from a bullet grazing, Mr. Hurst says, but it had scabbed and healed when they arrived at Badajoz. Kitty and I come and feed him carrots daily. Now you should come also."

The General grinned and nodded to the girls, "We must find a way to repay Mr. Hurst for his thoughtful care."

Kitty said, "He wrote that he was not as good as Darcy at lifting your spirits as you journeyed to Lisbon, but that he knew his orders and instructions about Night and your other effects would be done properly. Look in your right coat pocket." The General did, and, withdrew a cube of sugar which he gave to Night.

"Thank you," he said.

"So, shall we ride?" Kitty had hold of the General's arm on one side. Georgiana had the other, as she stroked the horse's mane with her free hand.

"It would be too much... Oh you are joking. Let us tarry here for a moment more, perhaps longer, then let us see what else we have to inspect." Which had been the plan initially. When they returned to the house, the General was tired, but quite fulfilled.

* * *

"I daresay, the house is getting full up. I have had a letter from my sister," The Earl said at dinner after the Sunday service. Another week had passed and the General had walked to service in the morning and back, a good half mile, and the length of the lane to the house. Mr. Darcy and the Earl had walked with him, whilst the ladies had taken Darcy's young boys in the carriage. "I think perhaps we should have purchased something larger for you." The Earl had been thanked by his son for the generous gift of the manor, but learned that the rewards of being a General had allowed his son to pay for many of the expenses that such a manor required. It lessened the burden that the Earl had anticipated.

"Aunt Catherine? Do you mean to say that she is coming to stay?" The General connected his father's remark about the house getting full, with his aunt's letter.

"Yes, you read me too well. That is it, precisely. She, of course, is bringing Anne. Now there are seven rooms, yes, and the Countess and I have one as do the Darcy's. You, of course, have yours, and each of the young misses have one. That comes to five. We shall be full up, come Friday."

"My lord, I am afraid we shall be over-crowded in that regard. You will recall our friend Sir Chamberlain Fairfax has become engaged to Miss Caroline Bingley." The Earl cleared his throat as the General continued, "He travels on his way to Netherfield for a fortnight and has asked to call here on the weekend, wishing to pay his compliments. I am afraid we shall now require some doubling up."

"Oh." Kitty now looked around from the Countess, who exchanged looks with her. They sat at the foot of the table, to the General and his father who sat at the head. That it was the General who faced his mother as host and she, hostess, while Kitty sat in the place of honor in the opposite corner to that of the Earl of M—K, was an amusement to the Darcy's and had been so for the four days that they had been back at Silverponds.

"While you gentleman have been arranging things, I fear that Kitty and I have, also, tendered invitations, though we should say that they were with your blessing, Stephen. You will recall how, shortly upon Mrs. Darcy's return, we were discussing the Gardiner children. Yes, you did allow as they should visit, as they have been your devoted friends these years that you have been away." The countess always referred to his time fighting as his being away, or as if he had been on holiday travels somewhere.

"They too shall be joining us on Friday," she concluded.

The Earl was shaking his head, for if he were to open his house, he could hold more than twice this number of guests, as could Pemberley.

"No trouble then, none at all," The General spoke as the diners wrestled with the thought of guests and rooms. "I believe that the nursery can handle this number of children, though I believe the baby will have to return to his parents' room, as he has done some few nights before." Young Charles was not quite six months and this was something the parents were used to.

Stephen continued, "I can have a trundle bed placed in my suite for Sir Fax, it will be more spacious then our digs at school and I shall remind him of that, when he comes. If Kitty and Georgiana would share a room, officially, for the weekend, then we can have one available for the Gardiners and all is taken care of," the General had a solution.

"Officially, share a room?" Kitty looked to the General.

"Do not look so mischievous Kit, you know well that in the time you have been here, you and Georgiana have shared one another's room, or sat all night in one another's room until the very early hours of the morning, several times. If you were still in the schoolroom I should set you down with a scold, but, as *young ladies,* I am only to smile, indulgently." Kitty and Georgiana joined in with the rest of the family in laughing about the matter.

Sir Chamberlain was the first to arrive that Friday. The household had spent the week preparing for all their guests. Fortunately, the General reflected, that in the event of more friends and family descending upon him, the Inn was but a half mile away and had eleven more rooms. Dining that many people, however, would require additional plate, and, though a mismatched set, the General had acquired some few services that could handle such a crush.

"Fax, you got my note? Good. I shall show you what it is like to rough it as if you were on campaign, eh?" The General had walked down the steps to greet his guest. Stephen could see that Sir Fairfax noted the stiffness of his gait.

"Yes, old man, but we are to be full up, is it? And, your aunt, again. I met her at Pemberley some years ago. Oh Miss Bennet, your servant." Kitty had come down the steps, seventeen, he had informed her as he had struggled up them many times now. Though, he told her, treading down them was more painful.

"Sir Chamberlain, my good friend. It is a pleasure for you to come to our little hospital." Kitty took his hand in both of hers and gave him a dazzling smile. Much had changed in the years since he had offered for her, but this was, certainly, the warmest they had greeted one another since that fateful event.

"She must regard you as a friend. To those whom she wants to berate me, she calls this our little sanatarium," the General had them all laughing. "Come. Let us show you the house and we'll take you to my rooms, there you can freshen up. My man will show yours the way." Half an hour later, Kitty and the General had returned to the base of the stairs, the tired General leaning on his cane.

The Gardiners had arrived and the children were all excited to see their hero. "Why, sir, are you not in uniform?" "Does it hurt much." "How many Frenchies did you kill." To which Mrs. Gardiner, firmly, said, "Enough of that. Mind your manners children."

The rest of the household came soon, too, to welcome the Gardiners for not only were they Lizzy's favorites, but the Countess had taken to them as well. As his mother had, so too had the Earl, and each time the Earl was in residence in London, the Gardiners would find themselves invited to many dinners. Georgiana treated the young children as if they were her own younger siblings, and as she had been the youngest of all the cousins, it had been a great joy to her to have new siblings. Much had changed for the Gardiners in the years since Lizzy had married into Darcy's family. For now, when the Darcy's, the Bingley's, the Earl and his son, the Viscount, were in London, the Gardiners might find invitations to so many dinners, that they, invariably, would have to refuse some.

The children helped the General back up the steps to the hall. The adults exchanged glances which provided what information they needed as to the General's physical recovery. The questions did start again and the General took time to answer them. The children did not ask the questions their mother had told them, previously, that they were not to ask. "My uniforms are in my closet, and I shall wear one on Sunday for church. Yes, there is often pain. The doctors say that it is to be expected. Night, he is in the stables and you all shall ride him tomorrow, yes?"

* * *

They were quite happy at that prospect. Once the party reached the hall, the General went to a drawing room accompanied by his father. Kitty then took over showing the Gardiners to the Nursery and then the parents to their room on the first floor. "He seems pale," Mrs. Gardiner whispered to Lizzy as they walked down a hallway.

Kitty heard and said, "Already, this had been a physically challenging morning. He stills tires easily."

"He still is building his strength, then," her aunt Gardiner understood.

"Yes. The Doctors say that he may never has as much strength as he had before the wounds. They have taken their toll," Lizzy supplied.

It was not much later that the third set of guests arrived, Lady Catherine and Anne, along with a small collection of footmen, coachmen and servants. Housing the staff was something that the house could not accommodate, and, so, six would be staying at the local inn.

"My dear boy, you are pale. You must get some sun. Come help your cousin down. Miss Bennet," Lady Catherine acknowledged her for the General clutched her tightly for support on this trip to the carriages.

"You'll forgive me aunt..." the General struggled for breath.

"Lady Catherine, I am afraid we have overtaxed the General at the moment. Pray allow Grimes to help," Kitty said. She motioned for the servant to give his hand to Anne.

"Cousin, good to see you," it sounded more of forced air, rather than words when Stephen spoke. Anne just nodded her head in acknowledgement. She did have a smile for Kitty who placed a free hand over Anne's arm, for a moment, then was back to bearing the weight of the General. She was a little worried for he had not been so weak for some time.

"Lady Catherine, the Earl and Countess are in the drawing room, which is just off the hall. It has a wonderful prospect. Pray proceed and we shall catch you up, or join you in the drawing room." Kitty nudged her head in the direction of the stairs.

Lady Catherine looked from the stairs to her nephew, then back to the stairs. She clucked and then looked to Kitty, shook her head once, and began the ascent, "Come Anne. I am sure Stephen will join us in due course."

The General slowly turned to follow his aunt, who was already on the third step. Kitty's arms not only supported him they restrained him. "You wait a moment, General!" she whispered. "You are overtaxed and we shall just rest a moment, shall we?" She turned her head, "Grimes you get her ladyship's footmen to lend a hand here, then they can trot around to servants' entrance and dispense with the bags. I think that you men shall be enough to help the General..."

"That is enough, Kitty," the General wheezed.

"As if you can say a whole sentence through, you are so exhausted. You let these men help you up to the hall, or I shall confine you to your room 'til dinner tomorrow, and don't see if I don't." She gripped his arm extra hard and leaned against him close, "And I will, too General, so just you be easy for you are quite close to overtaxing yourself." She released her grip and allowed the three men to help him up the steps and to the threshold of the drawing room where Lady Catherine could be heard talking to all those assembled.

"No, Mrs. Gardiner, I assure you I have never seen my nephew so, and you sister, why you can not have a nurse..."

"My dear Catherine," the General, and Kitty could hear the Countess as they approached the room, "Kitty, and Georgiana, too, have been the best nurses in the world for Stephen. We could not have been more fortunate should the best of Harley Street be made available to us."

The General waved off the help he had received and took a deep breath, "Hello, mother." He took the three steps into the room and was able to firmly grasp the back of a settee and support his weight. Kitty followed him in. "Perhaps Aunt, Anne, you would like to be shown to your rooms. We are a bit overcrowded," he paused for breath, "But we are able to give you each your own room, tonight. I believe Kitty and Mother were planning to do the honors. You see, we have divided up the duties of hosting until I complete my recovery."

Lady Catherine nodded silently and finally found her voice, "Of course Stephen, of course. Come Anne," Lady Catherine was out the door with Anne, the Countess and Kitty quickly following.

* * *

The Earl was quick to step over to his son, "Sit." And he guided the General to his seat.

"Georgiana, Aunt Gardiner, perhaps you would like to walk with me." Lizzy had stood, "I would like to check on the arrangements for dinner." Deftly the men were left to themselves.

"I believe that your wife expects we will have some need to comment on Lady Catherine's behavior?" Stephen looked to his cousin, Darcy.

Mr. Darcy was smiling, "What could possibly be spoken on a subject that we never raise?"

"Gentlemen." The Earl looked to them and shook his head.

While Mr. Darcy chuckled, the General spoke, "Sir, we never speak to our aunt's choice of phrase, though by discussion with the women who are acquainted with Lady Catherine I am sure, as is Darcy, that they all believe we do discuss it. This leads me to believe that in their parlors such matters are discussed."

The Earl, still shaking his head, "I fear it has been ever thus since we were children. Your grandfather said near enough the same after her first season. In any event, what drink can I get you? You know that you are not going to your room for some time, so best get comfortable."

"It's true," Mr. Gardiner spoke, "I have been here a few hours and I can see what would happen if Kitty were to find you had climbed the stairs to your room. Such a change these last few years. She was never this way as a child. I think Mr. Darcy you have done well with your guidance of my niece. Mr. Bennet would be quite proud."

Mr. Darcy had walked to the decanters, that held some liquors, ready to serve at the hand motion his uncle had used. "No Uncle Gardiner, I do not believe that is the case. Sherries I think? Kitty was much different when I left for Badajoz. I fear, she was much as we all remember her when I wed."

The General took a sip from the glass that he was handed. "I must believe you to be wrong. Her letters changed nature these last years."

"Yes Mr. Darcy, you are too harsh. I dare say I can see it from better perspective than you. She was self indulgent as a child, and perhaps the influence of Mrs. Wickham was the cause. But these several years she has matured much..." Mr. Gardiner began.

"Yes, Darcy, I have always thought her of a level of maturity," Sir Fairfax added.

"Oh I give way to the common opinion. My reservations are perhaps clouded by being too close to her. Perhaps I can not perceive her much beyond the girl I first met," Darcy said.

The General had something to add. "I believe that has been a failing of your's before. But you do treat her and Georgiana both as young women grown, it does seem."

Mr. Darcy nodded his acknowledgement.

The Earl finished his sherry, "We most likely will have the young lady back presently, once she has done her duty, and she will coddle you for exerting yourself. Perhaps you should close your eyes for a moment to regain your strength? Gentleman, *The Times* arrived a short while ago, should any wish to peruse it, I am retiring to the library." The Earl took his leave and was followed by the others who left the General, quietly.

Left alone, the General did close his eyes to rest and was composed quietly when Kitty came back to the room. She checked on him and his resting and took up a seat behind him. A needle and frame was nearby and she took that up, working on a blackwork sampler that she had begun weeks before. Every few stitches she would raise her eyes to see how the General rested.

* * *

"If you please, sister, to accompany me, Stephen will join us at the table," the Earl said when the party formed to proceed into dinner. The Countess took over arranging the other guests. She, taking Sir Chamberlain's arm, while Mr. Darcy had that of his cousin Anne's.

Soon enough, all was organized. Kitty and Georgiana brought up the rear, stopping long enough to motion a footman, who was stationed close, to bring the General to the dining room. After an hour's sleep the General had rested enough to continue to his rooms and dress, but Kitty had ensured that he would rest again until dinner was ready. His level of exhaustion was worse than it had been at any time since his arrival at Silverponds.

When seated, once again with the Countess, as hostess, and Kitty at her side, the host's place waiting for the General to arrive, the Countess looked to her husband's sister, "Catherine, I would like Kitty to tell you something of tonight's dinner, so you will be prepared."

"Dinner, why young lady what ever can you have to say?" Lady Catherine turned her attention towards Kitty.

"Just this Lady Catherine, the General has only been this fatigued thrice since arriving at Silverponds and we have developed a routine to ease him and our society that neither is tasked."

Lady Catherine shook her head, "What are you on about?"

"Please Catherine, Kitty is quite clever," the Earl admonished his sister.

Kitty paused, collecting her thoughts, knowing that she had but a few moments before the General would join them, "We dine on but three courses, the portions are small and meant for us to be finished with our meal in less than an hour entire. The General will then feel able to retire with dignity. When we withdraw, the General will return to his room and recuperate, whilst we will have coffees in the drawing room. This shall be supplemented with cakes and fruit to provide a more fulfilling nourishment, should you desire."

"I never. Three courses..." Lady Catherine was one to make her opinions known.

"Well done, Kitty," Mrs. Gardiner said, at the same moment. "Oh I am sorry, Lady Catherine, I did not mean to step on your words. But what an achievement. Now, is this all your idea?"

The Countess and Lizzy both said, "Yes," while Georgiana looked to her hands and smiled. The Countess continued, "A bout came over the General last week and we had to insist he retire after the fourth course. This is a much more accommodating plan, and we adopted it just three days ago when my son was infirm. It worked wondrously. Ah Stephen. Yes of course we were talking of you, who else would we talk of in this house. Take your seat, and don't embarrass Kitty for she has planned a very good meal and supervised Cook in its preparation."

"Of course mother, I apologize for keeping you all waiting. I have welcomed you all to my home earlier, but here let me share with you some of our triumphs. Kitty has taken a hand in planning all our dinners at Silverponds. Georgiana has become our chief decorator in charge of all our floral arrangements. Mrs. Darcy ensures that the children are attended to, and Mother ensures that father, Mr. Darcy and myself do not get out of hand." This brought some light laughter from the assembled diners.

Sir Fairfax recognized that a silence was sure to follow this but gave a practiced witticism to fill the void, "What great achievements indeed. Why, I shall have much to talk of when I reach Netherfield. Now I understand that Miss Bennet is in charge of the kitchen, why this is a singular achievement."

The Countess placed a hand on Kitty's arm and nodded towards the butler. Kitty motioned with her hand and the butler began having his staff, which had been augmented by some of the young people from the village, serve out the first course; a cream soup of local vegetables with leeks, turnips, potatoes and small bits of fricasseed guinea fowl.

"No, Sir Fairfax, there is some mistake in your thinking," Lizzy had been talking, "It was my duty to ensure that Georgiana learn her ways of managing a kitchen, and knowing that my mother had not attended to this task, full well, Kitty and Mary were also included in this instruction this last year."

Lady Catherine had to voice her certainty, "When Anne shall take over Rosings, she, too, will be a great supervisor of the staff. She had, often told me of embellishments to our dinners at Rosings that assure me of this. Mrs. Darcy you will remember when you were with us last? Miss Bennet, you have not had the chance to come to Rosings yet..." the conversation turned to comparing Silverponds in its comfortable size to the greatness that was Rosings Park.

As promised, the third course was served and finished before the hour had passed. The General had rallied to converse during the meal, but fatigue was clear upon him. "Why, how refreshing that all was. I must say I am quite full." Lady Catherine looked to Kitty who nodded. The Countess also acknowledge Lady Catherine and laid her hand once more upon Kitty's arm.

Kitty rose first, "Ladies, if you will join me, coffee is to be served in the drawing room. We can leave the men to their cigars and port. No, gentlemen, as is our custom here we do not insist that you rise at this time to see us on our way." Kitty eyed the

General, who nodded, as the other women found the way to their feet.

"Yes Kitty, I shall indeed find my way to my room momentarily. I am certain I shall be quite refreshed in the morning." Lady Catherine turned her head to look at her nephew and then back to Kitty. Lady Catherine had stopped her progress to the drawing room but found that Mrs. Darcy had come to grasp her by the elbow and was guiding her out of the room.

Seven ladies sorted themselves out about the drawing room and coffee was brought in to be served. As mentioned before, fruit and cakes were also on hand. The coffee was placed in front of Kitty to pour, and Georgiana served out the food. "You are quite at home with these arrangements of yours. I can not tell who is our hostess, you dear sister, Miss Bennet, or our Georgiana."

Anne covered her mouth, then reached for the cake plate in front of her. "Oh it is not so difficult, I would be here all on my own should Kitty have not been so resolute in attending to Stephen. Indeed, you should not be here either as his wishes were to remain alone here until the end of time," the Countess replied to Lady Catherine.

Lady Catherine said, "Well Anne, I wish we had come sooner, certainly you would have been immense help to your aunt in seeing to the management of General Fitzwilliam. Now, that all is so well in hand, I am afraid there is little for you to do."

"Lady Catherine, we should certainly find things for Anne to do in the supervision of the house. The General will one day interview housekeepers and we can all relinquish these duties, but until then, we have many that occupy us. I had understood though that you and Anne were to stay just for the weekend," Kitty said.

"Oh my dear Miss Bennet that was indeed the plan, but since arriving and seeing my nephew in such straits I wonder if we should not extend our stay to help you all with the burden of his convalescence," the Countess stood quickly and walked to Grimes, who stood ready to serve. She had a few words and turned back to her husband's sister.

"Dear Catherine, I am sorry but as we had only expected you

through Monday, we will indeed have to curtail your stay at that time. The household is overstretched for the weekend which we can just about endure. Further I did consult with the doctor when he visited this afternoon and we both felt that this brief intrusion upon our routine of the household is causing strain on my son's recuperation. The quicker ended, the quicker mended," the Countess said.

Lady Catherine stared up shrewdly at the Countess, "Perhaps Anne and I should leave in the morning, then."

"Nonsense," the Countess said. Smiling, when Lady Catherine's head had turned away, "Stephen has worked hard to make himself ready for all his guests this weekend. He would be greatly disappointed should you leave abruptly. Come Mrs. Darcy, help me implore Lady Catherine that she is getting a bee in her bonnet over naught."

"Yes Lady Catherine, the General's wounds are such that we should not resort to matters of tact and pride, but need to put that all aside and tend to his spirit and body. Many is the time I have found myself deferring to my younger sister over matters these last weeks as she sees, with a keener eye, all that must be attended to. There have been times when Darcy has come to me insisting that we too leave as we are a burden with the boys, but the mere mention of such an idea," Lizzy was saying.

The Countess then said, "And I go a shambles. Without Mrs. Darcy to support me, for I do not burden Miss Bennet or Georgiana with a mothers' fears as they have yet to know them, or without Mr. Darcy for the Earl to lean upon we all would be distraught. We have a certain equilibrium, Catherine, and the strain must, certainly, show on us all. I have not meant to upset you..."

Mrs. Gardiner had risen and gone to lend her hand to support the Countess' arm. They had become acquainted through the connection of family and were friendly, but this show of affection was a kindness that was indeed gracious and one the Countess had not experienced since Mr. Darcy's mother had died. Though Mrs. Gardiner had only reached the Countess one brief moment before Kitty had arrived at her other side.

"Pray your ladyship, you will forgive my intemperate words. I meant nothing by it. Miss Bennet and all, you do a wondrous job with the General and are to be admired. I hope your work here speeds his recovery and that he may return to the society of London, of your home, Countess, of Pemberley and Rosings Park in due time," Lady Catherine said.

The Countess had grasped the hand of Mrs. Gardiner as they rearranged themselves upon the settee. She smiled to Kitty who had helped her to sit. "Let us pray that your wish shall be come true quickly," the Countess said.

It was not long before the men came upon the ladies for coffee and the other nourishment. The Earl and Mr. Darcy were not in the habit of smoking at the end of dinner unless the General insisted upon it. Sir Fairfax had noticed that he had been the only one to indulge and placed his cigar out after but a few minutes' indulgence. The gentlemen confirmed that the General had retired moments after the ladies had left the room. His guests spent the remainder of the evening in a few games of cards, listening to Georgiana and Mrs. Darcy play the pianoforte. Kitty sing, and the gentlemen discussing the war, something they would repeat again, for though away from it forever, the General was keen to know how the campaign and his old companions faired in Spain.

TO YOUR GOOD HEALTH

"A letter has arrived for you Kitty. It is from the Inn." Georgiana handed it over. She had sorted the mail this morning.

"Oh," Kitty looked at the return, "Thank you."

The General chuckled, "From the Viscount again? That is the third this week, if I am not mistaken. He has become more constant in his letter writing."

It had been two months since Lady Catherine had first visited. She had returned one and sent Anne alone, twice, for weekend visits. The Darcys had gone to London and returned for stays also. At the present they were away.

The Earl and Countess were away at the present too, and the, chaperonage of the young ladies was in the hands of Mrs. Bennet who had arrived, with her husband, for her third visit at Silverponds. At the moment she had lain down in her rooms, whilst Mr. Bennet amused himself in cataloging the library and making a list of necessities to be added to it.

"How do you know?" Kitty asked.

"It is not much of a puzzler. You and Georgiana never mention whom the correspondent is with that particular stationary. You go all quiet when you see it, and it is clear, these three months, that the man must write you, else he would be not much of an admirer."

Kitty looked at the letter she held, "Father's year of examination is nearly up. The Viscount, I am sure, asks to be able to visit. His last inquiry, I told him it was no use..."

"Hmm. Certainly we can not receive him here at Silverponds, when your parents are present. It would be awkward, and I should not like them to know we acknowledge that he has our license to stay in the village."

"Now that you are named Baron Silverponds and both Mayor and Vicar defer to you, you have quite an inflated view of yourself." Georgiana spoke.

That act had changed how others addressed him. Now he could and was called 'my lord,' by those not on intimate terms with him, and those who were on intimate terms, did so to twit him. Those who were on intimate terms, stills referred to him as General Fitzwilliam, or General or Fitzwilliam, and a very few, Stephen.

"I think you have quite grown up from the demure miss I used to dangle upon my knee, cousin and ward. With such a lively tongue, it will be hard for Darcy to tie you off to the man who can tame you." Georgiana had three beaus herself that wrote constantly throughout the months, and who had also come to the Inn and then visited the great house. The General had proven fond of all three and had previously given her his blessing to have any of them, though he had his favorite.

"La, sir, is that not near enough to what you said yesterday, and last Saturday and last..."

"Yes Georgiana, I am but a poor soldier who has been shot up a bit and so my wits have all but left me. I am destined to be uncreative and repetitive."

They were all laughing, but this slowed as Kitty remembered she had the letter in her hand.

Stephen noted she held it also. He said, "Yes. That letter. Well you had best read it and quickly prepare a response before your mother comes down. I was thinking however of a stroll into the village after lunch. Mr. Dennis had promised to have that new riding crop for me. Anne is to be amongst us this weekend, again, and we are all to go riding with the Hunt..."

"Oh General, do you mean? You are too kind." Kitty stated. That he would escort her to the inn was unexpected.

Georgiana said, through a frown, "Too devious you mean. I shall write Lizzy and inform her so, for you both know I am her spy and have been placed amongst you to try to keep you both from too much mischief."

"At once that would have seemed true but now smacks, so much, of Pots, Kettles, and Black," the General smirked again, only to have a ball of yarn thrown at him.

"Are you sure cousin Anne is for the Hunt? I have ridden the Hunt and do not like it much, but cousin Anne, I should think she would be against it entire." Georgiana said. Giving an opportunity for them to talk of anything but Viscount Parkes.

Kitty saw the General pause a moment before beginning to

speak, and so used that time to say, "Perhaps it is more Lady Catherine de Bourgh's desire than that of your cousin, Anne. So much is the desire of Lady Catherine de Bourgh."

"As a woman whom we are to help have an assignation with her choice of paramour, I do not think it is fair to mention, with such innocent pleasure, what may turn into an alliance that is not of ones choosing or desire," the General's face seemed to have a grimace too.

"I beg your pardon," Kitty said and now she could be found staring at her hands.

The General nodded and turned his attention to opening his correspondence, "Perhaps Kitty, you should proceed with your letter from Parkes and contemplate this afternoon's adventure." He then went to peruse his letter.

Kitty and Georgiana thought better then to speak. Soon enough, the day was advanced and with the mid day meal partaken of, the three found themselves walking into the village. Mrs. Bennet was left behind for the promise that, today, the General was to push his walk to four miles, a distance much further then she would enjoy, and was thus, very easily swayed to remain at Silverponds.

Arriving at the Inn, the common room was sparsely attended but sitting with his feet up on a table the Viscount sat with a couple of companions. Each had a large pewter mug in front of him. "Ah, Parkes and Marrow, Barton... Well met. Here, do you gentlemen know my cousin Miss Darcy and her friend Miss Bennet? Of course Parkes does..." the General was all warm to the men at the inn.

"Why indeed," Viscount Parkes said then realized he was the only one still sitting and scrambled to his feet. The General smiled some more, "Oh terribly sorry. Kitty..." Parkes said.

The General cleared his throat.

"What?" Parkes asked turning to look at Stephen.

"Miss Bennet, surely Parkes. It is Miss Bennet," the General reminded him.

"Of course. Miss Bennet! Miss Darcy?" Parkes shook his head as he conformed to the correct mores.

The other two gentlemen mumbled greetings and bowed appropriately. Something that the Viscount was, also, forgetful of.

Stephen said, "Enjoying the local? I have had a few ales down here myself of late and find it to be very well done indeed. As I shall have this as my main staple, from now on, it is a good thing one learns to enjoy ones local beers."

The Viscount did not speak, so Mr. Marrow did, "You are quite right Lord Fitzwilliam. Congratulations on your elevation."

"Yes congratulations." Sir Barton echoed. There was a mumble from the Viscount. He had barely looked to Kitty since their arrival. The Viscount's eyes were on the General.

Stephen said, "Well I have brought the ladies into town for a small shopping excursion and for my exercise. They do not let me much out of their sight. I assure you that is a curse and, then, very much a blessing. They are such pleasant company." He paused. The other two men seemed congenial and had a light compliment to agree. Parkes was still silent.

"In any event I am off to the shop of Mr. Dennis. Georgiana and are all anxious to see a riding crop that he has brought us, but as we neared the Inn, Miss Bennet was overcome with the heat. Here Miss Bennet I did insist before that you sit down when we got inside and you stubbornly remain standing. This chair by the fire is quite nice and shall restore you in no time. Ah. Mr Stenson," he caught the eye of the innkeeper. "Some barley water for Miss Bennet. A large glass, please."

As the man scurried off to get it, the General turned his attention back to the three men. He said, "I say Marrow, do not take this as an affront, for I am sure your shops in London are much better at this thing, but you are the Hunt set and Mr. Dennis caters to them, perhaps you would join Miss Darcy and myself in our quest to the store? No, I too at one time would only patronize London stores but I found when, visiting the country, fine workmanship at prices much more affordable. I insist that you accompany me. Miss Bennet, I will leave in the care of Parkes and Barton." Barton turned his head sharply to the General, but surely saw the smiles on the faces of Georgiana and Kitty.

"Why capital idea. You know Marrow you were talking of just how shabby your whole outfit was while we came down here," Barton said.

"What? I don't remember saying any such thing." Barton leaned over to Marrow after that and whispered. Marrow then smiled and restated himself. "Oh yes, that is what I said, of course. I think I shall accompany you two. If you will forgive me Miss Bennet. Parkes, Barton I shall see you later."

The three were quickly gone with promises to be back in no more than half an hour. Viscount Parkes finally turned to Kitty when the trio had left the room. "That man is insufferable."

"Sir, you overstate yourself. The General took it upon himself to create such fictions as to give us this opportunity to meet." Parkes' head reared back and then he sat down. Sir Barton looked to his friend, Kitty wondered if he had thought of making an excuse to leave. The actions of the Viscount were such that she hoped he would stay.

"By your leave Miss Bennet," Sir Barton motioned that he wished to sit.

"Of please do." Kitty said hurriedly.

Which was followed by the Viscount saying, "What, can't you make yourself scarce for a time?"

Barton, not one to upset his patron, "Of course, how obtuse. Miss Bennet, if you will humbly accept my apologies, I find I must go in search of, of..."

"A Book, A newspaper, the privies... For gods sake man, it is not that difficult. Kitty and I should like our privacy."

"Yes, please forgive me Miss Bennet," he said.

"Just a moment, Sir Barton. I am afraid that I find these surroundings a little confining. I wonder if you might escort me outside. Yes, that is it. Oh, and my Lord Viscount, please don't trouble yourself to rise I shall take my leave of you, with great pleasure." Kitty grabbed Sir Barton's arm and was quick to have them both leave the common room, before the Viscount could recover himself. They heard a surprised call of "Kitty, wait Kitty." But her gait was so quick that they were out the door.

Kitty and Sir Barton left the Inn and found their friends just outside, but twenty paces away. They had not left the establishment too long before. They were all looking back to the Inn. "Oh Sir Barton, Miss Bennet, yes I expect the barley water was quite bad today. I shouldn't worry though. I say Marrow, Barton dash bad manners of me, but Cook has laid on a cold dinner, the heat you know. What say we take the ladies back to Silverponds after we see to Mr. Dennis and the riding crop. Then I should very much like to see you dine with us as the trenchermen I know you to be."

Marrow started, "But Lord Parkes..."

"Is quite ill..." Sir Barton supplied.

Kitty however was further inclined to add, "Has little desire to dine at Silverponds and I think good society has little desire to dine with him!" She saw Stephen give her a look she did not understand.

The party of five soon found that they had finished with the shopping. Not only the riding crop had been purchased, but so had several other accoutrements which had swelled the coffers of Mr. Dennis. As they approached the lane to Silverponds they found that a nice carriage waited at the turn. Sir Barton enlightened them, first, that it was their carriage. As they reached close enough to see inside, they were able to make out that Viscount Parkes sat inside.

* * *

The General waved the girls and nodded to the Viscount's friends to continue inside. As the Viscount's attention to the party was noted, the General held up his hand, "Do Not Speak Sirrah! No Do Not Say A Word. No! Not A Word! No!" The General turned to ensure that the other four kept on their way to the house. "Step down, else your coachmen shall hear a piece of my mind. I do not believe you should like that. Step down sir. Do it now." Stephen used the tone of voice he used on his new ensigns who had incurred his wrath.

When the Viscount had stepped from the coach, he motioned that they walk a little way back to the village, "You driver, go back to the Inn. The Viscount shall call for you anon. You need not look to the Viscount for instruction, follow my directions. I am the local magistrate." Another award that had been attached to him.

When the two men were quite alone, the Viscount could not resist being the first to speak, "What is your game Fitzwilliam? If you have driven a wedge between my affianced and I..."

"Oh do stop speaking, you fool. I have had some very stupid subalterns, but, you are the biggest buffoon. Oh I know where your smarts lie, but there is so much that you are just, well just a fool. Don't get your feathers in a ruff. If you want to win Miss Bennet you will keep your lips from moving and your ears open."

The General had his walking stick held in such a way that he could use it as a weapon and looked like he would, if pressed.

"Pray continue," the Viscount tried to look affable.

"You are a fool. Do you think you know Kitty, Miss Bennet? She deserves your respect if you wish to make her your wife, and that is by no means assured, for her father is opposed to your match. He and everyone he knows is opposed to the match. I am opposed to the match."

The Viscount shook, "I give her respect."

"I am sure you see it that way. Just how privileged are you, old son? Don't struggle with that, I was being rhetorical. By my counting you have slightly less than two more months to prove yourself worthy of being granted Mr. Bennets blessing. I should think that if Mr. Bennet had witnessed your actions this day, you would have found yourself shown the door. This is my house, here," the General waved towards Silverponds, "I would show you the door. Miss Bennet is a treasure. I can well understand developing an affection for Miss Bennet, and I should deem the man lucky who wins her affection, in return. Reconciling your previous life to the man that Miss Bennet has informed me that you have become I found difficult to credit. Yet here you are."

"How dare you speak to me so," the Viscount raised hands balled into fists as he swore at Stephen.

"Put your fists down boy. Not only could I thrash you, which I am sure you don't believe. You should believe that I have killed dozens of men these last years, and that should make you understand that I would have no qualms about doing you harm. Miss Bennet is my especial friend. You formed an attachment in her heart. As long as that attachment exists we will honor her wishes. As her friend, I believe your actions are not such that it nurtures that attachment. I am not your friend, nor will I advise you as such. As her friend, you may use words to repair your transgressions. Presents were appreciated when Miss Bennet was a girl.

She has matured to realize the difference."

"I don't understand," the Viscount shook his head, "But that is of little matter, your insolence is intolerable. I shall be having my seconds..."

"Enough, you insufferable peasant. You are in no way a lord, or a peer of this realm. I advise you against seconds of any sort or thought. I won't kill you in a duel. I would maim you. Can you live with yourself, looking in a mirror seeing a horrible scar across your face? Do you think being away at the war was some grand holiday? I have killed people, Parkes. Dead. It has not been a game."

The Viscount recoiled. Stephen continued, "Good I see I am having some impact on that arrogance you wrap yourself in. Now go back to the Inn and write your letter." The General shook his head, "Barton and Marrow, I do not understand the tamest members of your set. Have you dropped your other fast friends. In any event, I have them to the house so you shall have no interruptions for you to compose yourself and contemplate on how best to reconcile yourself to Miss Bennet." The General turned his back on Viscount Parkes and left the man standing alone in the lane.

When he entered the house and made his way to the drawing room, he felt sure that he would be beset by questions. He was greeted cheerily and found that the two chaperoning Bennets had joined them. Before Mrs. Bennet could utter a word, Kitty came up to him, and guided him to his seat, "I fear you have overtaxed yourself on our walk, pray let me evaluate your health and you may greet our friends who have this day come from London."

"Yes, but I assure you Kitty I am quite well indeed. No harm has befallen me, not any other, I assure you. I am as well as when we started out to the village, and have been no better since my wounding. So let me welcome Sir Barton and Mr. Marrow. It has been many long years since we have met, though not entirely of each others' set, I do remember some time spent with each before I left for my adventures on the Continent. Marrow, your younger brother and I served there together. He was well enough, last I heard."

"Yes General, he has his Majority now," Mr. Marrow referred

to a promotion that had happened sometime after the General had stopped keeping track.

"Wonderful news. He was a credit to your family, though not in my division you understand, quite an achievement indeed. You are the elder of course." Mr. Marrow would inherit the family fortune, and was not one who would be risked amongst the bullets and cannons as Stephen had been risked.

"Now, they were telling us about how ardently the Viscount pines from his separation from Kitty, for it has been fully three months since she has been nurturing you to health," Mr Bennet said, positioning himself so that only the General could see his face. One eyebrow was quite visibly arched.

"Indeed, has it been that many months? Perhaps we have reached the time when Kitty and Georgiana can return to London. I am quite happy to molder away down here in the country." The General returned the wry look of Mr. Bennet. He could not place one of his own upon his face as too many would see it.

"Mr. Marrow, Sir Barton you will forgive us for we have had this discussion from nearly the first. I will not speak for Georgiana, but I shall leave here, when you, General, will accompany us to London and society." Kitty sat forward on the settee, her back quite stiff.

Georgiana said that she too was so resolved. Stephen said to the two men, "You see, gentlemen, I am beset by great forces in my own home. You may assure the Viscount, when next you see him, that both these women have been urged to return to London and their many admirers. They will argue and use my abhorrence of returning to face society as their excuse. I am sure, though, that they have no other reason to flee the society of London."

Here, Mrs. Bennet was the perfect voice, "Faux, and no offense good sirs, but all the society I ever need is in the country. I have said so before and will do so again. Why, now with the General here, it is even more fine. Can you remember Kitty when we dined with four and twenty families? Now we dine at Netherfield regularly and here we can come to see the General and have been able to dine with his parents, the Countess and Earl of M----K. Then we have met several of the families here, and who knew they were such fine people. Is that not so General?"

"Yes, indeed, Mrs. Bennet. Why gentlemen, I should not have to tell you how much I find the quality of my neighbors here so enchanting that all thoughts of London society just fly from my mind," Stephen actually was sincere, but he was sure the Town swifts would think him sarcastic.

Sir Barton nodded, "I see the dilemma. Yet you have received us so cordially. Certainly my lord, conceding to the wishes of the ladies and accompanying them to Town would allow for the resolution."

"Perhaps, perhaps. Though I believe we have a period over the next few days when we shall see our way to taking such a trip," Stephen reflected on Sir Fairfax Chamberlain and discussions they had when Sir Fax had visited.

Kitty interrupted and informed the General that as their guests were staying at the Inn, they did not have proper evening clothes and this presented them with somewhat of a problem for dining. The General waved it off. In the course of three months, there had been several nights that the party household had eaten without dressing for a formal dinner. A cavalier habit, but useful and convenient. At the suggestion that the gentlemen's things could be sent for, or Mrs. Bennet giving her blessing to dine with less formality, dinner was seen to in comfort. It gave pause to both Sir Barton and Mr. Marrow and they happily said they approved.

Hours later when they were sent back to the Inn, they were in quite good spirits. They parted with a private admonishing for the Viscount from the General. "I gave your patron a stern talking to. That you two are the least of what was his decrepit circle does not surprise me as he seduces Miss Bennet. I expect that he shall put his best face forward from now on, but, gentlemen, I give you warning. Miss Bennet's happiness is important to me. You can see that her care has done much for my troubled mind. Her acceptance of the Viscount as her mate and her continual happiness shall be my concern and I shall have him out if he should jeopardize that. I believe when you allow him to know this, he shall understand, fully, my meaning." Stephen had killed men on the battlefield. If Parkes jeopardized Kitty in any way he felt tempted to show the man what a warrior was capable of.

* * *

The next day, before the post generally came, a messenger arrived with a long letter from the Inn. Mr. Bennet took notice of it, and took notice that it was from the Viscount. "Odd, his being at the Inn and not accompanying his friends last evening. Wouldn't you say General?"

The General made a noncommittal noise and returned to his bacon. The early hour ensured that the dining room held only the two men. "Come, come dear boy. It is clear that Viscount Parkes is in residence at the Inn. I wish to ensure my daughter's safety. I believe he has come to spirit her away to Gretna Green without my blessing."

This, the General had to notice, "No sir, I do not believe that is the case. I must admit to a fiction, I did encounter the Viscount yesterday on my walk."

Mr. Bennet looked at the man who was nearly as much a part of his family as his sons Darcy and Bingley. "Pray go on."

"I assure you I became entirely clear as to the Viscount's position in the country, here. I determined that his regards for Kitty were not enough to admit him to the bosom of our home. I made it clear that if he had Kitty's good regard, then he should solicit my acceptance of him as well, but otherwise he would have nothing from me. I believe I firmly established that I extended my protection to Kitty, also."

"Very well, though I should be obliged if you ensured the footmen were to watch for any adventurous activities on Kitty's behalf." Mr. Bennet might be remembering his youngest daughter's own misadventures, for he shuddered. Stephen had learned all about the Wickham's and their eventual marriage.

"Yes, sir. It shall be attended to, though, I wish to reassure you that Kitty is sensible enough that nothing shall happen," Stephen firmly believed that.

Shortly thereafter Georgiana made her way into the room and so they had to curtail their line of discussion. When the General left having finished his breakfast, he did ensure that extra precautions were made so that the Viscount could not come and spirit Kitty away, though nothing did come of it.

* * *

That afternoon as the small family gathered together, "I had a letter from the Viscount this morning," Kitty stated.

"Indeed, I should think he would finally correspond," Mrs. Bennet said. "Purports himself as your ardent admirer and begs your father for your hand, and where is he these three months? We see his friends last evening as they pass on their way to Town, but no sign of your most devoted servant?"

"Oh mama, he has written me before. I do not share everything with you." Kitty showed her defiance.

"Do not speak so, to your mother, that way, Kitty." Mr. Bennet intoned. "You agreed that, during this year, you would keep us informed of all of your interactions with the Viscount. That includes his writing you."

She looked down at her lap, "I am sorry, father. I forgot," she paused. Taking a few moments before continuing to speak, "In any event this morning's letter was filled with great prose and admiration for me. I am indeed the desire of his eyes..." She looked to the General, stopping her quotations.

"His eyes, is it," Stephen responded. "Just goes to show he's not a military man at all. Has a dash too much of the poet, I'd say. Why a man, such as I, could never compete with words like that." Kitty nodded her head in thanks, or acknowledgment.

"Well it is more than his eyes I want him to be using to admire you with, Miss Kitty Bennet." Mrs. Bennet intoned. "Should you marry the man and become Viscountess Parkes, I should have you know that I should want him to treat you as a fine lady indeed. Why General you say you are not a poet, but you've shown such amiable manners to all my family, why my brother a regular guest of your very own father the Earl's, in London. That, there, is admiration. You know the Viscount has yet to ask us to table or acknowledge the connection of such people as the Gardiners or the Phillips. Why we have tremendous examples of such actions with Darcy and Bingley and then the General here welcoming us with open arms. That, there, is admiration," Kitty knew she should not argue with that.

Mr. Bennet nodded, sagely, "I could not have said that better myself, m'dear."

"That is not fair, mama. Not many of our relations wish to

meet Henry," It was all Kitty could think to say.

Kitty saw the General nodding to Georgiana that making to leave might be done with his blessing. Georgiana then slipped away, but as he rose and pointed himself towards the door, her father said, "Please don't leave, General, you are a part of this." Mr. Bennet included him. "Kitty, what our family, our relations, have wanted is second to your regard. I have shaken hands with members of this family whom I might not wish to, and gladly accepted others who have quite surprised me. That I am resolved to ensure your heart remains constant, after this full year, is the least I can do to protect it as I have been unable to do very well, with your sister Lydia." Her father did not like to speak of that matter at all.

"Mr. Bennet, I shall have you know I heartily admire my son, Mr. Wickham..." Mrs. Bennet said.

"Yes I know your opinion of him." Mr. Bennet was resigned, "That does not mean, that though we hold opinions of the Viscount, he should not only ensure your regard for him, but should find means to ensure our regard for him. That it should extend only through you may cause the same relationship I have with Mr. Wickham. If you would be happy with that, then you chart a course, and that of the Viscount, somewhat adrift from mine." Her father was very blunt, she thought.

Kitty was clearly dismayed. The General said, "If I may, though it has been sometime since I was of an acquaintance with the Viscount, I am sure that once Kitty reiterates your feelings of being neglected by a man wishing to be your son, you will find invitations and introductions to the best of society the Viscount is connected with. And despite his reputation, as it stood when I left for Spain, I have seen no notices in the paper that he is as he was. Indeed, just last month I noted that he had been a key member of some fashionable charity event. Did I not, Kitty?"

There had been no such notice and, certainly, if there had, the General had not mentioned it. "Oh yes, you had brought it to my attention. Henry was too modest to write about it," Kitty said. She and Stephen had found themselves able to create a few such fabrications for their families.

"If that does not speak to a man making reforms of character,

I am not sure what would," Stephen said.

"Very well, then. Two more months. If your heart still wishes to have him, then I shall give you my blessing Lady Parkes. I shall certainly live by my word," Mr. Bennet said.

This ended the matter for two weeks. The end of which saw a small party ready to see the General to London and his parent's house. He had no need of his own residence there any longer, for being a solitary man without his serving commission, he was quite at his leisure. He not only was allowed to stay at the Earl's residence, but his brother's was equally available, as were rooms at the Darcys', the Gardiners', and the Hursts' should he wish it.

With the most recent stay of Anne at Silverponds, the General knew that he had recovered as much as he would, and the doctors said the same. He had agreed to stand for Sir Fairfax at his upcoming nuptials, which now had a firm date, coinciding with the end of the year whence Kitty and Viscount Parkes were waiting for Mr. Bennet's blessing. It had been the matter he ad Sir Fairfax discussed. The General knew Sir Fax hoped he would take longer to heal.

Treading on as many connections to the Peerage as she could, Caroline Bingley had invited a great many titled people to her wedding luncheon, and a few close ones to the church. The General decided to transition to London and meet his friends and acquaintances before the day, so as not to shock them. Only Kitty had the courage to speak openly to him about his fears and cautions, "You make too much of it. Those who love you will not care, those who do not, you should not care of their opinion." The General, however, could not separate those words from his concerns.

That he returned to London, however, saw the change of the happy group that had been at Silverponds. He had the giant house to himself in Town, as his parents were at their country place, and were not planning to attend the wedding or luncheon. Sir Fairfax, the Earl stated, he could put up with, but the soon to be Lady Fairfax he thought best to wait to meet until forces, such as a reception at the Darcys' or Bingleys' forced them to meet.

That seemed to be much of the prevailing sentiment of many of those who felt they did not have a strong acquaintanceship with Miss Bingley. The wedding feast was still to be well attended, though with not as many peers as Caroline desired.

Darcy settled himself into his the Earl's favorite chair. Stephen was well ensconced in the other chair. The library was well stocked but not many of the books in it had been read. Darcy remarked the same, and Stephen laughed, "Indeed you are right. Your Father, Mr. Bennet, was here to visit two days ago and I lent him some three dozen books. It seems few volumes have really been perused. Even of those the Earl has bought, since Grandfather's day. My father has read perhaps one a year, though these last five weeks I have read more than thirty."

Darcy said, "I have heard that you have come to London, but venture out very little. You receive visitors between two and four. You go to your clubs for a half hour every third day. You have ridden once in the Park, chaperoning Kitty and Georgiana whilst they stayed with the Gardiners. Though despite your reclusiveness, you have seen them quite regularly, twice for dinner each week, once each week with them to a box at the theater or opera, and all afternoon Sunday, you have them here so the children can play."

"You have too many spies, Darcy," Stephen said.

"Just one, just one." Mr. Darcy replied with a smile upon his lips. "Thirty books, that is very impressive, I do not read that many in a six month, though I do try."

"Hah, Mr. Bennet would say we are both uninformed," the General smiled.

"Yes, my Father is quite the scholar. He remarked that he missed some of your debates, since you have come to London, that you two used to have at Silverponds. He says that Charles and Hurst are not of use to him in that way when they are at Netherfield, and though he believes our friend, Sir Fairfax, will be the very best of a man to discuss current world events, he believes that you or I are the only two who care to sport with him on the classics. His words I assure you," Stephen had been shaking his head at such a compliment.

There was a tumbler of strong drink to hand, and the General had a long gulp before speaking, "I am heartily sorry that our time at Silverponds came to an end. It was past time that Kitty got on with her life, and Georgiana too. Her time of seasons are coming to an end of our indulgence, and I think once Kitty has settled with her Viscount, then our little Georgiana shall make her choice known to us. She was ever the one to make sure all others were taken care of, before she asked for anything for herself."

Darcy nodded and said, "And that was more your influence then mine. My influence as her brother was to ensure that she was protected, looked to, and taken care of. You are the one who taught her self sacrifice." Darcy sipped from his own drink.

"I shan't argue. For, when I do try to argue about our personal character traits you always get your feathers up and I can't ever win. So I won't do it. But as I wish to ensure that Georgiana achieves her happiness, and I think we shall know who makes her happy by the end of season..." Darcy grumbled as the Viscount chuckled. Saying, "Yes he is an officer... In any case once she announces her wishes, then I too shall settle down."

Darcy stood up, "Indeed, well congratulations Stephen. I am mightily happy for you. Do I know the happy bride to be?" Darcy had extended his hand so that they could shake.

The General had to stand also and after they had done so, he said "As a matter of course, I shall wed Anne."

Darcy stopped his motion entirely, "You joke? That is ill done."

Stephen said, "No, I am serious. Neither of our hearts would be in the match. But I am a..."

CHOICES DO MATTER

" '...beat up old soldier, and she meets no suitors that Lady Catherine will allow to get close.' He then said something about happiness really did not matter and that both would have some-one to talk to instead of ending their days alone." Mr. Darcy informed his wife that evening as they readied for bed. Now that they had returned to London, not only were the Bennets with them, but the two young ladies, Kitty and Georgiana had also come to stay with them. Mr. Darcy thought first of telling this news to Lizzy then discussing it with the entire family.

"Well that is a great shame," Lizzy said. "He is very arrogant, your cousin."

"Lizzy!" Darcy exclaimed.

"Oh," she folded down the covers for his side of the bed from where she lay beneath them. "Don't act shocked. But how dare he be so conceited to think that he could solve Anne's loneliness with an offer."

"He thinks of it as kindness," Darcy countered.

"He does not. He thinks of it as cowardice. I daresay you only married me to save yourself from Anne de Bourgh. Oh don't look hurt, I don't mean that. And he is not a coward, his war service shows that. But he is a coward should he just sit and let events, that he has an interest in, pass him by. And he is very full of his own self worth if he thinks that marrying Anne will somehow save her from loneliness. I should imagine that a marriage between them would have them speaking to one another, but I should also imagine it would be much less than even my own parents find conversation." Darcy had little to say to that and after some inconsequential discussion, he blew out the candle and they retired to sleep.

The very next instance that Lizzy had with the General was the day before Caroline Bingley's wedding. The General had been invited to a dinner party that Darcy had agreed to host at the last moment. Invitations had only been out one day and it was for the group of people that the General did enjoy surrounding himself with, also.

Included in the group were Lady Catherine and Anne, as they had traveled to London for the wedding. Caroline's net had cast them within it. Lady Catherine, invited because she was a peer with whom Caroline could claim acquaintance.

Lizzy made sure to get the General alone, "I do wonder if you wish me to have made your plans common knowledge? Do you know last night Viscount Parkes had us to dinner. He was quite pleasant. My father was even given a copy of Chaucer. Of course my father has at least three copies of Chaucer, but the Viscount thought it was significant. It is not a Caxton edition, but it might be mid 1600's, though the Viscount thought it was a Caxton..."

"Caxton... That would be a rare find indeed. And I do not want you to be speaking to my plans."

Lizzy said, "Of course, I did not think so. For why tell Darcy something that could wait until Kitty makes a decision that she can no way undo. She will have invested too much pride in defying the wishes of her family and friends. Of the one she loves and the one who loves her. Yes quite right to tell Darcy, whom you know would tell me of an instant." Lizzy's fan slapped the General's hand, with great force. He bit back the yelp of pain and exclamation that escaped, and then nodded with a false smile to those in the room who looked to their corner.

Lizzy let her own brief smile play across her features, then continued, "Ah, I see I have your attention completely, if not then perhaps another such hit will ensure it?"

"No, you have it," the General rubbed his hand.

"Do you think that I am your aunt, Lady Catherine? Darcy says that he gauged the information of Lady Catherine's midnight call upon myself, prior to our marriage, as a clear indication that I should accept him. Are all you Fitzwilliam blood alike, needing a woman to lead the charge?" The General shook his head.

"No, that is not it. Not it at all." Lizzy stroked her fan. The General noted it and rubbed his hand once more, then hastily added, "No, I don't expect anything from Kitty, not at this stage. As you said, you dined with the Viscount last night. He will make a match for her. Parkes has settled down." Joy was certainly not displayed on his countenance.

Lizzy tapped the General on his hand with her fan once more, this time it was a very light tap, "He is a grotesque ogre when I compare him to the man she should wed. Yes, you know I mean you. This entire assemblage, including your aunt Lady Catherine knows that it is you whom Kitty should wed. Lady Catherine holds her breath that my father will consent to Kitty marrying the Viscount, and thus being stripped from you forever just so you may live out her wishes, rather than either your own or Anne's."

The General turned to face Lizzy so that she could see his expression clearly. "I know all this. I am not so ill informed that I do not know the affection your family has for me, nor that they wish a match might take place between someone such as myself, whom they admire, rather than someone with such a dire reputation as the Viscount." The General had turned his back on the rest of the room so those who might look to the corner where Lizzy and he stood, would not see his emotions.

Lizzy nodded and then gave him one more scold, "I will say this last, before going to my other guests. Do not be such a fool. We don't want someone such as you... The family from my youngest Gardiner cousin, to my mama, to Kitty should she admit it, wants you to be made happy by Kitty and her to be made happy by you. And if you submit to such a truth, you will admit that you know this and have known so for many months. None of us, including my mama, will tell this to Kitty, though. This may be difficult for you, but it certainly can be no harder than what you did six months gone at the siege where you were hurt. You survived that." Lizzy turned even as she heard him murmur.

"I should think this harder, and the consequences of failure much worse..."

* * *

The General was not his lively self through the dinner. Often, he could be seen rubbing the back of his hand and looking away from the end of the table where Kitty sat. Asked, and he would say he was thinking of the toast he would give the following day for Fairfax.

After dining, when the men joined the ladies, it did not go unnoticed that the General sought his cousin Anne out and guided her to a quiet corner of the room. It was a different corner then the one that he and Lizzy had shared prior to dinner. Mr. Darcy and his wife exchanged significant glances. The General faced the assemblage for this interview and assured that his words were private and none would hear him.

The General began, "You will recall a certain plan that your mother had for you upon the night of the ball, in your honor, after Darcy's marriage?"

She smiled, not as pleasant and illuminating as some other's, but certainly an act that did her credit and something she should indulge more in. She only indulged in such smiles when out from the shadow of Lady Catherine. "Indeed, I do remember, for the plan involved yourself as well. Upon your becoming acquainted with the plan you did not even retreat, but were routed from the field, our brave General." It was as close to giggling as Anne came.

"Yes I am heartily embarrassed by those actions," Stephen said, though he had not felt embarrassed at the time.

Those nearest the corner would be able to hear Anne's laughter, "Come Stephen, you are not the first to have fled my mother. Look you to Darcy, who found a solution." She pointed her fan towards Mr. Darcy who was clearly looking to the two of them in the corner. The General eyed Anne's fan suspiciously. He moved his hands out of arm's reach.

"Yes, Darcy indeed. You do not hold him in condemnation for marrying Lizzy?" he asked.

"Not at all, she is a kind friend. She and I get along well enough, better, I expect, than Darcy and I should have got along should we have wed," Anne said.

The General nodded warmly, "I am glad to hear it. I believe her endearments to be genuine. Surprisingly, the Bennets have been a fresh wind amongst our family."

Anne looked at him and then used her fan a little more vigorously to cool herself, "So all you wanted to do is apologize for not becoming my suitor, as per Mama's plan?"

"Yes. No... It would be easy to ask for such forgiveness and were you to give it, then my course would be clear." He held up his hand to forestall her speaking. "No pray wait. I must do what is in my soul, my heart to do, whether I have your allowances to do such or not. You are a good woman, Anne, and deserve, and have always deserved to be seen, for yourself, instead of in the shadow of mine aunt. Should I have a household, and of course with Silverponds I do, you are always free to come to escape, a heavy word but correct I think, mine aunt's overpowering opinionations." Stephen knew if Lady Catherine ever heard any part of what he had just said, she would never speak to him again.

That Anne smiled encouraged him that he had said something pleasing to her. He added, "Again, I do not ask for your blessing, or pardon or allowance to act upon my course. I am sorry that Lady Catherine chose to set up expectation that we should marry. Perhaps she was the only one with a hope of that fruition, but it has damaged our relationship, these years. Or, at the very least, strained what had always been an interaction of camaraderie and friendship."

She laid her hand upon his arm so that she could stop him and, then, speak. It was an action Stephen noted that Lizzy saw and she tugged at her husband's sleeve so that Darcy noticed it as well. "Stephen, General, please stop. We are both victims of my mother's great plans and schemes. So many of which have failed and never come to pass. This was just another. And it has not damaged our relationship in a significant way."

Shaking his head he ventured, "I had thought to offer for you, and I do not wish to hear what your response would be, but I cannot do so. To do so would cause some sickness, a disease, to grow between us, I am certain of it. For my affections are with..."

He did not finish, for she smiled again and placed her hand once more on his arm. "You need say no more. Why, I shall leave you with little pain for, I am certain, that should you offer for anyone, there would never grow a sickness or disease between you and your wife. I will provide you with this. At present I find contentment in my life. I expect to find more so, anon. I will partake of your offer to avail myself of Silverponds should the need arise, though I shall not engage in the hunt, for it does not suit.

"Though, riding about your park and the lands of your neighborhood does. There are many find examples of oak, poplar and ash about your lands." She smiled, a third time, and the General realized that his estate did have some enchantment to it. But she tapped his arm lightly again, and, then, turned to make her way to a seat next to her mother.

* * *

Across the room Mr. Darcy found his sleeve pulled and then his wife motioning for him to attend to the General. The General however was in search of Kitty. But each having a private word with one another turned out to be impossible. The General was quizzed on his toast of the morrow, by all and sundry. Mr. Darcy was asked to fetch this item, or that, as host and often lost his opportunity to confront the General. Kitty always seemed to be in the company of someone and, never, alone.

In such a dinner, there is only so much time that one devotes to all the parts of it. There is the gathering of the participants, which takes place, beforehand. The dining itself, which would be of several courses, and would consume some hours of time. After the last course, the women retired to a drawing room so that they might have conversations away from the men, and the men with their port would discuss things that they felt were too sensitive for a woman's ears. This left the remainder for the two sexes to be together to share coffee, engage in entertainments, and have intimate discussions should they find quiet areas of the drawing room to do so.

In such a gathering, though, there were so many in attendance, and the size of the room being of such a nature, there were just two ends where private conversations could take place. The topic that General Fitzwilliam wished to explore was of a private nature. The availability of securing either of the two locations at a time when Kitty was free, also, came into play. That Kitty sat next to her sister, or mother for much of the evening, also, made soliciting a private moment difficult.

That their hot drinks, little bites of sweetmeats, and entertainment moved to fill time was evident, for shortly after the General had talked to Anne, Mary was asked to play some numbers at the pianoforte. In the first row, after the men and servants had arranged the chairs, Kitty sat next to Mrs. Bennet, Mr. Bingley and Mr. Bennet sitting directly behind, the General left standing. After the playing of three numbers, Lizzy asked for another to entertain, "Come, Kitty, a dramatic reading I should think, is in order, it will tide us until more tea arrives."

"I beg your indulgence, but I have nothing prepared," Kitty said.

"Surely an old favorite?" Darcy quizzed.

"Nay, if you will forgive me I fear I shall do anything with poor grace as the events of tomorrow, and my role for Caroline, fills my mind."

"Then perhaps Georgiana, you will play..." And the General's cousin took over from Mary. It was a wonder to note that Georgiana was more proficient then Mary, but the two had practiced together these last years and Mary's skill had greatly improved. Even Anne, as she followed Georgiana, had learned to play a tune, adequately, under the guidance of the other two ladies.

With tea following, Kitty asked to pour, whilst Lizzy took cups to each who wished to indulge. "I am sorry," Kitty apologized as one cup shook, somewhat uncontrollably, rattling amidst the conversations in the room.

"Is something wrong," Mr. Darcy was closest to her and was solicitous.

"No, it is nothing," Kitty had set the cup and saucer down for a moment. Then, stilling her jittery hands, began anew. Lizzy took the proffered cup to its intended recipient, having passed a thoughtful look with her husband. The General graciously accepted it and glanced towards Kitty, but she had become preoccupied with the next to be served.

The evening drew to a close and the only private moment the General had was thus, "I have something important I would like to discuss with you..."

"La, it will have to wait until tomorrow. Caroline has asked me to be present while she dresses and approve of her hair or some such fancy notion, so I must be there before ten. What an ungodly hour, and it near three, now." She turned and was off to her rooms.

The other guests who were to go to their homes, said their farewells. The General had moved into his brother's house in the city. Both parents and brother were away at their country estate and doing the best to avoid the wedding of Caroline Bingley and Sir Fairfax Chamberlain. When Lady Catherine had determined that she would come to Town and stay at his Father's house for the wedding, he found lodging at his brother's.

The General returned at half past nine to call to see if Kitty was available, but, found he had missed her. She, Georgiana and Lizzy had already gone to the Bingleys to help Caroline prepare for her great event. He did not have the footman tender his card, or report to Mr. Darcy or the Bennets that he had been at the door. Instead he went to the club and found Sir Fairfax there. They had arranged to meet at the club before walking to the chapel.

Fairfax however was in no condition to attend his wedding, "Fax, you must dress man, we have just over an hour..."

"Dress, why ever for. Oh that, yes I see you are dressed for a wedding. Uniform all shiny and polished. But I have had some thoughts about this marriage business, and what with the world as it is. You know Bonaparte still is quite strong despite the recent setbacks we have dealt him. Why should one think to marry and start a family with the world this way..." Sir Fairfax said.

"Quite enough of that old man." The General held out his hand for the newspaper that lay upon Fairfax's lap. It was handed over reluctantly. "Up. Yes, now." The General held out his hand, again, and Sir Fairfax took it cautiously and rose.

"Hendricks, help Sir Chamberlain to his room and find some lads to help you with his dressing. Half an hour Fax, then I am coming in to take charge. I don't think you will like that," Stephen used the tone he employed in Spain.

Sir Fairfax could see that there was little that he could say to escape, "Should have left for the American Colonies..."

"They haven't been colonies for thirty years, Fax. Now get dressed. It is high time you were married. High time, indeed." There was a distinct caliber in the tenor that was delivered in. The others in the room took notice. That some were previously military men showed, for they stood taller, or sat sharper in their seats. The General took the vacated chair once his charge had been marched from the room.

The General expected Hurst to arrive by half eleven and two others of familiar acquaintance who were to stand with them for Sir Fairfax, and then they would be off to the chapel. He did take the liberty to write a note. "Send this round to 11 Breed St. Yes, the Bingleys. It is for Miss Catherine Bennet. Here, a half crown."

* * *

All is well. Tell Miss Bingley that Fax will be in church on time. I still need to speak to you.

A reply came to him by way of Mr. Hurst upon his arrival, "Here, Miss Bennet asked that I give you this. At least she wrote it. Caroline was much more vehement and vocal. Through the door she was... Oh quite right. Shouldn't say how she was in public. You get the gist of it, though, and I need say no more. To be expected amongst brides I should think. Hmm think back that one time she looked to you to be meeting her at the altar, if I recall right. Where is Fax, shouldn't we be off?" Hurst looked about for the bridegroom. The General hadn't betrayed the desired expression at this little bon mot. Hurst readily changed the subject.

The note from Kitty said:

We will talk soon. I have much to say to you, also. Caroline does look radiant today. I hope Fax and You will do us all justice.

After some more time, Fax arrived to greet his friends, with moments to spare from the General's time limit. "Well done Fax. Now, look here, I should give you some thoughts on what it means to be married to a Bingley woman..." Hurst began.

"Indeed you should Mr. Hurst," The General stopped him, "but perhaps that shall wait until we have a dashed bit more of time. 'Sides have you actually seen the house that Sir Chamberlain has selected. Well, I guess it really was selected by your sister. I understand that the suite of rooms for you and Mrs. Hurst are quite extensive. A private study for you and, surely, nearly twice as big as the rooms you have when visiting the Bingleys..." Hurst's head snapped back and then he nodded three times with his lower lip jutting forward.

Hurst took Sir Fairfax's arm, "Indeed I had quite forgot. Why ever are we still here at the club, come now, you can't be late for your own wedding. Bad form indeed. And this wedding... Oh Indeed..."

That got the party started out the door with Fax not being able to say a word. Upon careful inspection though, Sir Fairfax did not give the appearance of being happy, or physically well, at all. Fax was certainly guilty of the appearance that his clothes were wearing him. Slumped in them, eyes downcast looking at his feet. His gait more shambling then a stride.

The two other gentlemen walked ahead breaking what little traffic there was, while on one side Hurst supported Sir Fax, and on the street side, the General. They had three blocks to traverse and amidst the normal noise of noon time, a boisterous singing ahead could be heard. As they neared the disturbance, an open carriage with six men was seen across the street. The General looked and could not determine more, but on his side of the street a few paces ahead, he could see Sir Barton and Mr. Marrow looking directly across at the carriage.

They shook their heads, "Hello my lord, Sir Chamberlain, gentlemen." Marrow said not intimate enough with Sir Chamberlain to call him Fax or Fairfax, and Sir Barton followed suit .A general exchange of honors was made. "Your wedding is it, saw the announcement in *The Times*. Good luck." Sir Barton intoned.

With a nod of the head, the General indicated the noise from the carriage. "What is going on? Too much merriment?"

Mr. Marrow supplied, "It is Viscount Parkes. He is celebrating." At that moment the man himself stood in the center of the carriage and caught site of the wedding party. His coat was awry and his cravat was undone, with a very visible stain upon it and his shirt.

"Well hello. It's old General Fitz, the Baron of the Ponds is it?"

Sir Barton had placed a restraining hand on the General's arm. "Steady, my lord. He is rather drunk." The General also felt his friend, Sir Fairfax, needing a little more support. A quick look showed Fax's knees a little wobbly.

The Viscount raised a bottle of champagne in one hand and a glass in the other and while pouring continued to shout in the street. "You must congratulate me, old man. Yes, indeed congratulate me. I have had wonderful news!" He lurched as his carriage moved forward in the opposite way of the General and the wedding party. "Congratulate me..."

"We must be off." Mr. Marrow was already walking after the carriage.

"Wait what news?"

The General hurriedly asked even as Mr. Hurst said, "General Fitzwilliam, we shall be late. Oh we can't have Caroline upset..."

Sir Barton turned back to say even as he walked away, "Oh Miss Bennet has given her answer. The Viscount had an interview with Mr. Bennet just a short while ago..."

The General felt Sir Fairfax tug at his arm as Mr. Hurst pulled Sir Fairfax forward. Even as the General turned about looking one way, he was being dragged the other. "Wait. Hold up."

"No time General, no time. We must to the chapel." Mr. Hurst said, from the other side. Worry clear upon his face as was a sheen of sweat. "Caroline must be wed. Today's the day. Eh Fax, today's the day."

With an illness in his stomach, the General faced the direction he was being forced in and marched with the others to the fate that awaited Sir Fairfax and the doom that he knew he would soon hear. His thoughts were full of Kitty. None were spared for the closed door of Anne de Bourgh, but later when he did pause to reflect on that, he smiled wryly, for Anne had never taken a hold in his heart. An offer for her would only have been an expedient of the mind.

His mobility he noted was such that the ill effects of his wounds were in the past, enough so that Stephen had sat a horse in the Hunt. He had recovered so well that he could walk for more than an hour. Certainly he knew of other serving officers who had less stamina. With all hope lost, sending a letter to Horse Guards citing his availability to return to any foreign duty might have some effect. When presented with the desire to leave England for a time, he was sure that some colleagues would take him up. Either that, or a return to his country seat and disappearance from view.

They rounded the corner and saw the chapel ahead. Several carriages were lined up in front, and a few fortunate friends who had been invited to witness the nuptials were gathered about. Some were seen in the doorway, and an impression was made as the men neared that the bride and her party awaited within. They had arrived even as the General glanced at a nearby clock face to see that they still were ten minutes ahead of Fairfax's appointed meeting with destiny.

"I shall share with you these words, Fax," the General whispered. "It is from a friend," It wasn't but Fax did not need to know it. "We all must marry. That we do so is but form, not function should we choose it to not be so. Now for my own thoughts. At some point you chose Caroline. She will partner you and provide you with a household for all the rest of your years. She is such that she will leave you to the club and all your newspapers which will please you. She will ask you to attend her much less, I think, than your mother asks, which will please you. You will eventually gain an heir, which will please her, and you will be remembered, which may not please you now, but I think will one day, please you greatly."

Fairfax nodded, "Nothing for it, then?"

"You must go through with it now, or you shall be the talk of the Ton. Already there is much speculation about the matter. I do not think you relish that. You yourself do not want to be newsworthy, do you?"

Fairfax looked about, and shaking his head, "Heavens, no!"

The General smiled and guided him and the rest forward, "Then onward, onward to glory." Though the General did not think that Caroline Bingley was really such. Getting Fairfax into the chapel to face his intended and become married was worthy of any medal he had ever won. And he had achieved several...

Well-wishers slowed their progress but still they entered the church before the appointed hour. Hovering about were family members, and close friends of Caroline. The Bennets were not in attendance, though the General did see his cousin Darcy standing next to his wife. The crowd was large enough that as he searched for a glimpse of Kitty, even as he walked at the side of Fairfax forward to the altar, he could not spot her.

Georgiana was next to Caroline and behind Jane Bingley. There was Mrs. Hurst, and another woman behind. Surely, that was Kitty, but too far for him to reach and speak to her. He would have to approach her later, but what use with Viscount Parkes already having been promised her hand.

Though there had been a series of wedding ceremonies prior to his service in Spain and Portugal that he had attended, the General had not been to such an event for the four years since Darcy and Bingley had been married. "Oh, by the way Fax, I got you a wedding present."

"Oh yes, well, jolly nice that."

The General's face was all seriousness, "Yes, a set of shooting rifles, inlaid with embellished silver etchings of pheasants in front of a ruined castle, on a darkly stained mahogany stock. And for Miss Bingley, a small book of poetry with gilt lettering on the cover and spine."

Mt. Hurst broke out in laughter, and Fairfax looked to the man wonderingly, "I say those are capital presents. What ever is so amusing?"

The general retracted his previous statement, "No. Sorry, I got you something else entirely, but never fear, I do believe that Miss Bingley has received several books of poetry as gifts and you will probably receive the odd shooter. I purchased you a very nice table with some sort of slot where you may store your papers. Saw it in a shop on Bond Street and just had to have it for you. For Miss Bingley, well I got her a copy of Debretts for your library. She'll need her own copy now that she is setting up your house."

By then they had reached the entire party and the time for such little discussions were past, though Miss Bingley asked of her brother, "Whatever is so funny Mr. Hurst? You must share it."

Being placed in the center of her regard was something that had a perpetual withering effect on Mr. Hurst. He responded in a small voice, "Oh, General Fitzwilliam brought to mind a prior instance of some few years ago and this was mirthful, only in context. I should only make a dashed fool of myself trying to explain."

"What," Sir Fairfax didn't catch the implication of trying to obscure from Caroline an event, "Indeed I think that I could attempt to tell..."

The General rescued himself, "Perhaps Fax some things that I mention are ill advised to repeat. My sense of humour has been somewhat degraded by my experiences in the Peninsula. You will please forgive me, but I do say the silliest things in the hopes of a good guffaw from Hurst. It sets my mood lighter."

Mr. Hurst was smart enough to catch on, "I am always one to oblige, General, always happy to."

They smiled, with satisfaction, to each other. The women clustered behind Caroline Bingley seemed to bristle, chief amongst them, Mrs. Hurst, who might take some effort to talk to her husband later in the day. And, who might not.

The Vicar was near enough, and he assembled the party for the vows. Here was the first moment that the General was able to see Kitty without obstruction. As he had found the first time he had seen her, she was fresh and beautiful, smiling and full of life. A contrast to his moods since the first moment he had spent in conflict.

Twenty minutes of service and vows was more than adequate to see Sir Fairfax and Caroline wed, and then a recessional to the carriages for the wedding party that had been arrayed in front of the chapel. "Kitty, perhaps you would accompany me on the walk back to the Bingleys..." The General asked her as he maneuvered to her.

"Oh, I am sorry General, I am for the second carriage with Jane and Mrs. Hurst. But look you to Georgiana who is in need of rescuing. There are some men she would rather avoid here and they all desire to fight over her escort..." She turned quickly to go to her carriage and left the General staring at her back. He then turned and found himself securing his ward from the men who hovered about her.

A passel of suitors who had learned of her excursion to the church that day had ensured to be about in hopes of engaging her good graces. Shooing the men off, whilst looking for Darcy, and seeing him nowhere, the General separated Georgiana from the admiring men.

Shortly he spoke to his cousin, "I am given to reflect, through observation, that soon all the folderol from these suitors will be over for you, and you will speak your mind to Darcy and myself." He was ever more certain that she had fixed one in her mind to accept.

"Oh yes, and this reflection came upon you, suddenly?" Georgiana and he were in the middle of the group that strolled back to the Bingleys, house. She did her best to smile in the same manner that she had done when she was a schoolgirl.

"Indeed no. I spent fifteen weeks in your close proximity, and have known you all your life, fair one. I believe I know the direction of your heart." She smiled, now, as the adult she had become. "Something amuses you." He said. He felt the tug of a smile upon his own lips, but shook his head and the feeling left.

She smiled even broader, "Oh, yes, very much. Though I shall admit that perhaps your suspicions are correct, I thought that my brother was ignorant that my heart leaned a certain way until someone recently revealed it, and I know it was neither Kitty nor Lizzy." He now nodded gravely.

"Yes, the subject came up in conversation. I sought to prepare him for what will be a wrenching separation. When you leave his house an era will have passed and he will not know how to separate his protection of you. I would happily wager that you desired someone, whether myself or perhaps Lizzy to have such a conversation with Darcy. But pray, this is not why you smiled."

She laughed gently, "No, for recently I remember a man, a man very dear and close to me citing Pots, and Kettles and Black..." She laughed without holding back.

The General thought for a moment and then remembered the instance at Silverponds. If he only was the type that harrumphed. Instead he retreated to a mumble, "Yes, well..."

She laughed even more gaily. "Oh, cousin, you are too easily marked."

His demeanor was serious and not as open as it usually was, "I am, thus, so readable to all?"

She patted his arm, "No, not all. Some do not know you half as well as they should."

He nodded, and noted their present location. Two more blocks until the house was reached. He would have to find Kitty alone. "I can not proceed along a line of questioning that touches me as this does currently. I do not chance revealing information that would be as the abyss for me, nor do I wish those who might help lift me to the heavens provide such an easy way. It is too close with me to bear."

"There, you are completely yourself again. I shall tell Darcy so. Even returning to London, I was sure you were not the old Fitzwilliam I have loved nearly as much as I love my brother Darcy." She dragged a glove enwrapped hand across his cheek, "There is still some remembrance of your battlefields and the horrors behind those eyes, but your spirit is healed. I am happy for it."

He continued walking but was quiet for a moment, then added, "You regard me as healed that I hold some topics at bay? I must think that I was ever thus, though I thought myself more open. I had not realized that there was such concern on your part..."

"Oh I think if you were not so preoccupied I would resent that remark and make you pay. We, all of us, have been concerned and well you know this. Else why spend so much time in your melancholic presence..." She smiled again.

"Ah, you tease. I was not so melancholic..." He shook his head lowering his voice.

Georgiana gripped his arm, "Certainly you were not, what with Kitty and myself to cheer you at every turn. But come, we have arrived and I must announce my triumph to all and sundry who should know, and then I must bedevil my brother with the names of my many suitors, especially those he has a great dislike for."

This left the General with a smile and a laugh despite his preoccupation in regards to his pained heart. He followed Georgiana up the stairs and was greeted by the new lady Fairfax, Sir Chamberlain, his mother and Caroline's family. Other guests had moved further into the house gathering in the three rooms that were open to them. In the first he had no sight of Kitty, though several of his friends and family stopped to ask after him and he, of course, acknowledged them.

He was stopped by Mrs. Bennet. "What a pleasure to see you, General, I am so looking forward to your toast. Now you must tell me simply everything about Sir Fairfax this morning. We did not attend the vows, but you will know that having come from there. I am sure I told Miss Bingley, no Lady Fairfax she now is, that Mr. Bennet would not have been able to attend, though he is about somewhere, I should think looking at the library, if anyplace. You know how he is with his books. Though he did fancy the collection you were building at Silverponds. Why to think we were there just a month ago, and what wonders you are doing with the place. Why I was telling my sister how you have had us to visit for more than six weeks all told and what a singular honor for us, who are not even your relations, to do that."

The General might have been overwhelmed if this had been his first encounter with Mrs. Bennet. But as he was sure that with the advent of Kitty's marriage to Viscount Parkes, he would be retiring from the society that included the Bennets, and so would not see her for some rather lengthy time. He took her hand and with a courtly bow, gave it a kiss as if she were one of the Princess Royals. This had the effect that Mrs. Bennet came to a slow stumbling halt in her discourse. "I am afraid, my dear Mrs. Bennet that our days all together at Silverponds shall now be but happy memories for me to cherish. I have something that I must discuss with another of the guests, and then give my toast to the blessed couple, then after that... Well after that, I am uncertain just what will come." He could not tell her it was Kitty he sought, and with a little deft maneuvering left the woman's side to quest for her daughter.

Lizzy was nearby in that first room, and went to her mother's side who was left somewhat speechless. "Stephen, Stephen, oh General Fitzwilliam," Lady Catherine de Bourgh called him, nearer the doorway. "Pray come here, I should like your opinion about something."

He hardly slowed for he had determined that Kitty was not in the room, "Pray aunt, if you will give me a moment, I have a matter that requires my attention. I promise to return." He did not pause for that would have provided an entry to a dialogue.

Still, questing for Kitty, in the second room he saw her, and she was radiant.

Her gown was crème, now that he took a moment to admire it. It had fine red knit work to accentuate her bosom, and her neckline. In her hair was a piece of jewelry that looked somewhat familiar. He noted that his cousin Anne seemed to hold Kitty in one spot alone talking and sharing some little laughter between the two of them. He was stopped twice, again, on his way to her, or rather, two times friends tried to engage him in conversation and he was as deft as he had been with his aunt in escaping the situation.

"Ah, cousin. You have made it. Why it has nearly been an entire day since we have spoken and this is the first you have been able to complete your mission. You, a successful leader of men?" Anne giggled.

Kitty looked confused and the General took this to mean she had little inkling of what Anne was talking of. Anne said, "Well I am off to find a punch bowl. No, General, do not fetch a glass for me, though I see you are slow to answer. Our Kitty has much to discuss with you and you with her, best you do it soonest." Anne did allow the General to help her up. "Pray," she turned as she left. "The garden is through there," Anne pointed the way.

"Anne is acting quite bold. I am sure Lady Catherine will not be pleased." Kitty said.

"Pleased? Indeed my aunt's pleasure is of little consequence, as Anne is showing us, as Darcy has so before. Will you stroll with me a ways?" He offered his hand for her to take so that he could help her rise, also.

She smiled at him briefly then her eyes took on a stricken look and she turned her head away even as she laid her hand in his and rose. "Yes, umm..." He had no other words until they were in the garden. Here a few other guests strolled or stood, but there was enough room to have a private conversation.

"I am sorry, I was just remembering..." She said and he looked once more and saw the smiles he was endeared too.

"Kitty, no Catherine."

She gripped his arm, "All serious? Pray Stephen, is it time for that?"

He smiled, this time, and his eyes were alight, "Past time... I hope though that there still is time." He paused and fully faced her. "I passed Viscount Parkes prior to the wedding ceremony this morning. He was in spirits." His smile was whimsical but he remembered what he was about.

Stephen continued, "I was made to understand that Parkes had an interview with your father this morning, and he had reason to celebrate. Pray wait. I have something that touches my soul that I must say first. No, it must be before you speak." He had got her to nod, demurely, and close her lips. For she had started to talk twice. He had touched one finger to those lips to beg for her silence just then. The pain was even greater than he had imagined, and certainly hurt as much as the sword cut he had taken at Badajoz.

"I am too late, I fear, and my revealing this truth may cause you distress in all our years henceforth. Yet, yet... Kitty, Catherine, I love you and have for as long as I know. From first we took to the back of Night so long ago at Lizzy and Darcy's wedding. I cannot let you marry Parkes without you knowing, and one word, one syllable from you and I will do all in my power to send him off so that you would be free to make me happy."

There was a tear now in Kitty's left eye, and then a track from her right. "Oh Stephen, Stephen." He brought his finger up to gently wipe the tears away. Another fell.

She was smiling. She was radiant. "You need have no worries. I let papa send him packing."

Now he felt wetness upon his cheek and she reached up to wipe it away. "How could I ever be content with nothing but a title when my heart was stolen by a dashing Colonel five years ago? How could there be any other man when I have loved you for so long?"

That seven people in the garden saw them kiss was no small matter. That the tale was circulating the wedding party moments later was cause for great joy amongst many of the attendees.

Lady Catherine de Bourgh was heard to say, "About time, if you ask me. Now if my nephew had been raised by me, we wouldn't have had to wait so long to see him wed. I do not know what my brother has been thinking, indulging his boys so..."

Darcy, when he heard that remark, said a silent prayer, and later made happy remarks to Lizzy that it surely must have been his example that led the General to a Bennet daughter.

Mrs. Bennet was heard to murmur, "Lady Silverponds, Lady Catherine Silverponds, no Lady Kitty Silverponds..." Not quite making up her mind which she liked the best.

Caroline Bingley, informed by Mr. and Mrs. Hurst as she began to sit down to her wedding luncheon, was heard to say, "I will not let another Bennet girl take my day away from me. Mr. Hurst send them away." He was delighted to return, "Can't Caroline, he is to give the toast, having stood up for Fax and all that. Why without the General, I think Fax would have gone missing again this morning and then where would we be, Lady Fairfax?" It was rhetorically asked, but Mr. Hurst seemed to enjoy the moment immensely.

When the news was related to Sir Fairfax, he had a laughing fit, stopped and then laughed some more. When the Gardiners returned from the luncheon and told their children there was much joy. Mr. Gardiner however had to be strict and tell his children that they would have to wait till the following day to visit their cousin and the General to wish them well as it was much too late to venture out. Mrs. Gardiner however took her time in telling her children of the General's toast to the married couple. She asked that they not interrupt, then she began her tale:

"Throughout the lunch there was much discussion of not only the happy couple, but also your cousin and her happiness. Lady Catherine de Bourgh spent a good fifteen minutes saying that it was more than time that the General make it official. She told one and all that the first time she visited Silverponds, Kitty and the General acted so in concert that if one did not know they weren't married they would be surprised by it." The children had laughed and this brought discussion of that same weekend as they too had been at Silverponds.

"When it was time for the toast, General Fitzwilliam rose. He was very gallant looking in his Regimentals and all his awards displayed. He raised his glass and it became quiet. 'Fax married. Fax married? Fax is married! Just a few years ago, a certain lady asked that I remember her to Sir Fairfax for she was quite interested in meeting this man. A man who has been more at home at the club, with his paper. And happy with yet his other other paper.' The General paused and there was another good chuckle."

Mr. Gardiner asked his children, "Do you remember how many papers were delivered when Sir Fairfax was at Silverponds? He reads that many each day." The children laughed at that too. They had not thought one person could read so much at all.

"'It took some time from that meeting,' the General, our General continued, 'some years, but romance came from that introduction. Something that comes to us all apparently.' This happy remark got applause from the company." Mrs. Gardiner had to stop her recitation for her eldest daughter insisted that Kitty must have blushed at the General's statement. Mrs. Gardiner confirmed that her cousin did indeed turn a rosy shade.

"'When I first thought what I would speak too, today, I thought of the awe I find in constancy, for constancy sees us here today. But I find that the root of our gathering is based upon a different word. Happiness.' The General looked then to your cousin and she blushed some more. He then reached for her hand."

Mr. Gardiner had a good chuckle then himself, "Why do you laugh father?"

"Er yes, well you know your aunt Bennet, she gripped my arm then very tight she was quite happy herself I do believe, yes I do believe." He rubbed his arm where it had been clenched by his sister.

Mrs Gardiner shook her head at her husband then began once more. "Here the General looked to the couples that were seated about the room. 'This morning Fax and I had a discussion about this day's event. It is happiness I believe that we see at the root of the need to marry. Happiness that is the soul of marriage. It is why we men ask you ladies to make us happy. Fax, Lady Fax, look about you at those whom you see married here. They sit here happy with you and happy for you.'" The children shifted, the boys less interested then the girls.

Mrs. Gardiner however added the rest. "The General then said, 'It is why we now toast the Happy couple.' The General sat then and had some words with Kitty. I do not know what was said but they held hands for the remainder of the meal, quite unseemly, but, very pleasing nevertheless...'"

As Stephen had sat down and the toast was repeated by all, Kitty had turned to him, "Do you think they are as happy as we?"

"My dear, if they are a tenth as happy as we, they will have more happiness then anyone has a right to."

The End

Made in the USA
Lexington, KY
18 August 2011